'An unputdownable, intriguing story of vengeance with tragedy at its heart'   *Woman & Home*

'Combining a moving love story with a fascinating slice of US history, this powerful novel is hard to put down'   *Hello*

'Utterly immersive, I savoured every sentence of this wonderful novel. A love story which is both tragic and uplifting'

Juliet West

'I loved this dark yet sunlit story of love and revenge'

Lissa Evans

'With characters and a story as warm and colourful as its Key West setting, Vanessa Lafaye's *At First Light* illuminates a shady period of American history with panache, style and a hearty punch to the gut'   Jason Hewitt

'This is fa   y'

Express

Vanessa Lafaye was born in Tallahassee and raised in Tampa, Florida, where there were hurricanes most years. She first came to the UK in 1987 looking for adventure, and found it. After spells living in Paris and Oxford, she now lives in Marlborough, Wiltshire, with her husband and three furry children. Vanessa leads the local community choir, and music and writing are big parts of her life.

Find out more about Vanessa on her website
vanessalafaye.wordpress.com,
and follow her on Facebook/vanessalafaye-writer
and on Twitter @VanessaLafaye

Also by Vanessa Lafaye

Summertime

Vanessa Lafaye

AT FIRST LIGHT

An Orion paperback

First published in Great Britain in 2017
by Orion Books
This paperback edition published in 2017
by Orion Books,
an imprint of The Orion Publishing Group Ltd
Carmelite House, 50 Victoria Embankment
London EC4Y 0DZ

An Hachette UK Company

1 3 5 7 9 10 8 6 4 2

A CIP catalogue record for this book is
available from the British Library.

ISBN 978 1 4091 5543 0

Typeset by Input Data Services Ltd, Somerset

Printed in Great Britain by Clays Ltd, St Ives plc

www.orionbooks.co.uk

For James, still and always

ACKNOWLEDGEMENTS

As any author will tell you, the second book is the tough one. It took me a long time to find the right story, and figure out how to bring it to life. This book owes its existence to a host of special people whose support and encouragement kept me afloat and steered me away from the rocks: my agent and sounding board, Tina Betts at Andrew Mann Ltd; my editor, Kate Mills, who showed me how to make it better; my beta-buddy, Fionnula Kearney and the other Prime Writers who shared the ups and downs; Angus and Debbie at White Horse Books in Marlborough, for expert advice; Kyle Pennington for Florida legal and police procedure; Chris Bredbenner for checking my Spanish slang; and my husband, James, for giving me the courage to set off on this voyage . . . and staying up all night to read the first draft.

ACKNOWLEDGEMENTS

HISTORICAL NOTE

'Cayo Hueso', Florida, or 'Isle of Bones' was the original Spanish name for Key West. In the sixteenth century, the first Spanish explorers to the island came across beaches strewn with the bones of Native Americans, the result of bloody tribal territorial battles. They combined the Tainos Indian word 'cayo' for 'small island' with the Spanish 'hueso' for 'bone', which was anglicised later to 'Key West'.

This story was inspired by real events which took place there during 1919–21.

LA PAJARA PINTA

(The Painted Bird, traditional Cuban children's song)

There was a painted bird
Sitting in a green lemon tree,
With its beak it cut the branch,
With the branch it cut the flower.
Ay, ay, ay!
When will my love come?

I kneel at the feet of my love,
I get up, loyal, loyal,
Give me your hand, give me the other,
Give me a kiss on the mouth.

I'll make a half turn,
I'll make a full circle,
With one step back,
Making a bow.

But no, but no, but no,
Because I'm embarrassed,
But yes, but yes, but yes,
Because I love you.

❧ PROLOGUE ❧

KEY WEST, 1993

On her last day of freedom, she hurries, breathless, down Tamarind Street, and into her garden. The beauty of it briefly stalls her, one hand on the rusted iron latch of the gate. It seems so peaceful, on this of all days, the shady tranquillity almost surreal after the scene at the park. The guavas hang heavy and tempting, the bird of paradise flowers nod their orange beaks in the hot, blossom-scented breeze. The water trickling across the stones in the fountain whispers to her: *stay, rest*. But she cannot.

Even at ninety-six, she is used to going everywhere on foot, with the support of her old buttonwood cane, but the brisk walk home has been tiring. Her heartbeat thuds in her throat, as much from the knowledge of what she is about to do as from the exertion. If only she could rewind the morning back to daybreak, she thinks, and go to the market instead of the park. If only she could un-see what she has seen there, and install herself beneath the coconut palm in her favourite chair with a glass of lemonade . . .

But she cannot.

Leaning on the cane, she opens the back door and passes through to her bedroom, its plantation shutters closed against the mid-day heat. The air conditioner is off because she did not expect to be back so soon. In the sepia gloom she reaches into the farthest corner of the closet. Her hand knows what it seeks: the cigar box with the faded Gato factory label on the lid. She allows herself a short rest on the bed, torn between the desire to sit there, remembering, and the urgency of her mission. She strokes the lid. Finally the airless heat drives her from the room.

In the garden, she fills her lungs with the lush greenness, and pictures the last time she saw the gun in his hand. He held it naturally, the way a soldier does, the strong lines of his fingers wound in a beautiful curve round the walnut grip. She removes the Colt from the box and imagines it still bears traces of his fingerprints, maybe even the smell of his hair oil. But there is no time for such nostalgic self-indulgence. The gun sinks easily into her pocketbook. The weight of it is solid, insistent. It has lain in its box, wrapped and oiled, for seventy years, waiting for this day, this day which she feared, and hoped would never come.

A hummingbird buzzes past her ear. It is Pablito, the one who often visits her at breakfast to sip sugar water from her spoon. She whispers, 'Adios, mi amor.' Her eye alights on a weed, growing between the red bricks of the path. She wants to pull it out, but is not confident of getting up again if she stoops down. It will have to wait for the next owner. She hopes they will appreciate this cool, fragrant haven, and not turn the house into another chichi B&B. She has had plenty of offers over the years from developers, keen to exploit the property's unique history.

Her back muscles protest, her joints grind painfully. She leans against the mossy wall, eyes closed, gathering strength. The revolver nudges her hip. Its message is clear: *time to go*. She focuses on the task ahead, and takes up her cane. She feels calm, resolute. And infinitely sad.

She allows herself one last look, then opens the gate and heads back towards the park.

Two hours later, Chief Roy Campbell is woken at his desk by excited squawks from the police radio speaker. The air conditioner groans beside his good ear, making it impossible to discern actual words. His face is hot, his mouth dry. He must have been snoring. He shakes his head to clear it. It's a good thing that the squad room is empty, everyone at the park keeping order for the rally. He could have been there alongside his squad, wasting taxpayer's money to ensure a load of racist shitheads got their full entitlement of constitutionally enshrined rights. Instead he has opted to hold the fort and begin clearing his office. This suits him fine. Despite having upheld the law for his whole long, undistinguished career on the force, an actual, in-person confrontation with the Ku Klux Klan might just be the thing that ends it, a week before retirement. Even his iron discipline might have faltered at the sight of those ridiculous, hate-filled pointy white hats bobbing around Bayview Park in their officially sanctioned rally. He can imagine how that news would go down at home. *Hi, Clarisse, guess what? I punched a Klansman in the face! There goes my pension!*

And it is Sunday. Although it means time-and-a-half pay, he wants to be in the backyard with a beer, floating in the little pool Clarisse insisted they install, because everyone in the neighbourhood has one. She has never reconciled herself to the lifestyle sustainable on a policeman's salary. The evidence is there every month in her credit card bills. Nor can she accept that, even after all these years, and all the different stations on his glacially slow ascent through the ranks, he has yet to catch a really big case, the kind that makes the evening news . . . the kind that would give her the edge over the other ladies at bridge club. It had taken him a while to realise, after they married, that she wanted Jack Webb out of *Dragnet*: a glamorous, dangerous, sexy cop. Down the years, as the TV shows got more exotic, her mouth developed a permanent droop. *Hawaii Five-O* was a low point, *Miami Vice* even worse. Her disappointment in him is like a sore that never heals.

She blames his father for a career choice which is, with a lot of hindsight, completely wrong for his temperament. With a wry look at the heat-hazed parking lot, he concedes she is probably right. He should have been a fisherman. He really loves to fish, and wishes he was on a boat right now, with a big marlin on his line and a cooler of cold ones by his side. His whole life has been one long, unsuccessful attempt to live up to the image of his father, one Sheriff Dwayne Campbell.

Key West is his last station: the end of the line in oh, so many ways.

He stands up to get some blood moving, pulls at his shirt where it stretches taut across the bulge of his belly. It tells him that it's lunchtime. He thinks fondly of his Sunday treat, the fried shrimp po' boy sandwich waiting for him at Johnny's down by the dock. He reaches for his blood pressure pills.

The squawks from the speaker resolve into words. *One*

victim ... male ... Klan member ... suspect in custody. He wipes his face with the back of his hand and vaguely wonders whether he is dreaming. This is belied by an unfamiliar sensation moving through his limbs: adrenalin. He says to the empty room, 'Well, this is going to mean a lot of paperwork,' which is handy, because it happens to be his forte.

The doors of the station burst open in a rush of hot air, dark uniforms and raised voices. His sergeant, Big Mike, is first, followed by Javier and Meredith, all grim faces and taut jawlines. The rest of the squad piles in behind. Roy catches Meredith's eye, magnified by the thick lenses of her glasses. Known as Fisheye by the squad (but only behind her back), she looks bereft. And now he is worried, because Meredith is the hardest cop in the station. The tears of drag queens, the pleas of addicts, the threats of entitled frat boys ... all of it washes over Meredith like melted butter off a corn cob. Right now, she looks like she might cry.

Roy coughs to cover the rumble of his stomach and comes out from behind his desk. All he can see is a mass of blue shirts. 'What happened?' he asks. 'Where's our perp? Or was it one of y'all?' No one shows even a hint of a smile.

The blue shirts part before him to reveal a small, white-haired lady who looks to be at least ninety years old. The top of her head only comes up to the middle of Big Mike's chest. Her eyes are focused on the floor, child-sized hands bound by the cuffs which almost fall off her delicate wrists. She resembles a tiny bird trapped in a blue cage. The next thing he notices is that her skin colour, the light brown of *café con leche*, matches his own – exactly. That colour has defined his entire life. He knows what people say about him, that it's the reason why he made Chief, after such a lacklustre career; that he's been over-promoted by politically correct liberals who want a little brown to offset the white in their senior officer photos. But he knows why he made Chief: because he is a survivor, and because he avoids trouble. This little woman is a big, steaming plate of trouble. On the edge of her shoe, the comfortable slip-on kind favoured by the elderly everywhere, he notices a small spot of what looks like blood. It is still red.

Big Mike consults his notebook. 'Charlie "Bucket" Simpkins, Kleagle of the Klan, shot dead twelve thirty-four p.m. today in Bayview Park in front of . . .' he trails off, flicks a few pages, 'estimated fifty witnesses.' He glances up. 'And several TV crews. Paramedics called, but pronounced dead at the scene. Forensics on their way, but there doesn't seem to be much doubt.' He looks down upon her fluffy white head. In his paw, an evidence bag bulges with a Colt revolver which looks like an antique. A dark wooden cane nestles in the crook of his arm.

'Fuck me,' mutters a voice softly, from the back of the huddle. 'I thought the youth in this town were bad enough.'

'Mouth, Sanchez,' snaps Javier.

Roy cranes to see a new recruit, cocky and bright in his pristine uniform. They all look the same to him anyway, with their shiny enthusiasm and smooth, unmarked faces. 'Get out, Sanchez.' The young man shuffles through the doorway. 'Carry on, Mike—'

'I did it. It was me,' says the old lady, in a light Cuban accent. She raises eyes of startling, bright bluish grey, like the sky before a storm. She sways a little on her dainty, blood-stained feet.

'That's all she'll say,' says Big Mike, 'won't give us her name or anything.' His meaty shoulders rise in a frustrated shrug. 'And she's got a death grip on her purse.'

Indeed, the woman clutches an ivory leather bag closer to her side. 'I did it. It was me,' she says again, a tiny quaver in her voice.

Javier surges forward with a chair. '*Sientate, Mamacita.*'

She sits, but withers him with a glance, her voice firm. 'I am not your Mamacita, young man.'

For a moment, it seems none of the trained professionals in the room has the slightest notion of how to proceed. And in that moment, she focuses those eyes on Roy again. Now the colour looks like lavender. In them he sees a plea. And recognition.

'Get her some water,' he says to Javier. 'Take the cuffs off.' With a final look at those astonishing eyes, he says, 'And book her.'

Roy and Big Mike take their machine coffee into the office. The fluorescent lights turn the sergeant's face into a relief map of anguish. Roy has never seen him so upset. There are many hours of form-filling ahead, but they seem paralysed. A local public defender is on his way. Roy knows the others will be in the break room now, gossiping over their lunch boxes. He will need to crack the whip soon, but he calculates a small dispensation is allowed. There is a feeling in the air that something momentous has happened.

'Tell me again,' he says, 'from the beginning.'

Big Mike clears his throat. He doesn't consult his notes this time, his gaze is fixed on a water stain above Roy's head. 'The rally was winding down. There wasn't much interest, just a few from AIDS Action heckling from the side lines, and some idiot Fore Fathers practising their Nazi salutes.' The Fore Fathers were the local white supremacists, whom the residents delighted in referring to as the Foreskins.

'Suspect was seen approaching the victim, who was in a wheelchair. They spoke, exchanged maybe two sentences.' Mike's voice gets very quiet. Beneath his *Magnum, P.I.* moustache, his mouth turns down. 'Then she shot him. Once. In the chest. There was no way she could miss at that range. She had to put down her cane to hold the gun with both hands.' His wide, square finger scratches at the coffee cup. The sound seems very loud in the room. White flakes, like artificial snow, form a ring round the cup. 'Medics said death was instantaneous.'

Roy exhales, and realises that he has not breathed while Mike was talking. He sits back heavily, eliciting creaks of protest from the chair. 'It will go to trial,' he says, 'it has to. And if she continues to plead her guilt, the judge will have no choice. Unless, of course, she does a Nugent.' Floyd Nugent was a local legend, who murdered his wife and mother-in-law with a spear gun. He avoided a lethal injection by attempting to bite off his public defender's ear in court, and saw out his days in the Chattahoochee mental hospital.

Big Mike sucks air through his teeth. 'Jail time for Mother Teresa there?'

'Not our call. That's for our great justice system to decide. Our two priorities for the next twenty-four hours are to get the public defender in here before the Homicide guys turn up. I don't want her talking to anyone without counsel present.

She may turn out to be incompetent, won't know until she's seen the shrink.'

'I'm no psychiatrist, Chief, but the odds of that don't seem great.'

'Yeah, I know.' Despite the apparent craziness of a daylight murder and immediate confession, she is all too sharp for her age – hell, even for his age. His mind is working faster than it has for a long, long time. It is imperative to obtain a charge of second-degree, rather than first-degree murder, for her to have any chance at all. In the second degree, with the right judge and a reasonable prosecutor, she could be bailed, to somewhere more suitable than the county jail. Everything hung on the question of premeditation, whether she had planned the killing, at any time in the past. He did not want to be in the room when that question came up.

'And the other priority, Chief?'

'Stall the press, at least until she's been before the judge. Tell them the public is safe, we have a suspect in custody.' *Just as my career fizzles out, I catch my first newsworthy case. Clarisse will be happy, at least.*

Javier hurries in, agitation written clearly in his dark eyes. 'I can't get the purse away from her. Neither can Meredith. When we tried, I thought the *señora* was going to stroke out.'

Meredith has a way of separating perpetrators from their belongings, which members of the squad liken to snake-charming. If she has failed, then the situation is dire indeed.

She enters the room, shoulders bowed in uncharacteristic defeat. 'Think we'll have to leave it with her for now. At that age, it's too dangerous to upset her like this. I won't be responsible. I've called the doctor, to check her over, and bring her meds. I'll try again later, when hopefully she'll be calmer.'

'You got a name?' asks Roy.

She hooks her thumbs into her utility belt, her fish-eyes a twinkle. 'She wouldn't tell me, but she emptied her pockets and I found an old prescription. Folks, you're not going to believe who is sitting in our cell.' She pauses for maximum effect. 'It's Alicia Cortez.'

Coffee sprays from Javier's mouth, all over Big Mike, who upsets his own cup. Brown liquid flows across the desk into Roy's lap, and he shoves his chair back and slaps at the wet patches on his trousers.

Everyone begins talking at once. Having only been at the station for three years, Roy is not fully versed in the local lore, unlike the others all jabbering loudly. His head hurts, from the fluorescent lights, from the lack of his po' boy Sunday treat, from the fact of a homicidal nonagenarian in his custody cell. He must re-establish protocol, and fast. He needs the comfort of routine. His normally focused, duty-bound, if somewhat mediocre team seem to be in the grip of a strange, collective emotional thunderstorm. The air crackles with it.

Javier breathes, '*La Rosita Negra.*'

Roy stands and bellows, 'Everyone, shut up!' No one has heard him use that voice before. 'For the love of Jesus, will someone please tell me,' here he glares at the ring of surprised faces, 'who the hell is Alicia Cortez?'

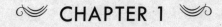

CHAPTER 1

KEY WEST, JUNE 1919

Alicia's first impression of her new home was that it stank. The reek of raw sewage permeated the air, which worsened as the ferry from Havana approached the dock. She wrenched a handkerchief from her purse to cover her nose and mouth.

'*Dios mio*,' she said to the elderly couple standing beside her at the boat's rail, 'where is that coming from?'

The woman pointed towards rows of wooden barrels lining the dock. There must have been thirty of them, topped by a seething cloud of flies. 'It's all the *mierda* from the outhouses. They're taking it to dump in the sea.' Her eyes surveyed Alicia with open curiosity, then slid away.

Alicia pulled the straw hat down low over her face. Her skin colour always drew attention, the product of her African mother and Cuban father. Even in cosmopolitan Havana, she attracted stares.

As she watched, shirtless men began to load the dripping barrels onto a boat, its gunwales sunk low in the water. Alicia tried not to gag but only partially succeeded. *They still have outhouses here?* Her family home, now ninety miles to the

11

south, had all the modern conveniences, indoor plumbing, brass electrical fixtures in every room. Mamacita cooked on a gas range. *It might as well be two thousand miles away. Or in a fairy tale.*

Already she missed the smell of Havana, that unique perfume of car exhaust, drains, cigarette smoke, Cuban cooking, and something indefinably old which pervaded every street and every building: the dust of centuries. Only now did she miss it, when she could never go back.

She was forced to wonder, as she had so many times since that awful night: *what have I done?* It had all happened so fast, the course of her life altered in an instant of desperation. It seemed impossible that it was only three days ago. Even up to the point of embarkation, she had thought there might be a reprieve, that Papa might find a way for her to stay. She had expected sympathy from him, when he learned of all she had suffered, when he understood the forces that pushed her to that single act of violence. Instead of sympathy and comfort, her tears were met with silence. He did not even come to see her off, remaining locked behind his study door when the cab arrived to take her to the port.

A tearful Mamacita had accompanied her and pushed a wad of crumpled dollars into her hand. 'You must go, *niña*. It is for your own safety!' she had cried. And so Alicia had taken her place on the Key West ferry, among the tourists heading for relaxation, and businessmen going to make deals, and families off to visit relatives. She might have been in shackles, so powerless was she. As the boat slid into the harbour, overseen by the ancient walls of Castillo el Morro, the gulls had mocked her, exulting in their freedom.

She had ample time to consider her situation during the crossing: banished from her home, with just a suitcase, destined for a hastily arranged job in a tea room run by her cousin Beatriz, who was a virtual stranger. They had met only once as children, long ago at a family wedding. With ten years between them, there was no common ground. Alicia retained a memory of a plump, confident girl with a knowing air and the bright eyes of a blackbird. There had been no contact since. At least, she thought, a tea room would provide a sanctuary in a town with a rough reputation, somewhere she could recover and decide what to do next. However hard she tried, the visions of dainty tables amid murmurs of polite conversation failed to soothe her.

She stared into the waves. In the patterns of blue and white, she fancied she saw faces: Papa's scowl, Raoul's teeth bared in rage, Mamacita's anguished farewell. She closed her eyes, but this only amplified the movement of the deck beneath her feet.

What is done cannot be undone.

For a moment she thought how easy it would be just to surrender. There would only be a quiet splash as she went in. It would all be over in seconds. Maybe the tides would carry her body back to Havana, where she belonged.

But no, she could not. Water terrified her, despite Papa's frustrated attempts to teach her to swim. Even just standing so near it made her hands white on the rail, blood crashing crazily around in her head.

Then, just at the edge of her vision, there was a flash of light, and then another, and another. Suddenly all around were airborne fish, leaping again and again out of the water on silver wings. She watched them fly and dive, fly and dive, from air

13

to water and back again. The crowd delighted in this simple pleasure, and she realised that, to everyone else, she was just an ordinary person making an ordinary journey. Her guilt, her family's shame, were behind her now, lost in the boat's foaming wake. Cheered for the first time, she thought: *if a fish can fly, then maybe there is hope for me.*

The ferry slowed, then stopped, remaining just beyond the end of the dock. The stench seemed to settle on her skin like the sheen of oil on the blue water. She straightened her back, which drew the foul air into her lungs and made her stomach heave once more. This time, her breakfast went over the rail, fish dancing excitedly in the remnants floating below.

The old woman patted her arm in a motherly way. Alicia wiped her mouth with the handkerchief. 'Why are we not moving?' Things must be better on land, she reasoned. They simply must.

The old man nodded towards the bulk of the troop ship which currently blocked their mooring. 'My guess is we must wait for that to get out of our way.' Soldiers lined the rails above them. White bandages – on heads, on arms, on torsos – flashed in the sunlight, giving the massed men a festive appearance belied by their grey, exhausted pallor. A few raised their cigarettes and whistled.

Her companion said, 'I have not seen a troop ship docked here before. It should have gone to the Naval station.' He adjusted his glasses. 'Ah, *sí*, look there.' His liver-spotted hand directed Alicia's eyes to an area of scorched metal near the stern. 'She has been damaged, maybe by a mine.' He removed his hat and passed a handkerchief across his forehead.

Alicia's gaze travelled up to the stack of coffins neatly

arrayed like dominos on the aft deck, each draped in the Stars and Stripes.

'Poor souls,' murmured the man's wife. Her hand made the sign of the cross over her shelf of bosom.

Up on the troop ship deck, there was some kind of scuffle. Shouts and laughter reached her on the noxious breeze, and then a big man with no hair tumbled right into the water.

'Oh! Is he all right?'

He surfaced, screaming curses at someone above, meaty arms slapping the water as he pulled himself towards the dock.

Alicia turned her eyes from the sad spectacle to survey Key West: *Cayo Hueso*, The Isle of Bones, The Rock. She had heard it called many things, but it was nothing like she had expected.

Crowds milled on the dock, tossing coins to small coloured boys who shouted and splashed in the harbour. Her eyes sought the rainbow colours of Havana's grand harbour, rose-pink and turquoise and gold, the stately arches and filigreed balconies, the elegant avenue of palms. Everywhere here was grey, from the grimy sewage workers to the weathered wood of the dockside buildings, so mean and poor in comparison with what she had left behind. The troop ship and its cargo of broken men were a study in drabness.

The island was flat, so flat that it seemed to float barely above the waves. No green mountains to soothe the eye, no rolling hills lush with banana trees. Nothing relieved this thin sliver of land, fringed with mangroves. Even the few trees in view seemed stunted in comparison to the magnificent, spreading banyans of home, and the spicy forests of pine. All was desiccated, dusty, bare. The Isle of Bones, indeed.

She touched the enamelled pendant at her throat, the *to-cororo* bird, hastily fastened round her neck by Mamacita just before the ferry pulled away.

'Our national bird,' Mamacita had said, 'to keep you safe and bring you back to us one day.' Alicia recalled that the bird was known to die of sadness if caged.

She allowed herself one last look at the sparkling blue of the Caribbean behind her, which led back to Cuba, and home. *This is my home now.* Slimy tentacles of despair coiled round her heart. Despite her resolve, she could not prevent a small sound from escaping.

The old man's watery eyes studied her. 'Is someone meeting you, *Señorita*?'

'My cousin, Beatriz. She runs a tea room.' There was no point in looking back. The boat's wake had vanished into the sea.

'Many people come here to begin again.' He gave her a consoling look. 'Welcome to America.'

Aboard the troop ship, John took a last drag on his last cigarette and threw it into the harbour.

So we're the lucky ones.

His comrades sat propped against the bulkheads, leaning on crutches or each other for support. Some of the most pathetic were the victims of the sickness that had raged through the field hospitals, just as armistice was declared. There was talk that just as many lost their lives to '*la grippe*' as to combat. Barely able to stand, their hacking coughs kept everyone awake at night.

At last, they were home, crowded onto one of the final transports to leave Europe. If the stormy Atlantic crossing hadn't been punishment enough, there was the explosion when the ship was almost within sight of Key West. He had overheard their captain say that although U-boats no longer prowled the Caribbean, the mines left behind by their vanquished enemy were still a hazard. And so it had proved. They were woken in the night by the noise, thrown from their bunks by the impact, and had been limping along at low speed ever since. It could have been much, much worse, but was the very last thing they needed.

The familiar smell of sewage washed over him.

I'm home.

Rudy appeared beside him, his hollow cheeks flushed. 'Want a smoke?' Rudy always had cigarettes, when everyone else had run out. It didn't seem to matter that his gas-ravaged lungs made him cough continuously. Smoking was his love, his hobby, some might say his religion. His grim dedication was impressive.

'Take the pack, man.' Rudy's hand shook slightly. 'Gotta do somethin' to cover the stink of this place.'

Rudy had attached himself to John as soon as they boarded, as if they were friends. John didn't have friends. Comrades, yes. Friends, no. Friends were a liability. Friends got friends killed. He had seen it hundreds, perhaps thousands of times during battle. Men stood up when they should have hunkered down. They ran into gunfire when they should have stayed back. They sprinted into no man's land, to rescue someone already blown to pieces too small to pick up.

That was not for him. As soon as he arrived at the Argonne

17

and took a good look around, he realised survival depended on one thing: staying free of entanglements. He couldn't afford to care about anyone or anything except doing his job, when the shells fell thick as raindrops and the ochre gas clouds floated into their faces. His job was to kill the enemy, to gain territory, inch by blood-soaked inch. That was his focus, the reason why he joined up, not to be anyone's babysitter.

Rudy hovered at his elbow. 'Hey, John,' he pointed to the ferry that wallowed astern, its deck full of passengers impatient to disembark. 'Will you get a load of those pins? Jeez.' There was a woman in a green dress at the ferry's bow rail, talking to an old couple. She was a spark of colour in the browns and greys of the harbour, her face shaded by a straw hat. Suddenly she rushed to the ferry rail and heaved over the side.

'All right, I guess,' John shrugged. That kind of entanglement he didn't need either. Pearl's girls were just fine for his purposes. He would head over there for some homecoming R&R, after he checked in with Thomas, and went out to see the old man. For the past two years, through all the mud and shit and blood, all the terror and hardship and pain, he would conjure the look on his dad's face when he came home, a war hero. As soon as he got cleaned up, he would go out to the woods to the charcoal kiln, and surprise him.

Rudy coughed so hard that his false teeth popped right out. At only twenty-two, Rudy had few of his own teeth left, and used old chewing gum to fix the dentures in place. They often fell out and John had become adept at snatching them in mid-air. These same quick reflexes had saved him many times in battle and earned him the nickname 'Lightning Jack'.

'Man,' Rudy spluttered, wrangling his teeth into position, 'you got charcoal in your soul?' He cast his eyes back to the ferry deck. 'She's swell.'

John didn't answer, didn't need to. Rudy was never bothered by John's silence. It was one of the few things which made his company tolerable. He could talk for hours with only grunts in response.

Not so the big, bald sergeant from Minnesota with the boxer's nose and the look of an angry pig, who sauntered over now with a crew of other hard-eyed infantrymen. Hicks, said the tattered strip on his uniform, but the others called him Psycho for his willingness to pit himself against any foe, in any number. He had been circling John for the whole voyage, prodding him, trying to provoke him, but so far John had dodged actual conflict. From Psycho's wide-legged stance, tattooed arms crossed over his chest, it looked like that was about to change.

'Morales,' called Psycho, 'we're heading to the Bucket o' Blood for some beers. You comin'?'

It was the roughest bar in a town of rough bars. He had no intention of joining the men for drinks – not tonight, not ever. The war was over, and with it, any reason they had to be together. Several of those standing there had John to thank for their survival, but he didn't want gratitude and he didn't want to relive old battles. He just wanted to be left alone, to go see the old man, and Thomas, and get on with his life.

'No, thanks.' He turned back to the rail to study the ferry. That girl in the green dress had finished puking, and was looking up at the troop ship deck, just where he was standing. Rudy was right. She did have good legs. He decided to ignore

Psycho in the hope he would get bored and find someone else to harass.

'Why not, Morales?' Psycho yanked him round by the shoulder and breathed in his face. 'Think you're better than us?'

'No . . .' John considered his options. He wasn't a small man, but Psycho had three inches and probably thirty pounds on him. Just the way he liked them: big and dumb. 'It's because you stink worse than those barrels of shit.' Rudy was all raised eyebrows and warning looks, but John carried on. 'And the reason I won't go on a date with you ladies is that I'd rather eat my own eyes than spend another minute in your company.' For good measure, he added, 'You fat fuck.'

The first punch went to his stomach. It was welcome, almost a blessing. For so long, he had only felt really himself when he was fighting and killing, attacking or being attacked. He was good at it, everyone said so. They even gave him a medal for it. And it was the only time he felt alive. All the rest was a blurry numbness.

Doubled over in pain, he waited for Psycho to make his mistake, and was not disappointed. The big man leaned in to uppercut John's jaw, but he flung his head back, catching Psycho under the chin in a spray of blood. While his balance was off, John used Psycho's weight against him to tip him over the rail. It was easy, fluid, almost like dancing. A stream of curses ended with a loud splash.

'Anyone else feel like a swim?' he gasped to Psycho's crew. His stomach hurt like hell, but the rest of him fizzed with adrenalin. A part of him, that part which had been awakened on the battlefield, wished they would all come at him.

But the others backed off, one muttering that they'd given

the Psycho nickname to the wrong guy. When they were gone, he slumped to his haunches against the bulkhead, breathing hard.

Rudy was at his side. 'You OK, man?' He helped John to stand. 'Jeez, would it kill you to make nice with the boys? How'd you get like this?'

John had successfully dodged this question all during the long sea crossing, and had no intention of enlightening him now.

'Give me a smoke.'

Rudy looked him up and down. 'You still OK to hit the bars and cathouses, right?

Damn. John had forgotten about his promise to show Rudy the town, one night when he had downed half a bottle of rum. Rudy was bound for New Jersey on the East Coast Railroad in a week's time, but first intended an epic round of debauchery. 'If you say so.'

'You're my local guide. I'm sticking like glue to you, Lightning Jack,' Rudy continued. 'Gals can't resist a genuine war hero. We're gonna be knee-deep in panties.' His gleeful chuckle brought on more coughing. 'Go on, show me yer medal.'

John slipped a hand into his pocket. His fingers closed on the familiar shape of the object, still with him even after all the miles he had put between himself and that ruined church in a small French town. 'Maybe another time.'

He and Rudy would make a comical pair, John thought, with his Spanish colouring and the build of a heavyweight, and Rudy as skinny and pink as a runty piglet. The women would most likely fall down laughing.

John resolved to pal around with Rudy for a few days and then lose him. He was an expert at losing people. Even in a place as small as Key West, losing Rudy would be no challenge at all.

From the dockside, Dwayne watched the soldiers make their way ashore. He had taken time out from his delivery round for Mr Jolovitz, but figured he could make it up if he ran all the way to Pearl's. It wasn't far, and it was his favourite stop. This was turning into a red-letter day after all.

It was a point of pride that he always turned out at the dock, with the rest of the town, to greet arriving ships. When rumour reached him that a troop ship had been diverted from the Naval base, he had high-tailed it over. And he was not disappointed. The town had hosted plenty of military personnel in recent times, but this was his first chance to see real fighting men up close, straight from battle.

They did not look as he expected.

For a start, their uniforms were dirty, torn and generally in poor condition. The men had a weariness about them which looked bone-deep. Several had the hunted expressions of game animals, and covered their ears to shut out the noise of the crowd. Some were crying, kissing the dock as others stepped over them. He had figured there would be wounded. That's what happened in war, people got hurt. He didn't really understand much about why they had gone to fight, except that Germany had done something really bad so everyone hated them. Why didn't matter. What mattered was that these guys, these exhausted, shambling figures, had won. But they didn't look like winners. They looked like sick, old men. All except one, a big guy with dark hair who stood taller and straighter than most. It wasn't just his posture that set him apart. He had the look of someone ready for another fight. He swept past Dwayne on the tide of khaki and was lost from sight.

Dwayne's attention switched to the ferry from Havana as it glided to a stop. The passengers spilled down the ramp, hurrying in all directions. One caught his eye, a woman alone, dressed in green, with a heavy bag and a hat pulled low over her face. A sharp gust of wind sent a group of seagulls into the air just in front of her. Startled, she let go of the hat, and it flew towards the edge of the dock. Dwayne leapt for it and just managed to catch the brim before it went into the water.

He looked up to find its owner standing over him. First he noticed her dusky complexion and heard his father's voice in his head: 'It's not natural for the races to mix, son. Remember that.' He knew Pa was right in this, as in all things. The Bible said so. Then he looked into the most amazing eyes he had ever seen, the bluish-greyish-purple of sea glass or storm clouds, which seemed to glow from the darkness of her skin.

A few spirals of hair had escaped the bun at her neck. They swirled around her face until she pushed them back with impatient fingers. 'Thank you.' She smiled. Even her smile was sad. 'Please, can you direct me to Pearl's Tea Room?'

'You want to go to Pearl's?' he said, with an embarrassing squeak on the last word. He stood and returned her hat. She didn't look like one of Pearl's girls, but you could never tell, as Pa liked to say.

23

She pulled the hat down over her face again. 'Yes, my cousin was supposed to meet me, but she's not—'

Miss Pearl ran up to them. 'Alicia,' she panted, 'I have been waiting over there.' She pointed to the dock occupied by the troop ship. Dark crescents of sweat marked her dress, whose buttons strained at her generous frontage.

Alicia, Dwayne thought. A pretty name, too.

'Beatriz?' said Alicia. 'It has been a long time.'

'*Momento, por favor.*' Dark curls stuck to her forehead. She produced a fan from her bodice and fluttered it with much agitation over her reddened cheeks. 'You are late.'

'Yes,' said Alicia, 'we have been waiting to dock for some time because—'

'Dwayne, you are late too,' interrupted Beatriz. 'Why is everyone late today?'

'You know this boy?'

'*Sí,*' said Beatriz, 'he does deliveries from Jolovitz's department store to the Tea Room. But since you are here, Dwayne, instead of where you should be now, I will give you an extra nickel to take *Señorita* Cortez's bag. *Andale.*'

He hefted the bag with a cheerful, 'Yes, ma'am, Miss Pearl!' and loaded it on his cart. Then he led the way towards the Customs House, weaving between piles of pinky-cream conch shells and ranks of patient dray horses.

Dwayne's eyes kept straying to the new one, Alicia. She was an awful strange colour, with that hat pulled low, as if she wanted to make herself invisible. It made him sad, almost as sad as she looked. He wondered what made her that way, a pretty girl like her. He remembered what Pa always said: 'Only the Lord knows the contents of a person's heart.'

But then he thought about what to buy with that extra nickel and cheered up. He had four of the five Zorro episodes from *All-Story Weekly*, hidden away under his bed. Now he could buy the last one.

A red-letter day, for sure.

CHAPTER 2

Alicia walked on into town with Beatriz and Dwayne on unpaved streets that ran with khaki. Hundreds of soldiers jostled past with duffels on their shoulders, and she was carried along by the tide, shoes whitened by the limestone dust from the road. A car swerved to avoid a large pothole and honked its horn loudly as it passed, a face leering from the passenger side, 'How much, darlin'?'

Beatriz just brandished her fan at him. Dwayne had moved ahead with the cart. He looked to be about fourteen, not yet grown into his gawky limbs, with the wary eagerness of a puppy used to being kicked. Never had she seen anyone with carrot-coloured hair before, and so many freckles.

'Why does the boy call you "Pearl"?' Alicia asked.

'Whoever runs the Tea Room is Pearl,' puffed Beatriz. 'There have been fifteen Pearls before me.' She stowed her fan, and wiped her face with a handkerchief. 'And there will be many more after.'

Competing for road space with the soldiers was an array of peddlers, weaving their carts through the crowd, drawn by horses or donkeys, others pushed along by their owners. Each called out the wares on offer, trying to be loudest: 'Fresh produce!', 'Fish, seafood!', 'Best vegetables here!' One sang lustily in Spanish about the ripeness of his avocados. A black man led a skinny, sand-coloured cow on a rope from door to door, all the while calling, 'Fresh milk! Get yer fresh milk here!'

'What's he doing?' asked Alicia.

'It's the walkin' dairy,' said Dwayne. 'That's Emily the cow, with Mr Clemens. Watch your step.' He swerved the cart expertly around a pile of manure.

The cow stopped at a shotgun house, laundry drying on the porch rail. A woman came out with a bottle, which Emily obligingly filled, and then shuffled on.

Alicia felt dizzy, like she had stepped onto a carnival ride when she disembarked from the ferry. She had met Americans before, of course. Ever since they had liberated the island from Spain, five years before she was born, they had been flooding in. Papa worked for an American railroad company, and insisted they speak English even at home sometimes. 'It is the only way to get along in the new Cuba,' he would say.

But these people did not resemble the cultured, sophisticated Americans whom she had met through Papa's work. They were more like the peasants who came down to Havana from the sugar-cane fields and tobacco plantations. Nothing was as she had expected. It felt like she had travelled to the far side of the world, not just ninety miles.

They strode on through the fading light. All the wooden façades were the same silvery brown colour, bleached and flayed by sun, wind and salt. The town had the flimsy, temporary, thrown-together look of a frontier outpost, so unlike Havana's solid longevity. Centuries of history were trodden into its streets, whereas Key West looked like it was erected just in the past five years – and would be blown to dust by the next big hurricane.

The exception was a large, handsome concrete structure topped by a sign: *Fabrica de Tobacos de Eduoardo H. Gato.* In the slanted sun of early evening, men and women streamed out of its doors and into the street on a wave of sweet tobacco scent. The smell reminded her so much of home, the longing was like a physical pain in her chest. Several of the men ogled her with open curiosity. A short man with a hooked nose tipped his hat to her. '*Buenas tardes, señorita.*'

He had kind eyes but she only nodded back, accustomed to ignoring the attentions of men in the street. Of course, she had been slighted and stung at times, but it was by no means universal, and always there was the circle of Papa's protection. Until she had met Raoul, of course.

'Who is that?'

'Hector Rubio,' said Beatriz, with a dismissive swat at a mosquito. 'He is the *lector* at Gato's, and my biggest headache. He reads to the workers all day, and gives them ideas, about rights and unions. He tried to tell my girls they should organise! Can you imagine?'

Beatriz halted before a two-storey structure which announced itself as Pearl's Tea Room. 'Here we are.'

Surely, there must be a mistake.

A tea room should be found in a quiet residential road, she thought, or an arts district, or amongst a row of pretty shops.

To one side of Pearl's was a rough-looking bar called The Last Resort, and on the other side, a tattoo parlour. Both were doing big business, the men with collars undone, fanning themselves with sweat-marked straw boaters.

A rickety porch hung off the front of the building like a fold of saggy skin. Draped along its length was a gaggle of girls in faded, shapeless dresses whom she took to be waitresses. Their eyes registered her arrival with mild hostility.

She checked again the sun-bleached sign above the porch. This was indeed her destination. But where were the tables with dainty china on flowered cloths? Where, in fact, was the tea? The grey of the building's weathered boards merged into the general greyness of the street, with no decoration to relieve its harsh, square silhouette. It was of good size, and might have been grand once, but it was gradually losing the fight against time and the elements. Termite holes and rusty nails peppered the boards. Her eyes, so accustomed to the colourful, ornate Cuban architecture, felt as dry and scratchy as her parched throat. This was no sanctuary; it was an outpost on the frayed edge of civilisation.

As the sweat dripped down her back, a sour surge of panic rose from her empty stomach, urging her to flee, back to the dock and the ferry for home. It took every ounce of will to keep her feet still. *This is home now. There is no back, only forward.* The girls' gaze followed her up the steps, prickling like the sweat on her skin. The boy Dwayne came along with her bag. He seemed nice enough, but there was something strange in the glances which he shot her when he thought she wasn't looking.

'Welcome,' said Beatriz. 'I will show you to your room,

you can freshen up a little and then I will explain your duties. Dwayne, she is in room four.'

The boy set off up the stairs, but Alicia remained immobilised in the doorway. Her senses registered the scene, but her mind, sluggish from exhaustion and shock, was slow to comprehend.

The salon was larger than it appeared from the street, with a high ceiling and well-proportioned windows. A heavy staircase rose from the back of the room to a landing with several doors leading off it. The salon was scattered with scarred tables, covered not with dainty china or flowered cloths but bottles of rum and smeared glasses. The only patrons seemed to be men in uniform. Through a wide arch to the right was a smaller room, in which squatted a plum velvet-covered sofa and armchair, shiny with use and nibbled by moths. Over everything hung an air of wilful neglect and decay, from the mismatched furniture to the cracked window glass, held together with tape.

Her attention was drawn back to the main salon when a lanky sailor swept a skinny white girl into his arms and stomped up the stairs with her, both cackling as they were lost from view. The air was thick with the smell of smoke, rum and unwashed men, most of whom had a girl on their knee or in intimate proximity. Their eyes appraised Alicia with professional interest, like she was a cow at auction.

'Hey, Miss Pearl,' called a man whose teeth matched his stained Army greens, 'who's the new girl? Ain't seen a brown in here before.' His hand reached out to pull Alicia to him.

She slapped at it and stepped back, shaking. That urge to flee now took over, a purely instinctive, animal need to get away, to be somewhere, anywhere else, with no thought for consequences or practicalities. All that mattered was escape from the stinking room and its leering, grasping occupants.

She turned to Beatriz. 'Give me my bag, I am leaving.'

'No, you cannot. I need you. Since Susan ran off with that *bastardo* real estate agent from Miami, I have no one to—'

Alicia's legs carried her out the door, onto the porch and down the steps. She would leave without her possessions. In some ways, it made things simpler. Now she had nothing, nothing at all. Heading towards the dockside, with no plan or even idea of where to go or what to do, her vision narrowed to the road just ahead of her limestone-dusted shoes. On the crossing from Havana, it had seemed her life had taken a wrong turn. Now she realised it had run right over the edge of a cliff.

'Stop!' Beatriz caught her arm. 'Wait!' Her face was flushed again.

Alicia spun round. 'You would make me into a *puta*? You would do that to me? Your own family?' She shook off her cousin and strode on, smearing away angry tears with the back of her hand. *There must be jobs here I could do. I have skills. I have good manners. I will find something.*

'No!' shouted Beatriz. 'Please, stop. Just wait, *por favor. Mi corazón*, my heart is not good.' She sat on the stoop of a derelict house. One hand clutched the front of her dress, her breath coming in harsh gasps.

Alicia turned. Despite herself, she noticed the bloodshot eyes and the pale, sweaty cheeks, set off by bright pink blotches. 'You should rest.'

Beatriz looked up, still breathing hard, 'So says the girl who made me chase her down the street.' She wafted her face with the fan. 'Susan was my greeter. She gave some class to the place. Of course, I did not expect you to work upstairs. I want you to take Susan's job. Look at you.' She wiped the sweat from her face with a grey handkerchief. 'An exotic "brown". Not pretty enough to cause trouble, but interesting. Just what the Tea Room needs out front. You will have them clawing at the door.'

'You lied to my family! You tricked them. How could you?' She thought of Papa and Mamacita sitting down to dinner about now, imagining their only daughter tucked up safely in the establishment with the dainty china.

'I did not lie, no, I did not.' Beatriz pointed a shaky finger, her other hand still at her chest. 'I told them there was a job for you in a tea room. And that is true. We even have tea on the menu. No one has ordered it in the ten years I have been running the place,' she conceded with a tilt of her head, 'but it is there. Listen, *chica*,' and here her face showed a mixture of calculation and pity, 'you should know, your precious family was desperate. They could not get rid of you fast enough.'

Alicia's eyes stung with the truth of those words. Papa's face, when he called her into his study, had somehow managed to look both pale and dark. Even so, she had not expected banishment, had not recovered from the shock of it, and wondered if she ever would. A mournful 'mooo' from Emily the cow reached her ears.

'I do not need your job. I can make my own way. Anything would be better than this.' And she turned to walk off.

'With what experience? What contacts?' Beatriz's voice followed her. 'Mark my words, you will end up working on your back, just like every girl who comes here alone. With me, you have protection and a home, and all you have to do is smile and flutter those pretty eyes of yours. Not so bad, eh? Think, *chica*. You know I am right.'

Beatriz's logic felt like a punch to the ribs. Winded, Alicia slumped onto the stoop. The street life flowed on by, peddlers and soldiers, beggars and hawkers, unstoppable as a river heading for the sea. If she attempted to swim it alone, she would surely drown.

'Yes,' continued Beatriz, 'your darling Mamacita told me everything. You cannot go back – not now, not after what you did. Maybe never.' With a shrug, she stowed the fan in her bodice. 'The Rock is not a bad place, once you get used to it.'

Something in her wistful, faraway tone made Alicia ask, 'Beatriz, why are you here?' She had a vague memory of Mamacita and Papa whispering over coffee after dinner. Beatriz's name was never mentioned after that, until the awful day when Alicia came running home, screaming, from Raoul's house.

'You are not the first problem Cortez girl to be dumped here,' said Beatriz, with a bitter shake of her head. 'I was younger than you, but enough of a woman to tempt my uncle.' She sat beside Alicia on the stoop. 'They sent me here to work as nanny for the Gatos. *Señor* Gato was the first good man I met, he taught me about business. I was terrible with children, but excellent with numbers. When he died, his wife threw me out in the street.' With a grunt, she stretched swollen feet in front of her. 'I worked as a maid in the Tea Room, then moved up to greeter, and finally became Pearl when the last one drank herself to death.'

Alicia found her own situation difficult enough, but she could not imagine the terror and loneliness of a younger girl forced to get along in this strange place, far from everything familiar. She knew Raoul's father wanted her dead, Mamacita had said so during the frenzied packing which preceded her departure. Now she wondered what would have become of her, had Beatriz not been willing to take her in. For the first time, she realised things could have been worse. 'Thank you, cousin.'

'Do not thank me.' Beatriz's glance was sharp again. 'You will curse me soon enough.'

They sat together for a few minutes in silence, while Alicia gathered herself. She forced herself to look around and see the place, really see it. The fish peddler stopped across the street to pick at a sore on his leg. His dog gave it an experimental lick. *This is my home now, these dusty streets, these scorched buildings, these odd people. For now, and maybe forever.*

'So what do I need to know, about getting along here?'

'Learn to shoot,' said Beatriz, 'and keep your back to the wall.'

Still a feeling of unreality would not be dispelled. Too much had happened, too quickly. Such was Alicia's sense of dislocation, she would not have been surprised to see an elephant stroll by, eating an ice cream.

The gorilla barged out of a side alley, an enormous sack of potatoes balanced across its bulging, black-haired shoulders. Alicia shrieked in surprise, hand over her mouth. The beast was dressed in faded blue overalls.

She turned, agape, to find Beatriz wheezing with mirth.

'What . . . what is that?' she croaked, eyes still on the blue-clad animal as it muscled its way along the street with seeming great purpose. From the top of its pointed head to its leathery feet, it was almost six feet tall. Its appearance drew not a single curious glance from the passers-by.

'He is Percy,' said Beatriz, wiping tears from her eyes. 'He works on the dock. The circus did not want him any more, so they gave him a job. Welcome to the land of opportunity, *chica*.'

~ CHAPTER 3 ~

John shifted the heavy duffel bag to his other shoulder. The journey of many weeks and thousands of miles was almost over. He muscled his way through shipmates, peddlers, workers from Gato's, and lunchtime drinkers on their way home to sleep it off, a head taller than most of the crowd. Rudy coughed and shuffled in the dust of his wake.

John lengthened his stride, impatient to be back on home territory and resume his place at the bar. Three years previously, he had been in a red-hot hurry to see the world, fight for his country, and have adventures. Now he just wanted to be back within the four walls of The Last Resort.

He had built the business over several years, after he won it in a crap game. Lots of the guys from the ship were interested when they learned he owned a bar. He would serve their drinks tonight and send them on their way, back to Iowa and Texas, California and Vermont. He bore them no ill will, but it was time to move on. Long ago, he had learned that distance, not time, was the great healer.

Distance, and work. There was plenty of work to do, of

that he was sure. He had received no letters from Thomas for months, and was keen to find out if this meant that there was no news, or that there was bad news.

Rudy panted beside him. 'How much farther?'

'Almost there.' Rudy was like a sea anchor, impeding his progress. The little guy had helped pass the time on the trip, always with a deck of cards and his inexhaustible supply of tobacco. But in exchange, John was subjected to Rudy's whole life story, about how his dad was killed by a trolley bus back in New Jersey, and how he worried about his mom's asthma in their mouldy tenement, about how his brother's rickets had made him medically unfit for the army. It was more than he needed to know, but it was a distraction from the endless miles of ocean in front of him, and he even came to look forward to their all-night gin rummy games. And Rudy had a stock of silly gags which shouldn't have been funny but were. He was one of the few people who could make John laugh.

Now Rudy's usefulness was ended, they could part as well.

As they turned the corner into Tamarind Street, the sun hit his face like a fist. His uniform was welded to his torso with sweat. Someone had cut down the big palm tree that used to grow beside The Lobster Pot, which he thought was a shame, as it was the only shade on the street. Soldiers lounged on the steps of Pearl's, hats off, collars undone.

He would need to work hard to re-establish his place in the local hierarchy. There was a time, before he went away, when The Last Resort was the undisputed favourite in town, with its proximity to Pearl's and the docks. No more, it seemed. At this moment, such a challenge was just what he needed.

'I'm done, man,' Rudy said, sitting atop his duffel bag.

'It's all right, we're here.'

He looked up at the sign. A little more faded, but otherwise The Last Resort looked much as it did when he left. It seemed that the hurricane seasons had been kind while he was gone. The roof was on, and there were no holes in the walls. He rested his duffel on the ground.

Rudy lit up a cigarette. 'Well, I – Jesus Christ!' he exclaimed and fell off his bag, as a huge shape blocked the sun. He dropped his cigarette and scrambled to his feet.

John grinned. Thomas often had this effect on people. 'Good to see you.'

'Welcome home.' Thomas enveloped him in a lung-crushing embrace. 'Wasn't sure you'd made it. Ain't had no letters for months.' He hung on, making it hard for John to breathe.

Rudy coughed.

'Who this?' asked Thomas, at last dropping his arms.

'Rudy,' said John, 'meet Black Caesar.' He pulled away to breathe and get a look at his old pal, who had taken the name of the famous pirate who terrorised the Caribbean as Black-beard's lieutenant. It was useful for business, but Caesar was born Thomas Lightfoot. They had grown up together, both with fathers who worked as charcoal burners in the woods beyond the salt ponds. Thomas was orphaned at five when his father's kiln blew up. His face was badly burned too. He had no one else, so John's dad took him in, put bacon fat on his burns, and let him sleep in the shed with the dog. People in town would have thought it kind of strange, a black boy living in a white house, but there was no one to see it out in the woods. Even though the native Conchs took a relaxed attitude to laws in general, Jim Crow included, some lines weren't for crossing.

Thomas didn't talk for a year after the explosion until one day when John came to the shed with food, and he said, 'Thank you.' John taught him his letters and numbers, and they hunted and fished together. None of the other kids wanted to be his friend anyway. He and Thomas, who was part Seminole and thought himself an ace with bow and arrow, ran wild and barefoot through the woods. With his scarred black skin and Indian features, he was a powerfully frightening sight until he smiled, which made him even scarier. There was no one else whom John could trust to take care of the place when he joined up. This was the longest they had been apart.

'Well,' said John, 'that's the US Army postal service for you. How's business?'

'Good,' said Thomas. 'We need to talk, boss. In private.' He spared barely a glance at Rudy, who seemed to become even smaller alongside Thomas's bulk.

'Later. Let's get a drink.'

Thomas lifted the heavy duffel bag like it was a cotton boll. They climbed the steps and pushed their way into the busy main room, which was already full of drinkers.

'You coming, Rudy?'

The little man had recovered his cigarette, wary eyes on Thomas as he dragged his duffel up the steps.

Thomas raised an inquisitive eyebrow.

'Just a guy from the ship,' John muttered, 'won't be stayin' long.'

Inside, the open windows channelled weak wisps of breeze through the room. John roamed its boundaries greeting customers. He savoured the aromas of rum, tobacco, and sweat.

The wooden construction was steeped in all three. If it ever caught fire, he thought, it would go up like a grenade. The place looked good. The bar had a few more dents, as expected, but the floor was swept and the row of demijohns sparkled in the setting sunlight pouring through the front door.

A group of Marines in the corner launched into a raucous rendition of 'I Don't Know Where I'm Going, But I'm On My Way'. Across the room, some infantrymen struck up in competition with 'Over There', pounding out the beat with their boots.

Thomas lined up the shots on the bar. John threw his back and closed his eyes to enjoy the fierce burn of the liquid in his throat. In France, he had tasted all manner of spirits, including Calvados, Pernod and absinthe, which once sent him on a bender where he lost three days to complete oblivion. But rum was the taste of home.

'We'll get situated and then hit the town.'

He turned to Rudy, but discovered he would be on his own after all. Rudy was asleep on his bag, the only still point in the middle of all the carousing. John snatched the cigarette from his fingers just before it touched the floor.

'Pour me another one, Thomas, and then I'll head out to see the old man.' His father still lived most of the year beside his charcoal kiln in the woods, tending the fire inside its smouldering heart. It required constant attention to prevent it from either extinguishing itself or setting the woods alight. It was a hard life – too hard for his mother, as it turned out. She had left when he was five, to live with a Brazilian coffee planter who wished to remain unencumbered by children. She had taught him the hardest, most valuable lesson of his life: trust

40

no one. There had not been a single word from her since she departed. When asked, he said his mother was dead.

'John,' said Thomas, with a slow shake of his massive head, 'I wrote you. Your dad, he gone. Bitten by a rattler. Some kids found him, when they was out huntin'.' He laid a hand on John's arm. 'Sorry, man.'

When Thomas's father died all those years ago, he didn't cry, little as he was. Now he looked ready to weep. 'We buried him out there, at the kiln. Figured he'd want that.'

'Yep, I see.' John nodded, ears ringing as if from a punch to the head. 'Well, then.'

Snakes were a constant hazard in the woods, just another reason why the men wore thick trousers tucked into boots, no matter how hot it got. The old man never bothered. As he had been bitten so many times already, he used to boast that he was part snake. It was just another example of his deep-rooted stubbornness, which John seemed to have inherited. His first thought now was: *what a stupid, stupid way to die*.

And then: *How can he be gone?*

He rested his weight against the bar. His father had seemed made entirely of sinew and bone, glued together with nicotine. He was the hardest man John had ever met, and that included all the men at the front. And he never seemed to age. For all of John's life, he had looked the same, with his lined face, wiry white hair, teeth yellowed by tobacco and hands black with charcoal dust. He had seemed immovable, as elemental as the coral beneath his feet.

The last time he saw his father was just after he had joined up. Out at the kiln in the woods, the mosquitoes were biting bad, so they sat in the driftwood shack which was the only

41

shelter. The metal screens of the windows were coated in engine oil to repel the insects, but still they penetrated. They had killed cats, dogs, goats, even a cow once. Some said that it was only a matter of time before they brought down a man.

John felt like a cork in a bottle within the cramped dimensions of the shack, but his father seemed to take up hardly any room. For a time it had looked like John might turn out the same. He was a small, miserable kid, always getting beaten up. It got worse after his mother left because he never wore shoes, hardly went to school, and ran around the woods most of the time with Thomas. Towards age twelve, he suddenly put on inches of height and pounds of muscle and the beatings stopped.

'Why you want to do this?' his father had asked. 'Ain't got nothin' to do with us. Them over there, let them kill theyselves. It don't make no matteration to us here.' Cigarette smoke veiled his face in the gloom.

They had been around the same circle of argument again and again. This would be the final time. It was decided. The enlistment papers crackled in John's pocket.

'Ain't nothin' for me here, Pa.' He waved away the smoke. 'It's a chance to do something important, and see the world.' The prospect had made him light-headed with excitement – or maybe it was the fumes from the engine oil. He was going to get off The Rock and fight for his country, in France. His mother had come over from Spain, and she used to fill his head with bedtime stories of the Old Country.

His father's eyes were shadowed but sadness creaked in his voice. 'You think you goin' on some big adventure. I tell you this, son, war ain't no comic book.' He had been a midshipman on the USS *Maine* when it was blown up in Havana harbour in the Spanish-American war of 1895. He rubbed the sweat from his face with the old rag that was always in his pocket. 'Look, I know this life ain't for you, son, but there's other jobs than bein' a soldier.'

'You know what'll happen if I stay here, Pa. Just more trouble.'

He didn't seek out trouble, but it always seemed to find him. Teenage fistfights escalated as he grew bigger and stronger, culminating in a bar brawl that nearly killed a man and earned him a stint in the county jail. He gained a reputation for being unbeatable, which provoked men to challenge him wherever he went. After that, he found most doors closed in his face. It felt like The Rock was eroding around him, and soon he would have nowhere left to stand. He was a fighter. The Army wasn't fussy. They would pay him to do what he did best. It was his only way out.

'Yeah, you've always been a hot-head, it's true,' his father conceded with a sigh. 'I blame your mother's Spanish blood. And you ain't been right since she went away.'

They never talked about her leaving, ever. This was the first mention that John could remember. Sometimes he wondered if his memories of her were just dreams.

'Maybe the war will cool you down.' His father picked some tobacco from his teeth. 'Could be the making of you, or . . .' He slapped at his neck and fixed John with eyes reddened from decades in the smoke. 'Son, I sorely wish you wouldn't go.'

It was the only time his father had ever asked anything of him.

John downed another shot of rum and wiped his mouth. If there was one thing he had learned from the war, it was that you couldn't stand still when someone died. You had to keep moving, always moving, unless you wanted to lie with them under one of those white crosses in a green field. And the old man wouldn't want him to moon around, grieving. John could hear him snort, 'Leave me here in the ground, and get back to work.'

'Let's go look at those books, Thomas,' he said.

'There's more,' said the big man with an apologetic wince, like he had been forced to deliver another slap. 'The government, they passin' a new law, called Prohibition. Gonna ban all the liquor in the whole country. Sorry, man,' he said again. 'A lot happened since you left.'

Incredulous, he stared at Thomas, waiting for the punchline. But Thomas didn't smile.

'Come on, now,' he guffawed, 'I ain't in the mood. How stupid do you have to be to think that would work? In America?' Any suggestion of a joke was crushed by the intense seriousness on Thomas's face.

The old man was gone, and now the government had targeted his livelihood for destruction.

'Sorry,' shrugged Thomas. 'What we gonna do?'

'Well,' said John, 'seeing as I own a bar, my plan is to get stinking drunk before they take it away.'

Thomas never touched a drop, which was just one of the things that made him a useful business partner. He also knew when to talk and when to shut up. Without comment, he reached behind the bar for the bottle of *Aguardiente*: 180-proof Cuban brandy. John filled the first glass. The clear liquid

promised to cleanse him of sins and memories. All he had to
do was drink enough of it.

Next door at the Tea Room, Dwayne was on his knees in the
side salon surrounded by a circle of women when Miss Pearl
and the new one, Alicia, returned. This was usually the high
point of his week, when he brought shoes for the girls to try.
Among the jumble of boxes, they giggled and preened in their
new footwear. And once in a while, if he was really, really
lucky, one would lift her skirt for him. A quick glimpse was all
he ever got, but it was enough to send him floating home to
treasure the image, alone in his room.

He slipped a patent leather pump onto Paulina's foot. She
had the nicest ankles of all the girls, a voluptuous figure and
a generous nature, but the rash of pimples on her face earned
her the nickname of Paper Bag Paulina. Although her knees
parted obligingly, for once his attention was elsewhere. Miss
Pearl was talking to Alicia, who looked like her best friend had
just died.

'Wassa matter?' asked Paulina, affronted. Her eyes followed
his. 'Oh, does little Dwayne like a bit of chocolate in his *leche*?
Hey, girls,' she called, 'Dwayne is sweet on the new brown.'

The others commenced squealing and making a fuss all at
once. Dwayne felt his face heat up.

Like the other houses in this part of town, Pearl's catered
only for whites and Spanish. The blacks stuck to the houses
over in Coloured Town, although it was known that white
men 'jumped the fence' all the time. This had been going on
for generations, much to the disgust of God-fearing folks like

Pa, but so long as it happened under the cover of night, and no one talked about it, the town tolerated it. The Rock would tolerate almost anything, Dwayne thought, if folks were discreet about it, and that's how it should be. He didn't hold with people parading their private business for everyone to see.

The mixed-race 'browns', on the other hand, had a hard time fitting in anywhere, what Pa called 'neither fish nor fowl'. They were the evidence of the night-time excursions, the living, breathing proof that could not be ignored. And they paid for it, always unwelcome, never accepted on either side of town.

Dwayne sneaked a glance at Alicia. Although he knew it was wrong, he couldn't stop staring at her. She was unlike any girl he had ever seen, so exotic with that skin and those eyes. She made the other girls look dull and ordinary, like finding a flamingo in a flock of pelicans. Somehow her sadness only added to her charm.

Flustered, he piled the boxes up in readiness to load them back on the cart. It was getting on for dinner time and he still had to return the stock to Mr Jolovitz, who was nothing if not punctual. There had only been one sale today, another pair of the new Mary Janes that were proving so popular. But his mind wasn't on business. He would make it up to Mr Jolovitz the next day when he went into Gato's factory. Business was better there. The stop at Pearl's was never really about business anyway.

Sure enough, when he got back to the store, Mr Jolovitz was outside waiting, big key ring all a-jangle with impatience. No matter how oppressive the heat, he never took off his black coat or his black hat outside the store.

'I hope you're going to tell me that you are late because of so many sales?' he said. A glance at the cart showed him otherwise. 'Ah, not so.'

'Sorry, Mr Jolovitz.' Dwayne shifted the shoe boxes into the storage room, where they would be safe until morning. 'I'll do plenty tomorrow at the factory. Today there was a troop ship at the dock, and I just had to go and see, you know—'

'Yes, my boy,' said the old man. 'I do know. All those young lives.'

Dwayne mentally kicked himself. Mr Jolovitz's son, David, had been on the USS *Maine* when she exploded. He was buried in the special section of the cemetery set aside to victims of the *Maine*. Or, at least, he had a marker there. His body was never found. No one could tell Mr Jolovitz what happened to his son. So every day, even after so many years, he watched and searched among the thronging faces on Duval Street. And he waited.

'Sorry,' mumbled Dwayne again. Mr Jolovitz had been good to him. The delivery round paid better than any other work offered to boys his age. And there were the other attractions. He'd certainly rather be paid to look up Paulina's skirt than rake seaweed off the beach or pound sea sponges to death on the dock. He was his own boss on his rounds, didn't have an overseer checking his every move. Mr Jolovitz trusted him to bring back either unsold shoes or money for the sales. Pa wasn't happy with the arrangement. Mr Jolovitz's father had opened the shop long before Dwayne was even born, when the Jewish peddlers were driven out of business. Pa said the Jew would always cheat his way to the top, and the success of their stores was proof of this.

He said, 'Mr Jolovitz, sir?' The old man didn't seem to hear. 'Sir, I best be gettin' on home.'

'Of course, Dwayne, of course. Run along. See you tomorrow.'

Dwayne left him there, still lost in thought. He'd have to run to be back on time. Pa hated it when he was late.

As he drew near the house, Dwayne saw his father leaning on the gate, looking down the road in his direction. The Reverend Neil Campbell's face was like a smooth, glassy lake, with snapping turtles just beneath the surface. His mother appeared in the doorway. It looked like she had been crying. Again.

After he washed up, Dwayne sat in silence at the dinner table while Pa said grace. He tried to catch Ma's eye but she just looked at her plate. The chirp of the crickets provided a counterpoint to Pa's prayers, which always took a long time as he had to mention every one of his afflicted parishioners. Powerfully hungry, Dwayne gave a prayer of his own, for the congregation to be healthier than usual.

'. . . and we give thanks to you for curing Mrs Saltby's lumbago,' his father continued, 'and for healing Jim Logan's toothache.'

Dwayne fell on his food, although it was the usual fried conch and grits. He fished for conch in his glass-bottomed boat, which Ma cooked in all kinds of ways, but it always tasted the same. Their yard was piled high with the rosy-throated shells, like a conch graveyard. Sometimes Dwayne sold them to tourists on the dock for extra money.

'Did you hear me say "amen"?' his father asked.

Dwayne's fork halted a few inches from his lips. 'No, sir.'

'Then I'm not finished.'

With reluctance, Dwayne lowered the fork to his plate. He knew, word for word, what would follow.

'And we ask thee, oh Lord, to cherish and keep our little Danny, whose light still shines for us, and who we miss every day.'

Danny was only three when he died of diphtheria. As soon as he was aware of such things, Dwayne understood his role was to live the life that beautiful Danny would have lived, had Satan not poisoned his tiny, perfect body with an awful disease. There was only one problem with the plan, and it was a big one: everything about Dwayne disappointed. He didn't look like Danny, who had silky fair hair and fine features. Dwayne's hair was coarse, curly reddish brown, his brows heavy and his freckled nose prominent. Danny smiled continuously for his three short years of life, according to Pa, whereas Dwayne had colic and screamed non-stop for three months after he was born. At church once he overheard someone say he was lucky not to have been drowned in a bucket. Danny was the dream child, and Dwayne struggled every single day to live up to his image. 'Amen,' he said, and shovelled some grits into his mouth.

'And we give thee a special thanks, O Lord,' intoned his father, his deep voice edged with satisfaction Dwayne hadn't heard since old Hal Hanlon was caught cheating at the dog fight, 'for ridding us of Satan's worst, most powerful scourge.'

Dwayne perked up at this change of tone. Something big was coming, because the Reverend Campbell maintained his measured delivery at all times, whether sermonising or counselling

49

his followers. In this, his public persona, he never wavered. At home was a different matter, as he had explained to Dwayne many times: a man's business was his own, and no one else's, especially with regard to marital matters. Dwayne loved his mother, but he respected his father. As pastor, he was the moral centre of their community. Everyone sought his guidance. Dwayne tried hard, really hard, to follow his father's example, but sometimes he stumbled. This was one of those times.

'The Jews, Pa? Ain't they mostly gone?' Many Jewish merchants had moved up to Miami, a town which had only recently emerged from the swamp. Jolovitz was one of the few left, and that was only because of waiting for David's return. Dwayne thought of his boss, sweating outside his store in his black coat and hat. For the second time that day, he felt unsteady. The Jews killed Jesus, everyone knew that. It was a fact, taught in Sunday school. But he could not rid his mind of Mr Jolovitz's eyes, in their continual search for David's face in the crowd.

Pa took Dwayne's shoulder in a tight grip. 'In time, they will be dealt with, in time,' he said, 'But first, God Almighty, through his servants in the US Congress, is going to cleanse this land of the demon drink – forever. A great, great day is coming to our beloved country. Join hands and say "hallelujah" with me.'

Dwayne obeyed. His mother's lips murmured the same.

'Amen.' Pa's eyes were lit by the passion, but his voice remained level. The bigger the words, the quieter he got, until the congregation had to lean forward and bring out their ear trumpets to hear. Dwayne wished Pa was a shouter, wished there was some warning before he lashed out. He just never knew when it would happen. Even a rattler gave warning before it struck.

'Amen,' said Dwayne. Ma still would not meet his eye. 'But Pa, what about all the bars in town? What'll happen if they cain't sell liquor no more?' He chewed hard on the rubbery conch, then washed it down with lemonade from the jug.

'They'll have to close, son, of course. And that will clear the way for pious, good, Christian businessmen to take their place.' Pa cleaned his plate. 'It's a great, great day. Delicious grits, Mother, as always.'

'A great day,' said Dwayne. 'Ma, please pass the salt.'

Pa wiped his plate with some corn bread. 'And then all that's left to do is fix the Negro problem, for our little town to become a shining beacon of God-fearing righteousness.' His face was lit by an expression of pure joy at the prospect, with a broad display of even white teeth that never failed to charm the ladies of the congregation.

'What's happenin', Pa?'

'In time, son,' he said, 'all in good time.' Through a mouthful of cornbread, 'I'll just say this. I've been praying for help, and it may be on the way.'

He looked so happy, so different from the frosty, tight-jawed person of earlier, that Dwayne started to smile too. Everything was better when Pa was happy. But then he saw his mother shudder. It was very slight, just a shift of her shoulders, but it must have been ninety degrees inside the house. Pa didn't notice, as he was focused on his food. As in all things, he approached eating with a single-minded determination.

She raised her eyes, only briefly, but it was enough. That morning, she had burned the milk for his coffee. If Dwayne had not intercepted Pa's fist with his cheek ... He couldn't fathom the random nature of Pa's explosions. They seemed to relate little to the actual offence, but usually followed a night of argument. From his bedroom, he couldn't hear the words, just the sounds of voices and thumps and muffled crashes. Sometimes, he left his bed and crouched outside his parents' door, but never had the nerve to go in. In any case, he knew it was a husband's right to discipline his wife.

He had once seen a man crushed to death between two boats during a storm. Sometimes he knew just how that felt.

⤜ CHAPTER 4 ⤛

Up in her room for the first time, Alicia began to unpack her bag. Her skin felt encrusted with travel dirt. She imagined sloughing it off and walking free, clean and new like a butterfly, to escape Pearl's and everyone in it. It seemed impossible that she had left home only that morning.

The sheet on the single bed might have once been white, and the coverlet might have once been pink. There was a wash basin, a chair, and a chest of drawers. The water in the jug looked brown. Everything felt damp. The drawers smelled of mildew. On the sill of the dirty window overlooking the backyard, a dead moth lay on its back, desiccated legs splayed towards the sun. The glass was smeared where it had bashed itself repeatedly, trying to escape. The view wasn't much: an outhouse in the far corner, partially submerged in a green tide of strangler fig, an expanse of trampled weeds and concrete peppered with a few palmetto bushes, a wild crimson slash of bougainvillea. A water cistern on wooden legs completed the desolate tableau.

Conscious that Beatriz waited for her downstairs, she sat on the bed, her limbs unresponsive as in a dream. Grunts, moans, and the sounds of creaking bedsprings filtered through the thin partition walls. She put her hands over her ears. Beatriz had prepared her for a busy night and introduced her to bartender Felix, who had the square face and dull gaze of someone who had taken a lot of blows to the head. He made a special point of showing her the baseball bat kept behind the bar, which he referred to as 'Isabella' and polished in a way that bordered on lascivious.

A knock on the door shocked her into motion.

She opened it to find three women. The first, who had a lovely figure but a badly blemished face, pushed past her and said, '*Hola*, I am Paulina, and this is Kitty and Maxine.'

Kitty was the very thin girl whom Alicia had last seen being carried upstairs by a sailor. Maxine's skin was so white that it almost looked blue. Atop her head was a pile of midnight-black hair, her hooded eyes fixed on Alicia with a stare of contemptuous curiosity. All wore thin dresses mended several times.

They began to empty her suitcase, trying on her clothes, her shoes. Kitty sprayed herself with perfume and sneezed loudly. Maxine put on the straw hat, which perched on her hair like a gull in a nest.

'Wait, stop!' Alicia called, trying to snatch her belongings from their grasping hands, but this only turned it into a game. The girls laughed and screeched with derision as they milled around her. She had to get her things back, they were all that connected her to home, to the person who she really was. A vision of her future flashed before her: a much-mended dress, dull skin, hopeless eyes, these four walls, and the incessant noises of the occupants on either side. She made a grab for her hairbrush just before Kitty pulled it through her dingy blonde ringlets. It had been her fifteenth birthday present, made of polished mahogany with her initials inscribed on the back.

'Stop!' she cried again. Her fingers closed on the brush. Some note in her voice must have changed, because Kitty released it. 'Thank you.'

'The brown thinks she is better than us,' said Paulina, as she smoothed one of Alicia's slips between her fingers.

'No, I—'

'The new ones allus do,' said Kitty. Up close, she looked barely more than a child. A sore disfigured her otherwise pretty mouth. Her collarbones were like two twigs that would snap with the slightest force. She looked in need of a big plate of Mamacita's *arroz con pollo*. 'Won't be long afore you realise you just the same as us.'

Alicia blinked and held the brush to her chest.

'Yeah,' said Maxine. She came close enough for Alicia to see the yellow sclera of her eyes. 'You no different. Got all the same equipment.' Her eyes travelled over Alicia's body. 'Except you a brown, ain't ya? Don't fit in nowhere now, do ya, Sugar Plum? That why you figure to try them pretty eyes here at Pearl's? Hmm?' Her rum-scented breath was hot in Alicia's face.

Her back met the wall. It felt like there was no air in the room. 'I . . .' She coughed. 'I mean, I, I am . . . I am taking over from Susan. The greeter.' The girls exchanged a look. 'What? I am on the door, that is all.' Her eyes shifted from face to face. Maybe they thought she was competition? 'That is all. I am not here to . . . I am not doing . . . what you are. Doing, I am mean, I—'

'You think your little *chacha* made of silver,' said Paulina. 'But it just like ours. You find out soon enough, first time you on your back.' The words sounded more sad than spiteful.

'No, I do not, it is just—'

Kitty sniggered. 'That what Miss Beatriz tell y'all?'

'Anyways,' drawled Maxine, as she deftly pinned up a stray swirl of black hair, 'she don't belong here. She belong over in Coloured Town, with the rest of her kind.'

Alicia had been warned that things were different in America. Coloureds and whites kept apart from each other, always. A marriage like her parents' would be illegal here.

Mamacita had said, 'When your Papa and I made you, we knew you would be special. But being special is hard. You must have thick shoes to walk this road.'

Alicia looked down at her feet: square, solid, whitened by limestone dust. Not special after all. An ugly silence settled into the space around her. She had no answer for Maxine, no reference point from which to navigate the treacherous seas in which she found herself.

I really have travelled to the far side of the world. She raised her eyes, with absolutely no idea what to say.

'Don't mind her,' said Kitty. 'She's from Georgia. She don't get how it works here on The Rock. Anything goes here – white, black, yeller. So long as you careful, you can get away with murder in this town.'

'No,' said Paulina, from under her lashes, head tilted to better appraise her, 'she could pass for white, I think, in some lights anyway.'

If Kitty was all sharp angles, then Paulina was like a comfortable cushion. Among the angry red pustules on her face,

Alicia thought that she spied a flicker of sympathy. Or pity.

She stared at Paulina's acne-ravaged face. For her, healing was a natural reaction, a reflex: if she saw someone suffering, she offered help. It was as normal as breathing out after breathing in. And it had been her life for quite a while, ever since the school sent her home for the last time. Oh, how she had loved her school uniform: the shiny black patent shoes, the linen stockings, the yellow gabardine skirt and the little straw hat. Dressed just like all the other girls, it was the only time in her life that she felt like she fit in.

But when that was over, she had sought out the local *santería* practitioner. She had no interest in the religious side of things, just his knowledge of how to unlock the powers in the plants and flowers.

Everyone knew that old *Señor* Castillo was a *brujo*, but because the government had outlawed *santería*, his official job was barber. One afternoon as he was closing up, she presented herself as his pupil. He laughed and shooed her from the door with his broom. She left in a flurry of hair and curses.

But she was not deterred. Unbeknown to her parents, she had kept returning to his barber shop until he finally relented. After many months of pulling together all the knowledge from *Señor* Castillo's head and his books, she started by helping Mamacita's friends, just with little things, like headaches, coughs and colds, menstrual problems. Word soon spread. She would never forget the day when she opened the kitchen door to find a line of people waiting there.

Another place, another life.

Maxine opened her mouth, but Alicia blurted, 'Paulina, would you like something to help with those pimples?'

Paulina's expression soured. A hand went to her cheek. 'I wash with carbolic every day, but it does not help.'

This was the worst possible thing to do. 'You must boil the sweet potato vines and wash with the water. Failing that, tea made from amaranth seeds. There will be some growing nearby, I am sure—'

'Why should we listen to you?' Kitty asked.

Three pairs of expectant eyes focused on her. *Why, indeed?* 'Back home, I was a healer. I know about plants and herbs. People came to me for help.' She studied Kitty's mouth. 'That sore on your face. Do you get them on your . . . *chacha* too?'

'Yeah,' Kitty muttered and scuffed the floor. 'Cain't work when I get 'em there.'

Alicia was pretty sure that Kitty had worms too. *One thing at a time.* 'Well, I can't stop the sores from coming, but I can give you a poultice to make them go away faster. And you, Maxine . . .' She turned to find her standing, arms crossed. For the first time since they entered the room, Alicia allowed herself to breathe. 'You feel tired? Soreness here, when you have a drink?' She laid a hand on her right side. Maxine nodded. 'You must stop drinking rum and I will give you an elixir that will turn your eyes white again, and stop the pain.' She would worry later about where to find some wild chicory, although there should be dandelions in the rough ground at the back.

'Ain't no one gonna take away Maxine's rum, Sugar Plum.' Her stare felt solid, like a shove.

Alicia stepped back. Clearly she still had much to learn, but if nothing else, she had bought herself some time. To fulfil all these promises would require access to the herbs and flowers in her garden back in Havana. Some things, like aloe, could be found growing wild. But for the rest . . . she pictured the back yard again, the uncultivated patch of ground below.

A burst of male laughter travelled up the stairs.

'Let's go, girls,' said Kitty, 'gonna be a busy night.'

'For some, more than others,' said Maxine, with a final adjustment of her towering hair. In the doorway, she turned. 'You scared of spiders, Sugar Plum?'

'Oh, yes,' gulped Alicia. Snakes she could tolerate, and even admire their brilliant colouring and smooth, silky bodies, but insects were a different matter entirely – and nothing worse than spiders. Maybe this would give her some common ground with Maxine?

'Best take Felix's bat with you to the outhouse, then,' she said with a cold grin. 'Got spiders out there big as baseballs.'

With a nod, Paulina folded her slip and left it on the bed.

Beatriz's voice called out: 'Alicia, come down, *ahora*! Now!'

Gone midnight, John was wide awake and still unaccountably sober. The alcohol consumed during the evening had no effect at all; in fact, the more he drank, the sharper he felt. His feet still felt like they were attached to the deck of a moving ship, which made everything seem off balance. Nothing around him seemed real, not the walls holding up the roof, not the mosquitoes which stung every bit of exposed flesh. Not even Thomas's weighty shape behind the bar was enough to anchor him. There seemed to be a glass pane between himself and the world. He had always been a fighter; war had simply given him a focus, and a purpose. Now it was over, he felt light as dust, like he could drift right out the door on the still, hot air.

Am I dead?

Maybe all of it – the ocean crossing, his conversations with Rudy, his walk through the town, the bar itself – were figments, illusions, and he would spend eternity here, in this vision made of the energy of his final thoughts. The men told stories of the lost souls of the battlefield dead who could find no rest because they had been ripped so brutally from life. They just drifted, tethered to the earth but not of it.

That was exactly how John felt.

He looked down at his hand. It seemed solid enough, heavily veined and tanned from the sun, but as he watched, the fingers turned red and slippery with blood. He grabbed a cloth and scrubbed and scrubbed, but when he took away the cloth it was clean. The wooden walls turned to stone, punctuated by jagged shell holes. The windows lost their glass and stretched from squares into grand arches. And he heard it, played on a dusty piano by a man long dead, the soaring melody of 'Amazing Grace'. He was there, in that ruined church in Exermont. He had never left. He would always, always be there, forever bound to it by the weight in his pocket.

'You OK, boss?' Thomas's voice seemed to come from far away.

Bile rose in his throat. He had to move, do something. Sleeping forms draped themselves around the tables, on the floor, looking like fallen corpses. He stepped over them and hurried towards the porch. He had to find out whether he was, in fact, still alive. The answer was to be found next door.

'I'll be back,' he said.

At Pearl's, the crowds had thinned. About half the tables were full, but there were chairs atop the rest. Felix the barman nodded to him as he entered, then continued to sweep the floor.

A brown woman rose from her chair to greet him. She looked familiar somehow, but also terribly out of place. Her hair in its demure bun was different to the other girls, and so was her stylish green dress. She smelled clean, not heavily perfumed, and she lacked the knowing weariness of the regulars. Her skin was an unusual colour, almost golden in the glow of the lamps. Right at that moment, she was exactly what he needed to forget the past two years. And so he gave her the slow smile, the one that always worked. He wasn't vain about his looks, just pragmatic, and used to instant success, but this girl's fixed expression didn't change. Eyes averted, she spoke as if to someone over his shoulder. 'Good evening, sir, can I get you—'

Beatriz appeared at her side. 'Go to bed, Alicia, you can leave this one to me.' She took his arm. 'John! Good to see you, *amigo*.'

Feeling a little foolish, he allowed Beatriz to lead him to the bar, with some of his attention still on the brown woman who climbed the stairs, slowly, like she wore leg irons. *Alicia*. There used to be another woman on the door, with a harsh New York accent and brassy blonde hair. *A lot has changed since I went away. What did I expect?* At least Beatriz was still there. They went way back, to the time when both were new to the business and trying to get established in the shark tank that was Key West commerce. They shared information on suppliers and compared notes on how much to bribe various officials. John and Thomas dealt with a disappointed customer who tried to burn Pearl's to the ground. They shared liquor stocks when deliveries were late. She taught him basic book-keeping, and gave him a free pass once in a while.

She went round the bar and poured him a shot.

'Who's the new girl?' he asked. Like the rest of the liquor on this seemingly endless evening, the shot had no effect, yet he trusted Beatriz to give him the good stuff.

She refilled his glass with a quizzical glance. 'My cousin from Havana, came on the boat today. Interesting, no? Good for business.' Her sharp black eyes took in everything.

Of course. The green of the dress stirred his memory. *The puking girl on the ferry.*

'Look at you,' she said. 'Some trip you been on, huh? What was it like?'

'It's over. That's all.' He would never talk about it. Never, ever. Nothing would ever persuade him to bring it into the light.

'But you won, right? So everyone is happy now, and we get back to normal.' She polished some already clean glasses.

He felt her waiting for his reaction. 'Speaking of business, I hear they're gonna ban this.' He raised his empty glass for a refill. It was such a crazy, nonsensical, even un-American thing to do, that it only added further to his sense of unreality. He felt himself drifting up to the ceiling, like a spectator, and rubbed the edge of the wooden bar with his thumb. A splinter jabbed his flesh. *So I am alive, after all.*

Her face grew serious. 'What we gonna do? How we gonna live? Most of my profits come from the booze, and whoever heard of a dry whorehouse? We need a plan.'

'Plan?' He shrugged. 'No one's gonna bother us, all the way down here. It's a smuggler's paradise. We just got to figure out who to pay off, like always. Probably the same ones as before, just with different hats on. Trust me, we'll be fine.'

Beatriz did not look convinced. 'You want another? Or maybe a visit upstairs? On the house. Maxine is still awake.'

It was the reason why he had come to Pearl's, to find the sweet oblivion in a woman's body, but suddenly he was hit by a wave of fatigue so powerful that it seemed to melt his bones. It felt like he had walked all those thousands of miles back from the Argonne carrying his sixty-pound duffel. Without the bar's solid support, he would have folded into a heap on the floor.

'Thanks, but I think it's time to turn in.' He pushed himself to his feet. 'Suggest you do the same. You don't look so good.'

'I am fine,' she said. 'Welcome home.'

As he went out into the humid darkness, his last thought was: *Well, I was looking for another fight. Seems like I found one.*

⌒ CHAPTER 5 ⌒

A week later, at the rooster's call, Alicia woke with no recollection of the room or its contents. Then, in a rush, it came back. It happened every night, as if her brain refused to accept the truth, forcing her to experience the shock anew each morning. She was not in the comfortable bedroom on Cuarteles Street with its view of the presidential palace; instead, she was on a hard, narrow bed that smelled of other bodies. Shouts from the hallway filtered through the door. Someone had taken someone else's soap. With a groan, she pulled the pillow over her head and wondered how much longer it would take to adjust.

Instead of the gardenia's perfume, the whiff of the outhouse drifted in her window, forcing her to full wakefulness.

Like every night, the previous evening had been long and boisterous, with all the tables in the salon occupied, and more men trying to get in. Most were in uniform, all were drunk or looking to get that way as quickly as possible. Her job was to manage the flow, entertain them until a table came free, and encourage them to buy drinks. Beatriz said the men came for the girls but spent on the booze. Felix was there in case of trouble, with Isabella at the ready.

By the end of each night, the men's faces had all merged into a single mask of pure, animal need. Their laughter had the coarse rasp of desperation, their grimaces strained, as if they were fleeing an invisible enemy and could only find refuge in the flesh of a woman. They pushed wads of stained dollar bills at her, which she deflected with the help of Felix's glowering presence behind the bar. Fragments of their stories drifted in the fetid air as she passed between them, trying to avoid their grasping hands. There were tales of friends lost and chances missed and, over and over again, of the stupid, shameful waste of it all.

Fascination and repulsion mingled in the men's stares that followed her around the room, and all through the long evenings, the words buzzed in her ears like mosquitoes: *mulatto, brown, morena, half- breed, high yellow.*

Mongrel.

She didn't flinch outwardly any more, because they enjoyed that too.

There had only been one exception, the dark-haired soldier who came at closing time on her first night. Beatriz called him John. A head taller than the others, heavy shoulders sagging with fatigue, he had seemed to disdain the sweaty raucousness of his comrades. His nose had been broken at least once and his chin was creased with a scar. There was a cold deadness in his dark brown eyes, even as he turned his practised smile on her . . . like it was out of habit rather than any genuine desire. He had been back a couple of times since to discuss business with Beatriz – something about a new law, banning liquor, too ridiculous to be true – but he never spoke to her, just stared like he was trying to recall her name.

You think you are different to the others, but you are not.

A kind of routine had developed already. During the day, she helped out with cleaning, shopping, whatever was needed, and made up the remedies promised to Kitty and Paulina. Beatriz was bemused by her bunches of herbs and pots of salves, but did not object. She was allowed a siesta in the heat of mid-afternoon, before the evening rush, and then she was on her feet until at least midnight. She was coming to recognise, from a glance or a gesture, which of the men would be amiable big spenders, and which would cause trouble. At her signal, Felix was there to brandish Isabella in the offender's face, even before the first punch could be thrown.

Through it all, Beatriz was in control, even command, of the room. Alicia marvelled as she swayed between the tables, joking and laughing, swearing and teasing. The customers never tried to touch her, just seemed to enjoy the banter. And it paid off. The tables she visited always spent more. When Alicia expressed disgust at their behaviour, Beatriz said, 'Give me men any day. They are simple, predictable animals. But women . . .' and here she scowled at the girls, who were fighting over a torn, faded robe, 'may *Dios* preserve me from them.'

After that, Alicia tried to adopt Beatriz's approach. The bald, beak-nosed sailor she saw as a tortoise; the soldier with the huge handle-bar moustache was a Schnauzer dog; the tubby cigar worker with the sleepy brown eyes, a bear just out of hibernation. It was fanciful, but it worked. No more did she cringe.

With a yawn, she pushed aside the clinging sheet and went

to the window. The morning air was already warm. Down below, the sun painted the yard yellow.

She heard it again, in a deep, slow Southern drawl: 'Half-breed.'

Mamacita had wanted a white husband for her, for the same reason she had married Papa.

'This is the best thing for your future, and for your children,' she had said. 'You will have an easier time because you are lighter than me, and your daughter will be lighter than you. And so on.'

Alicia knew of several neighbourhood girls who had bought things to bleach their skin, to improve their prospects of finding a better job, a better husband. At the time, she had felt fortunate not to need that, especially when a school friend was horribly burned. She trusted Papa, so when he presented Raoul, the boss's son, she had smiled a lot and said little, as instructed. Raoul had the right skin colour, the right family, and the right address. Not bad to look at either. Everyone said she was lucky, so lucky. She understood perfectly well what they meant, and from their first night together, he made sure she knew it, too.

Her time at the Tea Room had brought home what she already knew, but had refused to admit, even to herself: in the end, all relations between men and women came down to a transaction. Raoul had bought a wife with his pale skin and his good name. For the single year of their marriage, she had been his exotic pet, whom he could treat however he pleased. Fundamentally, she was no different to Pearl's girls. They worked for cash; she had traded herself for security and her family's propriety. At least Pearl's girls were honest about it.

The smell of fresh bread and coffee drew her from the window. A small mirror, spidered with age, reflected anxious eyes above a taut jaw. What was she, in this town where nothing was what it seemed, where her own cousin had deceived the family and a gorilla could find a job but she could not? Back home, her place was clear: the twilight land between white and coloured, as an object of curiosity. But here, in this wilderness . . . Maxine had declared her to be coloured, Paulina said she could pass for white.

'What am I here?' she asked the mirror and dragged her fingers over the smooth caramel of her cheeks. 'Good for business,' she answered, in Beatriz's voice, 'that is what you are.' It seemed her cousin had been right about that, on the evidence so far. Word had spread, of the Tea Room's striking new greeter, and trade was brisk. With a sigh, she washed with the stale water in the jug and pulled on a clean dress. Last night, a group of British sailors were in, and one asked her for a 'fag', which was not in her English vocabulary. She had always been a quick study, but there was so much to learn. Each day, Beatriz revealed a little more of the Tea Room's inner workings. She would be waiting, always first up, no matter how late the closing. She always collected the fresh Cuban bread from the porch where the baker left it, and put on the first pot of coffee.

But when she went downstairs, Beatriz was not to be seen.

Fumes of sweat and last night's rum lingered in the main salon. The girls were in the kitchen at the back, sprawled around an old table with their bread and coffee and cigarettes. The windows were opaque with the grease from the cook's dreadful attempts at food. So inedible were the meals that he slapped on the table, that Alicia had taken to cooking for herself while the cook snored on his cot in the next room.

The door was open to admit a damp breeze scented musky green. An old rooster strutted past, a scrawny specimen with only a single remaining tail feather. In a patch of sunshine rested the largest iguana she had ever seen. As if he felt her observing him, he blinked once and went to sleep.

Paulina followed her gaze. 'That is Miguel. He is mine.'

'Your . . . pet?'

'Oh, more than that. Watch this.' She pulled a scrap of fat from a ham wrapped in waxed paper. '*Miguel, venga aquí!* Come here, *amigo!*' She made loud kissing sounds in his direction.

Sure enough, the reptile opened its eyes and ambled with a rolling gait to the back door. Paulina dangled the fat from her lips. Miguel snatched it with a flick of his scaly head. A thick magenta tongue flicked over its jaws.

'You see,' sighed Paulina, 'we are so in love.'

Alicia's morning hunger evaporated.

'You got a boyfriend back home?' asked Kitty.

'No . . .' Unable to tell the truth, too slow-witted to lie, Alicia pulled her wrap around herself. She slept badly on the lumpy mattress, despite the exhaustion, with a recurring dream of being pursued down dark corridors of polished wood, treacherous with loose pearls under foot. 'That does not interest me.'

'Oh, she likes girls!' hooted Maxine, with a lift of her nightdress that caused Alicia to blush. Beatriz had since added to her advice, saying, 'Never turn your back on Maxine.'

'No, I—'

'Leave her be,' said Kitty, more weary than friendly.

Paulina studied her, but Alicia ignored her inquisitive gaze. Why should she tell these girls about her short, brutish marriage, or its end, that moment of insanity which had propelled her from Havana to this fly-spotted, grease-stained kitchen? Her remedies had begun to work for Paulina and Kitty – which Maxine continued to scorn, of course – and this eased relations somewhat, but Alicia still felt wary and very much alone in their company.

Paulina fed another morsel to Miguel.

Kitty said, 'Beatriz'll kill you, she see you doin' that,' with a long drag on her cigarette.

'She cannot see if she is not here,' said Paulina.

'Where is the lazy bitch?' asked Maxine as she refilled her coffee.

'Dunno,' shrugged Kitty, 'ain't seen her yet.'

'You're her kin,' Maxine said, waving her cigarette in Alicia's direction, 'you go wake her up.' She flicked ash onto Alicia's feet.

Upstairs, at Beatriz's room, there was no answer to her knock.

'Beatriz,' she called, 'it is Alicia.' She could hear snuffly sounds from behind the door, and then a faint cry. She went inside.

The room was on the shady side of the house. With the curtains drawn, Alicia could only distinguish the rough outlines of furniture in the gloom. Guided by the sounds of laboured breathing, she made her way to the bedside and spread the curtains a little. During the previous evening, Beatriz had been sneezing, complaining of feeling cold. Alicia knew how to treat that.

'Poor thing,' she began. It was already clear that Beatriz was not blessed with a robust constitution. Just climbing the stairs left her breathless. Alicia had offered to make her a poultice but received a brusque refusal.

'Sleepyhead,' Alicia began, 'some hot lemon and honey will make you feel much better and—'

She turned and gasped.

Her cousin's eyes were sunken and shut. From her open mouth came a gargly wheeze. Her skin had a greyish pallor – no, not grey, she realised, slightly purplish, like a bruise. Her whole face looked like a bruise, even to the tips of her ears. Beatriz coughed and shivered in the baking stuffiness of the room.

'*Ay*! Beatriz, what is this?' She put a hand to Beatriz's forehead. The skin was actually hot to the touch. She had seen similar symptoms of *la grippe* before, many times, but never this severe, and never accompanied by this odd flush of colour. And never so quickly. When Alicia had gone to bed, Beatriz was chatting cheerfully. From that, to this, in only a few hours . . . it was incredible. Her mind instantly went to work. Such a fever was extremely dangerous. It must be brought under control immediately. Garlic, willow-bark tea, elderberries . . . all would be readily available in her pharmacy at home, but where to find them here?

And was there enough time? Would they be strong enough to cool the fever? Just as she was wondering about her options, Beatriz gave a mighty groan and spewed red fluid down the front of her nightgown. '*Ayudame*,' she whispered, eyes bloodshot in her purple face. '*Por favor*. Help me, please.'

71

'Help me, John!' cried Rudy. 'I'm dyin'!'

John looked up from the desk where he and Thomas were working to find Rudy propped in the doorway, his face pale and sweating. The cigarette shook in his hand.

'You ain't gonna die,' said John, leaning back, arms crossed. 'You've got a cold, that's all. Get out in the sun, you'll feel better.' During his short acquaintance with Rudy, John had learned the only thing wrong with him was a terminal case of hypochondria. An ache in his back was polio. A stiffness in his neck was lockjaw. A bad batch of chow was dysentery. And although his lungs were probably pure black from smoking, his constant coughing never worried him.

'You're wrong,' said Rudy, with a hand on his forehead. 'Feel my head. I need to go to the hospital.'

'I ain't gonna feel your head.' John was in no mood to indulge Rudy's paranoia. At last, he had regained his land legs. The awful disconnected weightlessness had gone, and he felt solid once more: ready to fight.

He and Thomas were planning for the arrival of the coming liquor ban, the 'Prohibition'. Although he had reassured Beatriz it would be simple, they had much work ahead of them: to find new, reliable offshore suppliers, find out who to pay off and how much, get somewhere secret to store the stock. Of course, all his competitors would be doing exactly the same thing. It was going to be like a game of alcoholic musical chairs, and he had no intention of being left without a seat. And it was just precisely what he needed. In the heat of the rising sun, he had begun to see the ban as an opportunity, a challenge. First priority: buy a new boat. The Rock's long and illustrious tradition of smuggling had been founded on fleets of swift, nimble craft able to negotiate both open sea and mangrove swamp and evade more cumbersome official vessels.

He studied Rudy. The man was clearly unwell, but there was no reason to panic. They had just finished a long, tiring trip, after two years of bad food and exhaustion. The marine hospital was clear across town, and it would cut the heart right out of his day if he had to drag Rudy up there, even with the electric street car.

'Go to the hospital or not,' he said, 'ain't none of my business. You're the tourist. I've got work to do. Tell you what,' he said over his shoulder, as he returned to the papers on the desk, 'I'll take you to the hospital when you turn purple.'

Back in France, the medics had called it 'the heliotrope flush', a distinctive mauve colouring of the face that signalled the final phase of the Spanish flu. It sounded pretty, but there was nothing pretty about choking to death on the red jelly that erupted from their dissolving lungs. With supreme irony, it arrived right at the armistice, just in time to finish off many who survived the fighting. The men called it 'drowning on dry land' and it had nearly taken John, along with tens and tens of thousands of others. One morning, he had a sore throat and by that night was in the hospital, fighting to breathe, all around him the purple faces of the doomed. Once they turned that colour, the sign of terminal oxygen starvation, there was no hope. He woke a week later to find the men on either side were gone.

But that was nearly a year ago. Yes, it had been hideous but, like the war, it was over. *Time for everyone to move on.*

'He sure don't look good,' said Thomas, after Rudy shuffled off.

'He'll be fine,' assured John. 'What's up with you?'

'You still got that Colt?'

'Always,' said John. 'It kept me safe, through everything.' It was the only present ever given him by his father, on his tenth birthday, a fine piece with a walnut handle. In battle, the wood of the grip had come to feel like part of his hand and, despite many offers – some seriously large – he had declined to sell. It had proved its worth in close combat, when rifles jammed and bayonets got stuck between the enemy's ribs. There was only one time when he had wanted not only to be rid of the gun, but to see it smashed into tiny fragments of wood and steel, then ground to dust. That was in a shadowy corner of a ruined church in France, which still echoed to the strains of 'Amazing Grace' played on a miraculously intact piano.

'Good,' said Thomas. 'From what I been hearin' from my people upstate, customs men may not be the worst thing comin' to town.'

John thought he had never seen the big man so worried, not even when he announced he had joined up and was shipping out to France. 'What? Looks like you swallowed a hornet.'

'There's talk, comin' out of Georgia. People sayin' . . . they sayin' the Klan's comin', and not just for a rally. They mean to set up shop here.' His eyes flicked to the window as if, at any moment, hordes of white robes would burst forth, flaming crosses held aloft.

'Those clowns?' John barked, both amused and relieved. 'For a minute, I thought it might be serious. Why would they bother comin' all the way down here? And even if they do, they won't last five minutes, you'll see. This place is different. Folks here'll string 'em up with their own stupid robes. And I'll be first in the goddamn line to do it.'

Residents of The Rock had seen worse come and go, many, many times before, from the first pirates, to the Spanish, to the gangsters from up north. The locals had no interest in politics or big speeches; all they wanted was to be left alone, to fish and drink, and live by their own values – which meant making money and spending it however they chose, without interference from church or state. The rest of the country, and the world, could go hang.

If anything, his words seemed to make Thomas more anxious. 'From what I hear, won't be nowhere safe, once they get dug in. My cousin up in Tampa, he got lynched just 'cause a white lady say he looked at her sideways.'

'Trust me, Thomas. It ain't gonna happen here. When have I ever steered you wrong?'

Thomas just looked at him.

He stood. 'I'm gonna see a man about a boat.'

'I check on Rudy later.'

With a shrug, John headed for the door. Rudy was the sickest well man he knew. He would be fine.

It was early afternoon when Alicia managed to get Beatriz to the marine hospital, having been turned away at both the Maloney hospital because it was full and the Casa del Pobre because she was not poor. Felix helped her get the barely conscious Beatriz into a taxi, but there was no assistance forthcoming from the girls. With one look at Beatriz's face, they had shrieked and run to hide in their rooms.

'Help!' Alicia called as they pushed through the main hospital doors. 'Someone, please help!'

A nurse appeared, her entire body swathed in white, with only her eyes visible between her mask and head scarf. 'You can't bring her in here. This is only for military personnel. She should be at home with her family.'

Alicia's shoulder felt damp where Beatriz's head was resting. Blood trickled from her ear. In a low voice, she said, 'Her home is the Tea Room. I am her only family.' The sad truth of this made Beatriz seem even heavier. 'Please. We have tried everywhere else.'

The nurse opened her mouth and closed it again, then handed a mask to Alicia and said, 'Put this on, and don't take it off. Orderly!' she barked. 'Another one!'

The orderly wheeled Beatriz to the farthest corner of the ward, surrounded by screens, where the blinds were drawn against the sun. Another nurse appeared and performed a practised ballet around the bed involving buckets and cloths. She wiped the blood from Beatriz's neck, and from her nose, where it had started to stream. Last, she laid a compress on her forehead.

Beatriz looked even worse against the white pillow, already stained brownish red. Her eyes were closed again, her breathing loud and raspy, her entire concentration turned inwards.

'What is it?' whispered Alicia to the nurse, searching her eyes for reassurance. 'What's wrong with her?'

The nurse's eyes betrayed no emotion. 'Wait here. I'll get the doctor.'

Sitting beside the bed, Alicia took Beatriz's hand. She had sat with other gravely ill people before, whom others were afraid to touch, and knew the comfort it brought. Her cousin's eyelids flickered but remained closed. Despite their family connection, Alicia realised she knew almost nothing about her, this woman who had taken her in. *What use is all my healing prowess now, when I cannot help the one person who I know in this place?*

Around the room, nurses swished between the beds like ghosts in their white tents. Alicia noticed that the patients in close proximity had the same distinctive mauve colour in their cheeks. The air was scented with antiseptic and fresh blood, filled with the sounds of wet coughing and lungs straining for breath.

'Water,' said a hoarse voice beside her. 'Please.'

In the next bed was a woman of perhaps thirty, with a chestnut bob and bloodshot, bright blue eyes in a purple face. Alicia helped her to drink from the glass beside the bed.

'Thank you,' she wheezed. 'I'm sorry, for your friend.'

'The doctor is coming. He will bring some medicine. She will get better.' It would be true, because it had to be.

'You don't know,' said the woman, with a glance of pity that encompassed both Beatriz and Alicia.

Distracted, Alicia scanned the doorway for the doctor. 'Know what?'

'There is no medicine. Us here, in this corner. We're goners.' She coughed, trying unsuccessfully to cover her mouth. Red spatters appeared on the white sheet at her chin.

'What . . . what do you mean?'

'It's the Spanish flu, same as last year. This is where they put the unlucky ones, like me, and your friend. It's come back agaaaaaaaa—' Her words were lost in another fit of coughing. A stream of red jelly flowed from her mouth, followed by a high, horrible groan.

Alicia leapt up, a hand clamped across her mouth. '*La grippe*' had burned through Cuba, like everywhere else, but Papa had taken them to safety in the mountains. Everyone in Cuba knew people who had been bereaved, and the funeral cortèges had clogged the roads for months afterwards.

All the blood sank to her feet and she had to sit down again.

The nurse reappeared, pushed her aside and yanked a fabric screen between them. In her wake strode an elderly man in a white coat, half-moon glasses balanced on his masked nose.

'You must help my cousin,' Alicia implored. 'Her fever, she needs—'

'I'm sorry,' he said, sounding as if he had already said the words a hundred times that day. 'We didn't expect this to happen, not again.' He passed a hand over his balding head. 'We weren't prepared for another outbreak.'

Loud gurgling came from the woman behind the screen, then silence.

Millions died the first time. A balloon of panic rose in Alicia's chest, getting bigger and bigger until she thought it would explode. 'But how?'

'Just like the first one, my guess is that it came back with them.' He indicated the soldiers occupying the rows of beds. 'So far, it doesn't seem to be affecting as many people this time. Your cousin is . . . unlucky.'

A thought arrived to puncture her panic instantly. *Of course, Beatriz will be all right. This is America, not Cuba.* 'If it has come back, then you must have some medicine now, some treatment for it?'

He blinked as if she had spoken nonsense. 'There's nothing we can do except try to make her comfortable, with aspirin and fluids. We have whisky. It eases . . . things. A little.'

He bent beside Beatriz and held a stone jug to her lips but she jerked her head away, mumbling.

'My cousin does not drink.' In this dark corner of a modern American hospital, it seemed impossible that this was the best on offer. Even her herbal potions would be better, but she had none to hand and did not want to leave Beatriz.

'Aspirin will help the pain,' he said. 'It's all we can do. I am sorry.' And he moved on to the woman behind the screen.

Alicia slumped down beside Beatriz's bed. Her cousin's eyes opened halfway, misty and unfocused. In a barely audible voice, she said, 'I am dying.'

Alicia knew this to be correct, and nothing could be done to stop it. The speed of it, the terrible speed, left her mind in a state of reeling incomprehension. Only a few hours previously, Beatriz had been bossing her around in the salon full of soldiers and sailors, ordering Felix to bring in more booze. *How could this happen?* But it was happening. Words of comfort coated her throat like sand. It felt like she might choke on them. There was nothing she could say to help. For the first time, she had met a sickness beyond her power to heal. 'I am so sorry.'

'You must . . . you must . . .' Her lungs made a sound like paper being crumpled.

'Anything, cousin, anything. Tell me what you want, and I will do it.'

'The Tea Room . . . it is yours now. Promise me . . .'

'No!' Aghast, she shook her head. Beatriz didn't mean it. She was delirious. 'No, I cannot. *Lo siento*, I am sorry. One of the girls can do it, or Felix, or—'

'It must be you! Only you, you are a natural, I can see it.' A bout of coughing. 'Promise me!' Bloodshot eyes wide, cheeks stained with red tears, she clamped Alicia's hand in a grip of surprising strength. 'Promise me!'

'I will! I will! I promise!' She said the words in an effort to soothe, trying to wipe away the blood from her face, but there was too much of it, coming from too many places. Her handkerchief was soaked in it. As she watched, more of the life drained out of Beatriz.

Despite the heat, Beatriz's flesh felt cold. 'Please, please don't leave me, Beatriz! You are my only friend here. Oh, Beatriz, how will I manage without you?'

Beatriz fell back, exhausted. 'Go to John . . . he . . . will . . . help.' This was too much for her dissolving lungs. She coughed and coughed with such violence that it nearly tossed her from the bed. Vile red slime coated her lips. With a great effort, she gasped, 'You . . . you are Pearl now.' And with that, she closed her eyes. A long exhale followed, and she was still.

Alicia raised her head to find the nurse standing a few feet away.

'I'm sorry,' she said. 'But at least she didn't suffer as much as some.' She laid a hand on Alicia's shoulder.

'Thank you.'

'I mean, I'm sorry, but we need this bed. You can collect her for burial tomorrow.'

The nurses moved in to repeat their dance. They whisked

Beatriz away and remade the bed while Alicia stood to one side, at a complete loss. Within a few minutes, another purple-faced woman with frightened eyes arrived, and it began again. 'I'm gonna be all right, ain't I?' she asked. 'Someone, please, tell me I'm gonna be all right.' No one answered.

In a daze, Alicia left the women's section and made her way through the men's ward en route to the exit. Beatriz was gone, leaving her in charge of the Tea Room and all that went with it. It felt like a giant sinkhole had opened up beneath her feet and she was falling, falling, utterly helpless to stop herself.

Large blocks of sunlight fell on rows of men. Although pale and hollow-eyed, some were sitting up, others playing cards. A few were smoking. It seemed impossible that this could go on just a few feet away from the carnage in the corner, that these men suffered from the same disease that had claimed Beatriz. How, she wondered, could some walk away from this, while nearby there were the others dying every few minutes? What made them different?

There was no time to think about the question, nor would the answer help Beatriz. Her leaden feet continued to shuffle towards the door. She must return to the Tea Room, break the news, and somehow, somehow, get to grips with the place, whatever that meant, but the enormity of it weighed like a boulder on her chest. She had promised, and the words had been Beatriz's last and only consolation. At that moment, she would have cheerfully sold her soul to avoid honouring her cousin's wish.

The nurses brought in a chatty young man who tried to engage them, but they just ignored him while they made their preparations. 'Hey, gals,' he said, 'what ya say we hit the town after this?' He was slight, perhaps early twenties, almost cadaverously skinny. His face was a delicate shade of lilac, his eyes two shiny globes of terror. He was just one among so many doomed. She could do nothing to help him, or herself, for that matter, and so she continued towards the door in a fog of fatalistic dread.

His hand shot out to grasp her wrist. His whole body trembled. 'Please,' he said, 'stay with me.'

She looked into his face, so filled with hope and fear. And she sat down beside him, because he had asked, and because she didn't yet know how to face what came next.

ᘒ CHAPTER 6 ᘒ

John arrived at the hospital late afternoon, on learning that Thomas had sent Rudy there when his condition worsened.

On entering, John was immediately swamped by a powerful wave of déjà vu. The white-swathed nurses, the hushed voices, the sense of barely controlled panic . . . they were all horribly familiar.

He grabbed a mask and followed one of the nurses onto the ward, where he scanned the rows of beds for Rudy's slender form. A distinctive Jersey-accented voice reached him from a far corner. 'My pal will be here soon. He's a genuine war hero, ya know.'

Two pairs of eyes turned to meet him. Those bright with fever belonged to Rudy, and the others to the brown woman from the Tea Room, Beatriz's cousin. Alma? No, Alicia. The white mask on her face intensified her eye colour, a vivid hue somewhere between blue and grey, with some green mixed in. In the Tea Room, she had seemed separate, aloof, as if she were just passing through. Now, with her face covered, there was something so intense in her gaze that he could not look away. His head emptied itself of words.

'John,' said Rudy, 'meet my new pal, Alicia, she's been keepin' me company. Alicia, this is my old pal, John.'

'We have met,' she said. 'My cousin Beatriz is – I mean, was – oh, no.' Tears moistened her mask. 'I am sorry, you must excuse me.' And she turned to leave.

'Hang on,' said John. 'What's happened to Beatriz?'

Alicia wiped her eyes. 'She . . . last night, she had a cold, and just now . . . she is . . . gone.' She stared up at him in helpless desperation. 'I do not understand. No one has told me anything. How is this possible?' And she dissolved again.

John stood there like an idiot. In truth, he would cheerfully walk into German machine-gun fire in preference to watching a woman cry. He raised a hand and dropped it again.

It was Rudy who answered. 'We're sorry for your loss, miss.'

'Yes,' was all John could say.

Rudy's coughing broke the awkward silence. 'Guys, I think I'm starting to feel better already. Yep, I bet I'll be fine in a few days. Just need some sun and rest, and I'll be hunky-dory for the trip home.' More coughing shook his narrow shoulders. 'Like you said, John,' he wheezed.

John pulled a chair beside the bed. Rudy's whole face was now lavender. John reckoned he had a few hours left. 'You bet, Rudy. You're gonna be just fine.' It struck him that they had swapped places since their discussion that morning: John knew Rudy was certain to die, and soon, whereas Rudy had cast off his habitual hypochondria. John had seen the same thing before with mortally injured men. Some faced the truth head on, with terror or bravado or calm resignation, and others went on refusing to accept what was happening to them until their eyes closed for the last time. 'You're gonna be just fine.'

He felt Alicia's questioning glance but ignored it.

'John's always right,' said Rudy. He slumped back on the pillow. Blood leaked from his ear onto the white cotton as he mumbled, 'Genuine war hero, you know.'

Alicia and John stepped away from the bed. The setting sun lit up the walls with gold and bronze, catching silvery reflections from the metal bed frames. In its warm glow, the faces of the patients were returned to health, as if by a magic spell. The windows showed pure azure rectangles of sky. It was a beautiful evening to die.

Alicia's eyes were wet again. John said, 'You can go now.'

'Yes . . . yes, I should . . . I should go.' She looked around the room like she was lost. 'Beatriz said . . . she told me, I am Pearl now. I do not know what that means.' Her hands kneaded each other, her face twisted. She muttered something in Spanish, like she was arguing with herself. Then she seemed to remember he was there. 'Beatriz told me to ask . . . she said you would . . . that you might . . . help.'

The very, very last thing he needed at this precise moment was an apprentice madam to tutor, but without his help, the Tea Room would certainly go bust, even if this young woman tried to make a go of it, which seemed like long odds. He weighed the consequences of the Tea Room's demise: The Last Resort would inherit the drinking business, but it was a fact that men came looking for Pearl's and found his place, not the other way around. It was in his interests to help, even if it was a drain on his time. 'Yes, I will.'

'Thank you.' The line of her brows softened. 'I am sorry for your friend.'

'He's not my friend.' John glanced over at Rudy, who gave him a weak thumbs up. How many times did he have to tell her? This was exactly why he steered clear of entanglements, because of situations like this. He could feel Rudy pulling him down and down, like an anchor dragging him to the bottom of the sea. Sure, he wasn't bad company, and he was handy with a smoke, and a champion wise-cracker, quite a character overall, and . . .

No. This is not the time to get sentimental about a guy I hardly know. He's just one more.

Rudy's luck had run out, simple as that, just like the thousands and thousands, and thousands more men that he had left behind. He shook himself. Rudy would be gone soon, just like the others, and John would carry on. 'He's just a guy from the ship.'

Eyes narrowed, she studied him. 'He seems to think differently. He was telling me so, that you are great friends.' Her gaze travelled to the bed and back again. 'Maybe I will stay a while longer after all.'

He resisted the impulse to squirm under her intense bluegrey stare, which seemed to see everything bad he had ever done in his life. *What does she know about anything, this ignorant girl, right off the boat?* She didn't understand the first thing about him, nor had she any idea what he had seen. A sudden desire overtook him, unaccountably, to blurt out all his heroics, to impress her with the exploits and bravery in battle, the lives of his men he saved, the enemies he had killed. Whatever it took to erase that look. Instead he whispered, 'Why are you bothering? He's nothing to you.'

'I am bothering,' she said, 'because he is nothing to you.'

Death came for Rudy at around three in the morning. Alicia had been asleep in the chair beside the bed but woke with a start to find his eyes open and filled with fright. There was no moon, but the glow from the streetlight fell across his face, turning the red tears black. John was asleep in the chair opposite.

Rudy didn't speak, just wept and stared at the ceiling, as if something huge and terrible was about to swoop down on him from the rafters. She unclenched one of his hands from the sheet and began to stroke it. John woke but said nothing, just watched her from across the bed, his face unreadable in the weak light.

Slowly, as she stroked his hand, the tension ebbed from Rudy's body and his restless legs stilled. His grip on her relaxed. Just as she hoped he might be blessed with an easy passing, he took a massive gulping breath, hands at his throat, his whole body rigid. Then came violent convulsions, feet kicking, strangled sounds emerging from lips drawn back in a rictus over reddened teeth.

'Mom!' he gasped. 'Help me!'

Alicia leapt up. 'What is happening? Where is the nurse? The doctor?'

'They can't help.' John was by her side. 'He's drowning.'

He sounded so calm, as if talking about the weather. '*Dios mio*,' she sobbed. 'How can you just stand by, and watch?'

His voice stayed quiet, but above the white mask his eyes glittered darkly. 'It's too late. It's always too late.'

She thought he might be the coldest person she had ever met.

They stood apart in mute witness, as Rudy's moans rose in pitch and volume, then transformed into a scream of mortal agony. A few rows away, the card players stopped their game. There came a gurgling coughing fit which went on and on, in between desperate gasps for air, bouncing off the shiny floor and the black windows, up to the high ceiling, around and around the room. Some of the patients turned over in their beds, ears covered.

Rudy's teeth skidded across the floor to stop at John's feet, and then he fell back, eyes open.

A nurse arrived, but only to draw a screen around them.

John replaced the teeth in Rudy's mouth and reached out to close his eyes. His own eyes seemed blank, to all appearances a man unmoved, except for a tiny tremor in his hand.

'I am sorry,' Alicia said. She went to touch his arm but he shook her off.

Eyes on Rudy's corpse, he muttered something which sounded like, 'Just one more.'

Light-headed with exhaustion, John watched her move towards the exit. He should go with her, back to the bar. There was so much work to do, but still he sat there, as the business of the ward continued around him.

He had seen so much death, and walked away from far worse. So many faces swirled in his memory . . . their features flashed by, faster and faster, until they melded into a blur. Some were hopeful, some cocky, many just terrified. Often they called for their mothers at the end, as Rudy had.

Rudy was planning to surprise his mother with his

homecoming. 'The look on her face,' he had said, with his smoker's cackle, 'it'll be priceless!'

Typical Rudy, always with the drama.

There was no reason in the world for this to matter to him. None at all.

He's just one more.

And yet still he sat there, seemingly unable to move, staring at Rudy's last agonised expression. It was wrong, just wrong, that this little runt had survived the fighting that destroyed so many bigger, stronger men, only to make it home . . . to this. The anger took him by surprise, a powerful urge to smash something, to feel anything but this helplessness.

A commotion at the door.

'My boy!' cried a woman with a teenager slumped in her arms, 'Someone, please, help my boy!'

Alicia was by her side, trying to support him.

He crossed the floor in long strides to take the young man's weight and lower him to the bed. The woman nodded and hurried off calling for a nurse.

'Dwayne?' said Alicia.

John straightened with a grunt. 'You know him?' The boy was very pale, his breathing shallow, but as yet untouched by the purple flush.

'He does deliveries for the Tea Room.' More loudly, she repeated, 'Dwayne?'

'Miss Alicia?' Confusion and alarm registered in the boy's bloodshot eyes, his voice a hoarse whisper. 'Where's Ma?'

'She will be back in a minute. Try to rest. Help is coming.'

The words fell like ash in John's ears. Coughing shook Dwayne's whole body, and the blood began to seep from his nose. 'What's happening to me?' he cried, looking around wildly. 'I want my ma!'

'I'm here, honey.' The woman, now wearing a mask, reappeared with the nurse. 'We're gonna get you fixed right up, you'll see.' Her eyes beseeched the nurse. 'He's gonna be fine, isn't he?'

The nurse was only a few years older than Dwayne. 'We're going to do our very best for him,' she said, but seemed about to cry. 'I'll get the doctor.' And she scuttled off.

'You know my son?' the woman asked Alicia.

'I met him . . . at work. He is a good boy.'

'Yes, he is. I'm Lily.'

'Alicia, pleased to meet you. And that is John.'

Hands loose by his side, John stared down at the boy. The skin around his mouth had begun to change colour, just ever so slightly.

The doctor hurried over. He took Dwayne's pulse and listened to his lungs, then stowed the stethoscope in his pocket. 'He's strong, he's young, he could come through. We'll make him as comfortable as we can.' He half turned away, his mind already on another patient.

The anger still burning through John's body burst out in a single word, before he had time to think. 'Wait!'

'Yes?' said the doctor, his voice sharp with impatience.

'You have to help him.'

'I have explained,' said the doctor, with a glance at his watch, 'there's nothing we can do. He will either get better on his own or . . . now, if you'll excuse me—'

'There is something,' said John, 'but it has to be fast.'

'What do you mean?'

'There's something in the blood of survivors. I don't know what it is, but it can help, if you give it to others. Sometimes it works, if you do it before the flush comes.' When John had woken in the field hospital from his week of oblivion, it was to see a circle of exhausted, relieved, and frankly surprised doctors around his bed. They had separated plasma from the blood of a flu survivor, on the basis that it carried whatever had defeated the virus, and fed it into John's veins. John explained this to the doctor, whose eyebrows rose to his non-existent hairline.

'I've heard rumours about a plasma extraction, but we've never attempted it.' He studied John with new interest.

'What's he sayin'?' asked Lily, her head swivelling between John and the doctor. 'What's he sayin'?'

Alicia said, 'I think . . . I think he is saying . . . there is hope.'

'Oh, thank you, mister! Thank you!' said Lily to John. 'Do you know my boy too?'

'No.'

'Then why . . .?'

He couldn't explain why it mattered. After all, the kid was a stranger. But there was a chance, albeit very small, that this one could be saved. So many others were beyond his power, whole platoons of them . . . with luck, and some speed, there was just a chance for this one. With a shrug and a sideways glance at Alicia, he said, 'Because it's right.'

'You must understand,' said the doctor, to Lily, 'I give no guarantees about this. It's completely untried here. It may not work.'

'It definitely won't if we don't hurry.' John rolled up his sleeve. 'Let's get on with it.'

Dwayne was unconscious by the time they had drawn John's blood and removed the red portion to leave a clear liquid. It fell drop by drop slowly through a tube into Dwayne's arm. Lily sat beside the bed, holding his hand and talking in a low voice. His mouth and nose were lightly tinged with mauve, but it had spread no further.

As John was preparing to leave, sounds of shouting could be heard outside in the corridor.

A man dressed in black burst into the room, tall and powerful, with shoulder-length hair the same colour as Dwayne's. 'Where is he? I demand to see my son.'

Although his voice was not raised, John felt a prickle of alarm. He sounded like a man used to being right about everything. In his experience, these were the most dangerous.

At his approach, Lily went grey, as if trying to blend with the wall. 'Sweet Jesus,' she whispered, 'he didn't want me to bring Dwayne here, said he was in God's hands, but he was just so sick and I was so scared.'

'There you are, my family,' said Dwayne's father. Although spoken softly, it sounded like an accusation. 'I go to minister to the poor sufferers in my flock who have been struck down by this pestilence, and I come back to find that my wife and son have vanished. Dwayne doesn't belong here. He belongs at home, and so do you.'

'I'm sorry,' Lily began, her voice cracking with dread, 'I was just so worried—'

'You know my feelings on this. You know them very well.'

Lily seemed to shrink further with every word. She trembled, eyes downcast.

Of all the types of men, bullies riled John most. 'She did the right thing,' he said mildly.

'Who is this man and what is he doing here?' Dwayne's father looked at him like he was a stain on his trousers.

Alicia said, 'His blood might save your son's life.'

With a sigh, Dwayne's father turned to Lily, and his voice went even softer. 'You disobey me, and then I find you in the company of a brown, allowing them to give my son a stranger's blood.' As if with great sadness, he shook his head. The mantle of hair swished across his broad shoulders. 'You break God's laws. And mine.'

Dwayne opened his eyes. 'Pa? You're here. What's happening?'

'We're going home, son. All of us.'

Lily had stopped trembling. She was now completely rigid. Dwayne's father took her arm in a grip which must have hurt, but her face betrayed nothing.

As he led her away, she just managed to say, so quietly that John barely heard it: 'It was worth it.'

❧ CHAPTER 7 ❧

It was still dark when Alicia trudged up the steps of the Tea Room, but the baker had already left the fresh bread in its bag on the door handle. The smell of it set off a ravenous hunger, and she stuffed a chunk into her mouth.

Faint brightness in the eastern sky signalled the start of a new day, one which she had no strength at all left to face. The Tea Room without Beatriz was unthinkable. She almost expected to find her there in the doorway, hands on hips, demanding to know where she had been all night.

She paused on the porch, utterly at a loss to know how to proceed. It was oh, so tempting to forget her promise to Beatriz – after all, there were no witnesses – and flee to absolutely anywhere. But no, she could not, partly on principle, and partly because she had nowhere to go. She was trapped, with no option but to move forward.

Through the darkened salon she passed, with a few knocks against the furniture, to the kitchen for a glass of water. *Maybe I will wake up back in my bedroom in Havana.* In her delirium of fatigue, it seemed entirely possible. Lost in a memory of a gardenia-scented breeze swishing through her bedroom curtains, she turned on the kitchen light . . . and screamed. She screamed and screamed until she had no more breath.

Every surface of the kitchen was alive with a writhing carpet of cockroaches: on the table, the chairs, the worktops, the stove, in the jar of cutlery. They flowed over the sides of the metal sink in a living tide, scurrying to escape the glare of the light. In the moment that it took for the inky masses to disappear through the cracks in the floor, Felix was there with Isabella raised above his head, hair wild, clad only in an inadequate pair of shorts.

'Wha . . .? Who?' He flailed around him with the bat, searching for the intruder. 'Where is he?'

Alicia still could not breathe. Hand at her throat, she tried to speak, but could only manage to wheeze, 'No one. Here.' The chunk of bread rose up her gullet. She swallowed hard. '*Las cucarachas,*' she croaked, her eyes still imprinted with thousands of slithery bodies, '*en todas partes* . . . everywhere.'

Other sleepy faces appeared in the doorway behind Felix. First Paulina, with some white concoction on her face that made her look like a ghoul on the Day of the Dead, then Maxine and then Kitty, her hair tied in bows.

Felix lowered his bat. 'False alarm, girls. The brown is afraid of a few cockroaches,' he said over his shoulder. 'I'm goin' back to bed.'

'Might as well make coffee,' said Kitty with a yawn, as she busied herself at the stove. The pot began to hiss as the warm smell filled the corners of the room. She took the bread and laid it on the table with a crock of butter.

Alicia was quite convinced she would never be able to eat any food produced in the kitchen, or even touch anything in it. She could feel the insects crawling over her skin, in her eyes, her mouth. Her knees gave way.

Paulina scooted a chair beneath her and eased her down with a pat on the shoulder. 'There we go, *chica*. Seems like you had a night. How is Beatriz?'

Alicia had not planned what to say, so it just came out: '*Muerta.*' No time for explanation, because the three girls started talking at once. When the noise abated, she said, 'I am sorry. It was too late for her.'

Paulina crossed herself several times. '*Madre de Dios*, poor Beatriz. But we were with her! It is just like last time! We are all going to die too!' Tears cut tracks down through the white substance on her face.

'Did y'all die last time?' drawled Maxine, lighting up a cigarette.

'Well, no . . .' admitted Paulina.

'You were sick?' asked Alicia. 'With the flu? You had it before?'

'Yeah,' said Kitty, 'we was all really bad for about a week. Miss Beatriz took care of us.' And she began to sniffle too.

'That is good,' said Alicia. 'If you got better, then you will be fine.'

'But what'll we do?' asked Kitty, twisting the bows in her hair. 'Where'll we go? My people won't have me back, no ma'am, not now.'

Paulina simply looked at the floor.

In a quiet, almost thoughtful voice, Maxine said, 'We ain't goin' nowhere, are we, Sugar Plum?' She swung her arm in a grand gesture, cigarette held aloft, as if introducing a vaude-ville act. 'Girls, meet the new Pearl.'

Kitty seemed relieved, Paulina confused. Maxine gave nothing away, her hooded eyes shadowed by the light from the bare bulb overhead. Paulina put the hot coffee in front of Alicia, who gulped it down without thinking about it, eyes closed.

'It is true,' she admitted, staring into her cup. The coffee grounds looked like tar. Mamacita used to read them, much to Papa's bemusement. Alicia could see nothing but blackness on blackness. How long since she had left home? Her sense of time had both stretched and compressed. From the pale, straw-coloured light spilling through the kitchen windows, it could be either dawn or dusk. There seemed to be a layer of gauze over her senses.

'Beatriz asked me to take over from her.' A snort from Maxine. 'I know, I know. Believe me, I did not want this. I do not want this. But what could I do?' She scanned each face in turn, helpless to explain what she did not understand herself. 'She made me promise. But if any of you want to take it over from me, you may be my visitor.'

'Guest,' said Paulina. She flopped into the chair opposite. Kitty sat down slowly with her coffee, hands tight on the cup like she needed the comfort of its warmth.

It was clear from their vacant stares that they had even less idea than she of how to run the place.

'I must stay, but you are free, all free,' said Alicia. 'I cannot hold you here. I will not. So if you want to go somewhere else, do something else . . .'

'I got nowhere else,' said Kitty. 'And what'd I do? Tricks is all I done since I was grown. Nope, I'm stayin' right here with you, Miss Ali— I mean, Pearl. For as long as you'll have me, or I get another bun in the oven.' She picked at a scab on her hand.

The coffee helped to clear some of the fog from Alicia's brain, enough for her to feel pity and more for this girl-child. 'Another . . . bun?'

'Two so far,' said Maxine, sucking tobacco from her teeth with a scowl. 'And there'll be more, for sure.'

With a shrug, Kitty said, 'Miss Beatriz got rid of 'em for me. She always said I was too fertile for this job.'

'Kitty,' said Alicia, appalled by the girls' desperation, and their acceptance of this occupational hazard, 'we can stop it happening. All it takes is some honey in the *chacha*, and the sperm cannot travel. There will be no more . . . buns, unless you want them.'

'As easy as that?' said Kitty, sounding unconvinced. 'Why ain't no one told me sooner? I'm like to have a heart attack every time I'm waitin' for my monthlies.'

'As easy as that. But what did you mean, your people would not take you back?'

Kitty said nothing, just stared into her cup.

'They sold her,' said Paulina. 'Her papa sold her to the Tea Room. For fifteen dollars.'

'Was a lot of money, in them days,' muttered Kitty.

Alicia did a quick estimate. 'How long have you been here then?'

'Five years. Started on my fifteenth birthday.'

On Alicia's fifteenth birthday, there had been special cakes decorated with candied flowers, and indulgent smiles lit by a ring of candles. A mahogany-backed hairbrush. She turned to Paulina. 'What will you do?'

Paulina closed her eyes. A few seconds passed, and then a tear escaped from her left eye to thread its way down her cheek. She sniffed, and exhaled shakily, then pressed a hand-kerchief to her mouth to stifle a small sob.

Alicia was moved to lay a hand on Paulina's arm. 'What is it, *chica*? You need more time?'

'I was thinking of my old *nana*.' A loud snort into the hand-kerchief. 'She raised me, back in our village. She was killed in a fire on the sugar plantation. With her gone,' she wiped her eyes again, 'there was nothing for me there.' And she lit a cigarette with utter nonchalance.

Alicia asked, eyes narrowed, 'Is any of that true?'

'Of course not.' Paulina blew a smoke ring towards the ceiling. 'You pay me, I give what you want.' She fixed Alicia with a cool stare. 'I grew up in a suburb of Havana. I had a pony.'

'Then why . . .?'

'Why this life?' Her shrug hinted at a multitude of secrets. 'It suits me. One way or another, we are all selling ourselves. This is what I am good at.'

Alicia had assumed many things about Paulina, which she now realised were almost wholly false. They were far more similar than she realised. *Were you at my school? Did we pass on the street?*

'*Claro*,' said Paulina. 'I will stay. I have no family. I could go to another house in town, but I know girls at those places. Bad food, no protection, and so dirty. This place is clean at least. I will stay.'

Alicia felt faint at the thought of there being anywhere

dirtier, and resolved to find the money, by any means possible, to employ a maid. And a new cook. She turned to Maxine, certain she would be off to pack her bag. But Maxine said, 'I'm stayin', for now. Paulina's right. There are worse places than this.' She lit a new cigarette from the butt of the old. 'Much worse.'

'Maxine knows that better than all of us,' said Kitty. 'She has the scars.'

Maxine pushed back the sleeve of her robe to reveal a puckered burn, grape-coloured against the white of her skin, covering the majority of her forearm. 'Got that the night Hattie Malloy's burned down.'

'Hattie . . .?' began Alicia.

Maxine covered her arm. 'Was a floating cathouse, served the railroad camp in the upper Keys. Old Henry Flagler, he wouldn't have no whores in the camp itself, so Miss Hattie set up her house on a barge. It just floated offshore, moving down the coast with the men. I went to work there as a laundress when my husband got killed on the railroad.'

Alicia was not quick enough to stop the surprise showing on her face. Her reactions were slowed, her hearing dull. She was starting to feel uncomfortably warm, and unbuttoned the collar of her dress.

'Yeah,' said Maxine with a bitter chuckle, 'you thought I always been a whore, but I ain't. When my George got killed, they made me leave our house in the camp, me and little Sophie, said they couldn't have no single women or kids there. So I went to Miss Hattie and she took me on. I tell you, I washed some filthy linen in my time, but the linen comes out of a whorehouse takes some beatin'.'

The light from the window was now brighter than the bulb overhead. It hurt Alicia's eyes. Her throat felt dry and scratchy. 'So how did you . . .?'

Maxine crossed her arms and turned away, as if she had no more to say.

Kitty cleared her throat. 'Miss Hattie had her eye on Sophie, young as she was. There's men of all . . . tastes.' She now sounded a lot older than her twenty years. 'That's how Maxine got started. She went in Sophie's place. And then, one night, there was a fire.' She glanced again at Maxine, as if to ask permission. 'The place burned up and sank. Maxine floated all night on some wood. They never found Sophie.'

Alicia could think of nothing to say except, 'I am sorry.'

'Feel sorry for yourself, Sugar Plum,' said Maxine. 'Stuck here with us, now your fancy family don't want you no more. And don't try to fox us.' She waggled the cigarette with menace. 'Girls,' she declared, 'don't be fooled by her righteous act and her pretty manners, this one ain't hangin' around any longer than it takes her to trap some rich man.' She fixed her stare on Alicia. 'I know your type.' And she blew smoke into Alicia's face.

Alicia's bones ached with exhaustion. She just needed sleep, lots of sleep, maybe days of it. She would be fine after that. But she had to put this right. 'Not for me. Never again.'

'You were married before?' asked Paulina. 'What happened to your *esposo*? Did he die, like Maxine's?'

'No . . . he still lives. The marriage was annulled after a year, because—'

'He left you for another woman?' said Kitty.

'He left you for a *muchacho*?' offered Paulina.

'No,' said Alicia. 'It was because . . .' She had never told the story to anyone else. In her head was the sound of pearls skittering across a wooden floor in a Havana hotel room, as Raoul tore the wedding dress from her shoulders. In his dilated pupils, she had caught her reflection, arms trying to cover her chest, as he wound the leather belt tight around his fist.

'I am your husband now,' he had said, with a smile she had not seen before, 'who you swore to obey today, in front of God himself. Now you will obey, *puta*.'

She had lasted one year exactly. The violence of the wedding night was not repeated, but it did its job. She submitted to Raoul's every wish. When he came home from work, she washed his feet and put on his slippers. She served the food he loved, although her *arroz con pollo* never measured up to his dear, departed mother's. She kept the house immaculate and made herself pretty when they went out with his work friends, all of them eager to inspect his new *mulatta* bride.

When she managed to speak to Mamacita privately, she had no comfort to offer.

'*Niña*, I am sorry he is not more gentle, but it is how some men are, especially when they are young. They need to dominate everything. It is very tiresome, but hopefully he will mellow as he gets older. In the meantime, let me tell you a secret: men are terrible time-keepers. Have a supply of chicken blood handy, for whenever you want some peace.'

And that was all the advice forthcoming from her mother.

It had happened on the eve of their first anniversary, dinner time. She was chatting to Pablito, her tame hummingbird. Seeing his bright little face cheered her so, he was like a shiny green ray of hope, and her only company most days.

She did not hear Raoul come in the house. She should have been at the door to greet him, but she was concentrating hard on a new recipe, frying chunks of pork in a very hot pan.

'I am sorry,' she began, 'I did not hear you come in, Pablito was visiting and I—'

Without a word, he strode across the kitchen and took Pablito between his hands. For a small man, he had surprisingly large hands. He crushed the life out of her little friend, and dropped him on the floor.

A part of her died with him, and the cold, black void of the future opened up before her. She did not cry because she felt nothing, nothing at all.

'Mm, that smells good,' he had said, nodding at the pork in the pan. 'Give me a taste.'

Her thoughts were rushing like a runaway train, so many thoughts at once, colliding with one another. For one year, she had been his property, a year of total subjugation, which began on their wedding night. There would be a party the next day, with friends and family, everyone expecting her to play the role. And after the party, she knew exactly how the anniversary would end.

She held the steaming pork towards him on the turning fork.

He had smiled like it was a shared intimacy. 'Now feed it to me.' He opened his mouth, eyes half shut in anticipation of the pleasure.

She had taken the meat from the fork and placed it between his teeth. His eyes closed as he savoured the meat and the moment of total dominion. Night after night after night, she had thought, just like this one. Forever and ever, amen.

His face was a picture of contentment. With no conscious

control over her body, her arm drew back as if she were a string puppet. Just as he swallowed, she plunged the fork down with all her strength. His eyes opened first, in shock and pain, and then his mouth issued a pork-laden scream which went on and on as he spun around the room trying to remove the implement from his flesh.

She had run out the front door and did not stop until she reached her parents' house. And three days later, she was on the ferry to Key West.

Paulina's voice shocked her back to the room. 'Because why?' she prompted. 'Why was it annulled?'

Alicia breathed deeply, trying to clear the thick mist from her eyes. 'Because I stabbed him.'

There was a moment of total silence, and then the room erupted in exclamations.

'But if he's still alive,' said Maxine, 'you can't have tried very hard to kill him. If I stabbed a man, you can be sure that he'd be dead now.'

'I wasn't trying to kill him,' said Alicia, 'I wasn't thinking at all. I just wanted it to stop. I wanted him . . . to stop.'

'Well,' said Kitty, eyes wide with fascination, 'whereabouts did y'all stab him then? The stomach? The chest?' She paused. 'The whanger?'

'In the *cojones*. I stabbed him in the *cojones*.'

Paulina's mouth opened and stayed open. Kitty's eyes were large as the coffee rings on the table. Even Maxine forgot her cigarette. A long length of ash fell into her lap. She jumped up, slapping at her robe.

'*Es verdad?*' whispered Paulina. '*Cojones?*'

It had never struck Alicia as funny before, and certainly

was anything but amusing at the time, but for some reason, hearing Paulina say the word set off a fit of giggles. One by one, the others joined in until they were all rocking, crying with the hilarity of it. Alicia's head felt like it was filled with a gang of demolition men, busily excavating her brain with tiny hammers. Her face was burning up, but still she laughed and laughed, she laughed until her stomach ached and her throat was raw. She laughed at the stupidity of it all, at the winds and tides that had washed them all up together in a circle of light round the filthy, cockroach-ridden whorehouse kitchen table. She laughed for Kitty's dirt-poor family, she laughed for Maxine's failed attempt to rescue herself and her daughter. She laughed for Paulina's scaly white face and fatalistic acceptance of her place. She laughed for Beatriz and Rudy. Last of all, she laughed for herself.

She laughed, because it was better than walking into the sea with pockets full of stones.

Suddenly the room went quiet, and Alicia felt their eyes lock on to her face. 'What? Oh dear, my make-up must be a mess.'

'Miss Pearl,' said Kitty, her voice barely audible above the rushing noise in Alicia's ears. 'Your nose, it's bleeding.'

~ CHAPTER 8 ~

John felt like a prime patsy. After ten days of silence, he had received a note that Miss Pearl wanted to see him. He had been waiting for fifteen minutes in the side room off the main salon at the Tea Room, like a schoolboy summoned by his teacher. All because of his stupid promise to help the *morena*, Alicia, made under pressure during the confusion at the hospital. He had a business to run, important things that needed his attention. Beatriz had been sensible, practical. They had a good arrangement which benefited them both. But he sensed this one was different; she was trouble. He made up his mind to leave then, and to the devil with his promise. Better to save himself than have both of them go under. His father had schooled him well: never go in after a drowning person. In their terror and panic, they will clutch and grab and submerge anything that comes within range of their flailing limbs.

It was a quiet, cloudy mid-afternoon. There had been rain all morning, a miserable, drenching downpour that turned the street to a brown sludge which reminded him all too much of France. His boots were caked in it, a mixture of mud, manure, and limestone powder which dried cement-hard. He had been on edge for days. Each time he entered a room, it felt like Rudy had just left it ahead of him, his retreating back a khaki blur round the next corner. Sometimes John woke to the sound of his wheezing laugh, a smile on his face, to find himself alone but for a lingering whiff of smoke. It was the job of the dead to stay dead. He had no illusions about that, but could not shake the feeling of unfinished business.

Beyond irritated now, he turned towards the door. *To hell with you,* señorita.

Her voice behind him said, 'Thank you for coming, John.'

She had lost weight. Her lips looked dry. Her hair, restrained by the usual tight bun at her neck, was dull. But her eyes, her eyes were the same. Under her gaze, he felt completely naked. His gut, which he had relied on hundreds of times to keep him safe in battle, urged him to bolt, right then and there. *Just go out the door. Do it now.* But she glanced at him, just a flicker, really. Somehow her pallor intensified the colour of her eyes. And for the first time ever, he ignored his gut.

He took the seat beside her. 'I didn't know you had been sick.'

A slight lift of her shoulder. 'Unavoidable, I suppose. Like you, I am one of the lucky ones. Garlic and chilli got me through. I have always recommended them to my clients with flu . . .'

'Clients.' He smiled. 'Is that what they call "johns" in Havana?'

The uncomfortable silence was broken by a skinny girl who placed a teacup on the table next to Alicia's elbow, shared with a bowl of bougainvillea blooms. John remembered her, from before the war. Tiny frame, blonde hair in ringlets, like a pup taken from its mother too soon.

She said, 'There ya go, Miss Pearl. You need anythin' else, honey, just holler.' To John, 'I tell you somethin', sir, whatever ails you, this lady's got a remedy for it. Ain't never seen nothin' like it.' And she walked off, with a swing of her boyish hips.

Confused now, he said, 'Surely this ain't your first cathouse.'

She put down her cup with care and cleared her throat. 'That is what you think?'

''Course.' He leaned back into the spindly seat, suddenly very conscious of the filth on his boots. 'Why wouldn't I? You pull up a lobster trap, you don't expect to find it full of chickens.' And he tried another smile from his repertoire. From the look on her face, it was clear he had said something wrong, but for the life of him he couldn't figure out what it was. *What does it take to get this woman to smile?* He took another tack. 'I ain't got no problem with you bein' a whore. You're just doin' a job, like anybody else. Hell, I reckon y'all deserve a medal for services to the US Army.' And he chuckled, thumbs looped in his belt. To his own ears, he sounded ridiculous. She looked so prim, in her green dress with the lace collar, and her feet together just so.

He had to remind himself he was in a cathouse and not some la-di-da establishment. He longed for the simple certainties of Beatriz. It started to dawn on him that he might have taken a wrong turn. He was sweating, while her smooth brown cheeks were cool. His throat dried up. 'Y'all got anything to drink in this place?'

'Certainly.' And she signalled to Felix, who brought him a beer.

He drank it down in one long gulp, like he had just crossed the Sahara instead of a few yards of muddy road. A slight queasiness followed the gassy drink. His balance was off. He didn't like the feeling, didn't like it one bit. His gut was yelling now, but instead of doing the sensible thing and making his excuses, he dug in. No girl in a green dress was going to get one over on John Morales, not even one with eyes like hers, and skin like hers, and a shape like hers, filling out the folds of that dress . . . it was time for some home truths.

He wiped his mouth and leaned forward, elbows on knees. 'Listen, miss: however much you might wish things were different, you're now the madam of a cathouse. A nice rug or two and a few flowers don't change the fact that people come here to do two things: drink and fuck.' He enjoyed her slight grimace. 'If you don't like it, get back on the boat to Havana and find a rich man. Your choice. You want my help?' He slapped his knee. 'There you go, lesson one, completed.' He was pleased to see muddy marks on the rug beneath his boots.

Arms crossed, he waited for her reaction. He thought she might throw him out, or maybe cry, like she had done at the hospital. But something was different. She stared out the window at the side alley, her face closed. A few moments passed, and he thought he had been dismissed, but then she turned to him with a stare of pure determination.

'Choice? You talk of choice? Yes, I wish for different things. I wish I could go home to Havana, but I cannot. I wish Beatriz had lived and I did not need your help. Men like you have no idea . . . women like me have no choices. You think you know me? You think you know them?' With a jerk of her head, she indicated the girls near the bar, avidly eavesdropping. 'You do not. Every one of us has a story.'

'Then tell me,' he said. *Where on earth did that come from?*

He had no time for this girlish nonsense, and most certainly did not want to get tangled up in her personal life, whatever that meant. If he hankered for female company, he would make a straightforward transaction with one of her girls, where everyone was clear about the deal. Yet he remained in his seat.

'Why?' She leaned forward, mirroring his posture of a few moments ago. 'You have made up your mind already. Believe what you want. It is not important to our business here.'

Her breath was warm and sweet from the tea.

What irritated him most wasn't the slight purse of her mouth, like he smelled bad, or the way she tucked a stray curl into her bun. It wasn't the way she fiddled with the enamelled bird pendant at her throat, or the way she looked at the rug while thinking what to say.

It was the way he felt belittled in her presence. It was so colossally unfair. He wanted to shout that he was one of the few good men in a rough town, that there were plenty of others with far worse manners and far worse tempers, that he was doing her the most colossal favour and that a little gratitude wouldn't be out of line. He wanted her to know he could have just absorbed Pearl's into his operation if he had been so minded, as he had the strength and the means, and people in town were already wondering why he had not done so.

She doesn't know me, not at all.

His discomfiture seemed to go unnoticed. She smoothed the folds of her skirt and said, 'I would like to begin with book-keeping. We can use the kitchen table.'

And she got up and left him there, totally and utterly at a loss to understand what just happened.

By the time he left several hours later, Alicia was exhausted. It had been her first day out of bed, and the effort of remaining upright while concentrating on the numbers in the ledger had just about done her in.

There was still so much to learn, an overwhelming amount, and she tired easily. A rest was needed before the evening rush. But some progress had been made. As she lay on her bed, gathering strength, she felt a new sense of accomplishment, as with John's help she had deciphered Beatriz's ink-stained squiggles in the many closely written pages. Her cousin had kept meticulous track of all money that came in and out, whether it was for food or booze or bribes. On the last page, the day before Alicia's arrival, there was one income entry which caused her eyes to sting: 'Cortez fee $100'. Quite a costly sum to be rid of a troublesome daughter.

And still no word from Mamacita, which produced an ache just below her ribs when she thought about it. Never mind. They had paid good money for Beatriz to take her off their hands. Her parents were probably enjoying the peace and quiet since her departure.

John had been the first to notice the most important line in the ledger. On parting its flimsy covers, he ran a finger down to the last entry and whistled through his teeth. 'I always thought that Beatriz had a head for business, but this . . . it's a goddamn fortune. I'm in the wrong game, for sure,' he observed, with a wry shake of his head.

Ten thousand dollars Beatriz had accumulated, enough to live in comfortable style for some time.

Aghast at the amount, Alicia had said, 'I must go to the bank immediately,' and wondered why the Tea Room was in such disrepair, why the girls' clothes were threadbare, why every piece of furniture was held together with spit and string.

But John had just snorted. 'Beatriz didn't trust banks any more than I do. They're just store windows for robbers. Nah, she's like me, she liked to keep it close.' His eyes had travelled up and over the grease-stained kitchen ceiling. 'It's in this house somewhere, I'd swear it.'

As she struggled to arrange her aching limbs on the lumpy, uncomfortable bed, she thought about what the money could buy: new dresses for all of them, helpful for morale and for business; more hens, as their single ragged specimen was good neither for laying nor the pot; a new stove, because the existing charcoal burner had two settings: off and incinerator. Elated by the possibilities, she gave her imagination free rein. Yes, she would have a garden, maybe even – and here she got positively giddy, for the first time since arriving in Key West – maybe indoor plumbing. The very idea of a pristine porcelain commode instead of the spider-ridden hell-hole of an outhouse made her almost swoon. Maxine had only slightly exaggerated the size of those spiders. And there would be real toilet paper, instead of an old Sears Roebuck catalogue on a rusty nail.

Abandoning her search for comfort, she added 'new mattresses' to the list of purchases. The inadequacy of the bed had become excruciatingly clear during the past ten days of her illness, when she could do little except lay flat in a darkened room, while a series of blurry dream people forced her to drink revolting hot liquids. Burning up, she wanted none of it. All she wanted was to be left alone to sleep, even to die; nothing else mattered, just sleep. But every few hours, indistinct faces yanked her into wakefulness to drink more. Weak as she was, in her delirium she had fought them, and recalled someone's voice, maybe Felix's, grunting in annoyance: 'Dammit, hold her tighter, Paulina!' There was no sense of time, no day or night, only the feeling of being deep, deep under the sea, miles below the surface. That was the only place where she was safe from the pain, while every breath felt like her lungs were straining to move the tons of water pressing down on her.

The girls had told her that, before the fever took hold, she had ordered them to keep feeding her aspirin with garlic, and chilli tea, and not to stop, regardless of what she said. Her final command was: 'And no hospitals.' When finally she woke on a grey morning, with a sudden gasp and a blinding head-ache, Paulina was snoring in the chair beside her bed. Later, the girls told her of the town gossip, that the second outbreak had mostly affected the soldiers, not many locals. Beatriz, it seemed, was just very unlucky.

Carefully she sat up and rested her feet on the worn floor-boards, replete with termite holes. *Get a carpenter to replace the rotten wood. The stairs are a death trap.* Her body was slow to obey instructions, her muscles shaky with disuse, but the afternoon spent with John had helped to disperse some of the fuzz which had grown in her brain during the sickness. He was possessed of a strange nervous tension which she had not noticed before. His assumptions about her were offensive, but of no consequence. Men always assumed that a woman of her colour must be a *puta*. He was not the first to judge her falsely, nor would he be the last. All that mattered was a good working relationship. Clearly, it had benefited Beatriz, and she intended to take full advantage of it.

Because, as she stood and waited for the room to stop spinning, she felt changed, really changed. Something had happened during her ten lost days, while her body fought its battle for survival. This had been clear almost as soon as she woke from the fever, once the worst of the dizzy confusion had cleared. And seeing the 'Cortez fee' entry in the ledger, the transaction which had brought her to Pearl's, simply solidified her conclusion that the door to the past, her past, was closed. Another door lay ahead of her. Although it was not what she would have chosen, even in her weakened state she felt a fiery certainty about one thing: that she would be no one's property ever again, not her parents', not her husband's. She had been sold for the last time.

The key to it all was Beatriz's stockpile of cash. She was inclined to agree with John that it was secreted somewhere in the house. She went along the landing to Beatriz's room, untouched since her death except that the soiled bed had been stripped bare. She paused a moment in the doorway, remembering her cousin's mottled, bloody face and pleading eyes. It felt like a distant memory, from years ago, instead of mere days. She opened the window to let in air and light.

'Where is it, Beatriz? Show me where.' But the only sound was the soft rustle of the curtains and the voices of men in the backyard who had come to take the *mierdas* from the out-houses for disposal at sea.

She searched through the drawers and emptied the ward-robe, stopping regularly to rest, and feeling somewhat grubby as she rifled through a dead woman's underwear and trinkets. On her knees by the bed, she disturbed hairy dust balls which made her sneeze as she felt around under the mattress. Nothing but the sad detritus of an ordinary life. She sat back on her heels, breathless and despondent, and heard a strange sound from the floor, a hollow groan beneath one foot. The floorboard came up easily, beneath it the dull gleam of a strong box. With shaking hands, she raised the box from its hole on to the bed, excitement making her fingers clumsy. Lid off, a shaft of sunlight revealed a few papers, a string of pearls the colour of old teeth, and a bundle of letters. Nothing more.

She almost wept with the disappointment, so sure had she been of discovery. Then she realised the parchment of the letters looked familiar and turned them over to reveal her name in Mamacita's hand. There was a letter for each day she had been gone from Cuba. Now the tears did come, as she read them through one by one, taking in the achingly mundane details of her mother's life, of visits to the doctor, of a school friend's wedding, of another friend's new baby. Each one was signed, '*Te amo*, Mamacita'.

They were so powerfully redolent of home that she imagined she could smell Mamacita's perfume on the paper, hear the simmer of her *ropa vieja* on the stove. What if she had died of the flu, like Beatriz and Rudy? No one would have told her parents. They would forever wonder why she had never replied.

'How could you do this?' she cried at Beatriz, clutching the handfuls of paper to her chest. 'How could you?'

Then, as the tears subsided, she allowed her eyes to roam around the room once more. Her cousin was clever, very clever. Hiding the letters was just one indication of what she was prepared to do in order to protect an investment. How far was she willing to go to protect something truly valuable?

Alicia forced her thoughts to come to order. What things did she know about her cousin, besides her highly tuned business acumen? She counted them on her fingers: cleanliness was low on her list of priorities; she snored, because Alicia heard her through the partition wall; she was not vain, and often looked like she had dressed in the dark; and she liked very spicy food, although it did not agree with her, requiring frequent trips to the outhouse.

Noises from the backyard broke her concentration, shouts and curses and the smack of heavy barrels landing on a wooden wagon. With a flash of insight, she launched herself at the windowsill and shouted, 'Wait! Do not take that shit away! I am coming down!'

∾ CHAPTER 9 ∾

Dwayne woke in his bedroom. *I'm getting better*, he told himself. Every day, he felt a little stronger. The dizziness had abated and his breathing was a little easier. Never sick before in his life, he didn't know how to be idle. That first morning after he had come home from the hospital, he had swung his feet onto the floor, sucked in a big lungful of air, got up – and promptly crashed to the ground.

His mother had hurried in, all flustered and fussy. He saw her mouth move, but only muddy sounds issued from it, like she was behind a thick pane of glass. He had stared at her lips, trying to follow. 'There now,' her lips said, 'the doctor told us you'd be weak for a while. Got to take things easy.'

'Ma!' he had cried, but his voice barely registered. 'I cain't hear!'

She had helped him back to bed, speaking very slowly. 'You were awful sick, honey. They said it could take . . . a while . . . before you're all well again.' She pressed a cool palm to his forehead. 'But you're so much better than you were. I was so worried. And your Pa too.' She stood and smoothed her skirt.

'I'll get you some biscuits and gravy, just made a fresh batch. And then I'll change those sheets.'

Several days on from that, and the deafness was no easier to bear. Ma said he must have faith, that God had saved his life and would restore him in time. Both ears seemed to be clogged with molasses, but no amount of digging with his fingers did any good, nor did smacking his head repeatedly. Silence whittled down his faith some every day. It sent his focus inwards, where his mind was still sorting through the wreckage of his lost time. Ma said it had been ten days, but it felt longer, like he was old Rip Van Winkle.

He remembered a flurry of white-clad people who floated in and out of his vision like ghosts, only their eyes visible. He had known Ma by her voice, but there were others, shining lights in his eyes, looking in his throat. They seemed to be arguing, but he had been so tired, all he wanted was to be left alone to sleep. Then a pair of bright bluish-grey eyes had appeared above him, staring down with fierce determination. He recognised them as belonging to Miss Alicia, and he had wanted to smile, and ask her what she was doing in the hospital, but he couldn't move. Worse, he was finding it very hard to breathe. Panic flared with every laboured constriction of his lungs. His heart was beating fast, too fast. And then he felt a sharp pain in his arm, and looked around to find himself attached to a tube leading to a bottle of clear liquid. Beyond that sat a dark-haired stranger with military posture, who seemed to be waiting for something. Then there was Pa and a lot of raised voices, and then nothing until he woke again in his own bed.

When he tried to make sense of it, he felt about a hundred-and-two years old. His muscles shook so badly that Ma had to help him to the outhouse. With the morning sun warm on his face, and nothing else to do, he still felt so tired.

He had drifted off again, dreaming of grey-blue eyes in a brown face, when Ma bustled in with a tray. 'Rise and shine, sleepy head. Got your favourite here.'

Startled, he shot up in the bed. 'What'd you say, Ma?'

She raised her voice. 'It's pineapple, Dwayne, just picked this mornin', I—'

'Ma!' he exclaimed, and pulled himself unsteadily to his feet. 'I heard ya!'

She dropped the tray on the bed and hugged him. 'It's a miracle! Let's go tell your Pa.'

Although only one of his ears seemed to receive sound clearly, it was enough for now. He felt connected to the world again, by the clink of the dishes as Ma piled them back on the tray, the bark of a dog outside somewhere. It was enough. The rest would come in time, when the good Lord was ready.

Pa was in the kitchen with Mr Simpkins, known all over town as 'Bucket' because he was so good at making money as a child, and carried it everywhere in a bucket. Although a young man, he had the quiet confidence of someone much older and more experienced. Pa often spoke of him as a driving force for 'whitening' the town. Dwayne could sense Pa's excitement at having the man in his home, from the way he leaned in, arms folded on the old driftwood table, eyes locked on Mr Simpkins' face. The good china was out too, with slices of Ma's coconut cake, and cool glasses of lemonade making rings on the wood. Hunger jabbed insistently at Dwayne's stomach.

'I can hear again, Pa!'

His father looked up in surprise. For a moment, Dwayne had

the crazy notion that Pa didn't recognise him, as if his days in the sick room had somehow erased him from the family portrait. But there it stood, on the shelf above the stove, the grainy rectangle in its cheap cardboard frame that had captured them on Dwayne's thirteenth birthday. The studio lights shone on the thick layer of pomade which had failed to tame his curls. All three faces stared out with the same grim determination not to smile. The image flickered. Light-headed, he grasped a chair back, and wondered if this was another fever dream.

Pa glanced at him sideways, his face solemn as the photograph. 'Praise the Lord.' Then he turned back to Mr Simpkins. 'You were sayin', Charlie? You got almost enough signatures?'

The other man passed a pure white handkerchief over the square expanse of his face, then tucked it into his jacket. His pristine straw boater perched on the corner of the table. A pair of fine gloves draped themselves on his knee, like dismembered hands. He studied Dwayne for a moment, his eyes ice-blue in the palest face Dwayne had ever seen. Everything about him was immaculate, as if dirt would just bounce off him. 'We'll continue this discussion another time, Reverend. I can see you have family matters to attend to.' His manner was easy, friendly. Dwayne recalled the gossip on his rounds, talk of Simpkins as a potential candidate for mayor. Yes, indeed, he was a man going places.

'Not at all,' Pa protested. 'You're very welcome.'

But Mr Simpkins had pushed up from his chair and donned his hat and gloves. Although no taller than Dwayne, he carried himself like a bigger man, standing with legs apart and elbows out, as if to take up as much space in the room as possible. Dwayne decided it must be some trick of the light, or the fuzziness in his head, which caused their visitor to appear almost as large as Pa. And he had never seen anyone wear gloves outside of a parade.

With a disgruntled twist of his mouth, Pa said, 'I'll see you out.'

Dwayne watched them stroll to the gate, Pa talking fast, Mr Simpkins nodding. Then he laid a hand on Pa's shoulder and said something, but Dwayne could not see his mouth. Pa stood and watched while Simpkins mounted his green Oldsmobile and drove off in a swirl of limestone dust.

When Pa returned, his whole manner had changed to one of contented reflection. Gone was his annoyance and impatience. He pulled Dwayne to him with one arm, and Ma with the other, and stood there locked in a three-way embrace. Dwayne breathed in Pa's exhalation of tobacco and the liquorice candies that he sucked to sweeten his breath. Pa's eyes were closed, his lips muttering prayers. From Ma's expression, she clearly had no more idea than Dwayne of what had brought about this sudden surge of affection. It had been a long, long time since Dwayne could remember any similar kind of display. In fact, he was fairly certain that he had never seen Pa so cheerful. Ever.

Finally, Pa released his hold on them. With a cautious grin, Ma re-pinned her hair where it had been pulled loose. 'Everything all right, Pa?'

'Not yet,' said Pa with a sigh of intense satisfaction, as if he had just eaten the best dinner of his life, 'not yet. But it will be. Oh, yes, mark my words. Help is on the way. The citizens of the invisible empire are riding to our aid. All thanks to Charlie.'

Dwayne wasn't sure who he meant, but didn't want to ruin the moment by asking damn fool questions as usual. 'To drive out the demon drink, Pa?' he offered.

'Better than that, son. Even better than that. Our little town is about to be purified, at long last.' He clapped his hands together, eyes heavenwards. The sound was sharp in Dwayne's good ear. Ma's hand went to the cameo brooch at her neck. 'Charlie came to give me the news: we have enough signatures to petition for our own order, here in Key West. If the Imperial Wizard grants it – and we have high hopes of that – it will only be a matter of time before they come.'

'Who's that, Pa?' Talk of a wizard confused him. Pa often went out to meetings late at night, which he said were about important city business, but Dwayne didn't pay much attention, except to notice that these meetings always seemed to buoy his mood.

His ignorance earned him a smack on the side of the head. 'I can see you need schooling, son. I speak of the glorious empire of the Klan, of course. Now,' he said, rubbing his hands, 'who's for more coconut cake?'

After the plates were cleared, Ma led him back to the bedroom with an armful of clean linen. She parked him in a corner and said, 'Just a minute while I change the bed.'

But fragments of memories kept pushing through, or maybe they were dreams, he couldn't tell. A frowning, black-haired stranger, oblivious to an argument of some kind raging around him. There was Ma's stricken face, Pa's grip tight on her arm. And all the while, drops of clear liquid flowing into his arm.

'Ma, what happened, when I was sick, in the hospital? I cain't remember much.'

'Nothin' to worry yourself about, son,' she huffed, pulling the sweaty sheets from his bed. 'You just keep your mind on gettin' better. The rest'll take care of itself.' As she bundled the linens into a pile by the door, the cameo at her collar came loose and clattered to the floor, revealing several finger-shaped bruises on her throat. She replaced the brooch with shaking hands.

'Ma, something happened, I know it did. Why did he hurt you?' He was starting to feel dizzy again and sat down on the bare mattress. 'Was it because of me?'

She gathered herself and sat beside him. 'We lost ten from the congregation to the flu the last time, overnight. I wasn't gonna let that happen to my only child, no matter what it cost. Not after your brother . . .' She smoothed his hair, his cheek. 'If it hadn't been for Mr Morales . . .'

'The man with black hair? You know him?'

'No.' A sharp shake of her head. 'You got to understand, I was desperate. No one could do anything to help, and Mr Morales, he told the doctor that he had been sick too just like you, in the war, and something in another man's blood saved him. And he offered to save you. I don't rightly understand how it worked, but it did.' She massaged his hands between her rough, calloused palms. 'Whatever it is that he carries, that's what saved you, son.' Her eyes were wide and fearful, as if she were reliving that night. 'You see, I had to do it, but your Pa, he—'

'A stranger's blood, Ma,' he mumbled, both shocked to find how sick he was, and appalled at the means of his deliverance.

Now he understood his father's anger, and his coldness just now. Nothing was more important to Pa than the purity of the blood. The Campbell family could trace their line all the way back to the hardy Presbyterian colonists who came over from Scotland. He had been polluted. He withdrew his hands and tucked them between his knees.

With a sad smile, she said, 'God will forgive, in time, even if your pa won't.' She touched her brooch again. 'And, son, you owe your life to Mr Morales. When you're stronger, you must go and thank him. It's the Christian thing to do.'

It was a month before Dwayne was able to put Pearl's on his route again, in the humid swelter of mid-summer. Young and strong as he was, the heat pounded his head and shoulders as he pushed his cart through the streets. It now seemed he might never recover the rest of his hearing, but he didn't fret about it. His lip-reading skills were improving every day.

Passing through the Tea Room salon, he marvelled at the changes since his last visit: new tables and chairs, gleaming with polish, had replaced the splintered old furniture; colours met his eyes, where previously there was only brown and grey. Mason jars stuffed with flowers cut through a little of the usual odours of stale smoke and beer. He wondered what had prompted the famously thrifty Miss Beatriz to part with so much cash.

From the kitchen at the back, sounds of demolition and raised men's voices. A small woman with a broom and bucket pushed past him with a surly, 'Perdóname' and began to wash the front steps with vigorous, bad-tempered strokes.

'I've come with the shoes for Miss Beatriz,' he said. 'Is she here?'

'*Esta muerta*, of the flu,' said the woman.

Dead? How could Miss Beatriz be dead? And of the same illness that he had survived. A sudden chill ran through his body with the realisation of how close he had come to the same fate. If it had not been for that Mr Morales . . .

The woman banged the broom into his foot and said, 'Miss Alicia in charge now. That one is crazy. I prefer dead *jefe* to crazy *jefe*.' She strode to the foot of the stairs and bellowed in a voice that would suit a longshoreman, '*Chicas*, the shoe boy is here!'

They filed down the stairs. For a moment, while he took in the news, Dwayne thought Miss Alicia must have brought in a whole new set of girls as well as new furniture.

Pretty dresses in rose, leaf-green, and periwinkle swished around their calves and their hair shone; Paulina's skin was not exactly clear, but it was free of angry red pimples; Kitty's mouth had healed and she had put on enough weight to cover her ribs. Maxine looked much the same, but he figured it would take more than a new dress to tame her ornery nature.

As they settled in the side salon, there was a huge crash from the kitchen, followed by a stream of curses.

'What's going on back there?' he asked.

'New kitchen,' said Paulina. 'Miss Alicia making some changes. New everything.'

'So I see.'

'Hard to believe it's the same place,' said Kitty. 'My bed has a new cotton mattress. No more straw poking through! And there's even talk of a flush toilet! Can you imagine such a thing?' Her eyes sparkled as if she were talking about a diamond ring.

'And she paying us double what we got from Miss Beatriz,' said Paulina. 'I can buy all the shoes I want now.'

'Oh, it's the same old Tea Room, all right,' said Maxine, as she held out her cigarette for a light. 'Paint a pig gold, it's still a pig.'

'Who's the lady with the broom?' he asked, as he opened up the first box of shoes.

'Hortensia, the new cook,' said Paulina. 'She makes wonderful *arroz con pollo*. Almost as good as my mama's.'

'All this must have cost a lot,' he said, removing the shoe from its paper wrapper.

'Yeah,' snorted Maxine. 'Turns out Beatriz was sat on a pile of money we earned on our backs. Sugar Plum found it under the outhouse floor. Had to get up to her elbows in shit.' Here she allowed herself a grin of pure glee. 'That's just precious. Tickles me every time I think about it.'

Dwayne had never seen her look happy. He was not sure he ever wanted to see it again.

'Ooh, that one is pretty,' said Paulina. 'I want to try.' And she raised one foot.

As he leaned forward to ease her into the shoe, she obligingly parted her knees for him. *I'm glad that some things haven't changed.*

When he was finished with the girls, he went in search of Miss Alicia for payment. Mr Jolovitz would be overjoyed at the news that he had sold not one, not two, but three pairs in one afternoon. This earned the Tea Room a place on his regular round, up there with the Gato factory.

Hortensia was rubbing beeswax into the bar. 'Is Miss Alicia here?' he asked.

With a jerk of her head she said, 'Next door, with *Señor* Morales.'

He had never been inside The Last Resort, but it had the reputation for having the roughest clientele – quite an accolade in Key West – and the best drinks. Big plate-glass windows at the front, decorated with ornate script, announced 'Beer 5¢'. A painter was in the process of adding the word 'Root' to the sign. Raised voices led him into the back room.

Miss Alicia was at a table deep in conversation with two men: one was the black-haired stranger from his fever dream, whom he guessed to be Mr Morales, and the other was a huge Negro with the almond eyes of an Indian in a half-burned face.

'I told you,' Miss Alicia said, 'I am coming with you. It is my business. If you were me, would you leave it to someone else?' Before Mr Morales could answer, she carried on, 'Of course you would not. Just because I am a woman—'

Mr Morales pushed his chair back with a loud scrape. 'We've been over this. There won't be room for you in the boat once it's loaded. I need a drink,' he said, and stepped to the bar.

'There is room for you and Thomas.' She folded her arms. 'And, by the way, it is ten o'clock in the morning.'

He downed the shot and wiped his mouth with the back of his hand. 'Thomas and I will be humping barrels of rum and bottles of brandy. If you can do that, then take my place and I'll stay here, nice and dry. And, by the way, mind your damn business.'

The big Negro said nothing, just shifted his gaze between the other two.

Dwayne coughed.

'Yes?' she barked. She seemed different somehow to the demure lady whose bag he had carried from the dock. Her hair was still contained in its neat bun, her dress buttoned modestly, but she was leaning forward, her face animated. He wondered what Pa would make of that. On second thought, he knew exactly what his father would say: that it wasn't natural, that business was a man's concern, that there could only be harmony in the world when everyone knew their place and kept to it.

'I come for the shoe money, Miss Alicia – I mean, Pearl. Three pairs today. That's ten dollars, ma'am.'

She removed a roll of bills from her dress pocket and handed him two fives and a one. 'That's for you. And call me Alicia.'

'Golly, thanks, Miss Alicia.'

But she had turned her attention back to Mr Morales. 'As I was saying—'

Dwayne coughed again. 'I got a boat. She ain't too big but she's fast. I can take you, Miss Alicia, wherever you want to go.' He had heard there were no small craft to be had for miles around. Men had come offering good money for his old glass-bottomed skiff, but he had turned them away. With Prohibition enforcement looming, everyone was bringing in supplies overnight from smugglers out of the islands. 'And with two boats, you can bring back twice as much.'

'You're that kid,' said Mr Morales, as if just noticing him, 'from the hospital.'

Dwayne offered a big smile. 'Dwayne Campbell, sir. You saved my life when I was nearly a goner. My ma told me to come pay my respects. Much obliged to you, sir. I hear you're a genuine war hero, and—'

'And this is how you pay your respects? By interfering in my business?'

'The boy's right.' The Negro's voice boomed in Dwayne's good ear. 'We can bring back more with two boats.'

Up close, the burns on his face made a brownish-pink patchwork, extending from ear to chin and pulling one side of his mouth into a permanent frown. Everyone in town knew about Black Caesar, The Last Resort's dark enforcer, but never in his life had Dwayne expected to meet him. The Negro caught him staring and gave him a chilling half-smile.

Mr Morales glared at Black Caesar. 'So now you're on her side? So much for loyalty.'

'Not a question of sides,' he shrugged. 'Just good sense. And she's paying half, whatever.'

'Thank you, Dwayne,' said Miss Alicia, beaming. 'I accept your offer. Be at Smathers Beach at midnight on Saturday.'

Dwayne thought he would swim all the way to Cuba and back if she would smile at him like that again.

Once Dwayne had gone, Alicia stared after him. 'Such a nice boy,' she said. 'So helpful. Such a shame about his parents. Why do they fight so?'

But John just said, 'Hell if I know. None of my business, or yours. This town'd be a whole lot more peaceful if folks kept out of each other's business,' he added, with a pointed glare. 'Thomas probably knows. He hears everything.' And he stomped off.

It was the first time she had been alone with Thomas, who seemed ill at ease once John was out of the room, his eyes darting to the doorway. 'Do you know why, Thomas?'

The big man shrugged and dug a fingernail into the table. It seemed like he would offer no more, and she searched for another topic to engage him. He was an essential part of the operation, and it was in her interests for them to get along. And she was curious. He spoke like a coloured man but his features reminded her of the Taino people in Cuba, Indians who were there long before the time of Cristoforo Colombo. Round his neck was a silver panther head on a leather lace. She touched the pendant at her throat. *Like me, he belongs nowhere.*

Alicia waited, figuring he might bolt if she pressed him. It was her first time in the back office, and her gaze kept wandering to the open window where flashes of unexpected colour filled the frame. 'Thomas, is that a garden?'

'Yessum. Nothin' much. Just a few sweet potatoes and squash and collards and rutabagas, some tomatoes and pineapple and lemons and strawberries. John, he very partial to strawberries.'

'Will you show me?'

Together they went out the screened door to a rectangle of land roughly the same size as the waste ground behind the Tea Room, only this was planted in ordered rows, lush and verdant. And among the edible crops were bright blooms of hibiscus and gardenia, and the arching spears of bird of paradise.

'It is wonderful!' she exclaimed. 'Who works this for you?'

'I do. When John was away, I needed somethin' to keep myself busy. Now we grow enough to feed us, and then some. I reckon it's the outhouses hereabouts that do it.' The good side of his face registered a twisted grin.

'*Sí, claro*,' she spluttered.

His eyes appraised her for a moment, then looked away.

She bent to inhale the fragrance of gardenia. 'I used to have a garden like this. It reminds me of home. If I were to make a garden next door, would you . . . would you help me? I would pay for your time.' *It could work. There is enough space next door.* The new cook, Hortensia, had already made a vast improvement to the food in the Tea Room, but with such produce available free, she could cook wondrous meals at lower cost. And there would still be room for her medicinal plants.

'I reckon so.' Gaze fixed on the garden, he said, 'I know a girl, sometimes helps out Missus Campbell. The girl, she says Mrs Campbell touched by the tar brush, somewhere in her family.'

Now he had Alicia's total attention. 'You mean . . .?'

'Uh huh,' he nodded. 'It came out when the boy, Dwayne, was small. An old uncle of hers died, up in Georgia. There was some papers sent down.'

Lily Campbell's face came to her, eyes wide as a whipped dog's. Yet still she defied Mr Campbell, to save her child. Alicia said, 'Where I am from, that is no reason for a husband to treat his wife so.'

'You ain't lived here long, miss.' He straightened a tomato cane, his big hands surprisingly dexterous. 'Ole Jim Crow say it against the law. That little bit of blood make Missus Campbell black as me.'

'Then why does he not divorce her?'

'You got to understand how things work on The Rock.' He turned to her for the first time. 'For the Reverend, a man of the church, couldn't be no worse scandal than owning up to it.'

So Neil Campbell made his wife pay for her inheritance every day of her life. No wonder she had felt a sense of recognition on meeting Lily. *I know you, because I was you.*

And now she understood why the Reverend had reacted with fury to John's blood plasma transfusion.

'That means Dwayne, also,' she mused. His friendly, freckled face came to her, totally without guile. *He does not know.*

A disinterested shrug. 'Loads of white families 'round here got black blood in 'em, from slave days, and white men jumpin' the fence. Don't make no never-mind except, once in a while, little baby come out the wrong colour, then everyone act surprised. But this whole town built on a big swamp of secrets.' Thomas scanned the surrounding buildings as if they bulged with nightmare creatures, then stared at her again, serious now. 'Best advice I can give you, miss, is stay outta the swamp.'

❧ CHAPTER 10 ❧

A week later at Smathers Beach, and it was a fine, clear night, crowned by a smuggler's moon. The wind that had worried the palms all day had dropped, leaving only gentle wavelets to reflect the starlight.

Alicia had borrowed a dark blouse and trousers from Paulina, her hair stuffed into an old hat of Felix's. The moonlight washed everything grey and black, but for a cluster of yellow lamps bobbing at the water's edge. She hurried over, shoes clasped in one hand.

Dwayne and John stood in the shallows holding the boats ready as they rose and fell with the easy swell. Tiny silver fish glinted between their feet.

'I told you she'd be late.' John's voice.

'Come on,' said Dwayne, 'I'll help you up,' offering his hand to her.

Since insisting that she come along, Alicia had wondered if John had been right, that it was indeed stupid and unnecessary. It had seemed so important, and so much a piece of her new independence. Thanks to Beatriz's hoarded cash, she had the opportunity to effect long overdue change in the Tea Room, in a way never before possible in her life. This feeling of power was more intoxicating than any alcohol, not least because of its novelty.

But the sound of the water slapping softly against the hull forced her to acknowledge that she was about to trust her life to the element she feared most. Here on the beach, she could appreciate the ocean's beauty and majesty, but Dwayne's boat looked like a toy against the immense blackness behind it. Ever since she was a child, she had had a terror of it. Her only recurring nightmare involved drowning, forever fighting her way up through tons of water towards a light which receded and receded. She always woke gasping. Now she fought against the urge to dig her feet into the sand and clutch the safety of the land. Forever.

Of course, she had not told John about her inability to swim. He would have immediately – and now, she thought, quite sensibly – said she was insane. Even young Dwayne would have probably refused to take her. *It's not too late to change my mind.* She had nearly done so at least six times already, which accounted for her lateness. Despite the pounding blood in her ears, she knew she must go. She must swallow the bile in her throat, still the shaking of her hands, and give nothing away. At stake was not only her pride but somehow her whole future. She had learned that risk could not be avoided, only managed, and if she did not exactly embrace it, at least she felt ready to face it. The pull of it was no more resistible than the tide.

So she waded into the warm shallows of the treacherous, ever-shifting sea, to take Dwayne's outstretched hand.

'No, you don't,' said John. 'You're riding with me, where I can stop you doing any damn fool thing. Thomas, you're riding with the kid.'

As the boat cut smoothly through the dark water, John kept one eye out for José's light and the other on Dwayne's. Just about everyone he knew had been a smuggler at one time, of anything that was taxed: rum, gold, opium. People, too. Chinamen washed up regularly, their hands bound, thrown overboard when the traffickers were taken by the law.

John had grown up on his father's smuggling stories, told by the lantern light in the shed out in the woods. Some said the woods were one big treasure trove, just waiting to be unearthed, if only folks knew where to look. Others talked of unmarked graves for the unlucky or the unwary, with restless souls a-prowl at nightfall. One way or another, smuggling had been a proud tradition in Key West for over a hundred years, thanks to the many small mangrove inlets and coves that made perfect hiding places for booty of all kinds. It was a thread running through the fabric of life on The Rock, but the advent of Prohibition had brought hundreds of new people to the business. This was his first trip. He knew the risks and was, as always, prepared for a fight if it came to that. He and Thomas had seen off some serious bad guys in their time; he could anticipate Thomas's every reaction, and count on his strength, but having a girl and a kid along complicated things. In his experience, the best plans were simple. Complications meant casualties.

Nor was he reassured to see her hands attached like barnacles to the gunwales. Her back was rigid as steel, as if they were in the grip of a storm instead of moving easily through calm water. A nervous passenger was a liability. He had far too much on his mind to wonder why she should be so tense. His best hope was that she would stay out of the way; his worst fear was that she would get involved. That could be very, very bad for everyone concerned. *Let her see how it works this time, since she insists. Then never again.*

They were no more than half a mile offshore when he heard her cry out and point into the sea.

'What the hell?' he said through clenched jaws and slowed the boat, alert for the splash of a body.

All around them the water glowed bright blue-green, the boat's wake making sweeping patterns in the darkness that flowed and curled, sparkling like an underwater river of crushed emeralds, reflecting a soft, numinous light onto their faces. She leaned over the side to get a better look.

'Have you ever seen anything so beautiful?' She laughed and clapped her hands with delight. The boat rocked but this just made her laugh louder. She seemed bolder in the mannish clothes and hat, which only added to his problems.

'Quiet!' hissed John. 'You want to bring the Coast Guard right into our laps? And sit down! Or, so help me, I will take you back to shore right now.'

She took her seat, her expression unreadable in the gloom. They resumed their course, and within fifteen minutes had found José's men afloat in two boats, set low on the water. This far out, the wind was stronger.

John moved forward, Dwayne on his starboard side. A quiet voice wafted over the waves: '*Hola*, John.'

'*Hola*, José.' He could make out the barest outlines of three lamplit faces.

Dwayne's boat bumped into them. Sounds of consternation leapt across the few feet of sea between them. José said, 'We were not expecting company. That was not our deal. You should have stuck to the deal, John. *Andale.*'

This was a bad idea. Never again. 'Wait! *Amigo*, relax. I have good news. I've brought help because I want to increase my order. I know that wasn't the deal, but I'm hoping you won't mind taking more of my money?'

The voices conferred in Spanish, too fast for him to follow. A cloud floated across the moon's face, deepening the shadows on the ocean.

'Come closer, John, and we will discuss it.'

It felt wrong, all wrong, his gut told him so. And yet José came highly recommended, and his prices were lower than anyone else's. Suddenly he wondered why that was. Yet he was damned if he was going back empty-handed. He touched the motor's throttle. Instantly there was a hand on his arm.

In his ear, her breath soft as mist, she said, 'They mean to kill us and take the boats.'

Quietly, oh so quietly, he cocked his revolver, the one with the walnut grip that had seen him home safe. But there was so little light, he had no confidence of hitting anything but his own foot. He whispered back, 'I'll keep them talking, you take the throttle. At my signal, hit it.'

'I have another idea.' And she whipped off her hat and called in a throaty singsong, '*Hola, muchachos! Qué pasa?*'

A silence, then hoots of laughter. 'A woman? Hey, John, we heard you some mean *hombre*, but now we think maybe there is another John Morales in Key West – one who doesn't go anywhere without his *mujer*!'

'*Su mujer*?!' she cried, hands on hips, her hair turned into a golden crown by the lamplight. Her stream of Spanish invective just inflamed their laughter, which grew in volume and breadth, as José and his crew were enveloped in the hilarity, doubled over with it . . . incapacitated by it.

'Now,' she whispered to him.

John smacked the throttle and rammed the first boat. Three quick, gratifying splashes and a lot of shouting followed.

'Thomas,' he called, 'hop aboard and get those barrels into Dwayne's boat. Then dump their motor. They can row back to Cuba. Or maybe they'll be lucky and the Coast Guard'll pick 'em up.'

The big man moved with economy and agility and soon Dwayne's boat was filled and José's motor was on its way to the ocean floor. José's men were attempting to climb back aboard, but a few shots from John's revolver pinged off the gunwales to send them slipping into the water.

'Now, José, as you fellas have lost your motor, we're going to relieve you of all that heavy booze in the other boat. Thomas, bring the line round.'

Once the rope was secured to the stern and Thomas back aboard Dwayne's boat, John eased them away with a cheery, 'Have a nice day, *muchachos*!'

And they moved off into the night ocean. John took it easy to save fuel, mindful of the great weight of the boat dragging on the tow rope. As soon as they were clear of José's shouts, he allowed himself a huge guffaw. 'That was great! I only wish I could have seen their faces better. What did you say to them?'

She was in the bow, her back to him, hair streaming out behind. Turning her head, she huffed, 'I told them I was not your *mujer* because your *pinga* is the size of a baby shrimp.'

'Um,' he coughed. 'That . . . that seemed to do the trick. Good thinking. Well done.' *Baby shrimp, huh? What do I care? I'm the one sailing away with more than a grand's worth of free booze.* There would be consequences. There always were. And he would be prepared next time. He eased the throttle open a little more, eager now to reach the shore and examine the booty. The sea turned silver as the moon showed its face.

And then they were surrounded again by the luminescent water, and she let out a squeal of delight, and it seemed only right to slow down to let her enjoy it, but there was a real chop to the water now, and before he could open his mouth to warn her to stay seated, the wave was upon them. She went into the water too fast even to scream. All he saw of her was a cloud of hair, lit up by the glowing green sea, as she tumbled overboard.

He cut the engine and swung round hard, but the weight of the boat on tow was like an anchor, pulling him away from the bubbles still rising from her splash. Without hesitation, he grabbed his knife and slashed the tow rope, then headed for the bubbles.

Dwayne circled round and killed his motor, his face ghostly green. 'Where is she?' he cried. 'I cain't see her! Where is she?'

Silence, while they watched the light fade in the water and then, a few yards off his port side, she burst through the surface and screamed, 'Help—!' and went down again in a flare of silver froth.

Never go in after a drowning person. John heard his father's voice as clearly as if he were sitting right next to him. He was

139

over the side and swimming towards her before the sentence was finished.

He dove down, down where he had last seen her, salt burning his eyes as he strained to see in the electric lime water. A faint trail of bubbles rose before him and he swam deeper, lungs telling him that time was short, very short.

At the limit of his endurance, brain screaming for oxygen, his flailing hands brushed her collar and he grabbed and turned for the surface. With an iron grip, he swam up, up and broke through into the blessed air with a giant gasp. She was beside him, but so, so still, and he thought, *breathe, damn you* and then she raised her face from the water and took a huge gulp. Her arms grabbed his neck, tight as steel bands, her legs around his waist. He tried to speak but water filled his mouth. She was wild-eyed, unseeing. Crying and screaming, she climbed his body like a pole until his head was submerged. He went under, her full weight upon him. With all his strength, he tried to unwind her, but her panic was stronger and she clung on, immovable. He thrashed in every direction, but there was no escape.

The sea boiled around them like a green bubble bath. Even as he lost consciousness, he thought how pretty it was . . . and what a stupid way to die. *I'll know better next time. Oh. There is no next—*

Strong hands ripped him from the water and landed him in the bottom of the boat where he flopped and heaved among the barrels, coughed and choked, sucking great gulps of air into his aching lungs. She landed next to him in a tangle of limbs and hair, Thomas standing astride them both.

'If y'all are finished,' he said, 'best get back to shore.'

With all four of them on board, plus the cargo, water was lapping over the gunwales of Dwayne's skiff. John nodded, propped against a barrel, still trying to clear his windpipe. He expected her to cry, to scream that she would never, ever go out to sea again. Although totally understandable under the circumstances, he thought it rather a shame, as otherwise he would probably be at the bottom of the ocean with a bullet in him.

She raised her head, ropes of wet hair clinging to her face, and spat out a mouthful of sea water. After a few deep inhalations, she rasped, 'You will . . .' Another coughing fit. 'You will teach me to swim.'

A pink-and-gold dawn was just brushing the tops of the palm trees when Dwayne let himself in through his bedroom window. Every nerve tingled with excitement. It felt like his life had been smashed open in one night, like a coconut, all brown and dull on the outside, bright and sweet on the inside. Adventure. Even the word sounded thrilling in his head. He had been part of something, something wild and dangerous. At night. On the ocean. Men with guns. It all added up to the most – no, the only – exhilarating experience of his whole life, more so even than those glimpses of Paulina's girlishness.

Mr Morales had been magnificent, so cool and calm when things got rough with José's crew, and so noble, jumping in after Miss Alicia. He reminded Dwayne of Zorro. All five issues were stashed under his bed, the complete set of his exploits carried by *All-Story Weekly*. Like Zorro, he was of Spanish blood. Like Zorro, he defended the weak and vulnerable. And, like Zorro, Mr Morales was accompanied by a passionate, exotic lady. There was no black mask, of course, but he was prepared to overlook that detail.

Miss Alicia too had been so quick and fearless. He had never seen a woman act like that. Pa would no doubt whup him raw for the thoughts he had about her, being a Jezebel, and a brown one at that. Late at night, alone in his bed, it was her face he saw when he sinned against God and himself.

He was even losing some of his fear of Thomas. On their way back to shore, Dwayne had felt obliged to make conversation, just to be polite. His first few attempts were met by the broad expanse of Thomas's back and the whistle of the wind.

But then he had called, 'I hear Mr Morales was a war hero.'

Only then had Thomas turned to speak, the beginning of a wistful smile at the undamaged corner of his mouth. 'He the best man I ever known.'

Surprised to get a response, he had leaned forward, straining to hear over the thrum of the motor. 'Have you known him long?'

'Since I was a kid. We did everything together. And then he went away to the war . . .' His voice faded to nothing. 'He gone so long. I did my best, to keep things goin' without him, but it was hard. Very hard.'

He realised then that Thomas was a true friend to Mr Morales, even if he was a scar-faced half-breed, and wanted to cheer him up. 'And now he's home,' Dwayne said, 'and things can go back to how they was.'

'No.' Thomas had gazed into the darkness. 'No, they cain't.'

Back in his bedroom, Dwayne slid under the sheet in a state of blissful exhaustion. The light in the sky told him he had perhaps a couple of hours of sleep before Ma would call him for breakfast.

But it seemed only minutes after he settled his head on the pillow that Pa was there beside his bed, shaking him roughly by the shoulder.

'Get up, son.'

'But Pa,' he said, sleep coating his eyes, still dazzled by the night's activities, 'I only work a half-day today.'

'Get dressed.' He flung some clothes on the bed. 'You're coming with me.'

He knows about last night. I'm done for. He pulled on the clothes, every second expecting the first blow to land. *Please, God, I'll never do it again, I promise.* But the blow didn't come and he relaxed. He had lied. He had lied to God, and there would have to be a reckoning, somewhere down the line, but for now, relief banished his tiredness. 'Where are we goin', Pa?'

His father turned to him with eyes lit from within. 'To make history, son. To make history.'

 CHAPTER 11

The meeting room behind the courthouse was already full when Dwayne arrived with his father. A heady haze of cigar smoke hovered above the familiar faces: Jeb 'Snapper' Reynolds, owner of the turtle soup factory, next to Police Chief Baxter and Notary 'Slim' Smith. In another corner, recognisable by his braying laugh, was Bret 'Donkey' Hightower, owner of the Landfall hotel, in conversation with a group of bankers, lawyers, and businessmen. Dwayne was on nodding terms with most of them because of his delivery rounds, but had never been in close proximity to such a gathering of the town's leaders, outside of the Fourth of July. He reckoned it would take something really special to bring them together on a working day.

Everyone greeted Pa warmly but Dwayne felt their eyes sweep him with guarded curiosity as they made their way through the crowd. Gradually the noise of conversation abated, until Dwayne found himself the centre of their attention. He scuffed his feet and tried to make himself invisible.

Chief Baxter spoke first. 'There's no children allowed, Neil.'

Pa laid a hand on his shoulder and said, 'Luther, my boy is here with Charlie's permission. This is an educational visit. And,' he said, in a voice such as Dwayne had never heard, 'I hope him to become a Knight in future, if my brothers and God judge him worthy.'

'A fine ambition,' said Snapper Reynolds.

'None finer,' concurred the notary with a wink.

A little of Dwayne's embarrassment drained away, replaced by a tingle of pride in his pa for being so well respected among the important folk of the town; but he was kind of confused, as the only knights he knew of were in the story books of King Arthur, and the table in this room wasn't even round.

However, he was starting to enjoy himself. His shoulders straightened. He liked this feeling. Whatever they were selling, Dwayne decided he was buying.

The main doors opened to admit the diminutive figure of Charlie 'Bucket' Simpkins, who processed through the assemblage shaking hands and nodding, his blue suit freshly pressed, the usual white handkerchief in his breast pocket and fine gloves on his hands. He made the others look like a bunch of hoboes, Dwayne thought, in their crumpled, sweat-marked uniforms and shirtsleeves. Dwayne wondered if he could ever look as gentlemanly as Mr Simpkins, with seemingly so little effort. To see the way the others deferred to him made Dwayne newly impressed. *Not long since he was in our kitchen, eating Ma's coconut cake.*

Mr Simpkins took his place at the head of the meeting table beneath a large oil painting of George Washington crossing the Potomac. The general stood tall, foot braced on the prow, heedless of the snowy wind in his face. Around his knees, a miserable huddle of soldiers paddled like mad through chunks of river ice. Such cold was beyond Dwayne's comprehension. The only thing that ever came close was the time when Pa took him to meet the ice boat that had sailed all the way down from Maine, back before they had electric power, and he was allowed into the hold for a few minutes. He was only a little kid then. Much to Pa's embarrassment, the shock of that frigid air on his body had made him cry and run for the heat of the dock again. It struck him that his whole life so far had been a series of disappointments for his father. *It's about time I made Pa proud of me. From now on, I'm gonna be like General Washington, fearless and steadfast.*

'Gentlemen,' called Mr Simpkins, 'brother Knights. I bring this exceptional klonklave to order.' His voice reminded Dwayne a lot of Pa's, the same measured cadence, quiet yet laced with authority. Simpkins opened a drawer, and with precise movements, spread the Confederate flag across the table and laid a Bible in the exact centre. Everything about him was orderly, unhurried. Dwayne had been unsurprised to learn that he was the chief comptroller, with guardianship of the town's finances.

Pa indicated a chair for Dwayne set against the wall beneath the painting. With a finger to his lips, he said, 'You are here to listen, not speak.' Then he took his seat at the table with the others.

'Let it be noted,' Mr Simpkins continued, with a glance at Donkey Hightower who was scribbling, 'that also present today is Dwayne Campbell, son of our esteemed Kludd Neil Campbell.'

Dwayne sat a little taller in his chair. *First there was last night's excitement, and now this. By Jimminy, things were turnin' out swell ... But what in the world is a 'klonklave'? And why did he call Pa a 'Kludd'?* The words sounded silly to him, like a child's game. But none of the faces at the table looked amused.

Mr Simpkins paused while his eyes marked each man, as if daring him to speak out of turn. The silence held. It reminded Dwayne of a particularly well-behaved pack of dogs, ever attentive to their master. 'As Kleagle, I am delighted and honoured to report that our petition to establish the Klan of the Keys has been granted by the Imperial Wizard himself.'

Fists pounded the table. There were cheers and handshakes all around. 'God bless America!' shouted Chief Baxter as he jumped to his feet and threw his hat in the air. Mr Simpkins remained calm and cool, as if the show of emotion was distasteful to him. With a glance, he brought the chief to his seat again.

When all was quiet, Donkey Hightower asked, 'And when is the great day, Charlie? When will we finally free our town from its chains?'

'It is coming, Brother Klokard, still some months off. We have much to do by way of preparation, most assuredly in terms of recruitment, because – and this, my brothers, this brings me such joy to announce – the Exalted Imperial Wizard himself is coming to perform the mass induction of our new members.' And here even Mr Simpkins' face betrayed a broad grin while the excited exclamations swirled around the table. 'Now,' he said, 'I will ask Kludd Campbell to lead us in prayer.'

Dwayne's father stood and closed his eyes for a moment.

147

The men around the table bowed their heads. Then Pa raised his hands above the group and intoned, 'Dear Lord, grant us success in our mission to save our great country for the real Americans, and give us strength to cleanse our town of Negroes, Jews, Catholics, and all others not born as white Protestants, that we may transform this town into the southernmost citadel of the Invisible Empire.'

Heartfelt 'amens' followed from the group. Mr Simpkins was the last to raise his head. 'Amen, Brother. And now to our agenda, where the first order of business is the recruitment drive. I will ask our Klokard to read out the names of potential candidates.'

Donkey Hightower began to list the names in his high, nasal voice.

Of course, Dwayne knew of the Klan's reputation – but elsewhere, a long way away, upstate and out of state. Lynchings in Miami sometimes got reported in the local papers, with grainy photos of white-robed figures beside flaming crosses, or standing beneath the black legs of a corpse dangling from a tree. Everyone knew they hated the coloured people, but this mention of others was confusing. Jews were white, and so were most Catholics, as far as he knew.

And there were no robes in the room, no pointy hoods or mystical insignia, no crosses, flaming or otherwise. It was just an ordinary business meeting, attended by everyone responsible for safeguarding the town's welfare. So, Dwayne figured, there must be more to it than he realised, for such important folks to take it so seriously. His head rang with the strange words. The cigar smoke in the airless room muddled his thoughts and made him feel queasy. He settled his buttocks on the seat and focused his mind on staying awake. *I'll get Pa to explain. He'll set me straight, like always.*

Some hours later, they emerged from the meeting room into the noonday sun. Pa covered his head with his old straw hat that had seen better days and popped a liquorice candy into his mouth. They boarded the streetcar and rode it to the end of the line in silence, Dwayne grateful of the chance to marshal his thoughts. He had so many questions, but he sensed they were better aired in private. Pa had a look of otherworldly calm, his eyes far away, like he had spent the morning up in heaven with the angels, instead of in a hot, smoky administrative office.

They alighted and set off down the unpaved road to the house. Dwayne's steps were quicker than his father's, as he really, really wanted some lemonade. He forced himself to slow to Pa's relaxed amble. His father seemed in no hurry at all, like he was savouring the moment. Dwayne couldn't remember the last time that they had strolled along together in similar fashion. He tried to hug the sparse shade provided by a few coconut palms, careful to avoid the spreading branches of the monkey pistol tree outside old Mr Henderson's house. As a child he had been wounded by one of its exploding seeds.

'You know, son,' Pa began, hands in his pockets, 'when I was your age, the curfew bell rang at nine thirty every night.'

'What for, Pa?'

'It rang to tell the Negroes that it was time to be indoors, to protect them from themselves. It's a fact they can't control their base urges, especially at night. This is exactly the kind of sensible approach that's needed now. And those men who you met today are going to restore the town to its senses.' A pause, while Pa scrutinised him sideways. 'Until now, I have kept this from you, but you're becoming a man, and it's time you took your place at my side . . . if you're worthy, that is. Are you worthy, son?' The question was asked lightly, but loaded with import.

Dwayne had never been worthy, neither of Danny's memory, nor his father's love. This was his chance, for the first time, to make Pa proud. He determined that, in this at least, he would not let him down. 'Yessir, I am worthy!'

They walked on a few yards more. Dwayne imagined he could see the beginnings of a new bond shimmering between them in the heat. He searched his mind for intelligent questions that would indicate his worthiness. 'Why does the Klan hate so many people, Pa?' This was the main thing that troubled him. It seemed a whole lot simpler to stick to hating one group at a time.

Pa's feet came to an abrupt halt in a puff of limestone dust, and Dwayne immediately regretted opening his stupid mouth.

But Pa turned to him with an indulgent smile. 'You see, this is why I took you along today, to clear up these misconceptions. It's very important to get them out of the way now, before you seek to become a naturalised citizen of the Invisible Empire.' He took Dwayne by the shoulders and looked deep into his eyes, his liquorice breath hot and sweet. 'We don't hate anyone, son. The Klan is not a hate group. Now pay close attention, because this is the point: the good Negro, who knows his place and doesn't seek to stray from it, has no better friend than the Klan. As for the others,' he said as he resumed walking, still with an arm across Dwayne's shoulder, 'we save them from the disappointment of their thwarted ambitions.'

Emboldened by this show of affection, Dwayne asked, 'So the lynchings really do them a favour?'

'Just so,' said Pa, as if Dwayne had solved a tricky math problem. 'Just so.'

Dwayne felt very pleased to hear that the rumours of vicious violence, the newspaper reports of killings, folks tarred and feathered, were the result of a colossal misunderstanding: all that was required to avoid trouble was for everyone to know their place. 'And what about the others, Pa? Is the Klan also Mr Jolivitz's best friend?' His employer did seem to know his place. In fact, Dwayne had never seen him anywhere except at the store.

Pa turned to him with narrowed eyes and the hint of a scowl. It was the time of day when shadows disappeared, with the sun burning down from directly overhead. Dwayne could almost taste the cool, sweet drink waiting for him in the kitchen at home, but he didn't dare shift from Pa's icy gaze.

'Do you love your country, son?'

'Yessir! More than anything in the world!'

'Then you'd want to protect this great land from folks bent on destroying it?'

'Yessir!'

'What you need to understand, son, is that both the Jew and the Catholic are in league with the Negro to bring about the downfall of our nation.'

Almost too hot and thirsty to think now, Dwayne made an open-mouthed sound of surprise and blinked the sweat from his eyes.

'You see,' Pa continued, 'the Jewish religion only exists to control the wealth of the world, and the Catholic swears an oath to protect the Pope's interests above all else. I've seen this oath with my own eyes. They don't belong here, and it's the duty of every real American to drive them from this land. Together, that's what we'll do, son, once you become one of us. Together, you and me, and our brother Knights, we will take back America.'

Dwayne thought again of General Washington, battling to take America from the British oppressors on that freezing river. Even as he basked in this unaccustomed approval, something niggled like a maggot in his brain. Surely it was the same thing? Just a different enemy? *Then why doesn't it feel the same?* The words tumbled out of his mouth before he could stop them. 'But Pa, what about the law?' Notwithstanding the memory of Chief Baxter's hat falling through the smoky air, he figured there must be something more than a bunch of guys in white robes required to accomplish the grand task Pa had set for them.

'What you need to understand, son, if you're to join us, is that there's man's law, the written law, and then there's moral law, which is higher than anything man can devise.' The bright sun turned Pa's face to a chalk-white mask. 'That's the Klan's law, son. That's true justice.'

❧ CHAPTER 12 ❧

In the woods outside of town, the mosquitoes were biting bad as John arrived with Thomas and José's liquor. It was the first time he had visited the grave at the kiln. There had been plenty of reasons to put it off, but it could no longer be avoided. The driftwood shack, still steeped in his spicy tobacco, was the perfect hiding place for the booze, and the old man would have approved of using it to get round a stupid law.

John stood beside the rustic wooden cross which was the only marker of his father's remains, in the shade of the shack where he had spent so much of his life. It seemed puny, such a pathetic thing to sum up a man's existence. He had left nothing for John, no photos or keepsakes, no evidence that he had ever lived.

'This ain't much, I know,' said Thomas, with a contrite shrug.

'You did fine. It's where he'd want to be, where he spent all his time . . . the only place he was happy. And it's where you and I grew up.' Being back in these woods, he had a sudden flash of memory: Thomas at maybe ten years old, home-made

153

bow and arrow in his fist as he hurtled through the scrubby pines. 'You remember that day?'

Thomas knew exactly which day he was talking about. 'Was 'bout this time of year, I reckon. 'Skeeters were so bad, looked like sunset at noon.'

They had been in pursuit of a fawn which had easily eluded their clumsy efforts, its dainty hooves barely touching the sand as it bounded away. Just as they turned back, it flashed across their path in a streak of brown and white. John made a lunge for it, but it slipped right past, leaving him facing the biggest panther he had ever seen. Even after all the years, the hairs on his neck still tingled at the thought of it.

It was a big male, almost as tall as him. It smelled meaty and rank, with mean yellow eyes and fangs bared in a silent snarl. The beast crouched to gather all its power for a leap, but John couldn't move or speak or draw his weapon. Nor could he look away, nailed to the spot as urine soaked his shorts.

The arrow brushed his ear on its way to the animal's neck. It tore away with a cry but collapsed beneath a poisonwood tree, its honey-golden coat streaked with red, its breathing fast and shallow. Thomas had stroked the animal's flank, tears on his cheeks, muttering words John didn't understand. With trembling hands, John aimed the Colt but couldn't fire. Thomas took the gun and shot the animal in the head.

'One brother had to die,' he said, with a sad, twisted smile, 'so the other could live.'

It was the first of their adventures, and there had been many more over the years; he was starting to realise the bootlegging could turn out to be the most dangerous yet.

'Well, Brother,' said John, 'we best get this booze squared

away.' The risk of being robbed by other smugglers was about equal to the risk of being arrested by customs men.

Thomas grunted assent and loaded one crate on his shoulder and gripped two of the great glass demijohns in his fist. 'That José, he gonna tell tales on you.'

'Let 'im.' John puffed furiously on his cigarette to deter the mosquitoes. 'I dealt with much tougher guys than him before. There are other suppliers. And we have our own secret weapon.'

'You bringin' her out with us again?'

'She speaks Spanish, and gives us the element of surprise.' Although Thomas kept his eyes averted, there was disapproval in his posture. 'Why, you don't think I should?'

Thomas shrugged his burden to the shed floor, where it landed with a clatter of glass bottles. 'You the boss. I just think . . . maybe . . . maybe better for everyone if she stay dry. That one, she trouble.'

'I'll think on it,' said John, perched atop a crate to pull out a canteen of water.

Thomas squinted into the smoke around his face. His grandfather had been a runaway slave, sheltered by the Seminole Indians. Although he never spoke of his Seminole mother, who died of tuberculosis when he was a baby, John knew he still kept some of their ways. Every spring, he would disappear to the Green Corn Dance of the Panther clan and come back wild-eyed with exhaustion and excitement. But he wasn't superstitious, just cautious, and John had learned to trust his judgement.

Thomas hesitated, then blurted, 'What she got, this one? You ain't never been like this for no whore before.'

After a big gulp of water, John passed the canteen to Thomas. John also had reservations about Alicia's presence in the boat, despite what he had said. The fact was that the world was changing too fast around him, like a sand bar being devoured by the tide. He couldn't hold a thought in his head for more than a few minutes before something came along to change it. She made any situation much better and much, much worse, at the same time, and he had no idea how that was possible.

Nor could he rid himself of the image of her tumbling into the shining green water, hair aglow, and those endless seconds before his hand found her collar. His body had responded instantly, totally outside of his mind's control. *How can someone be such a liability and an asset at the same time?*

'You know what they say,' Thomas continued, 'best thing for gettin' a woman off yo' mind is to go with five mo'.'

John hadn't heard Thomas express this view before, and wondered how he came by such wisdom, as he had remained free of female entanglements all his life. It was another thing that bound them together. 'I said, I'll think on it.'

'You with the brown, with the Klan on the way—'

'I ain't *with* no brown, ya hear? But I'll tell ya somethin' else: if I was, wouldn't be no jerk-off in a white dress tellin' me who I can be with. Thomas,' he said more gently, 'you ain't got to worry about me. I'm a white man. If there's any kings in this country, I'm one of them. They'll leave me the hell alone, or face the consequences. For you, on the other hand, my friend, worst case, you go spend some time upstate with the tribe if things get hot here.'

But Thomas just shook his head. 'I ain't leavin' you.'

'Well, then, I guess that settles the matter. What now?'

'Show your old pal your medal?'

'Maybe another time. Tell ya one thing, when I depart this earth, I'm gonna rest under a big slab of white marble in the cemetery, with the other military graves. But I want a huge angel on top, ya hear me? Because that'll really piss 'em off. Yessir, they're gonna remember John Morales.'

A mosquito bit the sensitive flesh behind his ear. He slapped it hard and his hand came away with a smear of blood. He rubbed it on his trouser leg, then slipped his hand into the pocket.

The sinking sun brought out even more of the blood suckers. With a final glance at his father's grave, he said, 'Let's get back before they drink us dry.'

That night, as John lay in bed, it felt like the mosquitoes had swarmed in through his ears to infest his skull. Thoughts buzzed and whined, swirling in random patterns that made no sense. Faces from the past, faces from the present flashed across his vision, even with his eyes closed: the men of his unit, crowded around that French piano, white with plaster dust, Moscowitz at the keys beneath a noseless statue of the Virgin; the look of surprise on Jenkins' face when the German sniper's bullet found his neck; his dad, stoking the kiln, teeth white in a face blackened by charcoal; and weaving among all of them was her, falling into green water, over and over again.

Perched at the foot of his bed was Rudy, his toothless mouth still red, eye sockets empty. 'That's my pal,' he said, 'genuine war hero.' And he saluted, cigarette as ever between his bony fingers.

With a groan, John swung his legs to the floor and lit another cigarette.

They were coming for him, the memories, and it was all her fault. Like a termite, she had hollowed him out inside, leaving a shell liable to crumble at the merest hint of breeze. He had lost focus, somehow unable to concentrate on anything for more than a few minutes. Always a fighter, he didn't know how to fight this.

Thomas's advice returned: *try five more whores.*

He was right, again, dammit.

And so he decided that, for the next week, he would avail himself of a different cathouse every night, until he was free of her. His gut told him it was the key to restoring his sense of balance, and slamming shut the strongbox of memories that had started to bulge at the hinges. Once she was gone from his head, he felt sure the visions would stop, the voices would stop, and he would stop feeling like his next step would land him in quicksand.

It was late, but, he hoped, not too late.

At the end of this, I'll be free.

The bars were still open and busy when John went out to the street, as everyone made the most of the last time before Prohibition came into law. Under a light rain-shower, he made his way across town to Lottie Mae's, which used to be his favourite place, after the Tea Room. Lottie's girls used to be clean, and he still had his supply of reusable rubbers, thick as bicycle tyres, which he purchased after several of his comrades got the clap from the same French brothel.

Lottie met him at the door, cigar in hand. She was the only woman he knew who smoked them, right out of Gato's factory. 'Well,' she said, gold teeth in a broad grin, 'look who's back. I heard you had taken up with the new Pearl.'

He shook the rain from his hat. 'Evening, Lottie. Naw, not taken up,' he said, 'just business, that's all. Carla still here?' Carla had tits like ripe tomatoes and an ass like a feather pillow, plus an accommodating and adventurous nature which made her a favourite in the house. He ached to bury himself in her warm, welcoming softness. Already he felt better, more like his old self. *It's working. I'm going to be free.*

With a snort of disgust, she said, 'Carla? That bitch runned off with a cattle rancher from Okeechobee, him with another wife and kids, but she don't care.' She flicked the ash from her cigar with a sly chuckle. 'But Lottie Mae got what you need, honey, now you a man of the world. Got somethin' reeeel special. Jasmine!' she bellowed up the stairs. 'Get on down here!'

Although disappointed by Carla's departure, he trusted Lottie Mae's taste and turned his eyes to the stairs . . . to be met with a sight that caused him to take a step back, aghast. 'Not that one,' he hissed. 'Get another one.'

It was her, Alicia, or at least a woman close enough to be her sister. Same storm-cloud eyes, same brown skin, same wild bronze curls.

'What the hell?' Lottie Mae waggled her cigar in his direction. 'What's wrong with her?'

'No Cubans,' he said, eyes averted.

Now Lottie Mae stared at him with something more than confusion. 'You got shot in the head over there or somethin'? Jasmine ain't Cuban, she's a fucking Chinawoman! She and her husband got throwd overboard by smugglers when the Coast Guard found their boat. He didn't make it, and she washed up.' Eyes narrowed, hands on hips, she said, 'Look again, soldier.'

And so he did. Sleek, shiny black hair framed sharp cheekbones and slanted eyes, wary now, above a tentative smile. Her slender figure was highlighted by a tight black dress. In every way, she was as different to Alicia as it was possible to be. 'You come with me,' she said, hand out, 'we make good time.'

He felt the expectant gaze of both women on him. *It's going to work.* And so he followed Jasmine's petite, black-clad rump up the stairs, trailed by the smoke from Lottie Mae's cigar.

It didn't work.

If anything, his time with Jasmine, though a pleasurable release, simply made things worse. His body was sated but his mind raced ever faster and sleep became even more elusive. Never a quitter, he persevered, and thus the week unfolded. By day, he worked with Thomas, avoiding the Tea Room, and by night he made his rounds. Thomas shot inquisitive glances his way, but sensibly kept his own counsel.

After Lottie Mae's, he went to Miss Susan's, from there to The Pit Stop, and the next night on to Geraldine's place in Coloured Town. Then there was Pine Lodge, often mistaken by tourists for a modest hotel, and then The Titty Shack, which never was.

By the last night of the week, it was an open question whether desperation or exhaustion would finish him off first.

The faces and the bodies of the girls joined the procession of images when he closed his eyes. Thighs and breasts, open mouths and legs, round asses and skinny asses, pretty girls, plain girls, downright homely girls, white, black, and yellow . . . he tried them all.

But never brown.

Not only did their faces and bodies haunt his nights, their stories hijacked his waking hours. He saw Jasmine being thrown overboard with her husband, watching them go under, and thought of *her* again. The girl at Miss Susan's had scarred wrists, from a knife or shackles, he couldn't tell, and he found himself wondering. Another, at Pine Lodge, had a rag doll tucked beneath her pillow.

On one memorable night, after Geraldine's place, he went back afterwards to Lottie Mae's for more, thinking that it might just be a question of quantity.

It wasn't.

And so it was with some trepidation that he approached the House of Eve, the town's most exclusive brothel, located in a quaint cottage with gingerbread woodwork on a quiet, tree-lined residential street well away from the bars and clubs. He had an overwhelming sense of time running out, and all hopes pinned here. Although his body demanded rest, he was determined to complete his mission because he had absolutely no other plan.

Eve was on the porch swing as he approached, dressed in a turquoise kimono, an ornate fan in one hand and a cocktail in the other. She was the town's most notorious transvestite, a very tall Haitian formerly known as Pierre, who was ru-moured to have girls so skilful, they could make a man forget his own name. This was exactly what John craved: to have his mind wiped clean.

'I heard about *un grand soldat* with black hair,' Eve said in her rich accent, half French and half pure islander, 'who is fucking his way through every house on The Rock. Whatever you seek, *monsieur*,' she took a sip of cocktail, 'you will find it here. If you have any money left, of course.'

'I can pay.' Although only established since the war ended, in response to the demand from thousands of returning troops, Eve's had swiftly achieved the reputation for being the best, in a crowded market. This reputation was reflected in the price. He handed over the money.

She stood, and in her heels was easily a head taller than him. '*Venez avec moi*,' she said. 'I have what you need.' She inspired such confidence, he felt the tension of the week slip from his shoulders. Without a word, he followed her inside.

Less than fifteen minutes later, he was in such a hurry to get away that he was still doing up his belt as he raced down the porch steps.

'*Mais, attendez*!' Eve called after him, with a stamp of her towering heel. 'This happens sometimes, it is nothing to be ashamed of!' Her voice followed him down the road. '*Putain*!' she called. 'Next time, on the house!'

Burning with shame, he welcomed the cover of darkness. Usually, his problem was getting erections at the most inconvenient times. In fact, he had to concentrate very hard not to get them. It had never failed, not since he lost his cherry to the first girl ever, the one who his father bought for his fifteenth birthday, saying, 'Don't come out till you're a man.'

That started him on the road that he walked now, a series of girls, too many to remember, even if he wanted to. And he didn't want to remember. He got what he wanted, they got what they needed. A fair transaction, he had thought, everyone satisfied. Until now.

What the hell is wrong with me?

He wanted to blame her, Eve's girl, whose name he couldn't bear to think of, because that made it more real. The girl had been unremarkable, older than most, with an ordinary face but pleasantly rounded figure. When he hesitated, Eve bent to whisper in his ear, 'Trust Eve, she is what you need.'

And everything had started so well. When she stroked his temples, a feeling of deep peace stole over him like a fog. *Maybe she's a witch?* He wasn't asleep, nor was he fully awake. Moonlight suited her, and he understood why Eve said she had what he needed. She was indeed skilled, and as she went to work on him with her hands and her mouth, he gave himself over to it, looking forward to the complete emptying of his mind. It felt good, so good. Worth every penny. *This is going to work.*

But just when he was ready to take her, his eye had strayed to a photo on a table by the bed, of a small girl with unruly curls pulled up into a floppy bow, and a serious, downturned mouth beneath sulky eyes – the same eyes as the woman who opened her robe for him.

That was the end of it: no more activity south of his belt after that. Despite her most enthusiastic, acrobatic efforts, all he could see was the woman with a little girl in her lap, tying up her curls in a bow while the child struggled and the photographer looked at his watch. Alicia had said to him, 'Every one of us has a story.' Suddenly, he wanted to know hers.

It had never happened before. The woman was understanding, kind, quick and sincere in her reassurance.

He could not get out of there fast enough.

As he strode on through the quiet streets, he recalled her last words, as she pulled the robe around herself. With a small, sad shrug, she had said, 'The only way to be free is to stop fighting.'

CHAPTER 13

It was a week later, just as the sun began its descent, when Alicia finally puffed onto the fringes of the hidden cove where John had instructed her to appear. She could only assume he had chosen this secluded spot because he did not want to be seen with her in public, which was consistent, even sensible. Yet she was surprised to find she minded. Very much. She had started to think he was different. *He is not different. He is just like all the men who come to the Tea Room.*

The bathing suit bought specially from Jolovitz's was, she had been assured by the unctuous sales assistant, the most modern fashion. The collar of the striped dress chafed her neck, the folds of the black bloomers trapped hot air next to her skin, and the knee-high socks felt like winter garments rather than swimwear. At least she was covered, unlike some of the women whom she had seen on their way to Smathers Beach, their knees and arms bare for all to see. The floppy hat shaded her face, from the sun and curious glances. Yet still she felt eyes on her, as she rode the streetcar, and even now, as she followed the sandy path described in his note headed 'Swimming Lesson'.

They had not spoken since the night of the liquor run. He was never at the bar when she tried to find him. And then she received the note. She had been surprised at his willingness to teach her, after she had so nearly drowned them both on the first trip. In those few moments, before Thomas had pulled them out, she had been so close to death. She had not been calm or resigned or peaceful, filled with thoughts of heaven and angels, as she had heard from people with lucky escapes. No, as the blackness engulfed her, she had felt only the stab of pure, mortal terror through her heart. And when John jumped in, she had not even recognised him, overwhelmed by the all-consuming desperation to live, at the expense of anyone or anything else. Never before had she felt so utterly, completely out of her mind. The night had woken an animal inside her, and it would fight to live, harder than she had believed possible. She had never considered herself to be a fighter, preferring the softer road around conflict, but when death's sharp, pointed teeth closed round her throat, everything changed. The shock of that would take a long while to fade. If it ever did.

Her hand went to her neck. Even the memory of that night brought a panicked surge of adrenalin.

He had his back to her, ankles lapped by the shallow water on the small crescent of sand between the mangroves. A black vest looped over his bare shoulders, down to a belt which secured a pair of blue shorts, from which emerged thickly mus-cled legs. Strange, she thought, how much more streamlined he looked out of his normal clothes, almost like he belonged in the water. He sluiced his arms and hair, the droplets sparkling in the sunshine. Oh, how she envied his apparent ease with his body, and the freedom to preen in such minimal garments, while she itched and steamed inside her jersey cocoon.

Mosquitoes buzzed around her ears. She slapped them away, and looked up to find laughing eyes on her.

'What?' she said, self-conscious in just about every way possible. The water looked deliciously cool, but stronger than her discomfort was her fear. Still and always, the fear.

'Where did you get that . . . that costume?' he asked, arms folded. Black hair curled out of the neck of his vest. His limbs were covered in it, except on his right leg, where his thigh was bisected by a white slash of scar. The bright light caught on his head, his shoulders, and the rounds of his biceps.

'At the department store. It is very fashionable, I am told.' Starting to overheat inside the restrictive clothing, she felt like a stranded whale beside his dolphin-sleek composure. The gentle shush of the surf beckoned, the sea beyond mirror-smooth.

'If you say so,' he said with a grin.

More mosquitoes arrived to plague her. She barged past him to the water's edge and hesitated for only a second before wading in up to her knees. It was like standing in a warm bath, just slightly cooler than the air. That is all, she told herself, I am standing in a bathtub. Not on the edge of an unimaginably deep abyss filled with tons of water just waiting to fill up my lungs and take me down to everlasting darkness and dissolve my very bones. *No, not that. Just a bathtub.*

He joined her and removed the hat. 'You won't be needing this where we're going,' he said, and tossed it onto the sand. 'Come on.'

They waded out further and entered cooler water. It felt so good. She thought she would be all right, while he chattered away beside her, about the new supplier he had found, and his latest information about what bribes were needed for the ever-growing list of city, state, and federal officials with their hands out. But then the water was up to her chest and she was not all right, not nearly.

The dress floated up around her shoulders, the bloomers like weights on her knees. She was going down, down, and soon it would lap her chin, and then fill her mouth, and then – her arms were locked round his neck before she even realised.

'Hey!' he cried, and staggered in surprise. 'Cut that out!'

But his hands had a tight grip on her torso and the feeling of sinking abated a little, just enough for her to loosen the hold on his neck.

'This ain't gonna work if you try to drown me again.'

'I am . . . sorry,' she panted. 'For the other night, also.'

'Never mind,' he said, and returned her feet to the sandy bottom. 'My own stupid fault for comin' in after ya.' He regarded her, head on one side. 'See here, your get-up might be the height of fashion, but it don't seem right practical for our purposes.'

The dress was ample coverage, she decided, and underneath there was also her slip. 'Turn round.' While he obliged, she undid the fastening of the bloomers and kicked them off, to float away. Blessed relief followed. 'Ready,' she lied.

'Now,' he said, 'swimmin' is really just energetic floatin', so we're gonna get you to float. Lay on your back.'

'I cannot, I—'

'Trust me. Have I let you down so far?'

'No, but I—' And then she was floating. Above her, the sky, with a few wisps of cloud, edged orange by the setting sun, and below her, like two iron bars, his arms. She focused on their solid strength to calm herself. *He has not let me down.*

His voice was close in her ear. She could feel it resonate through his torso. 'There ya go. Nothin' to it.'

But then a little water splashed her face and it was back, the urge to clamp on to him like a monkey. The sky was too big, the sea was too big. She was a speck, a mote, a nothing in its vastness. Panic smouldered, ready to ignite. As if he sensed this, he said, 'Look at me.'

And there he was, above her, his face framed by dripping black hair, giving scale to the immense emptiness around her. Although she was rigid as a wooden plank, she fought down the urge, and slowly, slowly, accustomed herself to the sensation. *Just like a bathtub ... that is all this is ... a giant, fathomless bathtub, filled with monsters waiting to drag me to the bottom with them and—* NO. Eyes locked on his, she noticed they were not black after all, just very, very dark brown, with tiny chips of gold, like fine paintbrush strokes.

'Good,' he said. 'And now I'm going to let go and—'

'Wait! Not yet!'

'Put your arms out. Don't think about anythin', just relax and let the sea hold you up, like a feather bed.'

She was about to object and tell him it was all too fast, when a strange, weightless sensation took hold of her body. Arms extended like a starfish, expecting any minute to sink below the surface, instead she rested on it, moving easily to its gentle undulations. With only small adjustments of her limbs, she found it possible to maintain her position. *If only Mamacita could see me now!*

She began to laugh. '*Míra!* Look at me! I am—' The water poured into her mouth, choking her instantly. Her feet could not find the bottom. Her head went under. She tried to take a breath, but no air could find its way in.

Then she was up again, riding his shoulder like a sack of grain. Coughing, gasping, the water poured from her mouth and down his back. He dumped her in the shallows and she crawled, retching, up to the safety of the dry sand. He waited, hands on knees, while she sucked shaking breaths into her grateful lungs.

'You don't trust me,' he said, wiping his mouth.

'Of course I do not,' she spat, with yet more sea water. 'Why should I? I am useful to you, that is all.' Head in hands, she accepted defeat. Some things were not meant to be. The ridiculous, waterlogged dress was caked in sand. Salt stung her eyes, her skin sticky with it, her hair tangled around her neck. She wrung out the hem of the dress and a small crab skittered from its folds.

'Useful?' he said, eyebrows raised up to his hairline. 'I've owned shoes with more common sense than you have. And my life would be a whole lot simpler without your interference. I helped you because I owed Beatriz, but that debt is now paid.'

'Fine. I will ask you for nothing more.' Her degradation complete, she rose to her feet.

'Fine.' He shrugged, and slicked his hands over his dripping black hair. 'Was your stupid idea anyway.' And he turned back towards the water.

He had only gone a few paces when she heard her name. She decided to ignore him, as she struggled to untangle herself from the dress so she could shake off the sand.

'Alicia,' he said again, in the kind of voice used to avoid waking a baby, 'come here a minute. You'll want to see this.'

'If you think you can trick me into . . . oh.' She dropped the dress onto the beach and waded in beside him.

At first, all she saw was a shadow in the water, partly in the shade of the mangroves, but then John tapped his palms lightly on the surface and the shadow moved towards him. A whiskery nose broke the surface in a spray of droplets, then a rounded grey back emerged. The animal must have been seven feet long, cigar-shaped, from the snout nuzzling John's hand to the massive fluked tail which stirred the sand.

'Wha . . . what is it?' She looked down through the clear water to be met by a curious stare from an eye, round and brown as a pebble. The eye blinked at her once, twice.

'We call 'em sea cows. Thomas's people call 'em *manatí*. They eat 'em.'

Indeed, its snout reminded her of a cow. As she watched, it tore some grass from the sandy bottom and began to chew. Then it pushed its bulk against her leg, almost toppling her. Its hide was rough, its weight like the meaty shove of a horse.

'What is it doing?' Alicia completely forgot the water all around. She forgot her near nakedness. She had always enjoyed an affinity with animals, but since Raoul had killed Pablito, she had avoided becoming attached to another. This creature transfixed her with its huge, ungainly yet strangely graceful body, and ugly yet charmingly lumpy face. And that gentle, blinking brown eye.

'She's sayin' hello. Watch this.' He bent over and reached beneath the animal. 'She likes to be scratched under the flippers.' Suddenly the animal executed a barrel roll which exposed its pale belly to the sky. 'Go ahead,' he said, 'your turn.'

Alicia laid her hand on the belly, which was surprisingly

smooth, and scratched a few times. Another barrel roll brought the animal's head briefly to the surface again. Alicia stepped back with a start.

John said. 'Do it harder this time, under the flipper. Her hide's like a tractor tyre.'

Alicia followed his instructions and this time the creature rolled on its back and waggled its flippers in the air. Entranced, Alicia giggled and scratched harder. '*Es bonita, muy bonita,*' she cooed. The animal rolled over and over for her. 'She seems to know you.'

'I've been comin' here since me and Thomas were kids. Before the war, I found her as a calf, her ma had been butchered for meat. They're solitary creatures generally, like me, but the young 'uns are playful. I used to spend hours here with her.' He scratched the animal again and was rewarded with a powerful heave against his legs. It brought from him a laugh of pure delight which transformed the hard lines of his jaw and charged his eyes with a new warmth.

'Does she have a name?'

'I call her Pilar. My mom had a little dog by that name.'

Indeed, there was something almost dog-like in the way the manatee followed them around, its whiskery snout breaking the surface every so often. 'Does she still live in Key West, your mother?'

Something in his face hardened. 'She left, when I was five. Took the dog.'

Took the dog but left the child? What kind of mother does that? Alicia had a vision of the young John, scouting in the mangroves with a hand-whittled spear, skin toasted to deep umber by the sun, salt-stiff hair in his eyes. A lonely little boy, with his only friend, a little coloured-Indian boy with a burned face.

'I didn't think she'd remember me,' he said, with a fond chuckle, 'I been away so long.'

'But she does.'

'Yep, I reckon so.' His face was so open and relaxed, his eyes soft as he stroked her bumpy hide. 'I think she's beautiful too. And she likes you.'

'More than other . . . people you have brought here?'

'I ain't never brought no one else here,' he said, his gaze on the animal, whose nostrils broke the surface to spray his face. He laughed again and wiped himself clean.

Alicia became aware that they had drifted farther out, to where each wavelet lifted her from the sea bottom. Surprisingly, her body naturally adjusted position to keep her head dry. The *manatí* bumped against her again, which should have terrified her, to be so close to this enormous, untamed beast. Instead, the animal generated in her a deep sense of calm well-being, as if nothing bad would happen while it was near. She allowed her legs to rise up and straighten, head back, hair spreading around her like seaweed.

John's arms slid beneath her body again, warm and firm. The first star appeared above her. She released the fear she had clutched to herself for so long. It drifted away like fronds of sea grass. She could feel his eyes on her body in the transparent silk, and should have felt ashamed, but did not.

'You OK?' His voice sounded different, far away.

'Yes, I am,' she said, eyes closed, just rocking to the motion of the water. 'You can let go now.'

There was a time to fight, she decided, and a time to give

in. She felt light as a leaf, floating, supported by the infinite, timeless sea. And him. She imagined that Cuba, and home, were off the end of her right index finger, across ninety miles of ocean, but for once there was no ache, no magnetic pull. Afloat on the element which terrified her most, in the arms of a man she didn't know, for the first time in her life, she felt truly free.

His arms remained. She looked up at his face, suddenly serious, his eyes two dark glints in shadow. His mouth moved but her ears were full of water. She raised her head. '*Qué dice?*'

'I said,' and he swung her round to face him. 'I don't want to. Let go.'

Her legs naturally coiled about his waist, her arms around his neck, not in mortal terror this time. But she held back. Raoul had never kissed her, not once in that whole long year. *Putas*, he had said, were not for kissing. John showed no such inhibition. There was an awkward, salty clash of teeth and lips, his hands urgent at her breasts. She pushed away.

'What is it?' he said, eyes slightly unfocused.

'You must know,' she said, with as much dignity as she could manage, 'I am not a whore.'

A deep, shuddery breath. 'And you must know,' he said, equally grave, 'that I wouldn't give two hoots if you were.'

'But you brought me here, to this place, so that no one would see you with a *morena*.'

'Is that what you think?' He stared down in bewilderment. 'You really think I'd put up with such nonsense from anyone else, be they brown, white or purple? I brought you here . . .' he stroked her face, like she was a pearl plucked from the sea, 'I brought you here because I couldn't think of any other way to get you alone.' His hands found her buttocks and pulled her tight up against him.

'To have . . . to have your sex with me?' Men had always wanted her like this. It was nothing new. That she wanted him too, in a way that left her breathless with surprise, was not the point. *Please, please be different to the others.*

'Have my way with you?' He chuckled, and positioned her firmly on the shelf in his shorts. 'Yes, oh yes, that. Oh, yes.' He rested his forehead against hers. 'But you need to understand.' A deep, expressive sigh. 'I spent a whole week, and a lot of money, trying not to think about you. That night, when you fell in, and I thought you were gone . . . I went in after you, though I knew you'd probably get both of us killed, because I didn't care what happened to me. Because I was with you. Don't you see? My God, woman,' he groaned, 'don't you see what you do to me . . .?'

What she saw in him, for the first time, was fear, like a man on the edge of a precipice, and it was this that made up her mind.

She did not hold back when his mouth came down hard on hers, his fingers woven in her hair. It went on and on and on, the heat from his body gradually burning away the darkness. She poured years of sorrow and disappointment into that first kiss, all the desperate, lonely hours, all the times she wondered what was wrong with her.

He pulled her closer still, until finally she broke away to look at him in amazement.

'Well,' he gasped, 'that just proves it.' His delighted grin glowed in the fading light. 'No whore ever kissed me like that.'

175

She slapped him, hard. Then kissed him again.

'And none ever will.'

Dwayne saw it all from his hiding place inside a stand of sea grapes. He scrubbed tears of frustration from his cheeks, appalled to be crying like a little baby. All he had wanted was to see Miss Alicia home safe. He had tracked her from the time she boarded the streetcar in her strange bathing outfit, and then down the sandy path that wound through the palmetto scrub until eventually reaching the cove. He thought she might get lost, being unfamiliar with the area. Although her temperament was fiery enough, there was something fragile about her which he felt bound to protect, and there were plenty of bad men prowling the coastline, especially these days. A woman alone was asking for trouble. At least, that's what he told himself.

When he saw Mr Morales waiting for her, he could have left then. Mr Morales was a war hero, plenty brave enough and capable of escorting her back. Instead he had stayed. And watched. And now he felt so mixed up inside. He knew it was wrong, to watch them, but his eyes would not look away. And the longer he looked, the more confused and upset he felt, like having fire ants crawling under his skin.

Although he knew she was a Jezebel, it was still thrilling beyond belief to see her strip down to her slip and enter the water, like something from the lingerie section in the Sears Roebuck catalogue come to life, only better. He couldn't hear what was said between them – they were too far out – but he could sure tell what was going on when they started kissing.

Desire welled up, and he imagined that it was his mouth on hers, his hands on her breasts, his shoulders she clutched. He couldn't help himself. He had only ever used the catalogue before, and some old, stained postcards that some sailors sold him down on the dock. Other guys his age seemed to get girls, but Dwayne wasn't much good at it. They made fun of his red hair and freckles. He just froze and blushed scarlet when he tried to talk to them. Miss Alicia was the first one who was ever nice to him. To see her like this, not a girl but a real woman, clad only in some wet silk . . . it was too much.

Shame and anger joined the hot cauldron of emotions boiling in his head – shame at himself, at his weakness, anger at what she had made him do to himself. He was dirty, Pa always said so, dirty in his soul. He had thought she was different to the others he saw all the time at the Tea Room. She had seemed different, more modest and ladylike, despite her profession. But now he knew she was just the same, and it felt like something precious had been smashed beyond repair.

He had to be cleansed of her. He would read the Bible, and he would pay attention during Pa's sermons in church. He would devote his energies to the Klan recruitment drive, and make himself worthy of membership. And he would rid himself of the foul, disgusting thoughts that she gave him.

He would do all of this, he decided, after just one more look.

❧ CHAPTER 14 ❧

Encrusted with sand and salt, dazed and tired, Alicia arrived from the beach back at the Tea Room on John's arm.

Although it was well after dark, she was wary. 'What if someone should see us?' Raoul had been proud to show her off in public, keen to flaunt his striking bride with his friends, but the rules were very different here.

'It's my duty to see a lady home safe,' he said, as they climbed the steps. 'And, for the last time, I don't care what no one thinks, except you.'

Through the open door, the smell of Hortensia's cooking mingled with the inevitable sweat and rum, and she realised that she was very, very hungry. 'Stay and eat,' she said, with the distinct sensation of crossing a line. This would make a state-ment, which suddenly seemed rash. 'Never mind, stupid idea.'

'Not at all,' he said. 'I could eat a manatee right now.'

With a scowl, she pushed through the door ... and right into the arms of Mamacita.

A cry of surprise, followed by silence while they stared at each other.

'Alicia? Is this . . . person my *niña*?'

Alicia caught sight of herself in the mirror over the bar. Her head was a mass of tangled, sticky curls which had set hard during the ride back in John's boat. The bathing ensemble hung on her like a striped sack, dripping sea water into her squelchy shoes. At least John had changed into street clothes, but they too were stained with salt. They both looked, she thought, like victims of a shipwreck. Her own shock was reflected on Mamacita's face.

'*Sí, soy yo.*' Alicia didn't know what to say. There was too much to say. So she just stood there, gaping, being gaped at.

'You sounded lonely, in your letter,' said her mother. 'I decided to surprise you with a visit. But now, I see you have . . . other company.' Her gaze slid over John, but did not linger.

'Well,' he said, eyes dancing, 'I'll be seein' you, Miss Pearl.' He tipped his hat. '*Buenas tardes, Señora.*'

Paulina eased Mamacita into a chair, just as she looked about to faint.

'*Por favor,*' said Mamacita, 'some tea, please.'

With a helpless glance at Alicia, Paulina shrugged. 'I am sorry, *señora*, but we have no tea.'

'No tea?' She swivelled her head round, as if taking in the room for the first time. 'What is this place? Why is it full of men this time of the evening? Where is Beatriz? And why did he call you "Miss Pearl"?'

'Get *Señora* Cortez some water,' Paulina said to Kitty, and then whispered, 'with a shot of medicine.'

Mamacita drew a fan from her bodice and began to flap it with great agitation. 'Will someone please tell me what is going on!'

Alicia studied her dear face. 'Welcome to Key West, Mama-cita. We have much to discuss.'

After a bath, and over Hortensia's excellent *patitas de puerco*, Alicia provided as much explanation as she felt her mother could handle. At first, Mamacita had said she was not hungry, but as Alicia's tale unfolded, she grabbed a fork and began to shovel the fragrant pork into her mouth at speed. She des-patched with equal alacrity the creamy *flan de caramelo* which followed.

One of the regular customers put his head round the kitchen door. 'That sure smells fine, Miss Pearl. You got any more?'

Hortensia huffed and filled another plate, but Alicia knew she was pleased. Since her arrival, more and more of the regu-lars had begun to pay for food in addition to the Tea Room's other offerings. And thanks to Hortensia's knack for produ-cing delicious dishes from the cheapest ingredients, even pig's feet, the profits were handsome. The new kitchen was well equipped to produce bigger volumes of food. *If this continues, I will need to employ some waitresses.*

Finally, with a gentle burp, Mamacita wiped her mouth. 'Your Papa must never, ever know.'

'Of course. But since I will not be returning to Havana . . .' She waited for her mother to contradict her, but she just burped again.

'It is not safe, but one day, I pray, it will be. Time, *niña*. Just give it time. And meanwhile, there is . . . this.' Her sweep of disparagement went beyond the Tea Room to encompass the whole town. 'It is hard for me to see you here. I cannot bear to hear you called "Miss Pearl". Your hair, too, is different.'

'The name does not matter. It is just my job.' Not since the night of the boat trip had she tamed her hair into the bun, but instead wore it down, held loosely by a ribbon at the base of her neck. She thought again of it floating like a fan around her in the water, flowing between John's fingers . . . 'Many things are different.' For an instant, she wondered if her skin glowed where his hands had touched her, like the phosphorescent sea.

'I have missed you, *pajarita*.' She stroked Alicia's hand, just like she did when she was a little girl.

Sitting in the kitchen beside her mother brought back all the times they had conspired together to produce the special feast day treats which Papa loved, none more than the roasted pig on Christmas Eve. Alicia had been given the task of turning the spit ever since she was tall enough to reach. The memory was like a shard of glass between her ribs.

Her fingers closed on the bird pendant at her throat. 'Does Papa . . . does he miss me too?'

'Of course, he does.' But she sounded less than certain. 'Of course. He does. And we both hope . . . we hope that, some day, it will be safe for you to come home to us. But in the meantime, we must find you somewhere more . . . somewhere else to live, and a better job for you.' Her eyes went to the ceiling, which was pounding rhythmically to the activity in Maxine's room above.

A scuffle had broken out in the main salon. Alicia heard the crack of Felix's bat, a shriek from Kitty and a sound of angry protest. She viewed her life then, through Mamacita's eyes, in all its tawdriness. Her mother could see none of the improvements she had made, none of the obstacles she had overcome or battles won, how she had taken the filthy hand dealt to her and transformed it into something she was far from ashamed of.

'This is my life, Mamacita, the one you bought for me. And here I will stay. Excuse me, I am needed.'

Some hours later, too exhausted to sleep, she lay on the floor in a square of waning moonlight and listened to Mamacita's snores. Although the hard boards beneath the thin mattress would turn her into a mass of aches and bruises, it seemed she was still afloat on the soft rocking motion of the sea. Memories tumbled together: his mouth, his hands, his brown-gold eyes warm on her, fearful and amazed; her hunger for him, as much a surprise for her as for him; the sudden delight of joining with another person, and her utter inability to understand what that meant for her future. And then Mamacita's arrival, stirring up the silt of her past until all around was murky mud. She felt, in every sense, adrift from herself.

When she was with him, it had seemed so clear, so natural and right. But now, at the hour between night and morning, that grey time when nothing seems real, doubts sprang up all around her to whisper like wraiths in Mamacita's voice.

What do you know about him, really?

He is no different to Raoul, he just hides it better.

You are better off alone.

You will always be alone.

And Mamacita brought the scent of Havana with her. It was in her hair, her clothes, on her skin, so heady that it seemed Alicia had left only yesterday. And it made her believe, just as she drifted off into an uneasy doze, that all she had to do was wish, and she would wake up in her old bedroom, a hint of gardenia wafting on the breeze.

The next morning, Alicia found the fresh Cuban bread in its usual place on the porch, and stuffed a chunk into her mouth while waiting for the milk to arrive.

Every joint was sore. She kneaded the knotted muscles of her neck. At least yesterday's humidity and low cloud had been banished overnight. There might even be, she thought, the first sign that summer was weakening its grip.

Mr Clemens and Emily the cow strolled up just as Mamacita emerged on the porch, blinking in the sunlight.

'Good morning,' said Alicia, and held the bottle under Emily's udder while his expert hands produced the frothy, creamy milk.

She passed him a coin.

'Indeed it is, miss,' he said, and tipped his hat. 'Summer's finally over. Come on, old girl.' And he led Emily off down the street.

'What . . . what was that?' Mamacita asked, as Emily's generous backside swayed gently into the distance.

'Just the Walking Dairy. And if you wait long enough, you might see Percy the gorilla pass by on his way to work.' Still with the night's unease on her, she took childish pleasure in Mamacita's scowl. 'Breakfast?'

Before the others were even up, Dwayne had brought in more charcoal for the stove. He was first into the kitchen, even before Ma had made coffee. It was part of his new path to righteousness. No more lying in bed until the last minute. If he had not exactly vanquished the twin demons of lust and envy that tormented him during the night, he had at least subdued them somewhat. But he knew it would require constant vigilance to resist their whispered temptations.

'You're up early,' said Ma, with a fond ruffle of his hair, as she put the pot on the stove.

'It's a beautiful morning!' he said.

With a quizzical glance, she set a plate of fresh bread and a crock of butter on the table. 'You all right, son?'

'Never better, Ma. Got a full day of deliveries ahead of me. Good, honest work.' He had resolved to make his usual stop at the Tea Room but preserve his eyes from the sin of Paulina's girlishness this time on the grounds that they'd seen enough the day before at the beach. Unbidden, there she was again, in his head, Alicia rising from the sea like a mermaid, locked in Mr Morales's arms . . . under the kitchen table, fists clenched on his knees, he struggled to master the thoughts writhing like worms in his brain. *Get out, Jezebel, and leave me in peace!*

Pa entered the room, rolling up his sleeves. 'Glad to hear it,' he said. 'You can help get these into the right hands. I reckon there's several on your route.' And he extracted a pile of cards from his pocket.

On each was printed the message:

Brother: We have our eyes on you. You are being weighed in the balance! The call is coming! Are you able and qualified to respond? Discuss this matter with no one.

'What are they for, Pa?'

'They're the first step in bringing in the men we need. Kleagle Simpkins has entrusted me with them, son, and I'm entrusting them to you.' He produced a piece of paper with a list of names. 'Any of these on your route?'

The names represented the best families of Key West, and many of its public officials.

'Yessir, I can get to most of them.' He felt the mantle of responsibility settle on his shoulders along with Pa's right hand. They were both heavy, and rightfully so. He sat up straighter. 'And then what happens?'

'We let the message sink in for a bit, and then we follow it up with a second, and a third card. Each one softens them up a little more, until we bring them in to answer some questions. If they pass, then we get them signed up, ready for initiation.'

It all sounded kind of sneaky, and time-consuming. 'But why don't we just go up and ask 'em to join?'

'Because, son, our enemies will do anything, even pervert the law, to stop us achieving our goals. You must learn discretion. It's the Klansman's greatest tool.'

Dwayne had been known as Loose Lips at school because any secret trickled into his ear popped straight out his mouth. It was one of the reasons why he had few friends growing up. So far, he had amazed himself by keeping his nocturnal activities with Mr Morales and Miss Alicia from Pa's watchful gaze. Two things had worked in his favour: the first was that the rum-running trip somehow belonged to another time and place. All of it had felt unreal, like a dream or a story – there were even times when he wondered if he had imagined it all – so it took no effort to restrain himself from blabbing about it.

The second thing in his favour was that Pa was so distracted by the recruitment drive that he took almost no notice of anything around him. Dwayne thought he could probably dress up in a pink chicken suit and strut through the kitchen and Pa would still just hold out his coffee cup for a refill while he studied the list of candidate names. Still, it had been more than a week since there had been night-time scuffles in his parents' room, and longer since Pa had lashed out. So far, the Klan's anticipated arrival had been only good for his family.

He vowed to keep whatever secrets were entrusted to him.

'And Dwayne, remember: while you're going around town, you're our eyes and ears. I want to know of anything . . . unusual. Understand, Dwayne? Eyes and ears.'

'Yessir.' At long last, it was finally happening. Dwayne felt himself on the way to becoming a real man.

A few hours later, Alicia was preparing to take Mamacita to the dock to catch the ferry back to Havana. Her mother was already tearful, a damp handkerchief clutched to her chest.

'You can come again, Mamacita,' she said, and she meant it. Over Hortensia's delicious *huevos Habaneros*, her mother seemed to make a decision and, with fulsome praise for the cooking, engaged in animated discussion with Hortensia, Felix and the girls. She then bid each of the Tea Room staff an emotional farewell while extracting a promise from them to take care of her precious *pajarita*.

As the girls waved them off, Alicia heard a sniff from Kitty. 'My Mama never come down here to check on me. Not once.'

Dwayne arrived with his cart, now laden not only with shoes, but with sundry other household and personal goods from Jolovitz's store.

'Good morning, Dwayne,' Alicia said, 'this is my mother.'

'Mornin', ma'am,' he said, eyes down.

'Dwayne is very helpful, Mamacita,' she said, 'in all kinds of ways.' She expected this to raise a smile, as Dwayne had obviously so enjoyed the first rum run. It was such an adventure for him – for all of them – despite, or even because of, the danger. This was just one of the areas she had glossed over during her mother's stay.

'Yes'm, ma'am. If you don't mind, ma'am, I ain't got time to tarry.' He still did not look at her.

'Dwayne, are you all right?'

'Yessum, just got work to do.'

'Well, here's something to cheer you up. Mr Morales has another errand for you and your boat. Tomorrow evening, same place as before.'

John had told her about a different supplier, a bitter enemy of José keen to exploit any weakness, and they would need Dwayne's boat as well.

'My apologies, miss, but I will be unable to attend. Now, if you'll excuse me . . .'

'Of course, Dwayne.'

And he hurried up the steps with his boxes.

'Strange boy,' muttered Mamacita. 'At that age, they are nothing but walking *pingas*. At any age, in fact.'

Startled to hear the coarse slang from her mother, something still bothered her. 'Yes.' She stared after him. 'But I thought he was different.'

'And that *hombre* last night, the one who came in with you? That one is trouble.'

'My business partner, John Morales.'

'Business partner. Mm,' Mamacita nodded, 'I had one like that. A long time ago.'

Her all-knowing glance brought an instant flush to Alicia's face, along with the realisation that she knew little about the woman standing there. They had never spoken with such frankness, not even after Raoul. She had never questioned why her parents had separate bedrooms. It was simply not discussed. Comfortable, well-upholstered Mamacita was always cooking, always content to follow Papa's lead, ready with his slippers when he came home from work.

'You and your . . . business partner,' Alicia began. 'Did Papa know?'

'Your papa is a good man.' She looked away with a sad smile. 'A very good man. I chose him for the life he could give to you. But the other one . . . ay, *niña*.' Her eyes sparkled. Alicia had a sudden vision of her as a young woman, radiantly, ecstatically in love . . . walking away from it all, and towards her child's future. 'I have no regrets, none.' She laid a palm on Alicia's cheek. 'But to see how you are here, now, and how he looked at you last night. Be careful, *pajarita* . . . but not too careful.'

Alicia held her close and whispered, 'Next time,' she said, 'stay longer.'

'*Sí*, but in a hotel,' she whispered back.

The ferry dock was busy, with arriving passengers and street vendors offering all manner of treats and trinkets to tempt them. A mound of shark guts glistened in the sun next to a pile of carcasses. The coloured boys still dived for coins, the dray horses still clomped round the piles of conch shells and sea sponges.

It was the first time Alicia had been back to the dock since the day she arrived. *How little I knew then, of anything.* She recalled the hulk of the troop ship with its khaki-clad cargo, realising with a shiver that John must have been among them. And she remembered Beatriz, flustered and panting as she ran down the jetty, and Dwayne's cheery, open face. *So much has changed, in so short a time.*

'*Dios mio*,' said Mamacita, handkerchief to her nose. 'What is that terrible smell?'

But Alicia just smiled at the barrels of *mierdas* lined up on the dock. She could no longer detect their odour.

One set of passengers disgorged, the ferry was now ready to receive the next. Mamacita clung to her, wetting the front of her dress with tears. Over her shoulder, Alicia watched while a cart backed up to the boat's loading area, the driver patiently coaxing the horse. Then he removed the tarpaulin to reveal five plain pine coffins.

Mamacita dried her eyes yet again and crossed herself. '*Pobrecitas*, at least they are going home now, to be buried on Cuban soil.' This set off another bout of sobbing.

More sobbing echoed from behind, and a gaggle of black-clad women joined the coffins to watch, leaning on each other for support, as they were loaded onto the ferry.

'That will not be you, *niña*. I swear, by all that is holy, we will have you home with us, one day.'

Alicia steered her onto the boat's deck before she could dissolve again. The ferry's horn blared, drowning out her final endearments.

But as Alicia waved her off, in a cloud of diesel fumes and fluttering handkerchiefs, she thought of Mamacita arriving back at home, sitting down to dinner with Papa, her empty chair beside him. All would be exactly as she had left it.

Only a few months had passed, but her old life now seemed to belong to someone else entirely. Even if given the chance to go back – which seemed highly unlikely – she could no more pick it up again than she could fit into her old school uniform. And that naïve girl in the straw hat was someone she used to know, now nearly a stranger. If she met that person on the street, she would walk straight past, with only a slight, but troubling, flicker of recognition.

❦ CHAPTER 15 ❦

It the coolness of an early November morning, upstairs at The Last Resort, John turned to Alicia. 'My God, woman, you're so sweet, just like honey.'

She didn't answer, just lay back with a sigh on the single bed. This was his favourite view of her, naked and blurry with desire, her brown skin glowing against the twisted sheets, her curls falling in sinuous skeins across the pillow.

He was getting used to her sighs and her secrets. Both seemed to inflame him, when he least expected it, such as when he was catching up with his overdue accounts. As he completed the ledger, on its own, the pen would make lewd doodles in the margin, which Thomas noted with ill-concealed disdain.

This was a new experience. Never before had he cared or even wondered what a woman wanted or needed, except in terms of fee for service. It simply wasn't relevant to the trans-action; but once he learned the details of her short marriage, many things became clearer: why she never turned her back on him, why her face never completely lost its shadow of war-iness, even in the depths of passion, why she always chose to sit facing the door. He had bought her a pearl bracelet from a vendor on the dock, not a good one, but pretty enough. However, instead of the squeal of delight he had expected, she had handed it back with a small shake of her head and then: 'No gracias. Not pearls.'

He decided to learn her body to give her pleasure, like it was his job – the irony of this only adding to the enjoyment. A caress here, a touch there, fast, then slow, hard then gentle . . . she was like an uncharted island, infinitely fascinating to explore.

And yet, and yet . . . some part of her remained beyond his reach, something still withheld. He realised his map of her might never be complete, not even after a lifetime together.

Whenever she looked at him that way with her cloud-grey eyes, he felt his heart break. It broke open, like a seed from the monkey pistol tree. It hurt. Every time, it hurt, and every time he welcomed the pain. He should have run, and there were times when he felt like the happiest fly in the world, completely ensnared in her soft, warm web; but although the fear was there, it was distant, like a voice overheard in someone else's conversation.

Even more amazing was what happened the first night they were together, when her mother had turned up. Curled around her on his narrow bed, he slept, deeply and well, in a way he hadn't since the war, or even before. He could still remember, after his mother left, being afraid to close his eyes. She had tucked him into bed at night, and been gone in the morning. In his child's mind, it was clear that anything, even the worst possible thing, could happen while he was asleep. And so, from then on, he had never allowed his whole self to relax, always keeping one part of his brain alert at all times. It was effective for survival, but his first night with her made him realise he had felt exhausted for most of his life.

Until now. When he woke with her, he had no memory of anything from the night except the delicious press of her flesh against him. He no longer counted the minutes until the sunrise would drive his ghosts back into the shadows. They were still there, and always would be he figured, but quiet now, as if they too had been given permission to rest.

She cried out, 'Ay!' and got up, rubbing her shoulder. 'This bed is awful, worse than lying on cobblestones. Why can we not use my room? It is more comfortable.'

Her hair was a shining curtain between him and the world. 'Too many people at the Tea Room,' he said, and lay down in the space she had vacated, hands behind his head, the better to watch her move around the room. It was, he had to admit, furnished in the style of a particularly stingy monk. 'Don't like folks knowin' my business.'

She pulled the slip on over her head, clearly enjoying his eyes on her. 'Is this the man who cares nothing for what others think?' She splashed some water on her face from the jug.

'Just 'cause I don't care what they think, don't mean I want to give them a reason to think.'

No reply, just a guarded glance, while she did that unfathomable feminine thing of being more alluring for her mussed sleepiness. He felt himself wanting her all over again.

She noticed. With a slow grin, she bent over the wash bowl. 'If we do not want people to think things, I must be at breakfast next door, as normal.'

He knew it was true, but the rounded temptation of her

back view was almost overwhelming. With an effort, he turned his eyes away and his thoughts to the work ahead.

'We're taking the boat out tonight, hope it's better than last time. Why can't we use the boy Dwayne's boat again? He seemed keen enough to help out the first time.' The reason why José's bitter enemy was so willing to deal with them became apparent when they arrived back with the cargo and had a celebratory taste: it was more like liquor-scented water, a pathetic and unusable imitation of real booze. Other leads had proved futile. The situation was not yet dire, but heading that way.

'I do not know why.'

'Shame, coulda used the extra capacity. Donkey Hightower's bought up the best stock around here, offering to sell it on for around twice what he paid.'

She turned to him, drying her neck. 'That was clever of him.'

'I'd be more inclined to admire his initiative if I had other options. As things stand,' he stretched, enjoying the stiffness in his muscles, 'we're gonna need to get creative. And soon.'

The closer they got to the end of the year, when Prohibition would come into force, the greater the tension in the town, with everyone scrambling to secure their stocks before the coming drought. Bribes had already started to flow freely in anticipation. There was word of increasing violence too, as dealers double- and triple-crossed each other to earn favours from the new masters. He needed a trusted supply line.

With a tilt of her head, she asked, 'By any chance, are you friendly with the undertaker?'

'Friendly?' Sitting up, he scratched his chest. 'Not exactly, but Thomas knows everyone. Why?'

'I may have an idea. But we will need a much bigger boat.'

'Tell me.'

'Something I saw, at the dock, when Mamacita left. The coffins were being loaded onto the ferry, and it made me think . . . how big they are, and how much room there is . . . inside.'

His business brain was awake now. He could picture it: empty coffins loaded onto the ferry, accompanied by some suitably bereft females, full coffins on the way back. Backhanders would need to find their way into the right pockets, of course, but the scheme had several advantages over the dangerous night-time runs. And most pleasing of all, it would happen in public, in daylight, in front of hundreds of people.

It was this, he decided: her sharp mind together with her soft curves. Either of these on their own would be attractive. In combination, they were more intoxicating than any liquor he had tasted.

He spun her onto his lap to kiss her. 'You, *señorita*, are a mother-lovin' genius!'

She hugged herself with pure, girlish pleasure and he had a blinding image of her as a small child: wilful, smart, with chaotic curls and a shy smile, always into mischief, with few friends. *Very like me at that age.* He wondered how he knew this. And, in one thunderclap of a second, he wondered whether their children would inherit her eyes. He must have been staring, because she pulled back with a questioning look.

'So, you think it could work?'

Flustered, heartbeat uncomfortably loud in his ears, he shook the image from his head. 'Yes, I think so. I'll look into it. Pass me those pants. I got a business to run.'

As she picked the trousers off the floor where they had

dropped in their hurry, there was a metallic *clunk*. Her hand went to the pocket. 'What is this?'

'Nothin',' he said, lighting his first cigarette. He drew the sweet smoke into his lungs. 'Give 'em here.'

But she hesitated. 'Is it your medal? You are a hero, they say. You should be proud of it, what you did for your country. May I see?'

He rose and snatched the trousers from her more roughly than he intended and pulled them on. The easy relaxation of a few minutes ago was gone. He could not meet those eyes. *If she knew, she wouldn't look at me like that again.*

'You hungry?' he asked, reaching for yesterday's shirt. It was a long way from clean, but there had been no time for laundry lately.

She just sat on the bed and waited, knees together, with that patient, unyielding expression he already knew so well.

His hand went inside the pocket. With a powerful sense of impending loss, he leaned back against the window and took a shaky drag on the cigarette, arms folded across his bare chest. The morning sun was warm on his shoulders, so different from that day . . .

'Don't make me do this.' His voice croaked like an old man's. He picked some flakes of tobacco from his tongue. The taste always reminded him of Rudy. 'When you know . . . when I tell you . . . you'll cross the street to avoid me.'

'I will not, I—'

'You will.' But then a strange calm was on him, like he used to feel before a big battle, when there was nothing to do but go forward. He exhaled with a feeling that everything he had done since that moment, in that half-demolished French church, had been leading to this. It gave him some comfort, to know there was absolutely no way to avoid it, like being tied to the railroad tracks in the path of an oncoming train. The terrible burden was slightly eased by the knowledge that he had no choice. A fleeting thought, fast as a bullet: *this is why I've always been alone.*

For the ten thousandth time, his fingers traced the contours of the object in his pocket and then, before he had time to think, he brought it out into the light. It rested in his palm, heavy and real: a toy soldier, fashioned of lead in some long-destroyed French factory. It stood at attention, with the fixed, empty expression of infantry everywhere. Its uniform was from olden times, nothing like the washed-out blue of the French soldiers whom they had fought alongside every day. It had white trousers, and a royal blue tailcoat adorned with two rows of scarlet buttons, its head crowned with a tall blue hat decorated with a gold crest. Its once-bright colours were faded by the abrasion of his fingers. An old musket was clutched in its hand, pointing at the sky, but this soldier was from a different time, a different war.

Confusion clouded her expression. 'But, I thought . . . where is it?'

'My famous Victory medal?' He stared out the window, where the town was just waking. Thomas was in the garden, picking strawberries for breakfast. 'I gave it to one of the guys in my unit. This,' he hefted the figurine, 'this is my real medal.' The rising sun sharpened his silhouette on the dusty floorboards.

Already he felt his mind drifting back there, as the contours of the bright bedroom dissolved around him. He focused on her eyes, the only anchor as the scene before him wavered and shifted and reassembled itself into darkness and cold, and rubble and piles of bodies in a small French town.

His platoon had had no sleep for three days, making their way through the Aire valley towards Exermont. And they'd been shelled in open country, explosives and gas, and come under machine-gun fire in the woods.

'We had some food left,' he said, 'but no water, when we came into Exermont. The Krauts had poisoned every well and stream for miles around. None of this is by way of any excuse, understand?' He gestured with his cigarette. 'Nothing I say to you . . . none of it excuses.'

She nodded and folded her legs beneath her, leaning against the rough wooden partition. One hand twisted a hank of hair round her fist to rest on her shoulder. He almost lost his nerve and gave in to the urge to run, from the room, from the town, from the state, anywhere to avoid saying the next words.

His throat was parched, as he remembered the thirst that day, marching through mile after mile of untilled fields, untended orchards rank with rotten fruit, the whole countryside neglected after four years of war. There was a cold rain that day.

'We expected to fight our way through the streets, but there was no one. Jenkins was the first to spot the well. Guess he figured the Krauts wouldn't poison the water where they were holed up. The sniper found him just as he raised his canteen. Then O'Brien, on my left, went down, and we scattered. I tracked the sniper, up above the bakery, and dealt with him.'

John had found the sniper in what had been a girl's bedroom, wallpaper patterned with bunches of lilac tied with yellow ribbons, pocked with bullets. The floor had creaked beneath his boot, the sniper's rifle swung round – and smacked into the window frame. It gave John just enough time to fire the Colt, once again proving its advantage at close quarters. The sniper had slumped over with a grunt of surprise, his rifle clattering on the cobbles below, to cheers from John's remaining men.

And that was when they found the civilians, heaped on top of one another, anonymous and silent as pebbles in a roadside shrine.

'There was a shout from the church,' he continued, pulled along inexorably, knowing there was no stopping now until it ended, 'and we all scrambled over there, expecting more trouble, but it was just Moscowitz. See, he was the musician in the platoon, used to play in a jazz club in New York. Pretty good, too. He had found this piano, covered in plaster, but working.'

The floor had been a mess of broken pews and smashed glass, with a few paintings of saints being saintly propped among the debris. He recalled the noseless statue of the Virgin in her marble alcove, all-seeing face staring down at them.

He paused. Now the moment had come, he wasn't sure if he could do it.

'Go on,' she said, 'I am here.'

With a deep breath, like before a dive, he said, 'The boys were yelling for Moscowitz to play something cheerful, but straight away he started "Amazing Grace". Only it wasn't like I'd ever heard it before.' John was still haunted by the melody, recognisable but totally different from the version of his childhood that was pounded out by the church organist with hands like hammers. Moscowitz's fingers seemed barely to brush the keys, the notes rising like smoke to fill the spaces around them in the ruined room. Then the evening sun had broken through the shattered windows, gleaming on their helmets and the Virgin's frozen face.

He stopped, not certain he could continue, not even totally sure where he was any more, as the memories of that day rose up around him like water. He could drown in them, and resigned himself to it, as they closed over his head.

Her eyes were fixed on him, unwavering, and his field of vision narrowed further. Rudy's voice hissed in his ear, 'Tell her, man,' he coughed, 'tell her what a big hero you are. We're all here, listenin'.'

Jenkins was there on the bed beside Alicia, his neck a mass of red, and O'Brien over by the bedroom door, with a neat hole drilled in his forehead, and Moscowitz, killed a week later by a grenade, resting his hands on the keyboard while the notes faded . . . and another sound emerged from the far, darkened corner of the church. A soft, shuffling sound.

'I fired five shots before I even knew the Colt was in my hand.'

The shell casings had pinged like brass bells around his feet, echoing in the emptiness. Everyone else had their weapons raised by this point, but he had said to them, 'You're too slow, fellas! Kraut woulda had you if it hadn't a been for Lightnin' Jack!'

'Probably just a dog,' said Moscowitz, voice shaky with relief. 'They won't give ya no medal for killin' a stray dog.'

'Ain't no dog,' John had said. He knew very well the sound of bullets striking a person. 'Bring the light.'

The torch beam had found his foot first. He was still alive.

Scully, a devout farm boy from Minnesota who never swore,

blurted 'Jesus fucking Christ,' and puked on Moscowitz's shoes.

'What do you see, John?' Alicia whispered. 'Tell me, *por favor.*'

He looked up, the scene swimming across the familiar view of his bedroom, hands tight on the windowsill. 'A boy, about eight years old, trapped underneath a woman, his Ma, maybe. She musta been dead a while. One of my shots got him here.' He pointed to his chest. It had left a small, scorched hollow. The child had said nothing, face white in the torch beam, just held out his hand. 'He gave me this.' John looked at the toy soldier in his palm as if it had just appeared for the first time, as if he was noting the colours and the detail all over again. It had happened in the space of a second, and when he looked again, the boy was dead.

She said nothing, just cried silently into her arms, rocking back and forth.

'So now you see,' he said, 'now you know. They gave me a medal for what I did that day. John Morales, the big war hero.' His voice was hoarse from unshed tears, years and years of them. 'It's just like I said.' Still she didn't speak. 'You can go now.' And he turned to face the window, to hide what she had done to him, what he had done to himself.

He wasn't sure how long he had been standing there. He didn't hear her leave, but suddenly felt utterly alone.

Then her arms encircled him, her wet cheek pressed against his back. 'I am here,' she said.

'Stay with me.'

'Always.'

'No, I mean, not just for the night. I want you here, with me.'

'But I am only next door . . .'

'I know, but it's not the same. I want us to be . . . together. I've never done this before.' The only thing that mattered was having her near. It would make everything all right, he was sure, while completely unable to explain why. 'Live here, with me. That's all, just be . . . with me.' *Where the hell did that come from?*

His shock was mirrored in her face. 'No marriage?'

Oh, God. Girls like her, they expect to get married. She thought we were going to wed. Well, if that's what it takes . . .'

He opened his mouth to say the words he never expected to say in his whole life, but she got there first.

'I will not marry you, or any other.'

Relief mixed with a smidgen of affront. Over the years, women had tried numerous times to hook him, and he had always wriggled free. Her disinterest was disconcerting, to say the least. Bruised ego aside, he recovered quickly.

'OK then, no marriage. Whatever you say. Just be here, with me.' He took a breath. 'Please.' The word came from a place so deep inside that he could no more suppress it than suppress the need to exhale.

Cautious as a doe, still she hesitated. 'What about the talk? There will be talk.'

Her hand was on the pendant, a sure sign of nervousness. It occurred to him he might have come to know her better than any person in his life so far, better even than Thomas. In the old days, this would have been enough reason to bolt, and yet it just made him want to be closer. This made no sense, and the harder he studied the problem, the more it receded, like in those dreams where shadows seemed about to coalesce, but then drifted away at his touch.

'You think anyone's gonna take notice of us? With all that folks got goin' on here? Hell, we could hold a ticker-tape parade and they'd just think it was a good time to hide some liquor from the feds.' As if to underline his words, there came the sounds of angry shouts and smashing glass from the street below.

A frown in response. 'But is it not a risk?'

'Risk?' He shrugged and stubbed out the cigarette just before it burnt his fingers. 'Yeah, I guess so, but I survived a war that killed half the guys who enlisted with me. I think I can handle a few fat, old bigots.' He enfolded her in his arms, hoping his body would reassure her better than his words. 'They don't scare me.'

'They scare me,' she whispered. 'But I will be here, with you, on one condition.'

He waited for her terms, in what he realised was the biggest decision of his life so far, expecting it to be about respecting her independence, or maybe promising not to smoke in bed, which she hated.

'I will be here with you, *mi amor*,' she said into his ear, 'if you get us a bigger bed.'

And so he stood with her and watched the brightening day. *Mi amor*, she had said.

CHAPTER 16

A month later, Dwayne walked to the streetcar stop on his way to work. It was his favourite time of year. At last, the weather had turned cool and fresh, and Christmas was on the way. The anticipation, the decorations, the food ... he loved all of it, and it seemed somehow fitting that his new life would begin so near to Christ's birthday.

But even holiday preparations took a back seat to his main preoccupation: the forthcoming Klan initiation ceremony, where he was to have a special role as assistant. This only involved making sure all the props and equipment were in their proper places, but it was still a great privilege. He wouldn't have a robe either, as he was still too young for initiation himself, but in only a year or so, Pa had promised he'd be ready to take his full place alongside him.

His card deliveries over the past month had produced a surge of applicants, to the delight of his father and the other leaders, and an excellent turnout was expected. To cap it all, the Imperial Wizard was due at any time. Dwayne couldn't remember when he had felt so valued, so purposeful. After some thought, he figured a lot of it had to do with being part of something bigger than himself – bigger even than Pa. He had spent so much time alone as a child. Just being a small cog inside the big, sleek, whirring engine of the Klan gave him such a thrill, it tingled all the way to his fingertips. It made him feel, for the first time, like he belonged.

As he scuffed along the road, he considered that Charlie 'Bucket' Simpkins certainly ran a smooth operation. He approached the establishment of Klan of the Keys in the same organised, professional manner as if he were building a new bank or courthouse. Everyone had a role and clear responsibilities, everything was timetabled, all the discussions minuted. And yet, surging beneath this administrative propriety, Dwayne felt an electric current of excitement. Pa promised a spectacle such as he had never seen before, to be held in the field near the cemetery.

Sucking on a chunk of sugar cane, a familiar dread encroached as he came closer to the store. It had been hard lately, at work, to hide his enthusiasm for his new project from Mr Jolovitz – for that was how he thought of it, like a model airplane or a big, complicated jigsaw puzzle. And much as he tried to trap his employer into the typical Jewish acts of treason, as described by his Klan literature, it just never happened – no talk of colluding with Negroes to overthrow the government, or plans to steal all the Christians' money and force everyone to deny Jesus. Jolovitz simply remained his usual affable self, somewhat confused by Dwayne's attempts to engage in these topics. Several times, Dwayne felt himself being studied with a new sadness. In actual fact, he figured his days at the store were coming to an end anyway. Mr Simpkins had hinted at a position in his office which might be available, if the conditions were right.

And yet, and yet . . . despite his new project, there were still times when the memory of that rum-run with Mr Morales and Miss Alicia threatened to derail him from the path of righteousness. The thought of it gave him an empty kind of yearning inside, but his mind still returned to it, again and again. He once had an old hound who only ever wanted to sleep on a particular corner of the front porch, right where a big rusty nail had worked its way up through the wood. The dog just lay on the nail and whined and whined, the noise both pitiful and intensely irritating. Dwayne always wondered why he just didn't get up and move. And now he knew. These days, he did not tarry when making deliveries to the Tea Room. His stops there were a source of intense discomfort, watching her, all flirtatious with Mr Morales, hair loose and eyes flashing. Then, later, thinking about what they did together made him squirm like that time when he had poison ivy. Yet he found he couldn't stay away, because that was worse. He wondered what other adventures he had missed out on, and the wondering made him feel torn apart inside, right up the middle. He was due there that afternoon, already anticipating the sweet pain of it.

So deep was he in contemplation that he didn't even hear the car coming up behind until, with a blare of its horn, it flashed past him in a spray of coral grit before disappearing round the bend.

Dwayne just had time to jump into the ditch, and notice that it was the finest Oldmosbile touring car he had ever seen, black with silver wheels and headlights, all the surfaces bright with polish. As he climbed back to the road and dusted off his trousers, there came a terrible crash and a scream from up ahead.

He ran round the bend to find a scene of carnage. The Oldsmobile had come to a stop with one wheel embedded in Emily's side. The animal was on the ground, eyes rolling, agonised groans from her open mouth. Mr Clemens held her head in his lap, stroking her ears and trying to soothe her.

Several white men stood around the car, like they were at a baseball game. One of them flicked a cigarette butt at Mr Clemens and said, 'You're gonna pay for any damage, you got that?'

'Please, will somebody get a gun!' Mr Clemens wailed.

One man separated himself from the group and, with the calmness of long habit, drew a rifle from the back seat of the car. Feet braced wide apart, he fired one shot into Emily's head. The report sent a group of egrets into the air in a flutter of white wings. The silence echoed.

'Shame we cain't put the nigger out of his misery too,' observed one of the men, with a nod at the prostrate form of Mr Clemens.

'Might get your wish soon,' answered his companion.

'Remove that animal from my car,' said the shooter, 'and let's get goin'.' His voice carried the tone of command, very distinctive, with a coarse, nicotine rasp. He wasn't a big man, but something about his bearing told Dwayne he was in the presence of the Imperial Wizard himself. He wanted to call out a greeting but his mouth wouldn't open, and so he just stood by the roadside and gawped, like any ordinary small-town hick.

With some effort, involving protracted grunts and curses,

the men extracted the wheel from Emily's carcass and drove on into town.

Dwayne stumbled towards Mr Clemens, who was weeping inconsolably on his knees. 'They came outta nowhere,' he sobbed, 'just outta nowhere.'

The smell of blood and cow manure caught in Dwayne's throat. Flies had started to settle in Emily's open eyes.

They didn't come outta nowhere. You just didn't see 'em. Dwayne wanted to lay a hand on Mr Clemens' shoulder. He wanted to say how sorry he was. He did neither. After another moment, he just walked away.

In the Tea Room, an exasperated Hortensia ordered, 'Get outta my kitchen! *Hay mucho trabajo!* Let me get on with my work!'

Startled, Alicia put down the spoon she didn't realise she was holding. So many tasks awaited her attention, yet she seemed unable to do anything except stand still, stirring the pot, and gazing at nothing through the window.

Ever since John had given her the gift of his story, something had begun crumbling inside her, like chalk. He had expected it to drive her away, but instead it had bound her to him more tightly than any endearment. It left her feeling desperately sad yet elated.

In the arms of the most dangerous man she had met – a trained, experienced killer – she felt safe, truly safe for the first time in her life.

By unspoken agreement, they had made no plans. When she was away from him, like in this moment, she saw the years unfurl before them, but when he was there, she cared only for the present.

As she stirred, she thought once again how unlike he was to other men she had known, Raoul and the many, many who passed through the Tea Room doors. In the grip of intense desire, Raoul's face always transformed into an animal mask – a blank, unseeing film across his eyes. It felt like she could have been any woman. If anything, John became most himself, at his most open, almost painfully so. Afterwards, he put on the mask.

She had never thought of her body as anything but a liability where men were concerned, always at risk of attracting the wrong kind of attention at the wrong time, but then John made it his project. From a fairly rocky and all-round unsatisfactory start, as the weeks unfolded his attentiveness began to erase the past – his as well as hers. Like two blind people, together they were learning to see.

'*Vamos!*' A shove from Hortensia propelled her towards the back door. 'Be useful. Go help Thomas.'

He had arrived with his garden tools, and was setting them out, ready to begin work.

Since he broke ground, an unlikely rapport had developed between him and Hortensia which made Alicia feel somewhat excluded, as he was the next closest person to John. He loved Hortensia's cooking, and the old woman loved feeding him. She brought him treats while he worked, and they chatted like old friends.

'I will. I will do that,' Alicia said, and drifted out under the cloudy sky.

He was bent over the hoe, singing in a strange, angular

language she didn't recognise. The summer crops had finished, and he had cleared the earth for winter ones.

'I have come to help.'

He glanced up and, without interrupting his rhythm, said, 'You can weed them rows.'

They worked in silence for a few moments, moving up and down together. Having seen him shoulder heavy crates of liquor, there was an unexpected precision, even delicacy, in his movements.

'Where did you learn to do this?' she asked.

It seemed as if she weren't there at all, so focused was he on the work at hand. Up close, he smelled of wood smoke and sweat and something astringent in his hair oil.

'From my people on the reservation. They can coax anythin' from the ground.'

Bent alongside him, she had ample time to examine his face in close detail and remembered how his appearance had shocked her at first. He had seemed so fierce, so foreign, and so much the typical muscleman. Each time she thought to have his measure, he showed another side. He still had the capacity to surprise and disturb her by turns.

'You are a man of secrets,' she teased. He said nothing, just continued to hoe the earth. The silence made her bold. 'Why go to all this trouble for me?'

He turned his brown-eyed gaze directly on her for the first time. It felt like both a threat and a challenge. 'Because John wanted me to. I do it for him.'

She held his stare, full of pain and longing, and finally understood. 'I would like . . . I would like us to be friends. We both care for him . . . deeply.'

He said nothing, but didn't look away.

A pause, while she chose her next words with care. 'And we both want him to be happy.'

'Yeah,' he said. His great head hung down in something like defeat. Then he raised it, and said, with infinite sadness, 'I ain't never seen him so happy before.'

She saw what that cost him, in the twist of his mouth and the brief mist over his eyes. She wanted to ease his suffering, but it was not in her power. So she did all she could do, which was to acknowledge it. Leaning in, so their faces were inches apart, she laid a hand on his and whispered, 'I am very good at keeping secrets. And I will not take him away from you, I promise.'

'If you cared about him, you'd get him away from here. Bad stuff comin', maybe even here already.'

Rumours of the new 'Klan of the Keys' were everywhere. John dismissed them with utter contempt, but she had argued it was sensible to be cautious, at least until their impact was known. He would have none of it. She recalled the last time they argued about it. There was a principle at stake, he said. 'I didn't serve in France to take orders from a bunch of morons who like dressin' up and throwin' their weight around. Free is free.' And that, it seemed, was the final word on it.

For now, she accepted it, but she watched, and waited, and refused to walk out in public with him, on the basis that trouble would always find her easily enough on its own.

'He is not afraid,' she said. 'I think he even looks forward to a fight.'

Thomas leaned back, hands folded over the hoe's worn handle. The sun emerged from its veil of cloud and sent his eyes into shade. 'John ain't never run from no fight, even when he should. Just his nature. Once his mind made up, you'd sooner get a gator's jaws open than get him to change it.'

'*Exactamente*! I have never met a person so ... *como se dice*?'

Just a hint of a grin. 'Stubborn?'

'SÍ, *como un burro*!'

A little shared understanding warmed his glance, fleeting as the sunshine.

His face closed again. 'I worry about him, all the time I cain't see him.'

'Me also. And yet he only worries for us. What shall we do?' Her heart felt lighter, knowing John had such a formidable guardian, even if he thought of himself as everyone else's protector. There, in the massive shadow cast by Thomas's body, it seemed nothing bad could happen while he was around.

'If I had my way, we'd hog-tie him and sail for the islands. Failin' that, keep our eyes and ears open.' He faced her, cold and serious again. 'And a gun under the pillow.'

⁓ CHAPTER 17 ⁓

The next day, Alicia waited as usual on the porch for Mr Clemens, bottle in hand. He was never late, and she looked forward to their morning chats when she came back from John's place. She descended the steps to scan up and down the street for Emily's familiar swaying bulk, but there was no sign of her among the bustle of vendors weaving between the cars.

With a frown, she decided to wait for another five minutes, chewing on the fresh bread found in its usual place, and felt surprisingly rested after another night at The Last Resort. She had moved more of her things over to John's room, after he brought in the biggest bed she had ever seen. Its headboard was inset with a massive, ornate wrought iron panel twined with flowers and leaves, while the pine footboard could have made a dining table. And the mattress . . . it was the softest, most comfortable she had ever known.

In a rare moment of reflection under the morning sun, she remembered asking herself on arrival, *who am I here?* Just a few short months ago it was, no time at all to create a completely new life. Then, she was a young woman, on the run from men with power over her, defined mostly by her skin colour. The answer now, she realised, was entirely more complex: madam, bootlegger, restaurateur. The Tea Room had become her domain, its male clientele respectful, even deferential. No more did she hear the hiss of '*half-breed*' in her wake. She was Miss Pearl to everyone, not a poor, lost 'brown'. She had learned so much, and made the most of every opportunity. Beatriz had been right: she was a natural.

Outside the Tea Room, she was more circumspect. Yes, she negotiated hard with suppliers and officials, but was always conscious that the businessmen tolerated her in part because of John's support.

But that support had a double edge. She could see it in their faces, a 'brown' living with a man not her husband – a white man. In their eyes were curiosity, disdain, disgust, all overlaid with a hair-thin veneer of cordiality.

Back home, a white man with a *morena* would attract little attention. Here, she had felt it prudent to make no big announcement to the Tea Room staff about her new living arrangements. In passing, she had said, 'If you need me in the night, I am next door.'

The inevitable eyebrow-raising and rude guffaws followed, but soon died down. Felix barely paused in his polishing of Isabella to give a slight shrug. Only Maxine seemed to feel the need to make a fuss.

With a scowl, eyes narrowed against her cigarette smoke, she had asked, 'So you livin' over there now, is that it? With him?'

Even with the better conditions for the girls, relations with Maxine had only improved slightly, to the extent that Alicia no longer expected to feel her knife between her shoulder blades – if it came, it would come from the front. That counted as progress.

'This is my place of business,' she had replied, somewhat stiffly. *I should have known Maxine would be trouble.* 'Where I live, and with whom, is my concern.'

'Well, you'd best look to yourself,' she had said, with heavy portent. 'You ain't in the islands no more, Sugar Plum. You in America now, and folks here have standards.'

Alicia scanned the Emily-less street once more. Her balance felt off. Funny, she thought, how even the oddest things can, in time, become part of the normal rhythm of life . . . like waking wrapped in John's arms, his breath warm on her neck. 'You're still here,' he would sigh, with sleepy relief, as if every morning he feared to find her gone.

She stretched and took a deep breath. But she had no more time to wait for Mr Clemens now, and went inside to prepare for the busy day ahead. Once again, they were expecting a full house for dinner, and it would be Kitty's debut as a waitress. In her pretty dress, hair in ringlets, Alicia expected she could make more in tips than she could upstairs.

In addition, the first medicinal plants had filled out her new *farmacia*, some of which were also useful for the table: oregano for coughs, sweet potato for skin problems and plantains for digestion. Others, like mulberry for thrush and senna leaves for menstrual problems, plus hibiscus flowers for high blood pressure and aloe for almost any ailment, were to be found growing wild in the neighbourhood. They all seemed to spring forth in days from the rich soil under the warm, tropical rain and Thomas's expert care. And, of course, the plentiful supply of orange blossom honey from the local beekeeper had already proved its worth, soothing burns and bites, healing Paulina's spots, preventing pregnancies in the girls ... and herself. A large jar of it sat beside the new bed, much to John's bemusement.

She had dug up an old cabinet that had been left to rot outside, and scavenged a box-full of discarded bottles to hold her preparations. Already, news of her service had spread throughout the Cubans in the neighbourhood, those who followed the old ways of *santería* and those who could not afford doctors. To her delight, the first clients had begun to appear at the kitchen door. With that, she regained some of her old sense of purpose. And it felt good, in answer to the question of *who am I here?*, to add 'healer' to the list. For although there was grim satisfaction to be had from turning the Tea Room around, and its growing reputation as a restaurant, nothing gave her greater joy than dispensing the means to ease suffering.

In the kitchen, Hortensia darted between a full set of pots in action on the stove for the evening's menu. She stirred the biggest pot and offered Alicia a taste of coconut chicken, pushing steam-frizzed hair out of her eyes.

'*Excelente*,' said Alicia, wiping her lips. 'But I hope we have enough milk, there was no delivery today.'

'Did you not hear? The cow, she was killed. Run over on the road, out of town.' With the hem of her apron, she wiped moisture from her face. '*Idiotas*, everyone in such a hurry these days. In any case,' she said, adding a dash of key lime juice to the pot, 'we have enough milk for today.'

It shouldn't have mattered, a cow killed on the road. Such

things happened all the time. But for no reason she could fathom, Emily's death was like the toll of a faraway bell. Or the first flutter of dark wings.

But then, to her wonder and delight, it turned out that those wings belonged to a jewel-bright hummingbird. He hovered just off the kitchen windowsill, his magenta throat thrumming with the familiar rasping *chirrup*.

Pablito, you have found me!

Hortensia shooed him away with her dish cloth.

'What are you doing?' exclaimed Alicia, leaning out of the window. The bird had not gone far, it was just floating in the shelter of some bamboo canes, head tilted as if in recognition.

'He drives me *loco*, that one,' Hortensia grumbled. 'He is here every day, making that noise. We need a cat.'

'Nonsense.' Alicia mixed sugar and water in a saucer for him and went outside. With that, the balance of her day was restored.

Some hours later, at the field by the cemetery a beautiful evening seemed in prospect. Dwayne unloaded another oil drum from the truck. *It's God blessing our endeavours.* He had come straight to the field to help set up for the ceremony after he finished his rounds in the afternoon. Pa would follow with the other leaders, for the first time taking his rightful place in public. Dwayne was so proud, equal parts anxious and excited, and wished Ma had been there to see them, but no women were allowed. And anyway, Ma was strangely quiet whenever he gushed about the project, always seeming to find something else that needed her attention in another room. All she would say to him, when he brought it up, was, 'Remember, son, whatever happens, I love you.'

The huge pine cross was soaked in oil, ready to be fired at the exact moment of sunset. He had helped erect the altar and covered it with the Confederate flag, Bible positioned in the centre.

He was on standby, ready to provide any service needed by the organisers, but there wasn't much more to do except wait for the sun to sink and the crowds to assemble. A few enterprising vendors had set up stalls selling fried chicken and Coca-Cola from the local bottling plant. The festive atmosphere was more like a Fourth of July party than a sombre initiation rite.

But his pleasure was tainted now, by the conversation which had taken place that afternoon during his stop at the Tea Room. Its shadow dimmed the glorious sunset. Pa had told him that on no account could he say a word to anyone about the ceremony, but somehow it had slipped out. He had just been so damn keen to impress Miss Alicia.

It was the pastries that did it. He had always loved sweets, ever since he was little. When he entered the Tea Room, Miss Alicia had been there, with a tray of something straight from the oven, smelling heavenly.

'*Hola*, Dwayne! Would you like a *pastelito*? Hortensia just made them. These are filled with guava and these with coconut.'

And so he had sat down at the table with her, for the first time, not just a delivery boy, but like a guest.

She watched him eat with indulgent pleasure. 'Ay,' she said, 'I knew you were someone who liked his *dulce*. But why have we seen so little of you these past weeks, Dwayne?'

The buttery pastry oozed with sweet, gooey guava. He eyed the plate, and she handed him another.

'For later,' he said, and slipped it into his pocket.

'But there are plenty. Have another, or you will insult Hortensia,' she beamed.

'Well, all right, then.'

It was like an enchantment, sitting so close to her, as she grinned and chattered. All for him. She had missed him, that was clear. *She missed me.* A coil of hair had come loose from the ribbon at her neck. His hand was raised to tuck it back in for her, when this:

'There.' She wiped his chin for him. 'Messy boy.'

He swallowed. With that one small gesture, the pastry turned to mud in his mouth. Eyes on the table, he said, 'I been real busy, Miss Alicia,' and pushed the plate away. That was all he would ever be to her, a messy boy, while she consorted naked with Mr Morales. He started to choke and she handed him a glass of water.

'Don't eat so fast! There you go, drink that down. But I am sad to hear you are too busy for your old friends.' Arms folded, frowning in mock disapproval. 'What can you be up to?'

That was when it happened. He just so wanted to show her, once and for all, that he wasn't some little kid, to be dismissed so easily. He was a man, with an important job to do, taken seriously by other serious men in the town. She would see. Soon, everyone would see.

So he had blurted, 'I'm in charge of the Klan recruitment drive.' He enjoyed the sudden rush of blood from her face, making her look almost pale. 'Yessum, we got loads of fellas joinin' up, thanks to me. Hundreds, thousands maybe. And tonight,' he leaned forward, 'there's gonna be a spectacle like this town ain't never seen.'

That sure wiped the grin off her face. She cleared her throat. 'I see,' she nodded. 'I see how that would take, yes, a lot of your time.' A watery smile. 'You must tell me about it. And here, try the coconut.'

So he did. He told her everything: about Pa's exalted office as chaplain to the Klan, about how all the important city officials were involved, and about how the evening's ceremony would cement their place in the life of the town. He had filled her in on the conspiracy between the Jews, the Negroes, and the Catholics too, which was clearly news to her, from the shock written on her face.

To be truthful, when he said these words, they had sounded kind of strange to him, especially the conspiracy part, which he had never really understood. But she fixed those eyes of hers on him with such intensity that he carried on talking just to keep her there, listening like that. He would have said anything to keep her there. So rapt was she that even Mr Morales's entrance wasn't enough to distract her.

Only when he scraped back a chair and sat down did she turn.

'Mind if I join you?' He kissed her on the cheek. 'Dwayne, where you been hidin'?' And he stuffed the last pastry into his mouth, whole.

Dwayne was still reacting to a white man kissing a brown lady in public, and – much worse – imagining how her cheek would feel under his own lips.

'He has just been telling me,' she said lightly, 'about his new

. . . project, *sí*? He has been recruiting for the Klan. There is a big . . . *fiesta* tonight.'

Dwayne found his voice. 'Initiation ceremony,' he corrected her. 'And later a big parade, right down Duval Street!'

'Ya don't say?' Mr Morales scrutinised Dwayne with equal, but darker intensity, and he didn't enjoy it one bit, just felt extremely uncomfortable and a little sick. 'I didn't take you for one of them dumb-bells.'

Mr Morales showed his teeth, and all at once Dwayne knew exactly how the enemy must have felt when they met him in combat. For the first time, he felt sorry for them. And he really regretted eating all those pastries.

'John, *por favor*—' she began.

Mr Morales stood up, still smiling, and Dwayne became aware once again of the man's truly impressive size and strength. He could probably flatten Dwayne like a mosquito.

With a gulping breath, he said, 'I didn't mean no—'

'It's OK, Dwayne.' A large hand landed on his shoulder, fixing him to the chair. 'I'm just disappointed. I figured you for a smart guy. Why d'ya want to get mixed up with these clowns, with their silly dresses and secret handshakes? Hell, if you want a circus, I hear Mr Barnum and Mr Bailey are hiring at the moment.' He leaned in closer. 'Who got you into this?'

All the arguments and reasoning from the meetings and discussions went right out of his head, all the stuff about taking back America, and the big conspiracy. Nor did he want to bring Pa into it, for fear of sounding even more childish. Dwayne couldn't remember a single thing he had been taught over the previous weeks, as he felt himself wither under Mr Morales's inquisitive stare.

'Enough, John.'

'Just want to leave our young friend here with one thought: life ain't nothin' more than the sum total of your choices. Remember that, Dwayne.' Mr Morales let his eyes linger for a moment longer, then he said to her, 'You comin' home with me?'

'*Sí.*'

It was all Dwayne could do not to fall off his chair. *Livin' together as well? Pa would throw a silver-plated fit if he knew about this.* He stood. 'I got to get going anyway.' With a last look at her, he said, 'A lot of people depending on me.' And with that, he had fled.

Now, as he readied for the evening, the words kept revolving in his head, like a circus ride: *silly dresses, dumb-bells, clowns.* Mr Morales's offensive lack of respect for the institution was, he knew, designed to undermine his loyalty, and he conjured Pa's face and Pa's voice in rebuttal. When he struggled to square the theories about the Negro's low intelligence with the fiery smartness of people like Miss Alicia and Black Caesar, Pa's voice would say, 'That's because those mongrels have benefited from being only half Negro.' Nor could he take on board the Jews' supposed desire to strip the country's wealth and hoard it for themselves, when Mr Jolovitz turned up to work every day in the same dusty, creased black coat and hat, smelling of onions. But then Pa's voice would say, 'That's because Jews are the masters of deceit. Just look how they betrayed Jesus.'

Oh, how Dwayne envied the granite-hard certainties of Pa and the other leaders! He so longed to be certain of something, to join them in that place of calm assurance and rightness, not constantly sabotaged by doubts. Despite the weight of evidence at their fingertips, he had failed to silence a quiet voice which questioned their so-called facts. And he hardly dared admit to himself that the dizzying array of rituals, from the 'K'-shaped salute to the insistence on starting every word with 'K', just seemed goofy and odd – clownish, as Mr Morales had said. He wished they could just ditch all the paraphernalia and mumbo-jumbo, and focus on the mission, but no one seemed to share his opinion. Rather, the others seemed to revel in the trappings.

It confirmed his deepest fear: that he was not, after all, worthy. Mr Morales's comment about choices came back to him. With sweaty desperation, he pinned his hopes on the evening ahead. If it was as spectacular as Pa predicted – and Pa was never wrong – maybe it would finally silence the voice in his head. The cleansing fire of the burning cross would, at last, make him worthy.

Finally, it was time.

Shortly before sunset, Dwayne surveyed the field and marvelled at the fruits of his labours. Several hundred men milled around, many with the ragged, unwashed look of labourers, quite a few wearing remnants of military uniform, and a considerable number of police and other law enforcement officials. They smoked and chatted in small groups, hands in pockets. A sense of nervous anticipation flashed between them like heat lightning.

All eyes turned towards the road, where a phalanx of maybe fifty torch-bearing, white-robed Klansmen marched in and took up positions in front of the altar. This blaze of white and gold was a tremendously impressive sight, and instantly silenced the group of applicants. A soft breeze ruffled the torch flames and the robes. Dwayne stood straighter. *I helped to make this happen.* He didn't need any recognition for his contribution. It was enough to know he had played his small part.

Then came the sound of more marching feet. The leaders had arrived! Clad in robes of gold, red, green, purple, and blue which shone like jewels in the torchlight, they processed through the crowd. Last in line was Chief Baxter, the red-caped Nighthawk, custodian of the cross and head of security. The milling men parted like the Red Sea ahead of them, and closed again in their wake. Dwayne knew only that Pa would be in blue, but wasn't prepared for how it would feel to see his father, who sat next to him at breakfast every morning, as one of the few, the anointed ones who now inspired awe in so many faces. His heart felt so full of pride and excitement that it might actually burst through his chest and soar up into the clear evening sky.

Just as the sun touched the horizon, at a nod from the purple-robed Imperial Wizard, the Nighthawk laid his torch to the pine cross. The flames burst forth with a loud *whump* and cast a warm orange glow over the altar and its attendants. To Dwayne, it felt like the sun had risen anew.

'Who desires to enter here?' called the Wizard.

Dwayne recognised the voice as the shooter who had despatched Emily on the road.

The red-robed Kladd, or conductor, replied, 'We have these Aliens of the Outer World, who seek admission to the sacred realms of the Invisible Empire!' He suppressed a sneeze, which told Dwayne that it was Donkey Hightower beneath the hood. He had been suffering from a cold all week.

'And are they loyal to the Protestant God, and to white supremacy, and to Klancraft?' asked the Wizard.

'They tell us so, O Wizard!' replied the Kladd.

'You may approach the altar.'

The Klansmen in white broke formation to admit the applicants, who shuffled forwards in single file. Watching from a stand of oleander bushes, Dwayne so wished to be among them. He pictured himself there, in a few years, with the firelight flashing in his eyes.

'Honoured Kludd,' said the Kladd. 'I bring to you these candidates for exaltation to Knighthood!'

'Have they proven themselves true to the real America?'

It was Pa's voice! Dwayne stifled a cheer but could do nothing to prevent the grin, so wide that his cheeks ached.

'They have passed the scrutiny of the Eye of the Unknown, faithful Kludd!'

With a grave sweep of his hand, he said, 'You may proceed.'

This ritual was repeated before each of the other leaders.

Several seagulls landed on the altar and began fighting over something, their loud shrieks shattering the stillness. In horror, Dwayne realised their target was a scrap of pastry he had left that afternoon.

'Will someone get rid of those damn birds,' yelled the Kladd, 'before they shit on the Bible!'

A flurry of arm-waving from the white-robed attendants dispersed the birds in a noisy cloud of feathers.

Dignity restored, the Wizard continued, 'I hereby remind

you, before you take the sacred oath, that the penalty for treason to the Klan is death at the hands of a brother. If any here harbours motive other than the love of God and country, let them leave now.' The purple-hooded head scanned first left and then right until the entire assemblage had come under its gaze. Dwayne sensed a multitude of Adam's apples bobbing among the crowd, as the full weight of the ceremony's solemnity settled on their minds. A few nervous glances were exchanged, but no one moved.

Night had come. Beyond the circle of light from the altar, all was blackness.

'Very well,' intoned the Wizard. He produced a sword – an actual, full-sized battle sword – from beneath his robe.

Dwayne had only ever seen one in picture books. The blade gleamed silver in the flickering light, like an extension of the Wizard's arm, an actual part of his body. *Just like the knights of old!* All day, Dwayne had had the sense of being a witness to history. Now it was confirmed.

'Principal Terrors, join with me.'

At this, the other leaders, including Pa, moved to flank him in a rainbow-coloured formation.

'The prayer, O Kludd.'

Pa raised his arms. 'We ask of our lord, Jesus Christ, to look favourably on these honoured white men, soon to join us as soldiers in our sacred cause. May they always live as good Klansmen. Amen.'

'Amen' came the response.

'Kneel,' commanded the Wizard, 'all who seek to enter as Knights of the Ku Klux Klan! And repeat after me: In the presence of God and man, I most solemnly pledge, promise, and swear to obey faithfully the Constitution and Laws of the Order.'

The words came back from the throng in a disorganised babble. Some of the men appeared to forget what they were supposed to say halfway through, and there was a confused moment when no one seemed sure if they were finished.

The Wizard exchanged a whisper with the Kladd and then addressed the group once more. 'I can see we're gonna have to simplify things for y'all.' He adjusted his robes and straightened his hood. 'Do you swear to uphold the Protestant religion, and the flag of the United States of America; and do you, furthermore, pledge to use all your powers to uphold the values of White Supremacy and White Womanhood? Finally, do you swear to come to the aid of any Klansmen in any situation?'

A thousand feet shuffled. Whispers rippled through the crowd. A handful of heartfelt voices exclaimed, 'I do!' Then, 'Yeah, me too!' 'And me!'

'Everyone, godammit! Say "I do" at the same time!' exclaimed the Kladd. 'I'll give you a count of three: one, two, three!'

The massed chorus of 'I do!' boomed through the night. Dwayne could feel it resonate inside his rib cage.

'Arise, O Brothers of the Klan!' The Wizard raised the sword high above his head in an arc. 'Better that this sword should pierce your heart than you should prove false to your oath.'

And he swept forward to give each new member the special sideways handshake that always reminded Dwayne of a flapping fish.

This is the power, he realised. It didn't reside in any individual, nor even in the leaders, but in the vast, collective numbers of men. Such ceremonies were taking place all over the country. It was an army in all but name – it had a uniform, and a command structure, and a code of conduct. All it needed was some training and discipline to unlock its potential.

'I do,' he whispered to himself.

∿ CHAPTER 18 ∿

The next morning in the Campbell household felt to Dwayne like a continuation of the party. Pa couldn't stop grinning, and clapped him on the back more times than he could count. They kept going over and over the highlights of the ceremony together. Only Ma seemed to remain outside the circle of their jubilation; but then, being a woman, Dwayne figured such things were probably beyond her comprehension anyway. The Klan literature said that womenfolk were delicate, high-strung creatures, to be revered, and protected from the dark-skinned savages who coveted them, but it was a mistake to credit them with much smarts.

Pa demanded buttermilk pancakes for breakfast.

'I ain't sure if we got any buttermilk,' said Ma, hands twisted within her apron.

Pa's smile didn't falter. 'Well, go and get some, woman!'

Dwayne caught her eye. 'Bread and coffee's OK for me, Pa.'

'Nonsense, son. This is a special occasion. It's a new dawn for our town, thanks in part to your work. Gonna be big changes around here. For everyone.'

Ma scurried for the neighbour's house next door.

Dwayne had barely slept, with the residue of the night bubbling in his veins. All those men, all those expectant faces raised up to Pa at the altar, his arms aloft in benediction over the whole of the multitude, robe shining like a steel blue flame. The first Klan parade was planned for later that week, right down Duval Street. It would be the official sign that the Klan of the Keys had arrived and was open for business . . . but the meaning of that was still a mystery to Dwayne. His head was crammed full of Klancraft – the rituals, the history, the creed and all the arcane practices until he could just about recite the whole thing by heart – but he had been excluded from the planning meetings that Pa attended. And his father was a whole lot better than him at keeping his trap shut. Dwayne felt like he had been given a brand new automobile with no ignition switch.

He was itching to find out what was next, and his part in it. If the past few months had taught him anything, it was this: he needed to be useful.

'What happens now, Pa?'

'We clean house, son, starting with the obvious places, and then we'll work our broom into every nook of this town. We're putting the list together now. And your boss is at the top.'

'Mr Jolovitz? But he's so old, and he don't bother no one.' Reuben Jolovitz seemed to lead an utterly solitary existence, and for the first time, Dwayne wondered why. It had just seemed natural, like having the black folks live together over in Coloured Town. Everyone was happiest among their own kind. As Pa always said, problems only occurred when folks forgot that.

'He's a symbol, son, him and that store of his, of all that's filthy in this town. Symbols are important. You saw the proof of that last night.'

Dwayne could only nod in agreement, still dazzled by the spectacle, but questions hopped around his mind like a bunch of electrocuted frogs. *Why this fuss over one sad, old man?* Symbol or not, it didn't fit with the pomp and grandeur of the initiation ceremony. It seemed too small, too petty.

'Your boss has had ample warning to go join the rest of his tribe up in Miami, but he chose to stay.' Pa drained his coffee cup and leaned back. 'He's going to learn that, when we say it's time to move on, we mean it.'

Now Dwayne understood the hunted, haunted shadows on Mr Jolovtiz's face of late, the constant glances over his shoulder, the new tremor in his watery left eye.

'So we're doing him a favour, like those coloured folks who've already left town?'

'Exactly.'

Jolovitz would never leave Key West, of that Dwayne was certain, because his son would look for him there on the glorious day of his return. Never mind that everyone else knew David had become fish food years ago. Nothing but dynamite would dislodge the old man from his post. 'But what if he won't go?'

Pa's voice dipped to a register of quiet certainty. 'He'll go. Choices, Dwayne. That's what life's about.'

Almost the same thing that Mr Morales said.

'Should I quit my job at the store?' There had been no more mention of a position in Mr Simpkins' office. In fact, Dwayne suspected the Kleagle had already forgotten his existence.

'No, keep it. You can tell us when the message gets through.' Pa looked at his watch and stood up. 'Can't wait around for those pancakes. I'm going into town, meeting with Charlie and the others.'

'Can I come? I wouldn't make no noise, just sit there quietly.' He wasn't ready for Pa to go, taking with him all the glamour of the previous night, and leaving only a dull day of chores that stretched ahead like an empty road.

'Not this time.'

'What if . . .' he swallowed. 'What if I could help, with the list?'

Pa turned, hand on the doorknob. 'What do you know?'

'A white man, been livin' with a brown?' The words sounded more like a question than they did in his head. His teeth clamped shut, but it was too late. They hung suspended, floating with the dust motes in the cool morning light. But it was clear they had reached Pa's ears, from the way his attention sharpened.

'Are you asking or telling?'

'I seen it. I seen . . . them. Plain as day.'

He sat down again. 'We heard rumours of some such. What have you seen?'

Right then, Dwayne desired two mutually incompatible things with equal fervour: he wanted to bask forever in the fierce interest on Pa's face, to remain frozen in this one moment, the first time he ever had something of value to offer his father; and he wanted to claw back the words and lock them inside his head and seal his lips with wax.

'Dwayne?' Pa held his gaze, and in his eyes Dwayne saw it all, like on a newsreel. There was the desperate grief of losing little Danny, followed by the new hope at his birth, and then the unfulfilled promise, the bitter disappointment his life had been so far, made even worse by the lasting shadow of Danny's loss.

And so he told Pa everything about Miss Alicia and Mr Morales, about her living openly upstairs at the bar with him, and how everyone in the neighbourhood thought it was a scandal but no one would say so to Mr Morales's face because he was so big and good with his fists, always with Black Caesar by his side. He said how strong and scary Caesar looked, but how he had a soft heart.

He told everything, except the part about hiding in the bushes to watch them at the beach, or the part about taking his boat out at night to help with their bootlegging operation. And he neglected to mention how pretty she was. No word of that at all. Nor did he remind Pa that Mr Morales had saved his life in the hospital. Something in Pa's expression told him the episode was better left unrecalled.

As he talked, Pa's face remained blank of all emotion, so that Dwayne couldn't even be sure Pa was listening. When he finished, Pa said nothing for a bit, just stared out the window.

'How did you come by this information? Someone gossiping?'

'No, Pa. I picked it up myself, on my rounds. Like you said: eyes and ears.'

After another long pause, during which his father seemed to wrestle with his thoughts, he said the words Dwayne had longed to hear his whole life: 'Good work, son.'

And he got up to leave. Dwayne deflated like a leaky balloon. He felt empty and unaccountably tearful, like Pa had stolen something from him, something of value he didn't even know he owned. 'What'll happen now?'

'If you'll tie your shoes, we'll go to town and talk to Charlie. I expect he'll want to handle this personally.'

'You mean . . . I can come?'

A brief nod was all that signalled his change of status, but it was enough. 'You've earned your place.'

Ma bustled in with the stone milk jug, out of breath. 'I had to go all the way to Marshall's to find some.' She turned from Dwayne to Pa. 'But where are y'all off to? I thought you wanted pancakes.'

'Ain't got time for that now, Ma,' said Pa. 'Important business awaits us, thanks to our son here.'

They went out together, the shadows around the house still cool from the night. Dew dampened his ankles. A hummingbird flitted amongst the crimson frangipani blossoms. Dwayne felt he was right where he belonged. At long last, he belonged somewhere. Mr Morales knew the rules, and he chose to break them. So really, Dwayne reasoned, it was his own fault. And, he told himself, it was only a matter of time before his crime came to the Klan's attention anyway, being so blatant about it like that. In doing his civic duty, Dwayne had simply hastened the inevitable.

He felt Ma's gaze follow him to the threshold, like she was trying to fix a memory in her head. He let the screened door slam, enjoying its echo through the quiet street.

In the hall at Mr Simpkins' grand home, Dwayne waited as instructed. He had plenty of time to savour the anticipation, seated on a straight-backed chair with a needlepoint cushion that looked really old. Everything about the house had a reassuring solidity, from the shine of the floorboards to the fine carpentry of the window casings. It spoke of generations of the same family, of 'true Americans', as the literature said. All of it was so unlike his own home. There was no sand on the floor, no chickens, no termite holes or rust stains. Sunlight slanted through the shutters in gold bars at his feet. The heavy wooden door to Mr Simpkins' study, where the meeting was in progress, prevented all but a soft rumble of conversation from leaking into the hall. A tall casement clock ticked out the minutes, with a delicate chime at the quarter hour. Three chimes had rung since he had been sitting there.

A coloured woman in a starched uniform strode past, a pile of linen in her arms. She spared him not a glance.

Just as he started to wonder if he was invisible, or dreaming, the door creaked open. 'Come in, Dwayne,' said Pa.

Cigar smoke suffused the room, which was on the shady side of the house. Heavy panelling darkened it further, as did the closed shutters. It took a moment for his eyes to adjust to the gloom. Yellow lamps illuminated the faces of the leaders around a mahogany table. When his eyes fell on the distinctive figure of the Imperial Wizard, his throat, already dry, went to parchment.

Mr Simpkins spoke to him directly. 'I hear you have something interesting to share with us, Dwayne.'

'Just tell Charlie what you told me,' said Pa.

Dwayne swallowed. He had rehearsed it all, during his long wait in the hall, but the words just fled from his mind like a flock of startled sandpipers. He coughed. 'Could I please . . . could I have some water, sir.'

Chief Baxter poured him a glass from a crystal decanter on the table and he gulped it down.

'Go ahead, son,' urged Pa.

And so Dwayne repeated the tale he had shared with Pa, in abridged form, because of the current of impatience flowing between the men around the table, very different to the relaxed mood of the previous meeting he attended. This one meant business.

When he finished, he stood and waited, but no one said anything. It seemed for a moment like it was all for nothing, and he had embarrassed Pa again. The leaders just puffed on their cigars and exchanged knowing glances. He coughed again, starting to feel light-headed. He wished someone would open a window. Sweat collected at his hairline, and a single drop set off down his cheek. It itched but he didn't dare move to scratch.

Finally, Chief Baxter exclaimed, 'Didn't I tell you that Morales was a trouble-maker?' His fist pounded the table. 'We shoulda done something about this character sooner.' The water jug jittered against a glass.

'On the contrary,' said the Imperial Wizard, with a tap of his cigar, 'this is the perfect opportunity for the Klan of the Keys to make a statement.' His eyes swept over Dwayne. He alone seemed to lack the others' sense of urgency.

Dwayne knew of a fisherman who had once fallen out of his boat into a pod of sperm whales, down in the islands. One of the big males had hit him with a sonar blast, to check if he was food. The man said it nearly shook his bones loose. That's just how the Wizard's gaze felt, like he could see right inside Dwayne's body, every secret and every doubt revealed.

It was his first chance to observe the Wizard up close. He made the others in the room look like country bumpkins. Even Kleagle Charlie Simpkins was diminished in his presence. There was something fixed and immovable about him, from the thick neck to the feet planted wide apart. His eyes shone with the assurance of his unassailable, inarguable place at the top of the world. He struck Dwayne as the kind of man who never, ever changed his mind, about anything. For the first time, Dwayne felt himself palpably close to real power. The air around him thrummed with it.

'What do you have in mind?' asked Charlie.

'Just go and talk to him, first. Explain the situation, give him the chance to put things right. As a white man and a patriot, he deserves that.'

'John Morales?' snorted Donkey. 'You gotta be kiddin' me, a dirty, coon-lovin' swindler like that? Always with that big nigger-Injun by his side. And he's friendly with that agitator over at Gato's, Hector Rubio. White or not, a man like that has forfeit his rights. Been plenty of lynchings upstate for less.'

'Has this got anythin' to do with him undercutting your liquor price?' asked Chief Baxter with a wink of his good eye. Light chuckles followed, such that Donkey had to raise his voice to be heard.

'Now, that ain't fair, and you know it. And what if Morales won't listen? He's one stubborn sonofabitch.'

All eyes turned to the Wizard, who aimed a thoughtful look at Dwayne. 'According to this young man, the woman is mulatto?'

'That's correct,' said Charlie. 'Her cathouse is next to Morales's bar on Tamarind Street. The Cubans call her *La Rosita Negra.*'

'Ah, the Black Rose,' said the Wizard, and sent a plume of cigar smoke to the ceiling. 'That reminds me of what my old pappy used to say: white women are for marrying, black women are for working,' he roved his eyes over each man in turn, 'but the brown is best for fucking.'

A sharp hiss of admiration wound its way through the smoky air above the table. Dwayne fought to keep his face still, but felt his Adam's apple judder. Pa's eyes were trained on his glass. An image of Miss Alicia came to him, that curl of hair where it escaped the ribbon at her neck . . . Mr Morales's lips on her cheek.

'You'd better toughen up, boy,' grinned Donkey, 'if you're gonna ride this train.'

The Wizard said nothing more, just took a long drag on his cigar that sharpened the shadows on his cheeks, all-seeing eyes set on Dwayne. 'Oh I think our young friend here will be useful to the cause. Very useful, indeed. Now,' he said, and turned his back, 'I want to hear about plans for the parade.'

Clearly dismissed, Dwayne stepped from the room and slumped into the chair outside, feeling like he'd just run up a flight of stairs with a bale of bricks on his back. The door made no sound at all as it closed behind him.

ᖗ CHAPTER 19 ᖘ

It was closing time at The Last Resort when Donkey and Bucket came in.

John strode over to their table. 'Bucket,' he nodded to Simpkins. 'What brings you to this side of town? It cain't be the quality of my root beer. And I see you brought your mule.'

'I'm here on official business, John,' said Bucket.

Bucket had been a few years ahead of John at school, the only son of one of Key West's oldest families. John remembered him as extremely clean and quiet, pale and groomed amongst a gaggle of children who sometimes resembled feral animals more than human beings. From early on, Bucket was destined for great things. Not for him the lemonade stand or the newspaper delivery round; he relieved the other kids of their pocket money through a series of rigged games of chance. Bucket would take a bet on anything: cards, dice, crab races, whether a stray dog would pee on the playground flagpole. John never took part, because he had no pocket money to lose; and he never figured out how Bucket managed it, but there was definitely cheating going on. No one could be that lucky, all the time. Yet Bucket always managed to walk away from every encounter with a pile of coins to land with a *clink* in the bucket he carried everywhere. Anyone who complained about being swindled got a fat lip from one of the bigger boys he employed for such duties.

It was no surprise that he stayed behind when John enlisted. Bucket had just started in city government, on track for high office, maybe even mayor one day.

As if sensing the tension, the last few customers took their leave from the bar.

John turned a chair round and leaned his arms across its back. 'Is that city business, Bucket, or your new dressing-up club? I hear you and the other ladies threw quite a party over at the cemetery the other night.'

Donkey blustered, but Bucket just removed his gloves and tapped his arm with them. Then he laid them on the table and straightened the fingers until they lined up precisely.

'I'm here, John, because you're one of us, whether you realise it or not. We represent the endangered white majority in this country, which includes you, my friend. I'm here to give you the chance to do what's right, for your race and your community. America's founding fathers were white Protestants, and yet we find ourselves in danger of being over-run by the dark-skinned and the apostates. Surely, you can see that all we aim to do is restore the natural balance, and free this land for the people it was intended for?'

A clatter of breaking glass came from behind the bar. Thomas stood up, his already twisted face contorted in outraged disbelief. He looked about ready to leap across the bar, shoulders tensed to swing.

'Go on, half-breed,' said Donkey, hand on his pistol. 'And you'll get to see the ancestors, real soon.'

John shot a glance at Thomas which said, 'Hold. For now.' He turned to Bucket. 'I'm listenin'.'

Bucket settled back in his chair with a satisfied smile. 'I knew you would be reasonable.'

Donkey huffed and lit a cigarette.

'Now, the thing is,' continued Bucket, 'and it pains me to say this, but we've had notice that you're consorting with a woman of colour, that you've even put her up here, under your roof, in flagrant violation of the laws and moral standards of the state.' Indeed, he did look slightly pained, like he had eaten a bad shrimp.

'You've had notice? Where from?'

With a humble dip of his head, Bucket said, 'It's our job to know everything of importance in this town. Otherwise, how could we protect it? The point is, John, you must see that this kind of disgrace can't be allowed to continue, in full view of the good people of Key West. What kind of message would that send to our children?' He removed a pristine handkerchief from his breast pocket and dabbed his mouth, as if even the words were distasteful. 'We're all grown men here. We all understand about . . . temptation. And if you had been discreet, well . . . things might have turned out different.' With a sigh, he shook his head in regret. 'But you had to flaunt it, and now, here we are. As a white man, and a veteran, we're giving you an exceptional opportunity to put things right.' He leaned forward, his voice easy and light. 'Get that brown whore out of here, and out of your life, or so help me, God, there will be consequences.'

John nodded, deep in thought, eyes on the scarred floor-boards. He recalled all the miles he had marched through France, all the men blown to pieces around him, all the killing needed to gain a yard of ground, and then another and another yard; and the whole time, no matter how hard or sad it got, no matter how battered his body and mind, he always told himself it was worth it, it was all worth it, for the good folks back home. They were the reason, the whole and only reason.

He raised his head. 'Fellas, as you know, I'm just a simple soldier, so let me see if I got this straight: I'm really a racist cocksucker at heart, like you and your pals, just at the mercy of my dick, which has caused me to install a brown in my bed. And you and Numb-Nuts here,' he gestured at Donkey, who was glaring with naked aggression, 'are givin' me the chance to get back on the right path, to save all the young boys in town from doin' the same thing. Have I got the gist of it?'

Bucket's pursed lips so hard, they nearly disappeared. 'John, now you—'

'I take that as a yes. So, to keep things simple, here's my answer.' He unfolded his body to its full height. From that angle, he could see shiny scalp through the wisps of Bucket's blond hair. 'If you ever come here again, tellin' me what I can do and to who, I'll make you eat those fine gloves of yours, one finger at a time. Friend.'

Bucket tipped his great head back. His eyes were a blank pale blue, clear as water, empty as those of a sleep-walker.

Donkey picked up his chair to throw it. From across the room came the ratchet of a shotgun. Barrel raised, Thomas said, 'I got a reason. All's I need is an excuse.'

The front door swung open to admit Alicia, eyes down,

hands loosening the ribbon at her neck. 'What a day it has been, I—' She stopped. The smile wavered and then fell from her face, as she took in the room. 'Oh.'

Donkey's chair clattered to the floor, making her start. Thomas lowered the shotgun to rest on the bar.

With great deliberation, John went to her side and clasped her hand. To Bucket, he said, 'This is Alicia Cortez, who lives here with me, until she and I decide different. This ain't your town, and it never will be.'

Bucket stood, straightened his jacket, and replaced the handkerchief in the pocket, all with unhurried care. He blinked once at Alicia, as if taking a photograph to file away for future use.

'We tried, we can do no more.' Bucket turned towards the door, shadowed by the hulking Donkey, and John was struck by how little he had changed since the school playground, when Bucket surrounded himself with older boys to protect his enterprises. Bucket looked back, with something like regret. 'Discretion, John. It was never your strength. And that's a damn shame.'

Upstairs, it didn't take Alicia long to assemble her things.

John entered the bedroom, crackling with nervous energy. 'Oh, that Bucket has no idea what he's started now! Just wait till I—' He stopped when he saw her old case on the bed. 'What's happenin'?'

'We must leave,' she said. 'It is not safe here.'

She had known it couldn't last, that the dark wings would find her. She had just hoped to have a little longer before it was time to move on again. At least, this time, she wasn't alone.

'Come on,' he grinned, 'I can handle old Bucket. Why you wanna run away, just as everything's finally turning around for us? Ain't in my nature to run, darlin'. Besides, this is just a passin' shower. They'll be gone soon, just like all the others who've tried to own this town. Hey, you're shakin'.'

She allowed him to enfold her in his arms, but, for once, the warmth of his body couldn't ease the chill that had settled on her when she looked into that man's eyes. She was no more a person to him than the chair he had sat on.

'They're just bullies,' he murmured into her hair, 'and I know how to handle bullies, believe me. They won't get the better of Lightnin' Jack, I can assure you.'

A new note in his voice. It came from somewhere darker, somewhere deep inside a part of him she had never seen. It rang with battlefields and blood, of men locked together in the eternal rituals of combat, of a ruined church in a small French town. This was Lightning Jack. She pulled away. 'You are enjoying this.'

'If you mean, will I enjoy slappin' six shades of shit out of the likes of Bucket and his idiot pals, then yeah, I will, if it comes to it. It's all they understand, men like that. I seen it plenty of times in the war. While you're tryin' to parlay with them, they're getting' the knife between your ribs.' He stroked her cheek. 'Don't ya see? Someone's got to stand up for a man's rights.'

'But why does it have to be you?'

A lift of his shoulders. 'Just who I am. I didn't pick this fight, but I won't run from it, neither.'

'Ay, why not? Why not run? There is no shame in it, when someone puts a gun to your head.' Tears of frustration burned.

She clung to his arm. 'Let us leave, together, and start over somewhere, down in the islands, where there is none of this, where no one will even notice us. We have enough money to make a new life, a good life, together. *Por favor, mi amor*. Let us go away, tonight!'

'It ain't just about you and me. There's a bigger principle at stake. If we let the likes of the Klan tell us what we can and can't do, where will it end? I didn't fight a war—'

'The war is over!' she shouted. 'And you are not standing up for what is right – you are just . . . just . . . settling old scores!' A sob broke on the last word.

He removed her hands. 'That what you really think? Then you don't know me, not at all.'

No sound in the room except her ragged breaths. She stared hard at his beloved face, committed every detail of his body to memory. Then, with great deliberation to prevent a failure of will, she scooped up her belongings and shut them in the case. 'Then I must go alone.'

'What do you mean? Leavin' the bar, or . . .'

'I must go far away, far enough to make them lose interest in us . . . in you and me. Far enough to be safe.'

'Just like that? You'd leave me, just because things get a little rough? After everything we've done . . . everything we've said?'

'I do it for you! It is only because of me that they come. Can you not see that?'

'I didn't ask you to go. I thought . . . I thought you were different.'

And there, inside the warrior, she saw the little boy who woke, all those years ago, to find his mother had gone in the night, never to return. She saw how, ever since, he had wrapped that hurt in layers and layers of muscle and brawn, and a fear-lessness that bordered on suicidal disregard for himself. And yet there it was, still burning away inside him. She longed to extinguish it, but had no answer for the pain and betrayal in his voice.

'Have I let you down before?' he asked.

She recalled how it felt to be afloat in his arms, on the sea she had feared more than anything else at that time. She had felt safe, safe and loved, even before she loved him back. 'No, but—'

'And do you trust me?' He stepped a little closer. The space between them felt charged like the air before a thunderstorm.

'*Sí*, I do.'

He held one of her hands. 'Nothing matters more than being with you, but I couldn't sleep nights if I let the bullies have the run of the place. It's just how I'm made. I promise you this: there'll be a few scuffles with Bucket's crew, but then they'll cut out, like the cowards they are, and you and me'll be free and clear. Then we'll go anywhere you want – Jamaica, Aruba, Haiti. Hell, I'll even go to Cuba with you, if you want, and kick Raoul's ass into the bargain.'

He took her other hand. 'Don't go. Or it's all for nothin'. Please.'

For a moment, she balanced between yes and no, between stay and go. She saw the violence to come – because however he downplayed it, there would be violence – and then she saw herself, safe on some beautiful island without Jim Crow, with-out the Klan, without the stares of hostile curiosity . . . and without him. And she knew that every day would taste of ash.

She could no more walk away from this man than she could

learn to breathe under water, and so she leaned into him, and ran her hands over his back, his shoulders, his neck, using the solid strength and warmth of him to silence the clamour in her head. His arms pulled her close. His kiss was fired with all the longing and hurt and hope she had seen inside him.

When she had her breath back, she said, 'You will sleep with the Colt under the pillow?' He had been resisting her attempts to persuade him on this. 'And Thomas will stay downstairs at night too?'

'If it makes you happy, I will. And yes, he's been wantin' to do that for a while.'

She emptied the case onto the bed.

Delight and relief raced across his face. He lifted her from the ground and spun her with a whoop of exultation.

Before he could speak, she jabbed a finger in his chest. 'But you have made a promise to me, John Morales. And if you break that promise, then I will come for you, and make you wish I had gone. *Claro*?'

'*Claro*,' he said.

∽ CHAPTER 20 ∾

On parade day, Dwayne stationed himself on Duval Street in prime position to get the best view. Somehow the pomp and pageantry of it suited the season, with Christmas decorations going up in all the store windows, and people beginning their holiday preparations. Everyone was nicer to each other at this time of year, when the weather cooled off and they had a day's vacation to look forward to. It was like the town had put on its best face to welcome the Klan. If he had a tail, he would wag it. The celebration of Christ's birthday would coincide with the town's rebirth.

His heart soared as the first group of marchers appeared. There must have been at least two hundred white-robed figures, some mounted, each displaying the traditional circular emblem which gave the order its name. They must have accounted for most of the recruits who were able to afford the ten dollars to buy their robes. The parade started at the southernmost end of Duval and processed with stately dignity in the direction of Mallory Square, banners lifted by the cool breeze.

Dwayne kept pace with them as they passed Simonton

Street, expecting the place to be thronged with onlookers, but only a few passers-by gave the parade much attention. There were plenty of curious glances, but then most folks just went about their business. Oh, how he wished they had been in that field with him the other night, to witness the spectacle as he had done!

A woman came out on her porch, a basket of wet laundry balanced on her hip.

With a swell of pride, Dwayne called to her, 'That there's our own Klan of the Keys, here to clean up this town!'

The woman sniffed. 'From the smell of 'em, I reckon they need cleaning up first.'

Although the marchers were still impressive, Dwayne had to acknowledge that the daylight robbed them of some of the glamour he had experienced by the cemetery the night before. The pointy hats drooped, the hems of the robes were stained with the ordure of the street. It was clear that many of the men had never marched in step before, from the jerky motion and frayed edges of the formation. Small coloured boys played tag around them, darting in and out of the columns. Several marchers lashed out with bad-tempered kicks, hampered by their skirts. The boys just leapt clear of the boots, light as dragonflies. Their hoots of glee echoed off the buildings which lined the street, mingling with the marchers' curses and heavy breathing. Inside the hoods which restricted their vision, sweaty eyes swivelled.

The woman began to hang out her wet clothes on the porch rail. 'Always somethin' in this town.' With a grunt, she shook the folds from a limp, grey petticoat that put Dwayne in mind of a shroud. 'The crazies breed like mosquitoes 'round here. Be somethin' different next week, I tell ya, sure as Sunday follows Saturday.'

And then, with a whistle and a shout, from a side street appeared another set of marchers. Wearing the traditional white Cuban *guayabera* shirt, the men strode into the path of the Klan members, singing in Spanish.

Some of the horses shied and snorted, breaking formation. The columns dissolved, the Klan banners wobbled and dipped. Soon, all was chaos.

The woman paused in her labours to cackle. 'Ha! Now at least we got somethin' interestin' to watch.' And she settled back in her rocking chair to smoke a cheroot.

The lead Klansman bellowed, 'Get out of our way! We are the Knights of the Ku Klux Klan!'

'You get out of our way!' came the answer from one of the Cubans, arms folded over his chest. 'We are the *Caballeros de la Luz,* the Knights of the Light! And this is a free country, *amigo*! Or should I say, *amiga*?'

Dwayne recognised him from his distinctive hooked nose. It was Hector Rubio, the *lector* at Gato's cigar factory.

Much laughter flowed from the Cuban marchers, clearly very taken by the display of so many men in dresses. They minced up and down in mocking dances, bowing to each other. They tweaked the Klansmens' hoods and lifted the skirts of the robes as if to check the equipment beneath.

One of the Klansmen pulled a pistol from his robe but the parade leader slapped it from his hand with the command, 'Not here.'

A horse spread its back legs to release a fountain of urine from a penis the size of a forearm.

'Hey!' yelled one of the Cubans. 'Now there is a real *hombre*!'

When the first punch was thrown, Dwayne turned away and headed for home. It was, he reflected, very different to how it should have turned out. With a creeping despondency, he was starting to realise that a big part of being a grown-up meant dealing with this gulf, between how things should be, and how things actually were. It made him feel strange and stirred-up inside, like he couldn't trust anything or anyone, not even the evidence of his own senses.

But he was certain of one thing: sure as Sunday followed Saturday, there would be consequences to the march's disruption.

From his rooftop viewpoint, John watched the entire scene unfold in the street with increasing jubilation. When the mêlée erupted, he grinned and muttered, 'Well, how do you like that? This is how we welcome assholes to The Rock.' He surveyed the disarray below on Duval and exclaimed to Thomas, 'Didn't I tell ya that our welcoming committee would work a treat? I knew Hector would come through. He likes a fight almost as much as I do.' He stretched his arms to encompass not only the street, but the whole of Key West.

The Klansmen were in full retreat now, pursued by the raucous Cubans, hurling epithets and chunks of coral in their wake.

Yeah, that's right, run back into your hole, cockroaches.

But Thomas still had that hangdog look of concern, which was starting to irritate him. 'You got somethin' to say?'

'I just don't get why you had to stir 'em up,' said Thomas.

'Best policy when you find a hornet's nest is back the hell away, not whack it with a stick.'

'Hey, you heard Bucket the other night. Who's taking the fight to who? When someone threatens me, I don't sit there and wait for them to come good on it. You'd know that if you'd fought in the war.' His tone softened at the shadow of hurt in Thomas's eyes.

But Thomas just pursed his lips. 'Alicia know about this, today?'

He and Alicia had stood on the same roof a few nights previously, watching the sky light up to the Klan induction ceremony. Even several blocks away, the sound of hundreds of voices raised in unison carried over the rooftops. And young Dwayne's voice was among them. He shouldn't have minded. The kid was none of his business, but something troubled him about Dwayne's behaviour. Then he realised where he'd seen it before, that same powerful cocktail of bravado and ignorance. It was on the faces of the recruits he had joined up with, the same mixture of excitement and apprehension. Boys like that, he knew, were easy fodder for big causes; all of them in such a tearing hurry to become men . . . all wanting to belong.

Alicia had shivered and pulled a shawl around her shoulders. 'There is talk of the coloureds leaving town. Geraldine's lost four of her girls in the past week. Maybe we should think about going away, just for a while. We could—'

He had held her close and turned her eyes away from the glowing sky.

But there were others watching that night. Atop the Gato factory, John recognised the distinctive figure of Hector Rubio, his cigar a red eye in the blurry light of dusk. The two exchanged a nod . . . and John had an idea. Rubio was an agitator and a nuisance, but his workers represented the biggest Catholic community on the island.

'Nah, she's better off not knowin',' he said to Thomas, with another glance at the street below. Duval had regained its usual contours, as if nothing had happened. That's what those idiots in the Klan needed to understand: they might make a small ripple in the town, but no more, before the waters closed over and wiped away any trace of them.

He gave these latest goons a week before they packed up and headed back on the long journey to the mainland. 'She'd only worry, like you, old friend. Sometimes I think you two are in cahoots.' He had caught her staring at him several times, with an expression almost identical to Thomas's. And he knew all too well about her superstitions, drummed into her by dear Papa, about bringing bad luck, about it being her fault that Bucket had marked them. She wasn't bad luck. She was the best thing ever to walk into his sorry life, and in the unlikely event that he ever got to meet her dear Papa, he would thank the man for casting his only daughter so callously into exile.

But Thomas still wouldn't let it go. 'You could leave town, just till things cool off some.'

'Thomas, you know full well that even if I licked old Bucket's boots, it wouldn't stop, because it ain't really nothin' to do with me, or Alicia, or any of that. It's about power, pure and simple; those that have it shovin' it down the throats of those that don't.' He squinted at the horizon. 'The only way to deal with a bully is to push back twice as hard, and they'll look for an easier target. Come on, let's go get a root beer,' he said, with

a last look at the quiet peace of Duval Street spread out below.
This is my town.

The next morning, Dwayne arrived at Mr Jolovitz's house just
as the fire crew was packing up. The old man hadn't arrived to
open the store, and as the place did business every day of the
year except on the High Holy Days, Dwayne had come along
to find him. He had visited the house once before, when his
boss needed help fixing some storm damage, and been invited
inside for a glass of lemonade when he finished.

It had been obvious that Jolovitz spent little of his rumoured
wealth on his abode. The house was old, with evidence of several repairs to the roof, and a major termite infestation. The
yard was a mean, narrow rectangle of pounded earth beneath
a drooping jacaranda, with a jumble of weathered boards for a
fence. One of the front windowpanes was filled in with a square
of plywood, which gave the place a strangely piratical air.

It had looked a wreck from the outside, but inside was a rev-
elation. Dwayne had never seen so many books in his life, not
even at the library. Every wall was lined with shelves bowed
like ribs, every surfaced adorned with teetering piles of them.
The hall leading to the back of the house was stacked with
volumes up to the ceiling, the gap down the middle somewhat
narrower than Jolovitz's generous girth, by Dwayne's estima-
tion. They didn't have fancy covers or gold leaf. Mostly they
just looked ordinary, ordinary and very old.

Perplexed, Dwayne had asked, 'Why do you need so many?'

Jolovitz had retrieved a volume of Shakespeare's *Sonnets*
with a forest green cover lightly frosted with mildew. He

caressed the pages. 'They are my friends, my family. They keep me company and give me joy. Who can ever have enough of that?' And through the smeared lenses of his glasses, his eyes glowed with the only true happiness Dwayne had witnessed in his employer.

He recalled Jolovitz's expression now as he stood amid the smoking piles of possessions that had survived the fire. Some of the tin roof panels had collapsed; a few charred timbers still stood above the wet, smouldering remains of the house, sending up tendrils of smoke through the surrounding trees to smudge the early sunlight. The walls had caved in, and everywhere were fragments of belongings: clumps of charred papers, a cooking pot, half a rocking chair, a candlestick, and books, everywhere books, glued into useless blocks by the water. Dwayne thought he spied the outline of a black hat in the mire, but couldn't be sure. Strangest of all was the odour of burned pork cloaking the site. He coughed, but the smell lingered. A few onlookers clustered at the edges of the scene, handkerchiefs over their mouths.

All was dripping blackness, except for a white-draped mound towards the back of the property. Two policemen stood over it, making notes. In a daze, Dwayne stepped towards them, but a fireman stopped him with an arm across the chest.

'Can't go back there. Cops got a job to do.' His coarse northern accent grated in Dwayne's ears.

'What happened?'

The fireman's eyes shone porcelain white from his smoke-blackened face. 'You family? No one here seems to know him.' The label stencilled on his helmet read 'Lopiccolo'. He removed it to reveal grey hair drenched in sweat.

'He don't have no family. I just work for him.'

Dwayne was amazed at the level, calm tone of his voice. In his head clamoured a bunch of people all talking at once, Pa and Mr Simpkins and the Wizard, about warnings, and tribes, and over and over, the phrase 'time to move on'. Yet inside the storm of words, there was an awful stillness, a distance which made him feel like he was surveying the scene of destruction through a telescope, while his senses recorded it all, every bit of the stench and horror of it. It was like he was doing it from far away, in someone else's body.

With a feeling like he had swallowed a stone, Dwayne realised there might be no one left to attend to Jolivitz's affairs – or, for that matter, even hold a funeral.

Lopiccolo passed a dirty rag over his face, which took off the top layer of soot to leave him with a grey pallor. 'Early this morning, before sun-up, someone threw a burning pig's head through your boss's bedroom window. It was soaked in kerosene, woulda burned a long time.' A muffled crash as another timber succumbed to gravity. 'An old place like this, his chances of getting out weren't great, but by my reckoning, he'd have made it if it weren't for all them books.' He jabbed a grubby finger towards the heaps of ruined volumes. 'That's the best tinder you'll find, old books. The place was choked with 'em.'

But Dwayne knew the truth. Jolovitz was trying to save them, his friends and family. He would have been frantically loading his arms with them, unable to leave any behind, even as the smoke filled his lungs, even as the flames consumed them.

He nudged the toe of his boot under the cover of a tome

draped with some remnants of clothing and a half-burned pillow. The book fell over to reveal the title embossed on its crisped cover: *Treasure Island*.

Lopiccolo began to reel the hose over his shoulder. 'Ya know, I came down here from New York last year, thinkin' things would be nice and quiet, compared to the big city. I saw myself lyin' at the beach, surrounded by girls, waitin' for the next call to get some cat down from a tree.' He stowed the hose in the side of the fire engine. 'But the weird shit I've seen here in twelve months makes the Bronx look like a fairytale.' He shook his head and spat. 'An old guy like that ... what'd he do to deserve this?'

Around the blockage in his throat, Dwayne said, 'He must have upset ... someone?'

'I'd say so.' Lopiccolo snorted into a handkerchief, which came away black. 'Where I come from, if you wanna pop a guy, you shoot him in the face. You don't barbecue him in his bed. But as people keep tellin' me,' and here he affected an awful parody of a Southern accent, 'ya'll do things different down here.'

Dwayne's eyes went to the white mound on the ground just as a hand slipped from beneath the sheet. One of the policemen bent to cover it. Dwayne focused his attention on Lopiccolo's soot-smeared face. 'I guess the police will be ... they'll be lookin' into this?' And in his mind he saw Chief Baxter's hat, tumbling over and over through the smoky air above the meeting table.

'Sure they will, son. Sure they will.'

~ CHAPTER 21 ~

When Dwayne got home, Pa was chopping wood in the yard. The axe had been in the family for a hundred years, with only two handles in its lifetime. Pa liked to say it came over on the ship that brought the first Campbells to the colonies. It was a sizeable chunk of iron, with a handle like a small tree trunk, and Pa swung it as if it weighed no more than a length of sugar cane. Dwayne was still too rangy to heft it right, and used a smaller one to cut kindling, but he aspired to swing it like Pa. In his mind, it remained one of the true tests of manhood, and for years he had imagined how satisfying it would be finally to swoop it over his head in a big arc and slice through the wood like it was butter. The axe was part of his birthright, Pa said, part of what connected him to the generations of Campbells before him.

Ma's shape was visible behind the screened door, but she didn't come out.

Pa paused, sweat beading above his heavy eyebrows, and from the guarded look in his eye and the tight line of his jaw, Dwayne knew that he knew.

For a moment, he just stared, unable to corral his thoughts into sensible words, torn between wanting to punch his father right in that jaw, and fall into his arms to weep. Then it just burst from his mouth in a wail: 'Why?'

Pa wiped his brow with a handkerchief embroidered with his initials. 'You need to ask that?'

'You said we were sendin' a message. I figured that meant someone might talk tough to him, scare him a little. But not this. Burned to death in his own house?' Dwayne was breathing too hard, his voice rising too fast. He forced himself to slow down, calm down. Pa would explain, he would make it all right, just like always.

'That wasn't meant to happen, Dwayne. He could have got out. He should have got out. It was his own fault he didn't. If you want someone to blame, blame him.'

Again, Dwayne saw Jolovitz stagger through the piles of burning books, panting and wheezing, a stack of them balanced in his arms, while he bent to save one more, one more . . . just as the roof came down. He could taste the smoke in his own mouth, feel the flames sear his skin, smell the sacrilegious burning pork.

'His own fault? A burnin' pig's head? Through his goddamn window!' Tears of rage and frustration were close, oh so close. Dwayne bit down hard on his tongue.

'You will not blaspheme in my presence!' Pa sank the axe into the stump hard enough to make the ground shake. 'He forced us into this position! You know that! We gave him fair warning of the consequences, if he stayed.'

'So we didn't mean to kill him? Is that it, Pa?'

Pa came up close to him and looked down, still a good head

taller. 'What did you think, Dwayne? Hmm? That it was all gonna be ceremonies and parades and flags flying? The Klan's work is hard work, dirty work.' He planted his palms on Dwayne's shoulders. 'Men's work. And God's work.'

Dwayne looked up into the cool blue of his father's eyes, so different to the muddy green of his own. He seemed to have inherited almost nothing from this man, neither his height nor his colouring nor his strength nor his skills. Warmth from his father's hands, big and calloused and capable, flowed into his body. Once, he would have been so grateful for the touch of those hands. Now they made him feel soiled. He imagined they carried a whiff of pig.

He shrugged them off and stepped back. 'You get angry if I blaspheme, but not if an old man gets killed in his own house?' The tears came now, burning shameful tracks down his face. 'All my life, I've wanted to be just like you! Now I'm ashamed to be your son!' Pa drew his fist back to swing, teeth bared, eyes aflame in the way that had terrified Dwayne ever since he could remember. But now he just spat, 'Go ahead, beat me! Just like always, people smaller than you, who cain't fight back! That's all you know how to do, you . . . you COWARD!'

The blow knocked him completely off his feet. His head smacked into the base of the old oak that shaded the front of the house and everything went fuzzy. Blood swirled inside his mouth, and his tongue found a space where a tooth should have been. But his fingers still curled round a fallen branch, and with a shake of his head, he was about to raise it up when he heard Ma scream.

'Stop, Neil! Stop this now!' She flung herself across Dwayne, pinning him to the tree.

'Get off him, Lily,' growled Pa, big as a grizzly from Dwayne's prone position.

In a voice Dwayne had never heard, she shouted, 'It's enough, Neil! Enough, I say!'

Pa glared from Dwayne to Ma and back again, his face gone russet. Veins pulsed in his forehead. The axe stood not two feet away from his right hand, which opened and closed, opened and closed.

'You gonna have to kill us both,' she said, low but full of intent. 'Is that what you want? In front of all these people?'

Dwayne's vision cleared enough for him to notice several of the neighbours had come out to lean on their fences. Pa's breathing slowed. He smoothed his hair and straightened his collar. He gave them a wave and a big smile, the one that always charmed the parishioners and everyone else.

For the first time, he saw Pa, really saw him. The anger drained out of him, to be replaced by a sadness that brought no tears. It was like finding a tiny grey maggot grubbing around inside a grizzly suit. The sadness was so deep, so strong, that he thought it might choke him to death. A part of him wanted it to, if it meant he didn't have to know what he knew.

Still smiling, Pa said to Dwayne, deep and quiet, 'Get out of here, and don't come back.'

'I'll go,' he croaked, hand to his jaw, 'but Ma's comin' with me.'

'No, honey,' she said. 'My place is here. I'll be fine.'

'But Ma, you know what he'll do to you!'

'Don't you worry about me, son.' There was a hint of something in her eyes, strange and powerful. 'I'll be fine, you'll see.'

There was also resignation, even apprehension, but the cringing fear he knew so well was gone.

Without looking in Dwayne's direction or changing his expression, Pa said, 'I cast you out. You are no son of mine.'

Ma wiped some blood from his mouth and kissed his cheek. 'Remember, I will always love you.'

With one last look at her, Dwayne set off on the road back to town.

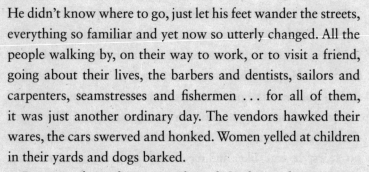

He didn't know where to go, just let his feet wander the streets, everything so familiar and yet now so utterly changed. All the people walking by, on their way to work, or to visit a friend, going about their lives, the barbers and dentists, sailors and carpenters, seamstresses and fishermen ... for all of them, it was just another ordinary day. The vendors hawked their wares, the cars swerved and honked. Women yelled at children in their yards and dogs barked.

Do any of you have any idea what's being done in your town, in your name?

Every bit of it remained unchanged, with one exception: outside the shuttered doors of Jolovitz's store, several customers milled. A young woman with a basket on her arm peered into the window, hand up to block out the light.

'We're closed,' said Dwayne.

'For how long?'

Dwayne blinked at her, the sun warm on his face. She was pretty, if a little thin, with bouncy blonde waves which he guessed were in fashion. He watched her take in the wound on his face, the blood on his shirt.

'Hey, are you OK? Do you need help?'

'I'm fine.' He couldn't think what else to do or say, so he just stared. Up close, she was on the plain side, but there was something pleasing in the arrangement of her features. He might have wanted to spend some time studying them, if the world hadn't just cracked apart.

'I'm Noreen Baker,' she said, and held out a slim hand with white-tipped nails. 'I just live over there. My momma's a nurse, and she can—'

'Thank you, Noreen, but I got to go.' And he turned away.

'You're Dwayne Campbell.'

The sound of his name rang strangely foreign in his ears, like it belonged to a different language. Or a different person. 'Yeah. How'd you know that?'

'Oh, we came to hear your daddy preach a couple of times, but we go to the Baptist church over on Fifth Street now.' She waited, bumping the basket against her knees.

Once, not long ago, he'd have given his whole collection of Zorro stories, plus a pint of blood, to have a girl like her talking to him like that.

'I'm sorry . . . Noreen? You're very nice, but I have to be somewhere. Good day to you.'

He walked on. The only thing that mattered was to keep walking, just keep moving, even if he had no destination. While his feet were going forward, it seemed like there might be a way to outrun them, the images in his head: Pa's open mouth, flecked with spittle, his fist hurtling through the air; Jolovitz spinning around in the flames, weighed down by his treasures; ranks of white-robed figures pledging allegiance in the darkness.

He stumbled. A hand came out, but he shook it off and kept walking.

His brain felt scorched by all that had happened in the past twenty-four hours, and yet there was something still worse, buried in a deep, dark recess which even now he strove to deny. This, he realised, was the real thing that his feet were trying to outrun. On the dusty pavement, they rang out a rhythm, 'You knew, you knew, you knew.' Over and over, the words repeated. He knew what the Klan stood for, what Pa was capable of, after so many years of living with him, and yet he had willingly chosen blindness. Just like a child, hands over his eyes. All those signs and rituals he had taken for manhood were simply ways for the leaders, Pa and the others, to wield their power over the weak and gullible . . . those like himself.

He had always known.

And what they did to Jolovitz, that was only the beginning. He saw that now. He had no choice but to see it, all of it. The enormity of it was like Pa's fist in his face again, only many, many times worse, and it halted him so abruptly that a fat woman leading an equally fat dog ran right into him. Both squealed their disapproval, but he took no notice.

God help me . . . what have I done? And is there any way to put it right, before . . . ?

His feet began to run, to the only place where he needed to be.

When he burst through the Tea Room doors, out of breath, with sweat stinging his eyes, there was no sign of her. The scary whore with the big pile of black hair, Maxine, was at the bar, painting her nails a shiny pink that glistened like shark guts. Paulina was reading an old issue of *Life* magazine.

'Where's Miss Alicia?' he panted.

'At the undertaker's by now, I expect,' Maxine said, without looking up.

'No!' he cried. 'My God, what happened?' The blood left his head in a rush. He put a hand on the bar to steady himself. *I'm too late, too late.*

Maxine snorted with laughter, head thrown back in a way that set her hair awobble. 'What the hell's wrong with you, boy? She and Felix are takin' delivery of more hootch off the ferry.' She blew on her nails, then waved them dry.

'Ferry? What? I don't—'

'It is their latest bootleg scheme,' Paulina chimed in. '*La Rosita Negra* is always somewhere else . . . everywhere, except where she should be.' She flicked the magazine pages without reading.

Maxine focused her fierce green eyes right on his. 'But you thought she was kilt. Now why'd you go thinkin' that, hmm?'

He took a few breaths, relief and adrenalin making him feel light-headed, his heart still thrashing inside his chest. 'I got a . . . very important . . . message, for her. I need to speak with her. Urgently.'

'Well,' she said, and uncurled herself from the bar stool, 'you can give the message to me. I'll be sure to pass it on.'

She reminded him of a huge black heron, all legs and dark plumage. At half a head taller, she made him tilt back a little to see her.

'All due respect, ma'am, I got to tell Miss Alicia in person.'

From behind him: 'You can tell me now, Dwayne.'

Miss Alicia came through the door that led to the kitchen, followed by Felix, face obscured by a stack of liquor crates. 'Put them in the usual place,' she said. 'Thomas will take them to the woods.'

'Oh, Miss Alicia, I sure am glad to see you!' A goofy grin took over his face, and for a moment he could do nothing but look at her. She was so self-possessed, so much in charge. In an instant, he was reminded of their first meeting down at the docks, and her straight off the boat from Havana, all alone, with no idea how to get along on The Rock. And now here she was, a prosperous business lady.

'You are always welcome here.' Her tone was cool, her gaze watchful.

And he recalled their last conversation, when he had boasted about all the Klan recruits he had brought in, and what a spectacle they would make. Then he thought of what the Wizard had said about brown women, saw again the supreme assurance glowing in his eyes through the veil of cigar smoke. In her presence now, shame burned through his whole body, all different colours of it: shame at what he had become, at how stupid he had been, at what a sucker he was . . . at what he had helped to set in motion. Of course, the Klan would target people like her. It was there, in plain sight, underneath all the big ideals and patriotic platitudes that he had been fed, like an infant from a spoon. It was hatred, in its purest form. And he had sat at her table and bragged about his part in it . . .

And then he had given them a reason.

His empty stomach rebelled. Bile singed his throat but he forced it down. At this moment, his feelings were of no importance. Those he would deal with later. The only thing that

mattered was alerting her to the danger on its way, the danger
he had brought down on her head.

'I come to apologise, for my behaviour. And I come to warn
you. Is there somewhere . . .' he glanced at Maxine, who wasn't
even pretending to mind her own business, 'somewhere private
we can talk?'

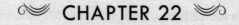

In the small storeroom off the kitchen, Alicia listened to Dwayne with an increasing sense of unreality. His mouth moved, and out tumbled words she had never heard before. 'Wizard', 'Kleagle', 'Klonvocation'. They sounded so ridiculous, like part of some silly game, she wanted to laugh, were it not for the deathly seriousness on Dwayne's bruised and bloodied face.

As he began to recount his tale, she noticed something different about him. Gone was the gleam of excitement, the talk of big projects, the puppyish enthusiasm. There was a new sadness, a new weariness in the way he carried himself. He seemed older suddenly, tipped over the brink of manhood by something momentous and terrible.

While he talked, she tended to his wounds.

'They're comin' for you,' he said again, 'you got to leave town.' His head drooped. 'And it's all my stupid fault. I am so sorry, Miss Alicia.'

She lifted his head. 'Hold still. John will not go, and so neither will I.' She dabbed the graze on his chin with a cotton square soaked in aloe. 'He can handle himself. No one will get past Thomas.' She sank back on her heels. 'And Dwayne, they would have come eventually. We are prepared.'

He grasped her hand and held it tight. 'You don't understand . . . you cain't prepare for this. You ain't seen what I seen. You don't know what they'll do.' His voice dipped to an urgent rasp. 'And there's no time. You got to go, tonight.'

With a sigh, she wiped her hands. 'I will tell John what you say, but I do not believe it will change his mind. And now I will make up a cot for you here, since you cannot go home.'

That word, 'home'. Her eyes roamed the kitchen, and called up a vision of how it had looked when she arrived, with the rotten cupboards, disgusting floor and fly-specked windows . . . and that seething carpet of cockroaches. All was now fresh, new, and kept spotlessly clean by Hortensia. Flowers and vegetables thrived in the garden beyond the window, where Pablito sipped at the dish of sugar water hanging in the guava tree. The ledger pages swam with black ink, and the liquor stocks in the woods had grown to the point where they were looking for new storage. The girls were healthy, and the restaurant did so well that Kitty was now working full-time as a waitress.

And all of it thanks to her hard work and determination. Not for a moment did she doubt Dwayne's sincerity, but as she stood there, her feet felt like the new roots of a tree, just beginning to bond with the soil. She was not ready to leave, especially at the hands of men whose only objection was her skin colour. Yes, there was fear, but for the first time, she could understand some of John's unwillingness to be driven away. She had been forced to leave her home in Cuba by men of power, and now a different group wanted to do the same thing, just as she was starting to feel settled. America was not Cuba. It was the Land of the Free. Surely that counted for something?

'Thank you,' he said, 'but you ain't listenin' to me. It ain't safe.'

'We have a right to be here.'

He was on his feet again, swaying. 'That don't matter! None of that matters, not now! Don't ya see, they're comin' for ya!' Then he sat down with a bump.

'When was the last time you ate? I will get Hortensia to make you something. Hortensia!'

'Forget about me, please! I'm fine! Just get packed and . . . go. Go anywhere, anywhere else. Please.'

She knelt, her face level with his, his pallor waxy, his eyes bloodshot. He needed food and rest. Beneath the veneer of maturity, he was still a boy, just banished by his father. 'When John comes back, you can tell him what you told me. He will know what to do for the best.'

The kitchen door banged in its frame. 'Ah,' she said, 'that is probably him now. I am in here, *mi amor*, with our friend, Dwayne.'

But the face that appeared around the doorframe belonged to Ricardo, a neighbourhood boy whom she had treated for worms. 'You must come quickly, *señorita*!' he said, eyes wide, breathing hard. '*Señor* Morales says, bring your medicines!'

'What is it?' she asked.

Dressed only in ragged shorts, feet bare, his little body vibrated with tension. A rapid stream of Spanish followed, which took the air from her lungs.

'What'd he say?' asked Dwayne, on his feet again. 'What's happened?'

She swept into the hallway and began to fill her bag with jars and tubs and potions. Dwayne hovered beside her. *Focus, focus just on what is needed. The rest will wait.* She had never treated someone in this situation before. Burn ointment, that was essential. She must mix up some fresh. But then, how to clean the skin?

'It is Hector Rubio,' she said, her mind sorting through the catalogue of preparations in the *farmacia*. 'He has been . . .' She lacked the English word, had never needed it before. 'I don't know how to say . . . they have covered him in the hot *alquitrán*—'

'Tar? Hot tar? Hector Rubio's been tarred and feathered?'

She looked up. 'They . . . do this . . . thing to people here?'

'Yeah,' Dwayne nodded, and passed a hand over his face. 'They do.'

From the doorway, Ricardo's voice, high and urgent: 'Please, come *ahora*! Now!'

🐦

It was almost midnight when Alicia returned with John and Dwayne. Hortensia thumped plates of *huevos Habaneros* in front of them under the glare of the overhead bulb. A moth circled it, drunk on the light.

'Eat,' she commanded, 'especially the skinny one.' She glowered at Dwayne as if being thin were a crime, then bustled out of the room, grey braid swinging in a grumpy arc across her back.

Alicia picked at the tar stains on her hands. Her ears still rang with Hector's screams as she had peeled it from him, strip by painful strip, made more difficult by the clumps of feathers tufted everywhere. Although it was only pine tar – *gracias a Dios* – and not road tar, it had to be removed, as it continued to burn while on the skin. He had been shaking so hard with shock that John and Dwayne had to lock him in their arms to hold him still. All of them were marked with tar and blood.

John stilled her hands with his own.

She had left Hector covered in cloths soaked in aloe, to protect the new skin that would grow. He would live, although the healing would be long and difficult; but she was fairly certain that the sight of his once-handsome face, torn to bleeding shreds, would stay with her always. She leaned on the table, glad of the solid wood because a tiny tremor had started up in her left leg.

'I want you to go,' John said, 'upstate with Thomas, to stay with his people for a while, just till things simmer down here.' The light cast heavy shadows over his eyes. His voice creaked with fatigue.

'When I wanted to leave, you wanted me to stay. What has changed?'

John cast a glance at Dwayne, of mingled anger and regret.

'It's because of me,' said Dwayne, 'because of what I did.'

He looked so miserable that she put a hand on his arm. 'You warned us. That is something.' She turned to John. 'It is simple: you stay, I stay. This is my home.'

'Godammit, woman!' His fist landed on the table, making the plates jump. 'I cain't take care of business and keep you safe!'

And then she saw it: there was real fear inside him – not for himself, never that, but for her – and she understood at last that her presence could be a crippling distraction for him.

She had not thought about it in those terms before. What if, in trying to protect her, he made himself vulnerable? It would hurt terribly to leave him, but now she realised there could be worse pain, if she brought harm to him.

'Very well.' Her throat closed on the words. 'I will go with Thomas—'

'Thank the Lord!' John rose to his feet. 'I'll get him now.'

She took his hand, trying very hard not to cling to it. 'I will go in the morning.' She looked up at him, his dark head haloed by the harsh light, 'but I will have this night with you. I promise, in the morning, I will go.'

Some hours later, John was dreaming of a pine forest in France. His squad were on the hunt for an enemy machine-gun nest. Tussocks of rough grass grew between the pillar-straight trees, in ranks close as bristles in a brush. Soft dappled sunlight lit the faces of his men, and everywhere was the fresh, clean scent of the fallen needles which silenced their boots. All his senses were alive to the forest. He had always been there, going back to primeval times, as much a part of it as the wolf and the hawk. It was beautiful, so beautiful and calm, that he stopped for a moment to take off his helmet, just to let the breeze cool his head.

A change of wind direction and there it was: man-smell, and close. He shouted at the others to get down and reached for his Colt, but it was gone.

Hands threw him to the ground, but instead of grass beneath him, the familiar bedroom floorboards grazed his palms. A woman's voice, screaming in his ear.

He opened his eyes to a circle of five white hoods, glowing above him in the faint light of the half-moon. Still partly fogged by the dream, he blinked and gasped, trying to get his bearings.

'Let him go!' Alicia shrieked. 'Let him go!' She pounded her fists against the nearest robed figure. With one hand, he shoved hard and sent her sprawling against the headboard. A loud *clunk* and she lay still.

'Alicia!'

The robed figures hauled him to his feet. One said, 'Your brown whore is doin' what she does best – layin' on her back!' His breath brought stale tobacco and cheap gin.

The others cackled in response, Donkey's distinctive bray among them, and began to shuffle him towards the door. John braced his feet and lunged again for his Colt but found only smooth, empty bedsheet.

'Lookin' for this?' One of the figures produced the revolver from under his robe.

'If you hurt her, I promise to kill you,' he panted, 'so help me—'

The blow was worse for the darkness. There was no way to prepare for the impact on his face, no way to shield himself in time. *Bastard hit me with my own gun. They're gonna pay for that.* Next came a fist to the gut and he crumpled to his knees, winded and heaving. Blood coated his tongue, dripped from his lips.

'She must be one damn fine lay, for him to make this much fuss,' said the figure closest to him. 'Maybe we oughta see for ourselves?'

'You first!' offered his companion.

With a roar, John sprang upright and stamped down hard on the nearest foot. The man yelped, releasing his grip just long enough for John to get his hands on the others' hoods.

'Halloween's over, assholes!' he yelled. 'Time to fight like real men!'

He managed to yank off two hoods to expose the furious faces of Donkey and Officer Maynard Cullen. Surprised, John's guard slipped, which cost him dearly. Cullen's startled expression was the last thing he saw before a blow from behind felled him into blackness.

It was early morning when the soft lap of the surf brought him to consciousness. The pain was everywhere, a whole continent of pain, worst in his lower back. He had a dim recollection of repeated blows from a baseball bat. The dawn sky was streaked with apricot and gold, as he lay in the sand, trying to summon the courage to inspect the damage.

The bruises would be awful, but he detected no broken bones. His most urgent need was to get back to Alicia. His last view of her, motionless on the bed, surrounded by white robes, spurred him on. Just getting to his feet made him cry out.

He began the long walk back to town, using the pain to fuel his anger, stopping every hundred yards or so to rest. And thinking, thinking of what he would do to them, how he would make them pay, for what they had done to him . . . and to her. He would find them, Donkey and Cullen, and the others who pulled their strings. He knew them, these men, had grown up with some of them, done business with others. He knew where to find them. He cursed them, cursed them all, startling chickens and stray dogs along his route.

In this fashion, he was able to place one foot, and then another, on the dusty road home.

The morning sun peeped over the horizon as he limped into Tamarind Street. With the last of his strength, he stumbled up the steps to the bar and fell through the doors into Thomas's arms. He looked up to see a gash on his old friend's forehead, one eye swollen nearly shut. Thomas lowered him into a chair. The pain in his back nearly made him lose consciousness again.

'They got you too,' he said, through swollen lips. Incredibly, he seemed to have retained all his teeth. 'How is she?'

'Miss Alicia!' called Thomas. 'Come quick!' His voice dropped. 'I so sorry,' he croaked. 'I was asleep when they came, I shoulda stayed awake, I shoulda—'

'They knew you were there. How'd they know that? And how'd they know about my gun?' The thinking part of his brain tried to work on the problem. There was something very wrong, beyond the obvious aspects of the attack, but it would take time to puzzle it out, and he didn't have the energy.

'I found it, the Colt, outside in the bushes.'

'Why didn't they kill me?' He remembered lying on his back at the beach, barely conscious, unable even to brace for the next blow. A voice in his ear, close enough to feel the man's breath: 'You ignored our warning, John. We gave you a chance to make things right. No more chances now.' It had sounded almost sad.

'The beatin' they gave you,' said Thomas, 'should've liked to kill most men. You just too ornery to cooperate.'

He would have laughed were it not for the agony in his ribs each time he drew breath.

Alicia sped into the room and flung her arms round his neck, causing him to gasp. She was unhurt, except for a nasty cut at her hairline. Relief took the strength from his legs and he slumped against the chair.

Her eyes brimmed with tears while they assessed his wounds with professional scrutiny. '*Mi pobre*, my poor love . . . who has done this?'

'I got a look at two of 'em, Donkey and a cop called Cullen. They're gonna be sorry for what they did to me, and to you. And Thomas. I promise you that. Very, very sorry.' All he needed was a little rest, and then he would make them pay. He went to rise, but only managed to straighten his legs before dizziness overwhelmed him and he crashed down again, nearly sick with the effort.

'No! No more!' she ordered. 'You must heal! As soon as you can travel, we will leave this place. Thomas, help me get him up the stairs.'

She cleaned his wounds and applied an array of salves and creams, some which smelled of flowers and others which burned the back of his throat. Soft cloths bound the torn skin. The worst was when she straightened his broken nose with a sharp twist. The pain still blared louder than anything else, but she gave him a bitter drink and it began to recede.

'You know,' he said, 'on my way back, I cursed 'em, all of 'em, who did this.'

A hand to his forehead, she said, 'I did not know you believed in such things.'

'I don't, but figured it couldn't hurt. And it made me feel better.'

He wanted to stay awake, to formulate a plan of attack. He

wanted to stare at her above him, safe inside the curtain of her hair. There were so many important things to say, about how he wouldn't let anyone hurt her ever again, and how he thought he was dead when he woke up on the beach, and how this hurt more than all his wounds because he was gone from her. The words were all jumbled up in his head, which throbbed to the beat of his heart.

He was with the old man again, in the time before the train brought fresh meat to the town, and the time before his mother left. At the butcher pen on the docks, where the cattle were driven for slaughter, the air was alive with the screams of animals and the iron reek of blood, which flowed down the dock and into the harbour. The water churned with sharks driven mad by it, the harbour walls ringed by ruffles of pink foam. His father turned to him, his face still unlined, his back as yet unbowed. John had felt sickened and wanted to go home, but his father's eyes were bright. 'This is it, son. Pay attention right here. It'll learn you how to get along in this town.'

Sweet music drowned the noise of dying cattle. She was singing in Spanish as she stroked his temples, either Alicia or his mother, he wasn't sure which. It was a song his mother used to sing at bedtime. Indeed, she had sung it to him on the last night before she left. Low and sweet, she sang:

> *Sleep, my son, sleep, my love*
> *Sleep, piece of my heart*

And he let go, and drifted away on the river of her voice.

CHAPTER 23

The next day, Alicia was at the Tea Room kitchen table, staring into the cup of cold coffee between her hands. Thomas had stationed himself outside their bedroom door for the night. Several times, John had woken in pain, but when morning came, his eyes were clear, and so was his determination.

'I'm goin' after 'em, Alicia.'

She had replaced the soiled bandages with fresh ones. Healing had already begun. It would only be a matter of a few days before he was up and ready to make good on his threat. 'We said we were leaving.'

'That was before this. I cain't just run away, like a kicked dog.'

To her eyes, he was a good likeness of one, with the bruises flowering over him like grotesque tattoos, and both eyes blacked. But those eyes shone with fierce outrage, which she shared but had no outlet for. And at least half the outrage was directed at the man in the bed with her. 'Yes, you can! People do, all the time, when the odds are against them!'

'I never have, and I never will. You should understand that, after what you did to Raoul. He wronged you, and you made him pay.'

'I did that to save my life, not my pride.'

'You think this is just my pride? Don't ya see? They've got to be accountable, not just for what they done to me, but for what they're doing to this town.'

'That is the job of the police!' She grabbed fistfuls of bed-sheets, near to rending them in frustration.

He had laughed bitterly, which turned into a cough, making him clutch his side with an agonised grimace. 'That's funny, the police. They're part of it, darlin', up to their shiny gold buttons in it.'

'Then you are even more of a fool.'

'In that case,' he had said, leaning back against the head-board, 'you won't want to hang around.'

She had stared at him for a long moment, all the love and fear and anger she felt for him churning together, over and over. She could no more walk away than sprout gills and swim back to Cuba. She knew it, and one look told her he knew it, too.

While he dozed, she had come next door to think, to breathe different air, to be reminded that some semblance of normal life continued.

Kitty and Maxine came in. Kitty exclaimed, 'Miss Pearl, what happened to you!'

Hands on hips, Maxine studied Alicia with cool detachment. 'I told her, didn't I? Y'all heard me,' she gestured to the room with her cigarette, 'I said no good would come of this.'

'Of what?' asked Alicia. Her blood still simmered. To come at night, while he was sleeping, and pull him from his bed. Such cowardice was beyond her comprehension. 'No good would come of what?' She could hardly bear to look at Maxine. It took all her will to suppress the urge to drag her from the room by her towering hair.

Something in her tone caused Maxine's smirk to wobble. 'I only meant, the races ain't meant to mix. Everyone knows that. And if you break the rules, gotta expect there to be consequences. Says so in the Bible. Ain't nothin' personal,' she added with a shrug.

A vision came to her, of John's bruised and bleeding body ringed by white robes. A fountain of rage surged up, up and sent a jolt of pure fire through her arm. She slapped Maxine hard across the face. 'There! That was nothing personal!'

With a gasp, Maxine toppled backwards onto the floor, legs pedalling the air. 'You crazy bitch!'

'Have you lost your mind, Miss Pearl?' Kitty bent to help Maxine right herself.

'It was you!' Alicia cried. 'You told them!'

Maxine held a hand to her cheek. 'Told 'em what?' Shock and fury in her eyes . . . and confusion.

Alicia continued, carried on by the momentum of the slap that left her hand stinging and her breath coming fast. It felt good, very good to see the glow of her palm's red imprint on Maxine's pale face. 'Ever since I came here,' she panted, 'you have been waiting for your chance. And last night, you took it. You told the Klan about Thomas, you told them where to find John's gun. Admit it! You told them everything!' Her hand drew back to strike again, but Hortensia blocked it with a sturdy forearm streaked with silver burn marks.

Alicia struggled against her. 'Let me go! How could you,

Maxine? How could you do this?' Nearly choking on the tears, she demanded, 'How could you?' Hortensia held her fast. Alicia leaned into her grip as her knees began to shake. 'How could you?'

'I didn't do nothin!' spat Maxine. 'But I sure as hell wish now that I did!'

'You LIE!'

'Miss Alicia!' Dwayne's voice behind her. 'She's tellin' the truth.'

Alicia spun to see him in the doorway, with a tight grip on Paulina's arm. He shoved her into the room. 'Go on. Tell her.'

'Paulina?' Alicia said, and pushed the hair out of her eyes, breathless and disorientated.

Paulina said nothing, just glowered at Dwayne.

'She was the one,' he said. 'She gave the Klan what they needed. She came to me because she figured I'd put in a good word for her.'

Alicia's hand groped for the back of a chair to steady herself. 'Paulina? *Es verdad*? Is this true?'

'*Sí*, it is true!'

Scorn twisted Paulina's face into an unrecognisable shape. She had been Alicia's ally from the start, the one whom she counted on to help keep the others in line. Cheerful, compliant Paulina, always willing, never any trouble. In some ways, she was the closest thing Alicia had to a friend. Winded by the betrayal, she put a hand to her chest. Her heart thrashed like a terrified animal inside the cage of her ribs.

'But why? Why would you do such a . . . such a terrible thing? Have I not been good to you?'

'Yes, and all was fine until *he* ruined it.'

'What? I do not—'

'You made this into the kind of house I dreamed of. I would have stayed until I was too old and ugly, because this is what I do. I am not a waitress,' and here she glared at Kitty, 'I am a whore, and a good one. He took you away from us, from where you belong. I wanted to go back to how things were, before.' Her mouth lifted in a half-smile. 'And now, we can.'

Despair seeped into her body, starting with her fingertips. It travelled along her limbs to spread through her bones and blood vessels, leaving an awful numbness in its wake.

'Oh, Paulina,' she sighed. 'I thought . . . I thought I was making things better. And he did not take me away. All he did was . . . love me. And they nearly killed him for it last night.'

'I did not know . . . I just . . .' Paulina blinked. Colour and defiance drained from her face. 'I—'

'You must go now,' Alicia said.

She nodded and, without another word, left the room. Alicia heard the front door close. Maxine righted herself and followed before Alicia had a chance to say a word.

Hortensia released her hold and removed the cold coffee. 'I will get you some fresh.'

'No,' said Alicia, 'I must go next door and check John's wounds.' She bent to assess the contents of her bag.

But when she looked up, it was clear no one was listening, because all eyes were focused on a column of black smoke several streets away, climbing higher than any of the surrounding buildings to sully the serene blue of the sky. A fire engine's klaxon shattered the stillness.

'Where is it?' she asked, leaning out of the window for a better view.

The breeze carried the smell of smoke and sounds of voices raised in alarm. Pablito swerved from his dish of sugar water and chirruped before diving deep into the stand of bamboo.

Felix appeared beside her. Taller than the rest, he narrowed his eyes and said, 'It's the church, St Cecilia's.'

Now she could see it clearly, the church spire atop its white pinnacle. It gleamed within whorls of smoke, which rose higher and higher until they dimmed the sun. For a few minutes, it looked like the spire would escape. Then more smoke billowed up, great angry gushes of it, followed by a booming crash which shook the window glass. When the smoke cleared, the spire was gone.

Around Alicia, a series of sighs, and then silence as more and more of the blue turned to grey. She picked up her bag. Dwayne still hovered in the doorway. 'Can I . . . can I come with you? I won't get in the way. I just want to . . . to pay my respects.'

He looked so hopeful, so keen to make things right. She doubted that was possible, but appreciated his desire to try.

'Yes, but you must not disturb him if he still sleeps.'

Thomas met them at the door of the bar, eyes frantic. 'He ain't up there. I was just comin' to find you. He went for a piss, I told him to take the Colt, because you cain't be too careful. But I just come from the outhouse, and he ain't there neither.'

'When did he go outside?'

'Fifteen minutes ago, thereabouts. When the church caught fire.'

'Ay, no, no, no.' Alicia walked in tight circles, cursing herself, cursing him. She should have realised, should never have left him alone. 'He cannot have gone far.'

'When he's a mind to do somethin',' said Thomas, 'won't let a little thing like gettin' beat near to death hold him back.'

'But where would he go?' asked Dwayne.

'He's goin' after your Klan pals, who did the beatin'.' Waves of anger radiated from Thomas's powerful body. He moved towards Dwayne, enormous hands flexing, each one easily capable of throttling Dwayne on its own. His eyes, filled with mortal hurt, sized Dwayne up. 'This your fault.'

Alicia stepped between them. 'Dwayne is sorry, Thomas. He knows he was wrong.'

'I am sorry,' said Dwayne, his voice barely a croak. 'So sorry. I want to help. Please, let me help.'

'Too late for that. You told 'em,' growled Thomas, 'you told 'em where to find the Colt.'

She laid a hand on his arm, which felt almost hot to the touch. 'No, Thomas. That was not Dwayne. It was one of my girls, Paulina. Think, Thomas. He will be found sooner with more of us looking. Where would he go first?'

With an obvious effort at control, he closed his eyes for a moment. 'John say them that beat him is respectable men of the town, so we try the whorehouses first, then the bars.'

John had to walk to the end of Tamarind Street to find a taxi. The road was busy, with cigar workers streaming from Gato's factory at the end of the working day, mingling with the vendors and automobiles. The exhaust made him cough, which created constellations of pain all over his body. The desecration of the burning church had brought him from his bed. Every step felt like a knife thrust in his back, but he kept going, driven on by the *haw-haw-haw* of Donkey Hightower's laugh echoing on and on in his head. Half-crazed by the pain, senses jumbled, the only clear image that emerged was of Donkey looming over him to swing his bat again and again, laughing. He had laughed too when he shoved Alicia into the wall, and now that grating bray was trapped in his head, drowning out all other sound. John harnessed the pain to fashion it into fiery determination. In his mind, Donkey became the focus for all the wrongs done to him, and his town. As the smoke from St Cecilia's spiralled into the sky, he swore to make Donkey stop laughing, if it took his last breath.

'Where you want to go, *señor*?' asked the driver, with a strong Spanish accent. The card on the dashboard said 'Jorge Martel'.

'House of Eve, Jorge, and there's an extra quarter in it if you make it fast.'

Jorge's eyes in the rear-view mirror took in the wounds on his face, his crouched posture and laboured breathing. 'You sure you no want me take you to hospital?

'Just drive.'

They turned into Duval Street, where the fire engines still clustered around the smoking carcass of St Cecilia, a scorched, trampled nativity scene arrayed on the lawn in front. The air was thick with burning. Jorge crossed himself and muttered, 'What son-of-a-whore would do this? In twenty years, never have I seen such a thing. This town is changing.'

'I got a pretty good idea, Jorge. And I aim to change it back.'

The car stopped in front of the House of Eve and John levered himself onto the street. 'Wait for me, Jorge. I won't be long.'

Eve came out to the porch as he made his slow progress up the steps. With a rueful glance, she tutted, 'Is this the *grand soldat*, come back for his free treat? I think not. This man belongs in a hospital bed, not a whore's bed.'

He leaned on the porch rail to catch his breath. 'Eve, I got business with one of your regulars. Step aside.'

'This is Eve's house. You have no business here.' Arms on hips, she blocked his path, easily six inches taller than him in her heels. On a good day, he would have struggled to take her down. This was not a good day.

He removed the Colt from his pocket. 'Eve, step aside. I'll get what I came for, and be on my way.'

She threw back her head and laughed, earrings like mini chandeliers swinging at her throat. '*Merde*! You think you are the first one to point a gun in Eve's face?' But her eyes flicked sideways, just once, and that was when he heard the back door slam, followed by the slap-slap of running feet. A car engine ground to life on the street behind the house.

John flung himself back down the steps and into Jorge's cab, gasping with the effort and pain. 'Round the back! Go round the back, now!'

They entered the side street just in time for John to glimpse Donkey behind the wheel, leaning forward as if to draw more horsepower from the car's engine as he turned onto Duval.

'Get alongside him!'

'*Señor*, I am not—'

'Just DO it!'

John rolled down the window. Wounds forgotten, pain a dim memory, every drop of energy went into his eyes and hands. His mind felt so clear, like it was filled with mountain air. An image of Donkey's face above him, red against the white of his robe, swinging a baseball bat above his head, again and again. He thought of Alicia, her lovely features taut and lined with worry, her eyes constantly on the door. All his training, all his experience, all his skill had been building to this one moment. Power flowed through him, every instinct tuned and ready.

Jorge's cab gained on Donkey's car, and for a fragment of a second, the two cars aligned.

The shot entered the back of Donkey's head to splatter the windscreen red. His car slammed into a lamp post with a shriek of metal and shattering glass, his body slumped over the steering wheel. Steam whistled from the broken radiator.

The Colt's report in the enclosed space made John's ears ring. The cab filled with the stench of cordite.

'*Madre de Dios*!' shouted Jorge as he braked hard, throwing John against the front seat. Pain surged back, wave after wave of it, enough to drown a man. He groaned, eyes closed, tried to breathe and waited for release.

'Get out! Get out of my cab!' Jorge's head swung from John, to the wreck of Donkey's car, and back again. 'Get out!'

On the pavement, a crowd began to cluster. A woman in a floral dress screamed, 'Someone call a doctor!'

'No point,' said another voice, belonging to a rotund man in a good suit. He removed his straw boater and placed it over his heart.

Jorge yanked open the cab door and pulled him out. As John leaned against the car, panting and holding his side, the eyes of the crowd turned on him. In them he saw shock, horror, excitement. Women covered their children's faces. It was only then he became aware of the Colt's weight, still in his hand.

'He did it!' shouted another man, skinny and sun-burned, with only a few teeth. 'I seen it all!'

A siren keened in the distance, high and insistent, and then another.

Duval was busy. Under normal circumstances, John would have easily melted into the crowd and made his way through the alleys and side streets. But not this time. The reports from his muscles and bones confirmed that running was not an option.

On the next corner, only a few feet away, was the Poblano building, topped by a high cupola with a good view of the whole street. It was the hour of dusk when light turns soft and shimmery, and outlines become blurred, which he reckoned would give him just enough cover to make it over there.

What he would do once inside was a complete mystery.

The first rule of soldiering, as he knew well, was never to enter a building without a clear exit.

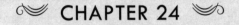

CHAPTER 24

John completed his slow climb up to the cupola to lean against a post, waiting for his breath to come, for the red spots to clear from his eyes, for his legs to stop shaking. The beating he received at the hands of the Klan had taught him a lot. He was now an expert in the different ways a body could hurt: the sharp stab of broken skin, the throb of joints wrenched from sockets, the deep ache of bruised organs. Each had a different character, each inspired a different dread. His body had never let him down before, not even through the worst punishments of the war, but there were clear signals that the end of its endurance was not far away.

From his vantage point, the whole town was laid out in front of him like a beautiful quilt, with its neat grid of streets, orderly houses and businesses. Ahead of him was the southernmost point, and the cove where he had taught Alicia to swim. To the east, he could just make out the weathered rooftop of The Last Resort, with the Tea Room tucked in beside it. The fishing boats were gliding out of the docks, lanterns bobbing, in search of the sweet, pink shrimp that only came out at night. On this short winter day, yellow lights showed in a few windows, where Christmas trees twinkled. It all looked so peaceful, even serene, with a spectacular sunset unfolding above Mallory Square. And where the streets ran out, at all points of the compass, there was the deep denim blue of the sea washing the shores of The Rock. The only thing which marred the scene was the dirty smoke that still hovered in the sky above St Cecilia's.

This is my town.

In the fading light, he searched for her among the faces in the crowd. Duval thronged with spectators now, their excited chatter rising up to him on the cool breeze. He counted ten police officers, plus several other armed men who he guessed to be Klan members. It almost looked like a party in progress; with a wry grimace, he realised in some ways, it was. The locals loved nothing more than a good drama. They would be talking about this night for a long, long time.

He couldn't find her, in the shifting mass of people. Whatever happened next, he needed to see her.

A shot pinged off the post next to his head, followed by a bellow like the sound of an enraged buffalo. He peered over the balustrade to see Thomas pummelling a police officer, on the ground with his hands over his face. It took three of his comrades to pull Thomas away, who then disappeared beneath a flurry of kicks and curses.

'Stop!' A woman's voice. 'Let him go!'

'Alicia!' John cried, waving. He stood up longer than he should have, willing his eyes to capture her image. There she was, a pure light in the dullness of dusk. A bullet thwacked into the post by his shoulder.

'John!' she called, her voice broken with sadness, 'Thomas is . . . I think . . .'

'No!' He fired into the huddle of blue uniforms again and again, until he heard the *click click* of the empty chamber. The returning shower of bullets covered him in shards of wood. One grazed his ear, coating his cheek with warm blood that felt like tears.

A cry came from below: 'Cullen's hit!'

Winded, he sank behind the balustrade. *That's for you, Thomas.*

A man's voice rose up, sounding strange and tinny. 'John Morales! This is Chief Baxter! We know you're out of ammo, so just come on down, and we'll talk this through like civilised people!'

John shouted back, 'I don't think so, Chief! I ain't healed yet from our conversation the other night!'

A short silence.

'Well, then, what's your plan, John? We got all the time in the world to wait you out down here.'

He stretched his legs, the useless Colt in his lap, and leaned his head back to think it through. Up until this point in his life, he had always been able to fight his way out of every tight spot, even when outgunned and outnumbered. All through the war, through the fields and forests, the devastated towns and villages, Lightning Jack had been able to count on his wits and his reflexes to make it through. *Well*, he thought, *my reflexes are shot to hell, but I still got my wits*. The first star appeared in the sky, right where the fading day met the arriving night. Never a believer in signs, it did give him an idea.

'I'll surrender to Sheriff Torrance, no one else!' he called. 'Get Catcher Torrance, and I'll come down.'

He and Miles 'Catcher' Torrance had joined up at the same time, and went through basic training together. Miles was older and already Deputy Sheriff, but still determined to do his part. They had shared a berth on the long Atlantic crossing, during which time John had been impressed with Miles' strength of character and ability to keep his mouth shut. The story went that a grenade landed in his foxhole and Miles, being a keen baseball player, threw it back. Another landed and he tried the same thing, but with less success. He lost an arm but earned himself the nickname 'Catcher'. On his return home, John had heard of Miles' promotion and raised a glass to him.

Shuffling sounds reached him from the street below, and then through the megaphone again came Baxter's exasperated voice: 'You'll come down for Torrance?'

'I will!' John shouted.

He didn't have a high opinion of law men generally, as a result of tangling with a few like Baxter, whose morals were lower than a snake's asshole; Miles at least tried to live up to the promise of the star he wore.

He settled down as best he could, to watch the sky, and wait.

On the ground, Dwayne strained for a glimpse of John up in the tower. The lights and decorations sparkled in the shop windows, everyone on their way home with last-minute presents and food for their families. Christmas Eve. He should be with Ma, watching her baste the baked ham with molasses, helping her peel the yams, stir the black-eyed peas. No conch and grits on this special night. He was now tall enough to set the angel on top of the tree without a lift from Pa. It was his favourite night of the whole year, which he looked forward to as soon as the summer heat loosened its grip. All that anticipation kind of spoiled Christmas Day itself, truth be told. He was always left feeling a little flat and disappointed. It was Christmas Eve that held the promise of magic.

And yet here he was, out on the street with half the town it seemed, everyone clutching packages, the atmosphere anything but festive.

The police still had their guns trained on the cupola, as did a bunch of others he recognised as Klansmen. He willed John to keep his head down, because he didn't trust them not to just pop him, for the hell of it.

Miss Alicia wept beside him without making a sound, just steadily. They had taken Thomas away. If anything, the crowd had grown in size, people leaning from windows, climbing lamp posts for a better view. From the comments swirling around him, the consensus was that John didn't deserve what was going on, but for sheer entertainment value, it was hard to beat.

He wanted to comfort Miss Alicia but didn't know what to do or say. Then she kind of leaned into him and his arm went round her, on its own, and he stood like that, her hair brushing his cheek. It seemed important to remain perfectly still, and so he did, while his arm gradually went numb and his feet started to hurt, but then her shoulders stopped shaking and he figured that was worth any discomfort.

A car arrived, and out stepped a man, lean and weathered as a strip of beef jerky. One sleeve of his sheriff's uniform was empty. He approached Chief Baxter and there followed a short conversation.

The sheriff took the megaphone from Chief Baxter. 'John, it's Miles here! You sure got yourself in a pickle!'

'I know, Catch!' came the reply. 'But I'm damned glad to see ya!'

'Come on down now! I guarantee your protection, but you know I got to take you in!'

'I do! And I trust you to keep those monkeys from gettin' too excited!'

Torrance swept the vicinity with a stern glance and barked at those with weapons drawn, 'Get back, all of you, back across to the other side of the street.' Pointing at the nearest Klansman, he said, 'And I tell you this, in case you're wonderin': ain't nothin' wrong with my gun hand. I swear, anyone who lets off a shot will get one from me.'

A silence, heavy with expectation, settled on the crowd. The street door of the building opposite creaked open and John emerged, hands aloft. There was a communal exhalation from the spectators, and Dwayne realised he had been holding his breath too.

With a cry of, 'John!', Alicia lunged forward. Half a dozen men swung their guns in her direction. Dwayne blocked her with his body, arms spread, adrenalin coursing through him so fast that it felt like there was a racehorse trapped in his chest.

'Alicia, I'm fine!' John called, walking slowly towards them. 'Just be calm. Don't want to give these fellas any excuse.'

He reached the kerb, where Alicia rushed to him and flung her arms about his neck. He whispered into her hair and took something from his pocket, which he pressed into her hand.

Torrance gave him a set of handcuffs. 'Do me a favour, John, put these on.'

John obliged. Dwayne stayed focused on Torrance, the first sheriff he had seen. He carried himself with such poise and assurance, clearly not the least encumbered by his horrific injury. The badge on his chest glinted under the street lamp. Just being in his presence made Dwayne feel better, for the first time in days. Torrance made it seem like things would be all right, like he could be trusted to do what was right, whatever malign craziness was breaking out around him. It wasn't righteousness, not that, but something better, and this caused Dwayne to remember his last view of Pa, wild-eyed, enraged and spitting.

Torrance marched John to the waiting car. 'Time to go.'

Alicia clung to John. 'Please, Sheriff, what will happen now?'

Torrance said, 'I'm takin' him to the jail, where he'll stay until we figure out which of his many crimes he'll be tried for.' He put John in the back seat.

'And he'll be . . . safe there?' Dwayne asked.

For a moment, it seemed that Torrance would just brush by without an answer, but he turned to say, 'Son, I got a detail of Marines comin' over from the base tonight for reinforcements. No one's gonna get past them. You can count on that.'

Alicia asked. 'May I come . . . visit him there?'

Torrance took an instant to make up his mind. 'Tomorrow. You can visit tomorrow. Let's go.' He rapped on the car's roof and took the passenger seat.

The engine started. Alicia remained by John's window, like she was waiting for the answer to a question. The reflection of the street lamps obscured his face.

As full dark descended, Dwayne stood with her and watched the sheriff's car drive away.

Back in their bed at The Last Resort, Alicia curled round herself, with the toy soldier clutched in her fist. His rifle pierced the skin of her palm and she welcomed the pain. It was so quiet. Although Thomas had never made a sound when he slept downstairs, his solid presence had filled out the air somehow. When he had fallen beneath the policemen's feet, she had tried to pull them off, but they were too strong and too many. He lay motionless on the ground until they took him away. It seemed no more possible that he was gone than if a chunk of The Rock itself had fallen into the sea. Without him, the stillness was so empty, it was like the place had been derelict for years.

Dwayne had wanted to take up Thomas's post outside her door, but she had sent him back to the Tea Room. He had done his best, throughout the day, to redeem himself. At some point, he would have to go back to his family, but she hadn't the heart to send him away just yet. He had faced down his own father and a troop of armed Klansmen, well on his way to becoming a fine young man . . . the kind of person his mother could be proud of.

She had never felt so alone.

The circle of yellow light made an island of the bed, afloat alone on a charcoal sea. Hortensia had urged her to stay in her old room, just for the night, but she would not sleep, and she had an animal need to be surrounded by traces of him. Pressing her face into his pillow, where the scent of his hair oil was strongest, she drew him deep into her lungs. The sheets smelled of him too, and she wrapped herself in them, tight. The mattress was imprinted with his shape, marked with faint brownish smears from his wounds. She laid herself down inside the outline of his body and stared out of the bare window.

The sky offered no comfort on this moonless night. He would be in a cell by now, which she knew neither frightened nor troubled him much, given his past wrangles with the law. Had this been Cuba, and him taken away by armed police, she would have been in desperate fear for his life. She would be at the jail even now, as people did back home, keeping vigil over their loved ones.

But this was America. That sheriff, Torrance, had seemed straight and upstanding, and John certainly trusted him. From everything she knew of American justice, his punishment would take into account the attack by the Klan, especially once John identified two of the men involved.

She could hear John's voice, as clearly as if his head rested on the pillow next to hers, his hair like an ink blot on the white cotton. 'I'm gonna be fine, darlin'. Torrance is a good guy, and no one's gettin' past a bunch of Marines. Those are some tough sons-of-bitches, make me look like a babe in arms.'

She pictured him, inside his concrete box with the metal bars, surrounded by a team of soldiers bristling with weapons. Only a few hours to wait. They would pass more quickly if she occupied her mind. *I will think about where we will go when he is free.*

Yes, the waiting would be hard. Very hard. But she had the skills and means to sustain herself. However far in the future, she would be waiting, and then they would leave, sell up the businesses and buy a boat to sail around the islands until they found a home. They would open another bar, on a beach this time, far away from the white-robed preachers of hate and their disciples, and the insanity of Prohibition and the sound of smashing bottles. And they would toast their good fortune at the end of every day, by the light of the tropical sunset. She saw pale brown children, with grey eyes and black hair, running naked in the sand, coconut palms swaying overhead.

I will see you tomorrow, mi amor.

It was still *Nochebuena,* the night before Christmas. How was this possible? she wondered. How could a single day last so long? They had woken together and now they were apart, almost certainly for a considerable amount of time. Back in Havana, Papa and Mamacita would be at the traditional neighbourhood feast, with the spit-roasted hog. It was almost midnight, when everyone would stagger down the road, singing, to mass, for candles and hymns and the blessings of a benevolent God.

Never devout as such, nonetheless during the long stand-off on Duval Street she had found herself praying more fervently than ever before, hands clutched in supplication: *Please, Father, keep him safe. That is all. I want nothing else, ever.*

And it had worked, she had been heard. John had come out of that building unhurt, and handed himself over to the people bound to protect him.

A clock chimed midnight.

Her hand had warmed the tin soldier to blood temperature.

Tomorrow is today. I will see you soon, mi amor, *very soon.*

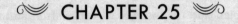 CHAPTER 25

KEY WEST, 1993

Alicia waits in her cell, the ivory handbag snug against her belly. Frigid air pours out of the vent, carrying the metallic tang of disinfectant. She wraps the blanket round her shoulders and suppresses a sneeze. Seated on the bench against the wall, her feet don't reach the floor. Still, her first experience of a jail cell could be worse. *It was worse for you, mi amor, was it not?* Her hand slips into the bag, her fingers sift the familiar detritus until they close on their quarry, heavier than the rest. She doesn't need to bring it into the light. Her hand knows every part of the toy soldier, now a dull pewter, its bright colours long burnished away. It waits there, among the tissues and cough drop wrappers and pennies and lint. As always, it soothes her to have it nestled inside her fist.

For all the years spent wondering how it would feel, she had been unprepared for the moment when it came. She had been walking through the park that morning, oblivious to the Klan rally until she found herself in the midst of it. White robes shone against the green field, pointed hats waving under the bright sunshine. In a panic of horrified disorientation, she had frozen, barely able to breathe, swamped by the tide of memories. She had willed her heart to keep beating, if only to deny them the satisfaction of having her drop dead during their party.

And that was when she heard his name.

One of the young acolytes in white bent to an ancient figure in a wheelchair and asked, 'Mr Simpkins, can I get you a Coke?'

The pounding in her head had stopped.

He was an old man now, of course he was, with big wraparound sunglasses beneath his hood, which together almost completely covered his shrunken tortoise face. His hunched body was of child's proportions, engulfed by the white robe.

His pitiful shape had threatened to derail her on the way back from collecting the Colt. Its insistent weight prodded her hip with every step, making her question once again if there was any point. It had been so long, so many years gone. A lifetime had passed. Her resolve had wavered, her steps faltered. So she forced herself to call it up, the memory most sacred and most feared: the full agony of the last time she saw John. And that had been enough to bring her back in front of the wheelchair to ask his name.

'Charlie Simpkins.' His pointy chin tilted up. In his lap, a pair of fine gloves. 'Who's asking?'

'Charlie "Bucket" Simpkins?' Her knees had begun to wobble. She gripped the buttonwood cane.

'Mr Simpkins to you.' And then he whispered, 'Brown.'

She only heard the last word thanks to the fancy hearing aids she had treated herself to on her eightieth birthday.

All these years, she had wondered if it would be hard, when

the time came, but it had been easy, shockingly so, to put her cane down and aim the gun with both hands at the circular emblem embroidered on his robe, right over his heart. His sunglasses had deprived her of his last expression, so she would never know if he had felt fear or surprise or anything else when the bullet tore through his thin old flesh, and shattered his fragile old bones. He had made a sound like 'Whoof!' and slumped sideways, a red bloom on his chest that grew and grew. She had stared at it, mesmerised, ears ringing.

More shocking than the ease of taking a life had been how she felt afterwards, as the police swarmed over her and the Klansmen roared at her and spectators and TV cameras took pictures of her. She had expected to feel some release, some relief now it was done, now the burden was gone from her shoulders. She had always imagined it would be different, once the scales of the universe were balanced; but it had eluded her, eluded her still, that sense of peace she had expected to feel when he was gone from the earth.

Now she feels nothing, nothing at all. Her eyes travel around the cell. This is the kind of featureless box where she could spend the rest of her days. Under the fluorescent lights, everything is washed to shades of concrete.

She turns to see Meredith enter, coffee cup in hand. *She is just doing her job.* But Alicia has no intention of giving up her bag while she has breath in her body. Her hand grips the soldier tighter, welcomes the sting of its rifle tip in her palm, where a faint scar still shows.

Meredith sets the cup on the table. 'Are you cold, *Señora* Cortez?'

'You know my name, then.'

'Yes, I worked it out.'

Smart girl.

'Your public defender is in the building, you'll see him soon. I'll get them to turn down the AC. They keep this place like a polar bear's—' She stops, blushing.

'Asshole?'

A burst of laughter escapes Meredith. She attempts to regain her composure. 'Indeed.' She sits on the bench next to Alicia. The lenses of her glasses are so thick, her eyes look enormous. Hands folded, one knee crossed over the other, she takes a big breath and opens her mouth.

Before she can speak, Alicia says, 'Meredith, I watch a lot of television. People my age do, you know.'

'Yes, but what—?'

'I love police dramas. They are my favourite. *Magnum, P.I.*, *Law and Order*, *Cagney and Lacey*. I tell you this so you know: I understand the process ahead of me.'

'I see.' She nods.

'You are going to tell me it is different in real life.'

'It is, yes.'

She has a pretty smile.

'If it were up to me,' says Meredith, 'you could keep the bag. I don't let mine out of my sight either, but Chief Campbell says—'

'Campbell? I have not heard that name for . . . a long time.' Everything around her shimmers. Images from seventy years ago flicker at the corner of her vision. Her hand tightens its grip on the toy soldier. 'I wonder, what does his father do?'

Roy studies the public defender across his desk. Kyle 'Snow-bird' Loughlin hails from so far north he might as well be Canadian, hence his nickname. Although he is blessed with old money and an Ivy League law degree, he has ended up defending the defenceless. The scuttlebutt says he was disinherited from the family practice. Roy isn't interested in the reason for Kyle's career choice, just glad to have his sharp mind on this particular case.

Kyle looks up from his notes. 'You were saying, Chief, that since her confession she has refused to speak? To be clear, all she has said is, "I did it. It was me." Nothing about premeditation?'

'Nothing. We didn't ask, she didn't say.' It was to *Señora* Cortez's advantage that she had kept her mouth shut. 'She went before Judge Mander today. She's charged with murder-two, bail denied.'

It was good to have Mander on the bench. He was past the ambitious stage of his judgeship, when everything was about the next election. He had nothing to prove, had tried enough high-profile cases that he didn't need this one to build his career.

'So I gathered. And how is her health?' asked Kyle.

'The doc checked her over last night, couldn't find anything to worry about except her blood pressure, not surprisingly. He left some meds.' In fact, the doctor had told Roy she was in better physical shape than he was. 'She doesn't seem scared or anxious, according to my sergeants, just resigned. She sits in the cell and waits for whatever's coming. And holds on to her bag like it's a life preserver from the *Titanic*.'

'Hmm.' Loughlin makes a note. 'What's your view of her mental state?'

'My gut tells me competence isn't going to be an issue.'

'I'll decide whether to call in the psychiatrist once I've interviewed her. There's a strong smell of crazy in what she did. That might be the best outcome for all concerned.'

Roy notes some southern inflections finally taking root in Kyle's speech. He leans forward onto his elbows. 'What do you know about Alicia Cortez?'

'Only what's in the case file.'

'You need to read up on the local history. I did as well, not being from around these parts. She lived here in 1919, with a man called John Morales. He was white.'

'I'm something of a history buff myself, mostly medieval Europe, but what's that got to do with yesterday?'

Roy can feel Kyle itching to move on. 'This was during the Jim Crow years. It would have been illegal for her, as a mixed race woman, to have a relationship with a white man. Plenty of it went on, of course, but never in public.'

'I get it, they broke the rules. Where is this leading, Chief? I need to see my client.'

'The Klan set up shop here during that time, and made an example of Morales when he wouldn't give her up.' He takes a sip of coffee. It's cold and bitter. 'I did a little digging. The man she murdered today, Charlie Simpkins, known as "Bucket" in the day, held the office of Kleagle for the Klan of the Keys, which was like a local organiser in their stupid lingo.'

He watches the wheels turn in Kyle's brain. He's smart, if a little impatient. Roy remembers himself at that age, always in a hurry. Nowadays he mostly hurries only to the bathroom in the middle of the night.

Kyle sits back, shakes his head and closes his notebook. 'I

understand now what you meant about competence. Thank God she's refused to say anything more.'

'Exactly. My suggestion is to head over to the library before you talk to her. That is, of course, if she's willing to say anything.'

'Thanks, Chief, I will.'

Kyle stands and turns to go just as Meredith raps on the door and enters.

'Chief, I – oh, sorry, Snowb— I mean, Mr Loughlin.'

Roy says, 'Meredith, I've just been filling Kyle in on the background to the case.'

'Something happened, Chief, just now, when I took her a drink. She's changed her mind about talking. Not to you, Mr Loughlin.' She shoots him an apologetic glance. 'There's only one person she'll talk to.'

Roy crosses his arms over his belly. 'Well, I suppose that's some kind of progress . . . but please, tell me it's not Oprah.'

'No, sir, not Oprah.' Her fish eyes blink once, twice. Her voice drops. 'The only person she'll talk to, Chief, is your dad.'

Thirty miles to the north, Dwayne sits on the edge of his bed, then stands up and walks around the room, then sits again. The phone call from Roy has obliterated his usual routine and he doesn't have the first idea what to do with himself. He would usually take a walk at this time of day, past the hurricane memorial and down to the beach for a game of chequers with one of the guys.

A change of clothes, he thinks, yes, that's the first order of business. But when he goes to the wardrobe, nothing seems right, these old man clothes, so he stands there and stares, his head fizzing with Roy's news.

Hearing her name again, after all these years, and under such circumstances, the past overwhelms him, until he feels so breathless, he has to sit again on the bed, and hold his head. *Bet my pacemaker is working double-time.*

So she has finally done it, what she had promised to do the very last time he had seen her, on that awful morning over seventy years ago. From what Roy had said, it looked like the Klan rally in Bayview Park had something to do with it. His son was on the right track, but he didn't have all the facts the history books left out.

Nor did he know his father's part in bringing about her crime at the park.

'By God, you did it, Miss Alicia,' he says out loud. 'You actually did it.'

It would come out, at last. Dwayne is glad of it. Roy said she has refused to speak to anyone but him, which Dwayne gathers has been more than a little frustrating. Roy is on his way to Heron Key to pick him up and drive him back to Key West, to help put the pieces together. And on the drive down there, along the highway beside the decapitated pylons of the old Florida East Coast Railway, he will finally share with his son the story he has kept locked away for so long.

And then, he realises, things could get really interesting. It will depend on whether the state takes the view that he was an accessory to the crime in any way, and that decision could hang on what his son decides to do with the information.

He turns back to the wardrobe and snatches a shirt at random, arthritic fingers fumbling with the buttons. In the mirror, a glimpse of his bald, age-spotted head brings him up short.

I look like a Galapagos tortoise.

She would still be beautiful, of that he is sure. He allows himself to relive his first glimpse of her, that summer day in 1919, on the dock when she appeared off the Havana ferry, so fresh in her green dress. And so sad.

He had tried to find her again, several times over the years, even calling in favours with someone who worked on the police database, but in the end concluded she didn't want to be found.

The shirt is wrong. He wrenches it off and grabs another, the white one he wears to church. He wonders whether he should wear a tie, a jacket. The AC in these stations is always ferocious. And he wants to look like a gentleman. But then he remembers he has only a black funeral tie left, which is called into service all too often nowadays. He opts for a blue sport coat which camouflages the worst of his gut. Turning left, then right in front of the mirror, he is satisfied for a moment, but then he pulls off the coat and shirt and throws them on the floor.

Here I am, worrying about what to wear, when she's locked up for a murder I helped her commit.

He goes to the window overlooking the ocean and stares at the surf. These days, the past is sometimes more real to him than the present, and he finds himself having more conversations with dead people than live ones. The view of his familiar beach dissolves into that other beach, and he is back there again, where it happened.

He had run all the way home, after they took John's body

away. A light rain was falling, more like a heavy mist, the droplets suspended in the air. They coated his face, masking the tears. It was an easy matter to retrieve the shotgun from the shed. Pa didn't know he'd seen him hide the key under the butter churn.

He and Ma were at the breakfast table when Dwayne burst in, gun raised. It was the first time he could remember ever surprising his father.

With a growl, Pa got to his feet. 'How dare you come here and threaten me with my own gun?'

Ma had cried out and tried to rush to him, but Pa blocked her.

Pa's voice had hummed in his good ear, the vibration travelling down his arms to his hands, which started to shake. Pa lunged forward, massive shoulders hunched.

'Stay back!'

But Pa had just roared with laughter. 'Oh, really? You gonna shoot me? Tell me, son: what did I do to deserve this insult, in the home where we raised you?'

Despite all the events of the past forty-eight hours, Dwayne felt like a little kid again. The smell of the coffee was so familiar, he wanted to sit down and drink a cup with a plate of Ma's buttermilk biscuits. Her eyes pleaded with him. He had missed her so much.

With a start, he raised the gun barrel again, trying not to stammer. 'You're gonna tell me . . . tell me who ordered it, what they did to Mr Morales. And then . . . all of you, everyone involved, you're gonna get . . . punished.' He despised the wobble in his voice, and clamped the gun stock harder under his arm.

'Well, how you gonna do that, boy? Tell the police? You're welcome to try. Or maybe point that shotgun in a few faces around town. I swear, it'll get you the same treatment that bastard got.'

'No!' Ma shoved her way to Dwayne's side. 'You will not allow them to harm him!'

'Just tell me who ordered it,' said Dwayne, 'and I'll go, and not embarrass you any more. Please, tell me.' He looked Pa right in the eyes. 'Was it the Wizard?'

Pa seemed utterly relaxed, perched on the edge of the kitchen table. He took up his coffee mug. 'You haven't paid attention to anything I've said, have you? Morales was a local problem, which required a local solution. And son,' he smiled, 'I'd have told you that without a gun in my face.'

Nausea boiled in his gut. Dwayne swallowed hard. 'Simpkins.'

'Now you're using your head.' Pa slapped his knee. 'Of course it was Charlie. He couldn't let that kind of disgrace go on, not under the Klan of the Keys charter. Now, son, you can holler and yell and carry on about vengeance or justice or whatever you want to call it, but I guarantee you this: nothing will come of it, except to make you a whole posse of powerful enemies. Do you see this town rising up in protest about what happened to Morales? You do not.'

Pa was right, and he knew it. Nothing would happen, nothing would change. Even if he went to the police, the Klan would find a way to buy the result they wanted. He was a fool to think he could stand up to Pa and his pals. He could never raise a hand to his father. He was weak, weak and pathetic, and always would be.

In disgust, as much at himself as at Pa, Dwayne tossed the gun onto the floor and turned to go.

The boom rattled the window glass, accompanied by a puff of grey smoke and a burned smell. Ma screamed and knelt by Pa, who had been blown off the table by the blast to land on his back. The shot had gone up right through his throat and out the top of his head, leaving a red starburst on the ceiling.

Ma rushed to Dwayne and hugged him tight. He closed his eyes, sure it was just a nightmare, but when he opened them, there was his father, sprawled before him. The impossible had happened: Pa was gone. The air felt charged with static electricity. Everything was different now. He wouldn't have been surprised to see the sky turn red and fish walk on the land.

A great pillar had toppled, leaving the world – his world – teetering on collapse.

He cain't be dead.

But he was, and it was all Dwayne's fault. Pa had fallen with arms splayed, in a grotesque parody of benediction, face frozen in astonishment. His coffee cup lay beside his cooling body.

Dwayne's legs wouldn't support him. He began to slide down the wall, but Ma pulled him up. 'We got to get out of here,' she said.

They had gone to Sheriff Torrance. After a careful examination of the scene, and hearing Ma's testimony, he had concluded Pa's death was a tragic accident and reported it as such to the inquest. Dwayne had Torrance to thank, not only for his lack of criminal record, but for encouraging him to choose a career in law enforcement.

Even after all these years, and all the things that have

happened since, the memory of that day still has the power to make Dwayne's knees wobble. He sits on the bed. Pa's death didn't break his hold over him, not in the least. In some ways, it made it stronger. For a long time after, he dominated Dwayne's dreams, berating him, quoting scripture in his resonant timbre, with a giant hole in his head.

Dwayne has never spoken about that day to anyone except Alicia. It was just one of the secrets that bound them together during that awful time. In the confusion after John's death, they had met once, as she was about to depart for Cuba. He had given her the only gift in his power – just a name – and watched her board the ferry for Havana, in the same green dress as her arrival, certain it would be the last time he would ever see her.

And now she was back, in the worst possible circumstances, because of his long-ago gift.

Roy's car pulls up to the carport. His son is the proudest accomplishment of Dwayne's life. Once the awful shock of Roy's birth had passed, and his peace made with it, he had resolved to be a better father to Roy than Pa had been to him. In most ways, he had succeeded, but there were chapters in his life he had never expected to share with Roy.

He puts on a plain T-shirt over his chinos and faces the mirror. When his heart started to go five years ago, it seemed like that would be it, but the pacemaker keeps it chugging along. Many times, more often as the years roll on, as friends and loved ones pass away, and his body deteriorates a little more each day, he has come to feel that he has lived too long.

But on this day, as he watches his son walk up the path towards the front door, he is very glad to be alive.

CHAPTER 26

'Hello, *Señora* Cortez, my name is Kyle Loughlin and I'll be representing you.' The harsh fluorescent lights of the interview room make him look older than his years. 'You've given a statement to the police and appeared before the judge charged with second-degree murder, bail denied. We're here today for you to tell me in as much detail as possible how you came to shoot Mr Simpkins in Bayview Park, after which you will be arraigned in the next twenty-one days. Are you comfortable? Any questions? Do you need anything before we start?'

Alicia settles into the hard chair of the interview room, handbag tucked between her ankles. At least it's a little warmer than the cell. Mr Loughlin seems like a nice young man, eager but not with that sweaty sheen of ambition so often seen on the upwardly mobile youth. The judge was nice too. Everyone had been nice since her arrest, despite the horrible mess she had created for them, but they all shared the same expression of puzzled angst, from the sergeants to the judge.

'Thank you. You can call me Alicia. I am fine. All I need is Dwayne Campbell.'

313

'He is en route. You understand, *Señora*— Alicia, I must be present when you talk with him?'

'I do. You will forgive me, please. My past experience with the law in this country has made me, shall we say . . . cautious.'

'Of course.' He straightens the pile of folders on the table with blunt, square fingers. On the left hand, a gold signet ring.

She studies that ring. *A young man from a good family, privileged even. He knows nothing of why I am here.* She composes her face into an expression of polite resignation.

His voice grows quieter, his gaze intent. 'The last time you saw John Morales alive, he was in the sheriff's custody, with a detail of Marines to protect him.'

Something is wrong with her eyes. The room suddenly seems terribly bright. She coughs. 'May I have some water, please?'

Pouring a cup from the jug on the table, he says, 'The library here has some good history books. It's kind of a hobby for me, digging through the past.' He puts down the jug. 'Alicia, are you all right?'

His voice carries a strange echo. Although the water takes away the dryness in her throat, it does nothing for the sudden vertigo. Her hands grip the metal edge of the table because the room is falling away, and then she is toppling backwards, over and over, out of control.

The lights go out.

We found you, Dwayne and I, at sunup on the beach where they left you. Oh, dear one, how they left you . . . broken, bloodied, shot to pieces. They had tried to hang you too, but the rope must have come loose in the night, because you lay at the base of the coconut palm. Your beautiful face, so smashed it was barely recognisable; the body that had given me so much pleasure, torn and riddled with too many bullets to count. Even so, my belief in you was so strong that I fell to my knees, searching for a sign, for any remaining spark, calling your name, over and over, pleading with you to stay, even just a moment longer. You were so powerful, and you had survived things that would destroy an ordinary man, I was certain that something of you must still remain. But I was too late . . . too late to save you, too late to tell you I loved you, or even to say good-bye. I gathered you to me and rocked you, my screams causing the birds to flee the trees. I stayed that way for a long time, as the rising sun revealed that they had killed you several times over. I lay down and wrapped myself around you, just like we used to sleep, and might have stayed there forever, if Dwayne had not brought help. They tried to pull me from you. Awash in your blood from head to foot, I fought them, I fought so hard to stay with you, like a mad woman I kicked and snarled and bit anyone who came near. I remember little else, except begging to be shot. Dwayne told me I shrieked vengeance on all involved. It was he who finally persuaded me to let you go. And it was he who gave me what I needed, to do what had to be done. And now, at last, it is done.

She wakes expecting to find herself on a patch of blood-stained sand, John's body cold in her arms. Standing over her are Mr Loughlin, and the chief, and an old man with lots of freckles and muddy green eyes. 'Dwayne,' she breathes, 'you came.' His whole face crumples into a smile of pure delight, and suddenly she sees him again, as the man-child of fourteen, so desperate to do the right thing. She focuses on his face, and the beating of her heart settles into a more comfortable rhythm.

Meredith kneels beside her with a first aid kit, hand to her wrist. 'Pulse coming down, thank the Lord. Doctor is on his way.'

'No need.' Alicia shifts up from her slumped position and wills the room to stop spinning. 'Please, let us carry on. All is well now.' She hears grains of time, slipping down, down.

Dwayne sits beside her and she grasps his hand. It is warm and dry, gnarled and covered in spots like hers. *We were young, so young.* With him at her side, her balance returns and breathing becomes easier. His presence makes her feel that, whatever happens, it will be for the best.

'Of course, I had to come,' says Dwayne, beaming. 'Look at you, still beautiful. How are you, Miss Alicia?'

'As well as can be expected. Thank you, for being here, my friend. And Chief Roy is your son? You must be very proud of him.'

'I am. But when did you—?'

The chief clears his throat. 'I'm sorry to intrude on y'all's reunion, but I'm afraid we've got to continue the interview. If *Señora* Cortez feels well enough, that is.'

Mr Loughlin says, 'I apologise for earlier, Alicia, if I said something to cause distress—'

She flaps at him. 'It is not your fault. I have not spoken of this for nearly seventy years, although I have thought of it every day. And hearing you say . . . his name, it just . . . brought back some memories, of that day.' *My life is now history, for others like this young man.*

Meredith and the chief step out and close the door with a quiet *click*.

Loughlin consults his notes. 'I realise this is upsetting for you, but we need to focus on the events of yesterday. My job is to negotiate the best position I can for you with the state attorney. I want to give the SA grounds to grant bail while the wheels turn, but I need your help. Is that all clear?'

'Yes, that is clear.'

He turns to Dwayne. 'I have to ask you, Mr Campbell, in what capacity are you here?'

'He is my friend,' she says, 'I trust him. And he was there, with me. He knows everything that happened.'

Dwayne squeezes her hand. 'I'm here to help, in any way I can.'

'And you're a retired sheriff? In Heron Key?'

'That's correct.'

'Hmm. Could be handy. Would you be willing to appear as a character witness?'

'Of course. Mr Loughlin, what do you think will happen?'

'That all depends on what I can tell the SA about Alicia's actions, and intentions yesterday. So please, Alicia, talk me through it, from the time you woke up, until your arrest. Start from the beginning. But before you start, I must ask Dwayne to step out. If we want him as a character witness, he's got to be free from any knowledge that could hurt your case.'

Dwayne scrapes his chair back, and with a squeeze of Alicia's shoulder, leaves the room.

Loughlin waits, pen poised.

'To start at the beginning,' she says, 'we need to go back to that Christmas Eve, so long ago . . .'

An hour later, and Loughlin seems ready to wrap things up but does not look happy. As Alicia related her story, the crease between his eyebrows had deepened further and further. He closes his folder and pulls his hands down his face. 'This is very important: everything you say to me stays between us. It must not leave this room, because if it does, we will have very few options. Alicia, you must never mention that you went back to collect the gun, because that is the definition of intent. That means—'

'Murder-one,' she says. 'I watch a lot of television.'

'Then you know you're into a whole different kind of problem, regardless of your age or situation.'

She gathers herself to say the thing that matters most, the thing she has been waiting all these years to say. 'Mr Loughlin, I appreciate your efforts, very much, but you must understand this: I stopped caring about what happens to me a long time ago. I killed Charlie Simpkins because he ordered John dragged from that jail and murdered. The law failed him, Mr Loughlin. No one was ever held to account, not then, and not now. I knew I was committing a crime, and I would be punished for it in a way they never were. So be it. I had the motive and the opportunity, and I went home to get the means. It does not make me happy, it does not make things right. But it had to be done.' She pauses for breath. 'Is it safe for Dwayne to come back?'

'Yes, I'll call him in, but Alicia,' he says, with a stern glance, 'it's very good that he left the room when he did.'

A moment later, Dwayne is beside her again.

Loughlin consults his notes with a rueful grimace. 'I've been back through the court records of the Morales case. A grand jury found only that "person or persons unknown" carried out the attack, and Morales was blamed for bringing the attack on himself.' He closes the folder. 'How I would have loved to be there back then, to do the right thing.'

'They would have killed you for it,' Dwayne says, with a slight shrug, 'or run you out of town. Just how it was, back then. But it's not too late now, for you to do the right thing.'

Alicia senses a shift in Loughlin's demeanour, like a small flame has come to life.

'You make a compelling case for clemency,' he says, 'which doesn't change the nature of your crime. I sincerely believe things have changed for the better. I will do my best to communicate the facts of your extraordinary story to the court.' He rubs his chin. 'One thing I'm still not clear on. How could you be certain Simpkins was responsible?'

'I told her,' said Dwayne. 'My pa held the office of chaplain of the Klan. I went to him, and persuaded him to divulge who ordered it.'

A pained expression from Loughlin. 'You must never volunteer that knowledge, or you'll be of no use to us. As far as the court is concerned, you're a dear, old friend and that is all.'

'I'm aware of that.' Dwayne continues, 'You've heard of Sheriff Miles Torrance? No? Well, he was a wise lawman, and maybe the only honest one on duty that night. It haunted him until the end of his days, what the Klan did to his prisoner. I never forgot something he told me, which was his sanity check, if you like, when a murder such as this was committed. He said, you got to ask two questions: Did the right person die? And did the right person do the killing? Try askin' yourself those questions, Mr Loughlin, and see where that leads.'

A week later, Roy takes up his pen to make what is perhaps the most important signature of his career. Loughlin has persuaded the judge to grant bail with house arrest, with a very unusual condition: that Alicia Cortez remain at her home until the arraignment, accompanied at all times by retired Sheriff Dwayne Campbell. Sergeant Big Mike is on his way with Dwayne to pick up some things.

On the drive back from Heron Key with his dad, each passing island, like a pearl against the blue, had been accompanied by a disclosure of something new about Dwayne, and his family, and himself. Some of the story had shocked him, but so many things had fallen into place, things he had wondered about his whole life, like what really happened to Grandpa and Grandma Campbell, and why Dwayne had left Key West.

He has always respected his father, but now he feels he knows him.

The press, locally and even nationally, are hailing the case as a victory for common sense, and a validation of the modern judiciary. In his office, surrounded by boxes stacked and ready for removal, the high point of Roy's long career comes just as the sun sets on it. Clarisse is now the toast of the bridge club, happier than he has ever seen her.

He adds his name to the release authorisation with a flourish and says to Loughlin, 'You're confident of getting a reduction to manslaughter?' This would be the best outcome possible, opening up the possibility of probation.

Loughlin leans back in his chair. 'We're not there yet, but

I'm hopeful. The SA has indicated her willingness to consider leniency, given the circumstances. Still a lot more to do though. Having your father on board has definitely helped.'

'You've done the hard work, Kyle.'

'I can't take much of the credit, really. Her story did the job, I just told it.'

'What about the Simpkins family?'

'There's a son in Australia, estranged for years. He's not even coming over for the funeral, seems to have washed his hands of the old man long ago. And, so far, the Klan has seen fit to keep their outrage to themselves. Might have something to do with the talk of reopening the original investigation.'

'I doubt there would be much local support for that. It's not exactly good for tourism, and most people here seem happy for the story to stay forgotten, from what I can tell.'

The door opens and Meredith escorts Alicia Cortez inside. The men get to their feet.

'Please, gentlemen, sit down. I just wanted to thank you for your help.'

'Just doing our jobs, ma'am,' says Roy. 'We wish you well in the final round of discussions. Meredith here will take you home.' He glances out the window. 'And there's Big Mike, back with my dad.'

'May I have the Colt, please?' she asks. 'It has great sentimental value, and I promise never to use it again.'

Roy thinks he detects a sparkle in those grey eyes, still astonishingly bright as sea glass. 'No, ma'am, you can't. But we'll take good care of it for you. I'll see you out.'

Meredith steadies her arm as they cross the car park, heat waves rising from the asphalt. '*Señora* Cortez, I don't want to seem nosy, but I'm dying to know: what's in the bag that's too important to let go?'

They reach the car, where Dwayne is waiting with a suitcase. He gives a little wave, like they are off on an adventure together. Roy has never been so proud of his father.

'Meredith,' she says, 'that is a story for another day.'

CHAPTER 27

The Tea Room is just as she left it, a little more than a week ago, except for a few more weeds in Thomas's garden – the garden she thought never to see again. Pablito flits into view, chirruping over his empty saucer.

'I will see to you, *amigo*, very shortly.'

'Who are you talking to?' asks Dwayne, as he wheels his case over the rough bricks of the path.

'My little friend. Come in.'

The building has changed, of course. She lives downstairs, having sold off the upper storey as apartments. And like everything else in town, the woodwork is no longer grey and sun-warped, but glowing with seaside pastel colours of sand and turquoise, aquamarine and white. The old porch she first climbed with Beatriz is graced by urns of rampant crimson geraniums on polished boards. Fortunately, the property holds enough value to satisfy the bail demand, several times over. *A very good investment, indeed.* The Last Resort has been gone as long as John. After he died, it was turned into a pool hall, and is now an over-priced B&B.

Dwayne climbs the steps as if in a trance. Once inside, he says nothing, just sweeps his eyes around the comfortable home she has created. The old side salon, where he used to fit the shoes for the girls, is now her bedroom, shutters drawn as she left them that afternoon. Hortensia's kitchen is still the kitchen, with the back door into the garden. The main salon she divided into a living room, spare bedroom, and bathroom. The old staircase is gone, but its ghost still travels up the living-room wall.

The air is stale and hot after her absence, so she opens the windows. There are probably some horrors to dispose of in the fridge, as she had no time to empty it before she went to the park that day. That day . . . that day she had thought never to see.

'I will get us a drink, and then we will catch up properly.'

She brings a tray with a dusty bottle of rum kept for cooking, and two of the surviving original glasses. 'I believe this is what we need for a toast.'

The aroma of rum fills the room, for the first time in nearly seven decades. It is almost too much to take in, with Dwayne sitting on her sofa. She sees him again as he was on her first day there, taking her bag upstairs, back when she still expected the Tea Room to serve tea. She sees him kneeling in the side salon, surrounded by shoe boxes and the bare feet of squealing girls. And she sees him at a table, chomping through Hortensia's *pastelitos* while enthusing about the Klan's upcoming parade. *Another lifetime ago.*

He looks up, and she can see he is reeling as well. She raises her glass. 'To old friends.'

'Old friends.'

A clink of glass, and they drink in silence. She feels his eyes on her.

'I tried to find you,' he says, 'several times after you left for Cuba.'

'I hid myself away until Daniella was born.' On her last night with John, the bedside jar of honey had remained unopened, both of them too preoccupied to notice, and by the time she had buried him and boarded the ferry back to Havana, what she thought was seasickness was not. She was met at the harbour by Mamacita. Raoul's father had withdrawn his threat when his son remarried. When her pregnancy became apparent, she expected Papa to send her away again, but instead he just sighed and said, 'You will always be trouble.' He had delighted in Daniella from the moment of her birth, and there followed several settled years in the narrow, sunshine-yellow house on Cuarteles Street, in the shadow of Batista's presidential palace.

'You have a daughter? Where is she? Can I meet her?' His eager interest causes a pain in her ribs, on the left side.

She removes a ragged, creased black-and-white photo from her wallet. Daniella was a teenager then, with John's black hair and her grey eyes, shielding her face against the sun with one hand, the other on her hip in a stance of pure defiance which always reminded her of him. Already she was a rebel, embracing the fashion for trousers, much to Mamacita's outrage. The photo doesn't do justice to her skin colour, which Alicia recalls as being likened to very milky coffee, what people these days called 'latte'.

'My lovely girl . . . she was a fighter, from the time she was born. She drove Mamacita to distraction, always causing trouble. When *La Revolución* came, she was one of the first to volunteer.' She stroked the photo. 'And one of the first killed.' The news, when it came, claimed another victim. Mamacita went to bed that day, saying she needed a siesta, and didn't wake up. Papa stopped eating after she went, and followed soon after. 'I left Cuba for Spain, and from there on to the Azores, and other places, so many places. Nowhere could I settle.' Living on the money left by her parents, she left a trail of empty rooms and disgruntled lovers, always packing her small bag when they got too interested.

'But why come back here, after everything . . .?'

It was a question she had asked herself so many times over the years. She was tired, tired of running from the memories which trailed her from place to place, all around the world, like a flock of crows. It was time to stop running. The Tea Room, for all its faults, was somewhere she had been happy, albeit for a short time, and it was still her property as the last 'Miss Pearl'.

'When I got old, I wanted to stop moving, and be near John again, I missed him so. I visit him most days now. But what about you, Dwayne? You married, I assume?'

'I did.' He twists the glass in his hands. 'But I wasn't good to Noreen, when Roy came out that colour. She didn't deserve the treatment she got from me.' He grows thoughtful. 'The funny thing was, I loved him straight away, and I think I've only just realised why . . . it's because he reminded me of you.'

She deflects this with a wave of her hand. 'From what you say, Roy was lucky to have you as a father. But what of your mother? I only met her once, but I remember it so clearly. A strong lady, your mother.' Alicia recalls that day in the hospital, Lily desperately afraid for her son, and afraid of her husband.

'After a while, it got too much,' he shrugs, 'the memories and the gossip here. We moved up to Heron Key after I got engaged to Noreen. Ma passed in '33, of cancer, the year before Roy was born. She never got to see her grandchild.'

'And how is Noreen now? It is very kind of her to spare you like this.' She pictures them together, enjoying the fruits of long companionship, joys and hardships shared, in a cosy house near the beach. Years ago, she resigned herself to a lonely old age.

'I lost her, in the Labor Day hurricane, in 1935. I barely managed to save Roy.' He drains the glass and pours another.

'You didn't marry?'

'No. I turned John down, I could never take another. And you? Did you find someone else after Noreen?'

'I figured I didn't deserve a second chance, after what I did to her.'

Things have not turned out as we hoped, for either of us. 'I am so sorry, Dwayne. But I do believe everyone deserves a second chance, if they are willing to change.'

'Even Simpkins?' he asks, with a wry twist of his mouth.

She recalls Simpkins at the park, the sneer, the way he had hissed at her: 'Brown.' 'Yes, even him. If he had shown any humanity, the Colt would have stayed in my pocket.'

He says nothing for a long moment. She waits. They have been apart for so many years, there is no hurry. The air conditioner hums and creaks. The sun shines right through the ornate glass of the front door to cast the shadow of a hummingbird on the floor. His hands pick at lint on his chinos.

She notices his white shirt has been carefully ironed, the sun spots on his neck dark against the collar. Just as she opens her mouth to speak, he takes her hand.

'I had such a crush on you, Miss Alicia.' His voice is fond, his eyes softened by decades of time and thousands of miles of distance. 'And you never knew.'

She folds her hand over his and looks into his dear face. 'Of course, I knew, Dwayne.' She thinks about how they used to be, and how they are now. Friends, still and forever. 'I always knew.'

One month later, Loughlin brings the news in person.

On this bright afternoon, Alicia sits under the sun umbrella, a full saucer of sugar water for Pablito by her elbow, a magazine open in front of her which she has been pretending to read. Loughlin's phone call is overdue. Dwayne sits in her favourite chair under the coconut palm, also pretending to read. He says the sound of the fountain makes him want to pee all the time. Never having shared more than a bedroom with a man, she is surprised at how easily the routine has settled on her. He doesn't talk too much, and goes to the market for her every day. They enjoy watching TV cop shows together, with his running commentary on everything the programme makers got wrong. He likes to cook, and does it well, whereas she has never taken an interest.

Loughlin comes around the side of the house, sunglasses on, expression unreadable. She stands to meet him.

'Good afternoon, Mr Loughlin, may I offer you a cold drink?'

He has prepared her for the eventualities: worst case, the original charge of second-degree murder sticks, possibly followed by a jury trial, or at least incarceration in a facility; best case, manslaughter with probation. She had thought herself to be at peace with both of them, until now. A tiny tremor starts in her left eye and she rests a hand on the back of her chair. At the edge of her vision, Pablito's wings whir inside the stand of bamboo.

Dwayne is by her side. A vein throbs in his forehead, muscles working in his jaw.

Loughlin removes his sunglasses and grins, a full-sized, teeth-baring grin. 'They went for it. The State Attorney agreed with my argument to take into account the whole bushel of mitigating factors, combined with your age and history as a good citizen. The terms are that you plead guilty to the charge of manslaughter and accept at least ten years of probation.'

'That is optimistic.' She sits and waits for her heart to quit its mad hammering. 'But very good news. What else?'

He takes a card from his pocket and reads: 'You are a convicted felon. As such you can never own a firearm, or vote, or get a job in public service. Nor can you use drugs or take part in any activity that violates the terms of your probation. If you do, the judge has the right to incarcerate you for the full term of a murder conviction. Do you accept the deal?'

'I do.'

Dwayne kisses her cheek and rests a hand on her shoulder. 'Thank you, Kyle.'

'Yes, thank you. Very much.' *Free*. Although she has traipsed across the globe, she has never really felt free since that morning on the beach. She stands. 'And now, we must tell John. Gentlemen, would you accompany me on a short walk, please?'

Loughlin shifts uncomfortably. 'That's technically a breach of house arrest . . . I should really call for permission . . . ah, hell. Make it fast.'

They turn onto Duval, past the shops selling tourist tat and bathing suits and marijuana paraphernalia and sex toys, past the old Poblano building, its cupola now painted cerise with gold trim, past the lamp post where Donkey Hightower's car came to its final rest. Jolovitz's department store is still there, now called Bentley's. A man dressed as Blackbeard, reeking of liquor, tries to push a tour brochure into her hands but she moves on, lost in the memory of her first ever sight of Thomas. How fierce he was outside, and how tender inside.

Her pace is slow, but John will wait. He has been waiting a long time already.

Left on Fleming, then right on Elizabeth where there is more shade. This is her preferred route, which leads directly to the main gates.

The cemetery is laid out like a town within the town, its own streets and avenues on a grid, its own sign posts and maps showing places of interest. Marble sarcophagi rise up all around, like miniature dwellings, filled with the remains of generations of wealthier inhabitants. Thanks to the high water table, many graves have collapsed on themselves, now home to emerald iguanas that skitter between the broken lids and leaning headstones.

They always remind her of Paulina, feeding treats to Miguel from her own lips. Paulina went on to start her own cathouse, which was extremely successful until a hurricane destroyed it a few years later. Kitty married a Navy man and had many children, more than enough to make up for the 'buns' she lost; Maxine drifted away, whereabouts unknown.

So many ghosts. This is a ghost city for me now.

She leads them on, past the area encircled by black railings reserved for military personnel, including the victims of the USS *Maine*. In silence, they file past the Jewish and Catholic sections, where she veers onto the grass, heading towards the fence. A dachshund-sized iguana makes a stand atop a tomb inset with a sepia photograph of a scowling man with fierce moustaches. Then it swoops into a broken grave with a meaty flick of its tail. She misses her sun hat, as the sweat gathers on her forehead.

A few steps on, and she arrives. There, in the shade between two grand tombs, she kneels on an anonymous strip of grass.

Dwayne is clearly feeling the heat as well. 'Is this the place, Alicia?'

Loughlin has removed his jacket and stands over her, arms folded.

Around her are the resting places of the men who put her John in the ground, all given proper, even grand memorials. While there is some consolation to be found in the success of John's curse – their ends were uniformly painful and untimely – the disgrace of it hits her anew, just like every time she visits. He should be in the military area with the other heroes, with its neat, clipped grass and orderly rows of marble headstones, with the full name and rank of the deceased inscribed. Not here, in this unnamed piece of earth.

'This is the only marker they would let me leave for him.' It is a rough square of cheap metal, almost hidden by spears of uncut grass and weeds. She passes her sleeve over it to remove a sticky collection of dead insects. *John Morales, 1890–1919.*

'John,' she says, 'it is done. I brought Dwayne to see you, and Mr Loughlin, who has won my freedom. You can rest easy now.' They move closer, throwing welcome shade across her. Eyes closed, she leans her palms on the hot grass, over the place where his heart had been, and thinks of the last time she held him in her arms.

My tears fell so heavy, they washed some of the blood from your face and I kissed you. Your cheek was cold. I sang to you and thought about what you would want me to do. I took all the rage and pain in my heart and turned it diamond-hard, to lodge there and make me strong, strong enough to live without you, and strong enough to find a way to punish them. It took a very long time, nearly until the end of my life, but I did it. At last, I did it. Be at peace. I come to join you soon. Adios, mi amor.

'Please, will you help me up?'

Dwayne takes one arm and Kyle the other, and she is restored to her feet.

'I think we need to get you home,' says Dwayne, his voice thick, his cheeks wet.

'Yes, home,' she says, winded and sweating heavily now. 'I wonder . . . Mr Loughlin, is it necessary for me to serve my probation in Key West?' A great weight is sliding off her chest, making her feel she could fly up like one of the stone angels watching over the graves. She has held on for so long. Now she can let go.

Loughlin raises a hand to shade his face. 'If you stay inside

Monroe County, I think we could work it out. Why, where are you thinking of?'

She looks up at Dwayne, where the tears have started anew. 'I hear,' she says, 'that Heron Key is nice. And I have an old friend there.'

AUTHOR'S NOTE

When I first came across the story of Manuel Cabeza (see link to Pinterest below), I was instantly intrigued by its elements: an epic inter-racial love story during a time of segregation, and an unsolved murder at the onset of Prohibition. Cabeza, a decorated WWI veteran, was murdered in 1921 by the Ku Klux Klan in Key West because he would not give up his mixed-race lover, a madam called Angela known as *La Rosita Negra*, the Black Rose. No one has ever been held accountable for the crime.

The Jim Crow laws of the period made such a relationship illegal, but Key West was far more tolerant than the rest of the South. People could get away with all manner of outrageous behaviour, as long as it was discreet. Cabeza was not discreet. Known as a tough character, he lived openly with Angela, which was a moral as well as a legal violation at the time.

What turned a scandal into a tragedy was the arrival of the Klan, invited by the city fathers to set up a new chapter in 1921. Contrary to popular perception – including my own – the Klan of the Keys directed more of its persecution towards Jews and Catholics than it did blacks. They were convinced of a grand conspiracy by these three groups to destroy America, and saw themselves as the only true patriots, with a sacred mission to rescue the country for the 'real Americans'.

The most infamous episode of their tenure in Key West is the one dramatised here. As the story goes, the Klan warned

Cabeza to cast out Angela from his life, or face punishment, but he refused. They came at night dressed in Klan robes and hoods, tore him from their bed, and beat him nearly to death. During the fight (which included being tarred and feathered, according to some reports) he managed to unmask some of his attackers, including one William Decker, and swore vengeance on them.

This was fulfilled soon after, when he murdered Decker in cold blood in the middle of town on Christmas Eve. He then holed up at the top of the Solano building, where he was surrounded by law enforcement officers and several armed Klansmen. A gun battle ensued.

It was common knowledge that the Klan counted among its members some prominent citizens of the town, including those charged with upholding the law. Understandably distrustful of them, when Cabeza ran out of ammunition, he agreed to surrender to someone from the military, and was guaranteed protection at the jail by a squad of Marines.

What happened next has never been fully explained. At some point in the early hours, the Marines were dismissed, and several cars full of Klansmen arrived. They broke into the jail and dragged Cabeza behind a car through the town, almost certainly killing him then, but this was not sufficient for their purposes. They went on to hang him from a palm tree (a lamp post in some reports) at a remote beach, and shoot him more than twenty times.

The grand jury convened at the time concluded that no one could be prosecuted for the murder because it was the doing of 'person or persons unknown'. Furthermore, Cabeza was blamed for bringing about the attack himself because of his intransigence. He is buried in Key West cemetery, not in the area reserved for military personnel who have served with distinction, but in an anonymous plot marked only with a handmade sign.

Cabeza supposedly cursed his attackers, and the whole island. The men he blamed for his death did fare badly: one crushed to death between two boats, another dead of tuberculosis, and another killed in the great Labor Day hurricane of 1935. Some took this to be evidence of the curse's effectiveness.

While I was considering whether to dramatise these events, I came across a news story from 2012 which documented the donation of the original Klan of the Keys charter to the local library. It also described the last known Klan rally in Key West, in 1993. What if, I wondered, the mysterious Angela was still around for this? Would she seek vengeance, given the opportunity? This hypothetical question, together with the historical pieces, gave me the story for *At First Light*. I was also fascinated by the prospect of having such an elderly perpetrator of a capital crime, who readily admits her guilt, and how this would be handled by the legal system.

I write in the introduction that the book is 'inspired' by the historical events. This is because I compressed the timeline and took other liberties to make the story flow. Many people are familiar with the 1918 Spanish flu outbreak, which resulted in 50 million deaths worldwide – four times as many as during the years of the Black Death. More American servicemen died of the flu (many before leaving training camps in the US) than died in combat. However, fewer people are aware that there was a second, smaller outbreak a year later in 1919. Just as people thought they could relax, that the worst was over, it came back with the last of the returning troops. Although of a lesser scale, it was still terrifying. It ended quickly, probably because of increased immunity in the population. This is the outbreak which I use to bring my characters John, Dwayne, and Alicia together. Dwayne is cured by the same method used to cure patients in the recent ebola outbreak. This involved administering plasma, extracted from survivor blood, which contained antibodies that could fight the disease – a method discovered in the field hospitals of France during WWI.

Very little is known about Angela, except that she ran a brothel and practised voodoo, which gave me wide scope to create the character of Alicia. I decided to give her Cuban nationality because Havana was a sophisticated, cultured metropolis, far more civilised than Key West at the time, and it seemed an interesting inversion of our current perceptions of the two places. I made her a practitioner of the Cuban tradition of *santeria*, a mix of religion and natural healing which is still followed today, because I became very interested in their use of plants and herbs as medicines.

More is known about Cabeza, whose family came from the Canary Islands, hence his nickname 'Ilseño' or 'The Islander'. He was survived by his father, whereas my character John loses his while away fighting in the war. Cabeza ran a coffee shop, whereas John runs a bar.

There was indeed a brothel called Mom's Tea Room on nearby Stock Island, where girls were trafficked from elsewhere in Florida, and beyond. I based Dwayne's visits there on the real account of a young man employed to deliver shoes to the girls in the Tea Room, always hoping for a glimpse of their 'girlishness'.

The Jews of Key West were driven out of street peddling by the punitive Merchant Protection Association act of 1889, and did go on to set up successful stores in town. Thereafter, many were drawn north to Miami when the town emerged from the swamp.

During the latter years of the nineteenth century, there was indeed a curfew bell which rang at nine p.m. to signal that all people of colour were required to be indoors. Any who broke curfew could be imprisoned or lashed, at the discretion of the mayor. I wasn't able to determine when the curfew was abolished, but did find a reference to it as late as 1944.

Prohibition was enforced from early in 1920. Key West had a long, proud tradition of smuggling, dating back to the eighteenth-century pirates; this, combined with rife corruption of public officials, ensured the free flow of liquor on The Rock while it was banned everywhere else. Smuggling methods were highly inventive, and included coffins and suitcases travelling on ferries – empty on the way to Havana, sloshing on the way back.

The scene where Emily, the 'walking dairy', is run over and killed is based on the experience of Stetson Kennedy, a white journalist who infiltrated the Klan in the 1940s and wrote about it in his book, *The Klan Unmasked* (see Further Reading below). He was in a car with Klan leaders, being driven to his own initiation ceremony, when they ran over and killed a mule belonging to a black farmer. It is a very powerful scene, and stayed with me for a long time. I recommend his book to anyone interested in an insider's view of the Klan's workings. His book brought home to me the strange combination of buffoonery and murderous efficiency which typified the

Klan's activities. Beneath all the costumes and rituals lay an extremely effective terror organisation which, at its height, boasted 850,000 members.

The Klan's reign in Key West seems to have been fairly brief, but it is interesting that they felt entitled to rally there as recently as 1993. It also struck me that their white supremacist rhetoric – keeping the country pure for the 'real Americans' – is still a loud refrain in contemporary politics. In addition, their means of recruitment, as portrayed here and in Klan literature, bears similarities to what is known today as 'radicalisation'. They targeted the angry, the disenfranchised, those who lacked a sense of belonging and needed to feel part of something bigger than themselves. By harnessing their disillusionment, they induced them to kill and maim the enemies of their ideology.

But at its heart, this is the timeless story of two people who wanted to be together, and were prevented from doing so by bigotry and hatred. It would have been so much easier if Cabeza had agreed to give Angela up, or at least moved away somewhere else with her. In this novel, I have tried to imagine the reasons for their choices, but we will never know why they stayed together. I like to think that the resulting tragedy says as much about the nature of love as the times in which they lived.

This link to Pinterest (https://uk.pinterest.com/vanessalafaye/atfirstlight/) will show you a photo of Manuel Cabeza, the real John Morales, and another of his grave in Key West cemetery. You will also find an image of the original Klan of the Keys charter, which is held by Key West library, amongst a host of images from the period.

QUESTIONS FOR DISCUSSION

- *'The sun shines right through the ornate glass of the front door to cast the shadow of a hummingbird on the floor.'*

  Hummingbirds fly in and out of the story. What do they symbolise?

- *'Her feet felt like the new roots of a tree, just beginning to bond with the soil. She was not ready to leave'*

  How important is the idea of 'home' to Alicia?

- *'They're comin' for you,' he said again, 'you got to leave town.' His head drooped. 'And it's all my stupid fault. I am so sorry, Miss Alicia.'*

  Dwayne is a complex character. How does he grow and develop through the novel? What kind of a person is he?

- *'All he did was . . . love me. And they nearly killed him for it'*

  Does love win over hatred in *At First Light*?

- *'I figured I didn't deserve a second chance, after what I did to her.' Things have not turned out as we hoped, for either of us. 'I am so sorry, Dwayne. But I do believe everyone deserves a second chance, if they are willing to change.'*

  Do you agree?

- Was justice done in *At First Light*?

- *At First Light* was inspired by the real story of Manuel Cabeza (see Author's Note). How important is it to remember the dark parts of history and bring to light the little known tragedies such as this one?

- To what level do historical novels such as this one allow us to explore and question our lives and our society today?

FURTHER READING

The Klan Unmasked, Stetson Kennedy, University of Alabama Press (2010)

Kennedy was an investigative journalist who became a folk hero in the South for his fearless efforts to expose injustice and corruption. This is his account of infiltrating the Klan in the 1940s. With a false identity, he managed to rise to the rank of Kleagle (local organiser). He took incredible risks with his own safety, and his book is a tremendous read, even if some have cast doubt on its authenticity since.

Grits and Grunts: Folkloric Key West, Stetson Kennedy, Pineapple Press (2008)

This is a quirky romp through two hundred years of history in the Conch Republic. It provided a lot of the detail and colour of everyday life that I needed for the book: what they ate, how they viewed Prohibition, how the town smelled – including the barrels of sewage collected from outhouses. There was something interesting on practically every page, including a retelling of the Cabeza story. Stetson collected the memories of Key West residents, so many of the vignettes are told in the first person, with swash and buckle and an ear for the local dialect. The whole book is a gem of micro-history which beautifully displays the unique character of the town.

Reyita: The Life of a Black Cuban Woman in the Twentieth Century, Maria de los Reyes Castillo Bueno, Duke University Press (2000)

This is the extraordinary biography of 'Reyita', one of Cuba's most famous natural healers. At the age of ninety, she looks back on her long life and recounts her struggles against poverty and racism. She married a white man deliberately to improve the prospects for her children, and used her herbal medicine skills to treat her whole community. Her work inspired Alicia's healing practice, and informed the choices made by her Mamacita.

Yesterday's Key West, Stan Windhorn and Wright Langley, E. A. Seemann Pub (1973)

This is a pictorial history of the town, with fascinating images of the docks, Duval Street, the 'shotgun' houses where the cigar workers lived, the Havana ferry and many more glimpses of life in the early twentieth century.

From Cuba with Love: Recipes and Memories, Ramona V. Abella Forcada, iUniverse (2003)

Cuban cuisine is so important to its people, especially for those forced to emigrate, for whatever reason. This book combines some nice personal stories with the recipes that I needed for this aspect of daily life. I cooked the *arroz con pollo* in the book, just for research.

Wild Key West, Donna J Robinson and Ben Roberts, lulu.com
(2013)

This is a compilation of some of the most extraordinary episodes from the town's history. What makes it special is the authors' dedicated collection of primary sources from the time. This included the grand jury report from the Cabeza case, as well as a detailed account of the entire incident. But this case is only one of twenty-five bizarre incidents covered in the book – further proof of what an incredibly unusual place Key West is!

Key Notes: A Collection of Folk Tales from the Florida Keys,
K.T. Dixon, Allusion Publishing (2009)

This is also an interesting batch of stories from the town's past, collected by the author 'during many hours of several barrooms and taverns'. He doesn't claim that they are all true, just entertaining. I can confirm the latter.

*Ku Klux Klan Secrets Exposed: Attitude toward Jews,
Catholics, Foreigners and Masons. Fraudulent Methods Used.
Atrocities Committed in the name of Order,* Ezra Asher
Cook, self-published (1922)

This short tome documents the history and lore of the Klan. Its author wrote it to expose the Klan's underbelly and its designs on society. It's a detailed view of how the organisation rose up out of the ashes of the Civil War to evolve into the organisation that still exists today. There are many practical details of Klan business, such as the wording for oaths sworn, and for recruitment cards, and a particular strength is the coverage of the Klan's paranoia in relation to both Jews and Catholics. The text is written with the urgency of someone living at the time of the events.

Quicksand and *Passing*, Nella Larsen, first published 1928 and 1929, this edition Wilder Publications (2014)

Nella Larsen was a mixed-race author and an important voice of the Harlem Renaissance of the 1920s at a time when few women could make a mark on literature. These two semi-autobiographical novels gave me a window into the life of a mixed-race woman in Prohibition-era society.

Return to Florida in

SUMMERTIME

A Richard and Judy Book Club pick.
Out now in paperback.

CHAPTER ONE

The humid air felt like water in the lungs, like drowning. A feeble breeze stirred the washing on the line briefly but then the clothes fell back, exhausted by their exertion. Despite the heat, they refused to dry. The daily thunderstorms did nothing to reduce the temperature, just made the place steam. Like being cooked alive, Missy thought, like those big crabs in their tub of seawater, waiting for the pot tonight.

She bathed the baby outside in the basin, under the banyan tree's canopy of shade, both to cool and clean him. His happy splashes covered them both in soapy water. Earlier that morning, asleep in his new basket, his rounded cheeks had turned an alarming shade of red, like the over-ripe strawberries outside the kitchen door. You could have too much of a good thing, Missy knew, even strawberries. This summer's crop had defeated even her formidable preserving skills and the fruit had been left to rot where it lay.

The peacocks called in the branches overhead. Little Nathan's cheeks had returned to a healthy rose-tinted cream colour, so she could relax. With a grunt she levered herself off the ground and on to the wooden kitchen chair beside the basin, brushed the dead grass from her knees. No one else around, only Sam the spaniel, panting on the porch. Mrs Kincaid had gone to see Nettie the dressmaker, a rare foray from the house, and Mr Kincaid was at the country club, as usual. He had not slept at home more than a handful of nights in the past few months, always working late. The mangroves smelled musky, like an animal, the dark brown water pitted with the footprints of flies.

Nathan started to whimper as he did when he was tired. She lifted him out of the water and patted him dry with the towel. He was already drowsy again, so she laid him naked in the basket in the shade. With a sigh she spread her legs wide to allow the air to flow up her skirt and closed her eyes, waving a paper fan printed with, 'I'm a fan of Washington, DC'. Mrs Kincaid had given it to her when they came back from their trip. Mrs Kincaid had insisted on going with her husband, to shop, and their argument had been heard clear across the street, according to Selma, who didn't even have good ears.

Even so, Selma knew everyone's business. She knew when Mrs Anderson's boy, Cyril, lost a hand at the fish processing plant, even before Doc Williams had been called. She knew that Mrs Campbell's baby would come out that exact shade of milky coffee even though Deputy Sheriff Dwayne Campbell had the freckles and red hair of his Scottish immigrant ancestors.

Selma had helped when Missy first went to work for the Mrs Kincaid's parents, the Humberts. She showed Missy where the best produce was to be found, the freshest fish. People told things to Selma, private things. She looked so unassuming with her wide smile and soft, downturned gaze, but Missy knew that those eyes were turned down to shield a fierce intelligence, and she had witnessed Selma's machinations. Missy was slightly afraid of Selma, which gave their friendship an edge. Selma seemed able to manipulate anyone in the town and leave no trace, had done so when it suited her. After Cynthia LeJeune criticised Selma's peach cobbler, somehow the new sewage treatment plant got sited right upwind of the LeJeune house. It took a full-blooded fool to cross Selma.

Missy sighed, stroked Nathan's cheek. His lips formed a perfect pink O, long lashes quivered, round tummy rose and fell. Sweat soaked her collar. When she leaned forward, the white uniform remained stuck to her back. She longed to strip off the clinging dress and run naked into the water, only a few yards away. And then she recalled that there was still some ice in the box in the kitchen – no, the *refrigerator*, as Mrs Kincaid said they were called now. She imagined pressing the ice to her neck, feeling the chilled blood race around her body until even her fingertips were cool. They would not mind, she thought, wouldn't even notice if she took a small chunk. There was no movement at all in the air. The afternoon's thunderclouds were piled like cotton on the horizon, greyish white on top and crushed violet at the bottom.

I'll only be a minute.

Inside the kitchen it was even stuffier than outside, although the windows were wide open and the ceiling fan turned on. Missy opened the refrigerator, took the pick to the block. A fist-size chunk dropped on to the worn wooden counter. She scooped it up, rubbed it on her throat, around the back of her neck, and felt instant relief. She rubbed it down her arms, up her legs, then she opened the front of her uniform and rubbed the dwindling ice over her chest. Cool water trickled down to her stomach. Eyes closed, she returned the ice to her throat, determined to enjoy it down to the last drop, then she became aware of a sound outside.

Sam barked, once, twice, three times. This was not his greeting bark – it was the same sound he made that time when the wild-eyed man had turned up in the backyard, looking for food. Armed with a kitchen knife, Missy had yelled at him to get away, but it was Sam's frenzied barking that had driven him off.

'Nathan . . .' she groaned, racing to the porch. At first she could not comprehend what her eyes saw – the Moses basket was moving slowly down the lawn towards the mangroves, with Sam bouncing hysterically from one side of it to the other. She could hear faint cries from the basket as Nathan woke. She stumbled down the porch steps in her hurry, and raced towards the retreating basket.

Then she saw him.

He was camouflaged by the mangrove's shade at the water's edge, almost the same green as the grass. He was big, bigger than any she had seen before. From his snout, clamped on to a corner of the basket, to the end of his dinosaur tail, the gator was probably fourteen feet long. Slowly he planted each of his giant clawed feet and determinedly dragged the basket towards the water.

'Nathan! Oh God! Someone please help!' she screamed, and ran to within a few feet of the gator. But the large houses of the neighbours were empty, everyone at the beach preparing for the Independence Day barbecue. 'Sam, get him! Get him!'

The dog launched himself with a snarl at the gator, but

the reptile swung his body around with incredible speed. His enormous spiked tail, easily twice as long as the dog, surged through the air and slammed into Sam with such force that he was flung against the banyan tree. The dog slid down the trunk and lay unmoving on the ground.

'Sam! No! Oh, Sam!'

The gator continued his steady progress towards the water. Missy swallowed great, gulping breaths to hold down the panicky vomit rising in her gut. Everything seemed to happen very fast and very slow at the same time. She scanned the yard for anything that would serve as a weapon but there was nothing, not even a fallen branch, thanks to the diligence of Lionel the gardener. The gator had almost reached the water. Missy knew very well what would happen next: he would take Nathan to the bottom of the swamp, and wedge him between the arching mangrove roots until he drowned. Then the gator would wait for a few days, or a week, before consuming his nicely tenderised meat.

She imagined the Kincaids' faces when they learned the fate of their baby son, what they would do when they found out that a child in her care had been so horribly neglected. The gator's yellow eyes regarded her with ancient, total indifference, as if she were a dragonfly hovering above the water. And then suddenly the panic drained from her like pus from a boil and she felt light and calm. She was not afraid. She knew what she had to do. *That precious baby boy will not be a snack for no giant lizard!*

She stood, and her thoughts cleared. Despite the ferocious mouthful of teeth, she knew that most of the danger came from the alligator's back end. She began to circle nearer the head.

She need only spend a moment within the reach of that tail, which was as long as she was tall, to snatch Nathan from the basket. If she succeeded, then all would be well. If she failed, then she deserved to go to the bottom with him. The gator had reached the waterline. There was no more time.

Movement on the porch, and suddenly Selma was running down the lawn towards her, loading the shotgun as she ran.

'Outta the way, Missy!' she cried, stomach and bosoms bouncing, stubby legs pounding. Missy had never seen Selma run, did not know that she could. 'Outta the way!'

Missy threw herself to the ground, hands over her head. Selma stumbled to a halt, regained her balance, feet spread wide apart, stock of the gun buried between her arm and her bountiful chest.

'Shoot it, Selma!' yelled Missy. 'For the love of Jesus, shoot it! NOW!'

There was an explosion. The peacocks shrieked, dropped clumsily to the ground and fled for the undergrowth. The air smelled burnt. And there was another smell, like cooked chicken. Missy looked up. Selma was on her back, legs spread, the gun beside her. The baby was screaming.

'Nathan . . .' Missy whispered, scrambling to her feet. 'Nathan, I'm coming!'

The gator was where she had last seen it. Well, most of it was there, minus the head. The rest of the body was poised to enter the water.

'Oh, Nathan!' He was covered in gore. It was in his hair, his eyes, his ears. She scooped the flailing baby from the basket and inspected his limbs, his torso, his head, searching for injuries. But he was unhurt, it seemed, utterly whole. She clutched his writhing form to her, which made him scream louder, but she didn't care. 'It all right, honey, hush now, everything gonna be all right.'

'The baby?' asked Selma, propped on her elbows. 'Is he . . . ?'

'He fine! He absolutely fine!'

'Thank the Lord,' said Selma, wincing as she got to her feet, 'and Mr Remington.' She rubbed her shoulder. 'Helluva kick on him though.'

Missy said nothing, just cooed and rocked Nathan with her eyes closed. He still cried, but fretful, just-woken crying, and it was a joyous sound to hear. She looked up suddenly. Her uniform was stiff with blood transferred from Nathan's little body. The Kincaids would be home in a few hours to get ready for the barbecue, and when they learned what nearly happened, she would be fired. And that might not be the worst of it . . .

'Missy,' said Selma firmly, 'come on, we got a lot to do.'

She felt cold under the hot sun. 'Oh Selma, I'm done for.'

'Listen to me, girl, this ain't the biggest mess I've seen, by far.' She shook Missy by the shoulder. 'Come on; now pay attention. First we get *him* cleaned up, and that basket too.' She scrutinised it with a professional eye. 'Yeah, this ain't too bad.'

The bundle at the base of the tree stirred, emitted a soft cry. 'Sam! He alive, oh Selma, how bad is he?' He had been an awful trial as a puppy, eating the legs right off the living room furniture and weeing in Mr Kincaid's suitcase, but Sam had been Missy's only companion most days.

'Give me a minute,' said Selma. She bent over the dog,

stroked his ribs, felt his legs, his head. 'Nothing broken,' she pronounced, 'just knocked out. Be some bad bruises; I'll give you something for that.' She straightened. 'Call him.'

'Sam, here boy! Come here, Sammy!' The dog's eyes opened slowly and he raised his head, whimpering as he struggled on to his front legs, then straightened his back legs. 'Good boy, Sammy, good boy!' Missy could not look at the carcass by the water's edge. 'What about . . . what do we do with . . . with that?'

'What do you think?' Selma was already striding towards it with great purpose. 'We eat it. By the time my people is done here, won't be nothin' to see but a few peacock feathers.'